# No Worst, There Is None

# No Worst, There Is None

Eve McBride

DUNDURN

TORONTO

Editor: Shannon Whibbs
Design: Jesse Hooper
Cover design by Laura Boyle
Cover image: © Mac-leod/shutterstock
Author photo by Carlyle Routh
Printer: Webcom

**Library and Archives Canada Cataloguing in Publication**

McBride, Eve, 1945-, author
    No worst, there is none / Eve McBride.

Issued in print and electronic formats.
ISBN 978-1-4597-1865-4 (pbk.). — ISBN 978-1-4597-1866-1 (pdf). —
ISBN 978-1-4597-1867-8 (epub)

    I. Title.

PS8575.B75N6 2014         C813'.54         C2014-901014-1         C2014-901015-X

1   2   3   4   5       18   17   16   15   14

Conseil des Arts du Canada    Canada Council for the Arts    ONTARIO ARTS COUNCIL / CONSEIL DES ARTS DE L'ONTARIO / an Ontario government agency / un organisme du gouvernement de l'Ontario

We acknowledge the support of the **Canada Council for the Arts** and the **Ontario Arts Council** for our publishing program. We also acknowledge the financial support of the **Government of Canada** through the **Canada Book Fund** and **Livres Canada Books**, and the **Government of Ontario** through the **Ontario Book Publishing Tax Credit** and the **Ontario Media Development Corporation**.

Care has been taken to trace the ownership of copyright material used in this book. The author and the publisher welcome any information enabling them to rectify any references or credits in subsequent editions.

*J. Kirk Howard, President*

The publisher is not responsible for websites or their content unless they are owned by the publisher.

Printed and bound in Canada.

VISIT US AT
*Dundurn.com* | *@dundurnpress* | *Facebook.com/dundurnpress* | *Pinterest.com/dundurnpress*

| Dundurn | Gazelle Book Services Limited | Dundurn |
| --- | --- | --- |
| 3 Church Street, Suite 500 | White Cross Mills | 2250 Military Road |
| Toronto, Ontario, Canada | High Town, Lancaster, England | Tonawanda, NY |
| M5E 1M2 | L41 4XS | U.S.A. 14150 |

*To all children whose innocence is seized*

No worst, there is none. Pitched past pitch of grief,
More pangs will, schooled at forepangs, wilder wring.
Comforter, where, where is your comforting?
Mary, mother of us, where is your relief?
My cries heave, herds-long; huddle in a main, a chief
Woe, world-sorrow; on an age-old anvil wince and sing —
Then lull, then leave off. Fury had shrieked 'No ling-
ering! Let me be fell: force I must be brief.'

O the mind, mind has mountains; cliffs of fall
Frightful. sheer, no-man-fathomed. Hold them cheap
May who ne'er hung there. Nor does long our small
Durance deal with that steep or deep. Here! creep,
Wretch, under a comfort serves in a whirlwind: all
Life death does end and each days dies with sleep.

— GERARD MANLEY HOPKINS (1844–1889)

# Author's Note

On July 25, 1986, in Toronto Ontario, vivacious Alison Parrott, an eleven-year-old budding track star, was sexually slain by Francis Roy, who had posed as a sports photographer to lure her from her home. He was a convicted rapist out on parole and in police custody shortly after the murder, but was released because he presented a falsified alibi. It was ten years before he was arrested, through matched DNA, a forensic technology that was not available in 1986. He was convicted in a sensational trial and given life imprisonment.

My daughter Clara was among Alison's immediate circle of friends. Our family was closely involved in the aftermath, both the mourning and the investigation.

Although *No Worst, There Is None* is a work of fiction, written from my imagination and based on my own experience and philosophy as well as extensive research, aspects of it were drawn from the events of July 1986 and it is certain that the book would not exist without Alison's tragic death. She is embedded in these pages.

# Part One

## MURDER

# *Prologue*

## A Thursday Morning in July 1986

The first thing she notices is the sky. For three days it has been aflame, the rising sun a glaring orange. And there have been violent thunderstorms. "Red sky in the morning ..." This morning it is subdued, benevolent, glazed: gold below blending into silvery blue above. There is not a single cloud. And even this early, this low, the sun is yolk-yellow and hot. There will be no rain.

Magdalena is walking from the stone farmhouse to the road. Her wellingtons are muddy and she splashes in the potholes to clean them off.

The long lane dissects a line of ancient maples with sprawling crowns. A few stray drops from the shimmering canopy run down Magdalena's neck, which already feels sticky in the humidity. She reaches up and touches her head. Her short-cropped grey hair is damp. Her khaki army shorts feel as heavy as canvas. Perspiration trickles down her torso and she pats it with her sleeveless T-shirt. The fabric clings. She runs her tongue over her upper lip and tastes salt. Walking the dogs will be an effort today.

She is a handsome woman, unusually tall and large-boned with elegant, curved cheek bones. A prominent nose offsets her strong, square jaw. Her mouth is full and toothy, prone to great grins. But it is her eyes that influence. They are dark and shadowy, heavily lashed, and though she wears no makeup, they appear lined. In them is a compassionate, profound, constructive warmth.

Magdalena is ambling down this laneway, as she does every morning, to get the city newspaper, her and Joan's only concession to the outside world. They are anxious to read it. An eleven-year-old girl disappeared Monday afternoon and is feared abducted. Lizbett Warne, actress. By yesterday morning's newspaper, she still has not been found.

Four years earlier, the Warne family adopted one of Magdalena's Great Danes, Mistral: daughter of Zeus and Artemis. She had helped to train the dog. Then, at two, Misty had to be put down … "put down" … she hates that expression. Misty was euthanized because of bone cancer. Magdalena had seen sorrow with the death of an animal, but this was … she wouldn't say excessive because she didn't doubt their feelings … more wrenching. Lizbett, seven at the time, had called sobbing, "We had to kill her, Maddie. It's not fair. I loved her so much." Meredith, the mother, weeping as well, said, "I held her in my arms while the vet gave her the shot. She looked at me with these scared, sad eyes. I know she knew what was happening. I watched the needle go in and suddenly she was limp. She was just gone. I've never experienced death so closely before. And Misty was so huge and heavy on me. She just lay there, as if she were asleep. I couldn't bear to leave her. I kept going back to her. I feel so guilty having such deep grief over an animal when there's so much suffering in the world. But I've lain on every place in the house where she slept." Thompson, the father, choked up, merely said, "She was a special dog."

Magdalena can't imagine their coping with a missing child.

A seven-month-old floppy Great Dane the colour of pewter is close at Magdalena's heels. She turns and checks the five adults behind, all "blues" as well. The two 180-pound males, Zeus and Apollo, are rearing up, growling and mouthing each other with their powerful jaws. Both dogs stand well over six feet with their front paws on Magdalena's shoulders. They are equine in bearing: magnificent, with enormous chests, great slabs of muscle and bone and thick, long necks. They even snort like horses. Their coats gleam.

Magdalena can just see the heads of the two smaller females, Artemis and Athena, above the Queen Anne's Lace and Black-Eyed Susans as they tear around the adjacent meadow. Their leaps are graceful and long.

The delineated symmetry of their shoulders accelerating their speed is wondrous. A third, Minerva, is prancing along behind, neck arched, satiny ears flapping (Magdalena does not crop them), proudly carrying a large, fallen branch.

Magdalena's heart soars at this time with her dogs. She revels in the secure freedom of her fenced fifty acres. And to her, her dogs are numinous, with their effortless, massive elegance, their unfettered zeal. Occasionally they bound up to her and she embraces their hugeness. They nuzzle her face with their big black leathery noses and whiskery jowls and kiss her with great wet slurps. Their eyes are sympathetic, soulful. These dogs are her life.

Magdalena and her partner Joan raise blue Great Danes. At the entrance to their property is a large sign:

CELESTIAL KENNELS
HEAVENLY BLUE GREAT DANES
CHAMPION STOCK KC REGISTERED
OWNERS: MAGDALENA WARD DVM, JOAN RICHTER RN
BOARDING AND TRAINING AVAILABLE

The puppy bounces in the puddles, unusual for a Dane. Normally they don't like water. This one is a return from Magdalena's last litter or, actually, Zeus and Athena's: the "O" litter — twelve puppies, four males and eight females. All were sold, this particular puppy, Ophelia, or "Lia," to a family with a teenage boy. Magdalena had had her doubts about the Lavernes because they had never had a dog. They had just moved into a recently gentrified neighbourhood adjacent to subsidized housing where there had been a lot of break-ins. Their son, Jason, an awkward, scrawny and sullen boy with raging acne, had not handled the transition well. His parents indicated that there were problems at school with bullies. And they were worried about the security of their home. They thought a big, strong dog would help give Jason confidence and also protect the house.

Magdalena watched Jason bend down and jostle with Lia and laugh at her licks. She was encouraged by his enthusiasm. She had seen the power of dogs to transform and since the Lavernes agreed to call Magdalena for the training, she let the puppy go.

But they didn't call.

Now Lia, whom they renamed Brunhilde, is back because the Lavernes have said they found her unmanageable. When she left Celestial Kennels at eight weeks, she was a twelve-pound, gregarious, curious puppy, with outsize, floppy paws and velvety ears. She has been returned as a gaunt, skittish, fearful animal with nicked ears who hides in corners and cowers and growls when approached. Magdalena suspects she has been abused and she is heartsick and enraged.

Yes, she has been abused. Magdalena can only imagine this scenario. Because Brunhilde was rambunctious and chewed the legs of tables and chairs, the corners of rugs and pillows, because she jumped on their white furniture, because she still peed everywhere, the Lavernes kept her in her wire crate except to take her out into their fenced backyard a couple of times a day. Whenever Jason went by he would run a large metal spoon back and forth across the side of the cage and poke it at the puppy. It was the same spoon they banged on the crate when Brunhilde yelped and whined from the confinement. When Jason was out in the yard with her, he chased her, raising his arms and yelling to get her to run. Or he'd hold out a toy and snatch it away if she went for it.

He was supposed to walk her morning and night, but he left it too late in the mornings and in the afternoons when he took her out, she pulled on the leash and he couldn't control her. He would take a rolled-up newspaper and smack her nose over and over to get her to obey, but that only made her cower. Then she didn't want to walk and he would have to drag her so he found a stick and beat her to make her follow, but she still refused. He gave up.

When the weather warmed up they had a doghouse built and simply kept her chained beside it, taking food out to her in the evenings although that was also Jason's job and he often forgot. He neglected to fill her water bowl as well.

Jason constantly tormented Brunhilde with a large stick which she grabbed and pulled. He yanked back. They played tug, the dog growling and Jason mimicking her. When she wouldn't give it up, he kicked her. Then he took the stick and shoved it at her again. After a while, Brunhilde wouldn't take the stick and he hit her with it. Soon she was curling her lip when he approached her. So he whacked her. She retreated into the doghouse and snarled and leapt at him if he got too close. Twice she had bitten his hand.

He thought this was great. Just what he wanted. A fierce dog. He enticed the bullies to come and see her and they challenged Jason to let her fight their dog.

Clobber, a Lab/Staffordshire Terrier cross was an intact, squat black dog with a broad, square face, heavy jowls, and muscular chest. The two dogs faced each other, tails erect, hackles raised. Clobber was a scrapper. In a few seconds he was on Brunhilde. She screamed and tried to get away, but was restricted by the chain and Clobber grabbed her by the neck and pinned her on her back, shaking her. Her cries terrified Jason who had never seen a dog fight and he yelled, "Get her off! Get her off!"

The boys hesitated, then grabbed a resistant Clobber by his choke collar and yanked him away. He strained, gagging, trying to get back at the puppy. She lay cowering on the ground.

"Here's what losers get," they said and the three of them jabbed Brunhilde with their cigarettes. Then they left, laughing, shouting back, "Let's do this again and watch him kill her!"

When Magdalena was called to retrieve Brunhilde, she had to muzzle her.

Now Magdalena sees the raw, red cigarette wounds. There are punctures in the flesh and a tear that bears the marks of stitches. But what causes Magdalena the most pain is Brunhilde's eyes. Where they once were animated, trusting, and responsive, they now reflect terror, mistrust, and ferocity.

Magdalena feels as she did when her mother was dying of ovarian cancer: helpless, distraught, and so influenced by her suffering, she incorporates it into herself. As with her mother, Magdalena wants to lie alongside the dog, to stroke the bony body, scratch the damaged ears and whisper reassurances. "I promise no one will ever do anything like this to you again." But Brunhilde is a shaking mass of frightened rage. She is dangerous.

Magdalena has been working for several weeks to gain the dog's confidence and she is beginning to respond, but it is going to be a great challenge to turn her into a safe pet. Magdalena is very careful about matching puppies and owners and she is utterly disheartened and ashamed that she made such a mistake with this one. Not every match is as successful as the Warnes and Misty.

Misty was one of her best Danes. She had character and beauty. She was a "solid," had no patches of white on her toes or her chest, as Brunhilde does. Of all the eleven puppies in the litter, Misty was the most outgoing and responsive when the family got down on the floor with them. She was all over Lizbett, but showed an almost instinctive gentleness with little Darcy, who was a teetering one-year-old at the time.

When Misty was six months old, Magdalena spent a week with the Warnes in their home to train her. Magdalena liked them and she liked their neighbourhood. It was a treed street of grand Victorians, but some of them were rooming houses and flats and since it was near the university, fraternities. The Warne family was a little like the street: privileged, but unpretentious, a bit haphazard even. The mother was loud, garrulous, the father taciturn, but to Magdalena, they had an innate, unerring, and affectionate sense of one another. They seemed mutually "plugged in." As a pair, they were clever, stimulating, she playing off his reticence, he quick with understatement. They hugged and kissed frequently and called each other "lambie" and "lovey." At least she did.

It was a family brimming with love and verve, with an unaffected sense of its charm, its comfort, a family where the children shrieked and jumped into their father's arms when he got home. He lifted them in the air. They danced with him on his insteps. He made them laugh with silly antics and nonsensical jokes. And they sat snuggled into him when he read to them every night.

The mother roughhoused on the floor with them. She constructed huge tents with sheets and blankets and played inside with them. She got behind the sofa and did puppet shows. She was always singing.

Lizbett, the eldest girl, was high-spirited and demanding, but respectful and responsible, even at age five, taking charge of Misty's food and water. The little one, Darcy, was placid, sweet-natured. Magdalena never heard her cry.

Even though Misty was imposing, with a noble forehead and a strong, square muzzle, she was obedient to the point where even Lizbett, with supervision, could handle her on the leash.

However, the Warnes broke a lot of Magdalena's rules. Misty slept on the couple's bed and curled up, as Great Danes do, on any couch or big armchair. She sat on laps. Magdalena decided she couldn't discipline away that much love. It seemed like a match of a perfect dog to a perfect family. Then Misty died from cancer at only two.

And Lizbett has been missing for two days.

Magdalena believes there is no such thing as perfection and she hates the disillusionment when occasionally she does.

Certainly her own family couldn't approach what she thought the Warnes had. It was that exuberant love that she had missed, a love without boundaries or expectations, where imperfections were accepted, overlooked, even. Magdalena's father, Nicholas Ward, a large animal veterinarian, had loved his patients, but he was a stern, exacting man whose only channel for affection was attending to them. When he was alive, the farm was a working one with horses, a small herd of Charolais, a dozen sheep, and Horatio, a donkey, all of whom he talked to unreservedly. But to Magdalena he was unreachable and unreaching.

Magdalena longed to be as beloved by her father as his animals. She has found that devotion with her empathetic, responsive Danes.

It made sense that she became a veterinarian. She loved the farm and her father had an established practice she could join. But when he died in 1980 when he was seventy-four, after a cow kicked him in the stomach, Magdalena felt freed, freed from a pressure to be the dutiful daughter striving to keep her father pleased, trying to win his affection. So she sold off the livestock and reduced her practice to part-time, treating pets only.

She lives with and loves Joan Richter, a night nurse in the ICU of the local hospital. They have had a joyous, concentric alliance for six years. They met when Magdalena treated Joan's Great Dane, Daphne, for bloat. Magdalena couldn't save her. The women became friends while Joan was grieving. Every time an animal died, Magdalena wept. Joan was attracted to the depth of her compassion. Joan sees constant death in her job and cannot afford to lose that much of herself.

When Joan moved to the farm, the two women decided to breed Great Danes. Great Danes suit Magdalena. They are dogs whose enormous strength and will are offset by their gentleness and generosity.

Joan, ten years younger, is small beside the great dogs. They could easily pull her over. But she brooks no nonsense. She is wiry and muscular with tawny skin and blond hair pulled back in a ponytail. In spite of the pressures of her job, the frequent dealing with death (or perhaps because of these), she is a beaming, enthusiastic woman, constantly on the move.

In the farm kitchen Joan is making muffins with cut-up peaches from their small orchard. She has already brewed a pot of coffee. She is just home from her shift. The evening before, a fifty-year-old farmer had come in, comatose from a stroke. He hadn't made it through the night.

At the end of the lane, Magdalena bends down to a puddle to pick up the newspaper, thankfully wrapped in double plastic. She shakes it, clucking, splattering muddy water on herself and heads back to the farmhouse. She yells, "Hello, paper's here," and places it on the back stoop. The urge to rip it open and see what's inside is pressing, but she is surrounded by five panting, expectant dogs. The news can wait. Their hunger cannot.

She walks to the barn and they follow, bounding through the stable door, swarming around her, tails waving like whips.

First, with a hose, she rinses out an aluminum tub and fills it with fresh water. The clean dishes are lined up on a bench and she orders the five adult dogs to sit. They do so, drooling, until she has measured out four cups of kibbles from a grain bin into each dish. (She will do this again in the evening.)

"Wait!" she commands. "Wait!" And the dogs' drool reaches the floor. Then she says, "Okay," and the great beasts lunge and gobble.

And to Brunhilde she says, "C'mon, Hildy, my girl, you get yours in the house."

Magdalena climbs the back steps with the puppy and they enter the kitchen, an old-fashioned, high-ceilinged space with a wood stove and pale green cupboards with chipped paint and an oversized, stained enamel sink. The room is filled with the delicious odour of freshly baked muffins. She smiles at Joan and goes over to embrace her at the Formica table but something stops her. Joan's face is grim. She angles her head toward the newspaper on the table. The headline reads, "Missing Girl's Nude Body Found Near Industrial Canal."

# 1

## THREE DAYS EARLIER: A MONDAY MORNING IN JULY 1986

*Melvyn Searle*

The first thing he notices when he looks out the window of his second floor flat is the sky. Red. Glaring, voluptuous red. A crimson sun. "Red sky in the morning ..." This may interfere with his plans. But the heavy rains will actually work in his favour.

Melvyn Searle's flat is in a red brick house on a square of similar two-storey houses with broad verandahs, constructed just before the First World War. The square is leafy and the small front lawns, most of them with low fences, have well-tended gardens. In the centre of the square is a lovely little park called Schiller Park, because Germans were the early residents here. There is the ubiquitous wooden structure for children to play on.

Many children go there: younger ones in the morning with their mothers, but in the afternoons, when school is out, older children come, as well, and use the big set-up for their games. Sometimes even teenagers hang around. On Saturdays and Sundays, the park is filled.

Melvyn's flat occupies the whole second floor. At the back, steep stairs lead to a driveway where he parks his grey Honda. It's more space than he needs, as he is single, but he can afford it and he likes the area. And it's only a short bus ride to the Courtice Museum, where he is head of the education department. He has an MA in ethnology. His specialty is masks. But he also earned a B.Ed. because he loves to work with children.

This morning he leaves his sparse bedroom with the dark furniture inherited from his parents and wanders in his striped pajama bottoms into his equally spare living room — except for the walls on which hang a great variety of masks. Besides those, the room contains only a couch and a chair. Above the couch are two inconsistencies: Arthur Rackham posters of Alice in Wonderland. On a side wall there is a shelving unit that holds a TV and a portable stereo on which he often plays children's records. "Free to Be You and Me" is one of his favourites as are "The Frog Prince" and "Honey on Toast."

The masks are impressive. He sometimes splurges on purchases, but his prized possession is a carved wooden Congolese kifwebe mask, whose intricately etched, angular shape gives it a Picasso-esque look. He also has a Chinese lion mask. And a glass mask from Poland. Most of his masks are copies he has made himself. An Indonesian Topeng Dalem mask. A Nigerian maiden spirit mask. A Hellenistic terra cotta mask. And several beautiful Japanese Noh masks, their simplicity, their apparent vacancy actually faces of restrained, secretive, exquisite revelation. Still others are his own creations, extensions of himself from a plaster mould of his own face. These are the masks he has used for his … what shall he call them? Escapades? Rituals? Rites? He wonders which ones he will choose for today.

His masks are an obsession. He loves their ironic duality: the wearer gives a mask life, but a mask also gives the wearer life, a wholly new life that sometimes comes deep from within and sometimes is external, something desired. A mask *knows*. A mask, though inanimate, has a subversive vitality. From the moment the wearer puts it on, a mask is born and finds its own voice. The mask overwhelms the wearer and the wearer injects that into mask. There is crucial intimacy between them. One cannot exist without the other. Without the wearer, a mask is simply a static aesthetic object. On him, he and the mask both come alive.

He leaves the masks for now, although still pondering his choices for today and goes into the kitchen. It is a former bedroom and is quite large, but has only one small counter with a sink, a narrow gas range, and a refrigerator that is covered with children's drawings, gifts mostly from his Saturday-morning classes. There are also pictures of little girls from magazines and there is a newpaper photo of Lizbett Warne as "Annie." A couple of Polaroids he took of his current mask class with Lizbett in them are up, as well. He also has a photo of her in one of the masks she has made, the star mask … as if she needed such an extension of her vivid self. The pictures of Lizbett give him a thrill every time he looks at them and imagines the time when they'll be together. But today, as he opens the refrigerator to get himself some juice, he feels much more. He feels a frisson of apprehension, a flip in his gut, a stirring in his groin. *This is the day.*

He flicks on the radio. The war between Iran and Iraq is still raging. Iran is supporting the Kurdish guerillas fighting for autonomy in Iraq. A car bomb has killed thirty-two people in Beirut and wounded 140 others. The trade and budget deficits are worsening. The Chernobyl clean-up is an ongoing horror. President Botha has declared a state of emergency in South Africa where millions of blacks have been on strike to protest Apartheid.

Melvyn turns to a classical music station and gets a Mozart clarinet concerto. He switches it off. He is too keyed-up for music.

He is a pale, small man, very thin but with a disarming agility, a child-like looseness. His face is almost beautiful, with high, delineated cheek-bones, a fine nose. His skin is smooth and taut. His limpid eyes, the colour of Wedgwood and defined by pale, thick lashes, are magnified by round tortoiseshell glasses that correct his far-sightedness. They give him a look of wide-eyed enthusiasm. And his hair is baby-soft and blond. No matter how he has it cut or what he puts on it, it is unruly, with cowlicks. His thin lips, when pulled back in a smile reveal small teeth with a space between the two front ones. If he were more mannish, he would be called handsome, but really, at age thirty-two, he is more boyishly appealing. This ingenuous physicality encourages connection. Children, especially, are drawn to him not because he is overtly affectionate but because he has a soft, highish voice. He inspires engagement and he exploits that.

He switches on the coffeemaker, which he has prepared the night before and decides to make scrambled eggs, which he does methodically, carefully cracking three eggs in a bowl so as not to get any shell. While the eggs are slowly cooking (he likes them soft), he butters whole wheat toast and then sits down at the wooden table with the carved legs and eats.

He thinks of Lizbett Warne. He knew of her, the way others did because of her role in *Annie*, but he never aspired to her. However, when she appeared at his mask camp, he was delighted. What unexpected serendipity. What fortuitous availability. All little girls appeal to Melvyn, but he aims for the ones who shine. That's why Lizbett fascinates him. Her intelligent sparkle, her sweet-natured vivacity set her apart. Her luscious girlishness is magnetic. She is generous with herself, standing out because she wants to, though not in a pushy way. She seems to ease naturally and comfortably into showmanship and other kids look up to her. He wouldn't say she is the brightest or the most insightful, but she is the most assertive. Where her fellow maskers seem reluctant to offer their ideas, Lizbett is full of them. He has worked on developing a rapport with her.

*We have a relationship*, he thinks, with a surge of confidence.

He cleans up the kitchen, meticulously drying each dish, utensil, and pot and putting them away in their proper places. He gives the floor a quick sweep and waters several pots of ivy on the windowsill. He goes into the bedroom and makes his bed, careful to smooth away all the wrinkles on the lavender coverlet.

Melvyn is not as preoccupied with his person as he is with his house. His clothes, mostly chinos and madras plaid shirts, short and long-sleeved, are clean and pressed because he takes them to the laundry, but he wears them longer than he should.

He does shave, closely. With a razor and a cake of shaving soap in a wooden bowl. He looks smooth-cheeked, but he actually has a blond beard which, if grown out, would be quite full. He dislikes his whiskers, sees them as detriments to his purpose (of appearing boyish), so every day he scrapes away the stiff hairs until his face is pink and shiny. His father, a captain who flew Lancasters during the Second World War, used to say, "a soldier always shaves, especially before a battle." Melvyn wonders if he is a soldier, if what lies before today him is actually a kind of battle; an assertion of desire and of supremacy not over an enemy, because Lizbett is anything but an enemy, but over the unsuspecting, smug society that claims her.

Melvyn doesn't shower. Once someone mentioned his body odour to him. Melvyn doesn't shower because he doesn't have one, but he does have an old-fashioned claw-footed bathtub. However, he hates to bathe even more.

This morning is one of those mornings when he feels he should have a bath. He tries to talk himself out of it, reminding himself he had bathed last week — was it Wednesday or Thursday? — but something pushes him and he runs the water until the tub is quite full, slips off his pajama bottoms, steps in, and slides back, immersing himself completely. In the hot surroundings he begins to remember, but it's when he washes himself that the images flood back. He washes his genitals and backside quickly, perfunctorily, as if it were painful there. This is where his stepmother began. At bathtime. In his earliest recall, he is three or four, an intense little boy with a cap of white curls and an angelic face. His wide, round blue eyes are filled with tentative curiosity. Stacey soaps and massages his genitals, pulling and stroking the little penis continuously. And then she inserts one or two soapy fingers over and over, deep into his rectum. Or something big and hard. He squeezes his eyes tight so he won't cry. "Good boy," she coos. "Good, sweet boy." He doesn't know if he's good or bad. He only knows that he doesn't like what she is doing; that it makes him sore. She gives him hugs, but he is afraid of her.

As he gets older and begins to bathe on his own, she comes into his bed late at night when his father has passed out from Scotch. At first she just fondles him. But when he begins to experience erections she starts to put her mouth on him. Eventually, he is entering her. And then it stops, when he is in high school. She no longer comes into his room because she becomes pregnant. And everything in his life changes. Stacey calls the new baby Alice after her favourite book.

He never wonders how his stepmother could have done what she did. She may not know. Or then, again, she might. Her father, Marvin, was a dentist, the youngest of six children, with five older sisters who wandered in front of him naked, mothered and bullied him, teased and used him as a little houseboy. When he was little, they flicked at his penis. And his mother either dressed him in girl's clothes or neglected him.

Marvin had three sons, and then Stacey, and though he doted on his little girl, as she got older he saw in her a personification of his sisters and that's when his violations began, in a kind of erotic rage. She was the one whimpering and sore then. It continued until she left home in her late teens. If Stacey's mother had any idea of her husband's mistreatment of her daughter, she never let on. She had enough trouble dealing with his erratic meanness.

Sometimes Stacey's mother would go to her sister's with Stacey and it was there that Stacey discovered little bodies when she slept with her much younger cousins. They would cuddle up close to her in the bed. One

25

night, three-year-old Cal woke up crying, and, to calm him, she caressed his genitals. She thought he seemed to like it.

In fact, Stacey had grown up believing sex was something males did to females, but because Melvyn was there and so passive, and perhaps thinking of little Cal, or in some kind of unconscious retaliation, she acted out against her stepson. Others tempted her, the little ones at the nursery school where she worked, for example. Sometimes when she took a boy to the bathroom, she would fondle his penis.

Melvyn's thoughts of Stacey recede when he is out of the bath. She lives in another city. Alice ran away when she was fifteen. His father died of pancreatitis, aggravated by his alcoholism, just before Melvyn moved here. He thinks of himself as being without family.

Melvyn steps out of the tub, reaches for a towel, and dries himself. He reaches for the deodorant in the medicine cabinet. Then he goes into the bedroom and puts on clean chinos and a pink-and-green madras short-sleeved shirt. In the drawer where he keeps his shirts there are several little girls' T-shirts, and on top, a pink sundress embellished with a cartoonish, sequined cat and words that say, "I'm A Pretty Kitty." He looks at them and wonders what Lizbett is wearing that day. A dress, he hopes. A dress makes things much easier. Besides, dresses make little girls more appealing. He can imagine their sweet legs all the way up to their panties.

Melvyn Searle's father, Ralph Searle, was a mid-level banker. He was a surly man and never sober once he got home from the bank at six. Melvyn tried to avoid him by staying in his room, but there was the dinner table where his father always seemed to find a reason to hurl insults at him or cuff him over the head. Once he dislocated Melvyn's arm when he pulled at it. "Straighten up!" he'd yell. "Or speak up!" "Don't chew like that!" "Clean your plate!" "You're a freakish little twerp fuckhead, you know that?" "Get up and help Stacey, you lazy chicken's asshole!"

Melvyn seems to think his father wasn't always like this. He imagines that when his mother was with them, his father was nicer. But his mother left them when he was only two. He can picture being on her lap, nestling into her soft chest, but her face is a blank. And there are no photographs.

His father's mother took over. She was like her son: never sober and always mean. His father brought Stacey home quite quickly and Melvyn's grandmother left. At first, Stacey seemed nicer than his grandmother. She did everything to gain his trust, especially reading him all the stories she did. He couldn't get enough of books. He loved the alternate worlds they offered him. Stacey was a wonderful, expressive reader, pulling Melvyn close in beside her, enveloping him with one arm. He felt so cozy and safe.

Being around children was the only time Stacey felt in control. When she was with them the insecurities, the shame, she felt around adults disappeared. And when she read to them, clustered all around her, her voice bringing them the power of the words, she felt assured and capable of love. And she loved to sing with them. Joy burst from her then.

Stacey first caught Ralph's eye when he was looking at schools for Melvyn. He watched her for some time. He thought she would be good with Melvyn, who was a shy, clingy boy.

She was a very thin, pretty woman with thick blond curls, but she was edgy. Her eyes flitted and she slouched. Stacey was young, at least ten years younger than Ralph's thirty-six and was slightly in awe of him, but also wary of him, looking up to him, but uncertain of his reactions. He was an overbearing man. She had rotten luck with men, especially the last one whose bullying escalated to hitting. She hoped Ralph would be different. He was handsome and could be affectionate, and he was older with a good, steady job and a young son. Melvyn grew up calling her Mom.

His favourite thing to do with her was make masks. She had a boxful of childish treasures: intriguing buttons, feathers, sequins, rhinestones and pearls, bright ribbon, silver and gold paper, raffia, myriad stickers, and, best of all, vibrant markers in many, many colours. She bought plain white masks, which he decorated lavishly. They cut holes in paper bags. He liked these because he could attach all kinds of hair from the Hallowe'en wigs Stacey found. Sometimes, if Stacey was in a mood to cope with the mess, he moulded a face out of papier mâché.

He loved putting on these masks and staring into a mirror. When he did this, he created an elaborate fantasy for the character he was portraying, a character far removed from himself. Like the red wizard with the ruby eyes and bright, full lips. He entered a world of power and magic whereby he could create new beings and make others vanish. The wizard had a mother, a shining queen in a pink and silver gown who smiled and sang instead of talking and caressed him and brought him gifts. When he put on his queen mask, he was beautiful.

He surrounded himself with other children who would do his bidding.

Ralph wanted Stacey to go back to work when Melvyn was in school, but she refused. She said she would need to upgrade her skills. So she sat in a big armchair reading all day long, smoking cigarettes. At first she only drank when Ralph got home, but then she began to pour something in the afternoon and by the time Melvyn got home from school, she was drunk.

Alice's birth sobered Stacey up, at least for a couple of years. It was then that Melvyn discovered how the happy loving innocence of a baby, how her little arms about his neck made him feel whole. Stacey taught him essential baby care and he became a big help to her. When he changed Alice, he was fascinated by her bottom, its minute, intricate, perfect folds. He would probe the tiny vagina with a baby-oiled finger.

His favourite thing was dressing Alice in the pretty, lacy pink clothes Stacey bought for her. Sometimes he and his stepmother would take the baby for a walk in her carriage. Melvyn thought this was what a family must feel like. Sometimes he would imagine having a daughter of his own one day.

But by his senior year, Stacey had relapsed and he'd arrive at the house to find Alice asleep or crying in the playpen and he had to take over a lot of her care. He was working toward a scholarship to get into a nearby college and he resented having her on his hands. And Alice was entering the terrible twos. She was no longer a pliable, responsive doll, but a defiant, tantrum-throwing toddler with huge needs he felt incapable of filling. The only way he had any control over her was to read to her, all the books Stacey had read to him.

And bathing her at night, it seemed right that he repeat his stepmother's acts. Everything about her body, pink from the hot water, seemed receptive. Except Alice wasn't. She flailed and cried. Why hadn't he? Maybe he had and he didn't remember because it became so routine. He took to giving her Double Bubble or cherry lollipops to quiet her. Once Stacey came in and caught him and she punched and pounded and kicked him almost senseless, screaming at him that he was filthy and disgusting and a pervert. He stopped giving Alice baths, after that. But he didn't stop wanting to do things to her, to her pale, smooth inviting little body. He found ways. Mostly he found he could sneak into Alice's room after Stacey had passed out in bed, the way she had to him. By the time he was near to finishing college, he was penetrating Alice, calling her "Sweetie," telling her she was his own "good, good little angel-girl." And reading to her. And buying her sweet pink dresses.

On this now menacingly hot July morning, Melvyn exits his house, already feeling excited and impatient for what is ahead. He hasn't questioned his motivation. What compels him is pure attraction, the enticing idea that Lizbett wants him. He is sure she does. Her girlishly scintillating reactions to his overtures have convinced him.

He has some time so he decides to sit in his park for a bit and watch the children, most of whom he knows and who know him. He feels this will calm him. He is always jumpy before one of his encounters. He plans them so carefully, but anything could go wrong. He'd phoned the Warnes yesterday and asked to talk to Lizbett, simply to make sure she'd be coming today, but she hadn't been in. He didn't identify himself. This will be Lizbett's third Monday. Her routine doesn't usually vary. She walks to the museum alone and then walks home. He feels pretty certain today will be the same.

He wonders if what he feels for Lizbett is love, if he knows what love is. Certainly, what he feels is powerful and he has the sensation she affects his heart. She does not make it beat faster; she makes it swell until it is painful. He wants to pound his chest for the pain. He longs to be with her, to take her in his arms. That's it, really, he wants to overtake her, to incorporate her existence into his. Not obliterate her, but possess her with every fibre of his being. If that is love, he loves her past comprehension. And he will have her.

Though it is some distance, he decides he will walk to the museum. In fact, he will walk through the university campus. It is an old, traditional university, featuring gothic stone buildings with ornate spires enclosing green quadrangles. There is a path that passes the music building and in the summer, when the windows are open, you can hear the students practising.

But bad weather threatens. Rain is imminent. So he decides to go back and get his car, after all. It will make what he is planning easier.

At 4:00 p.m. he will exit the building by the basement service entrance as quickly after Lizbett leaves as he can. It is a door that is little used, mostly deserted. Pete, the security guard, is an old and trusted employee, an alcoholic who sometimes drinks on the job and often sleeps in his small booth. Melvyn is counting on that. Then he will drive to the intersection where he is hoping to find her, just down from the museum. He may catch her a little farther along the street. No matter. He will offer her a ride because of the weather and he feels sure she'll accept. In fact, he's convinced she'll be flattered to be asked, to be alone with him. He knows she cares for him.

They will go for a drive. They will talk about masks. They will talk about each other. He will be so happy and so will she. He will see to it.

He isn't sure why he has chosen today. He is aware of an urgency within him to establish close, separate contact with her. It has been growing since the beginning when he was so surprised and delighted to have Lizbett in the class. But there, it's as if she belongs to everyone, so keen are her camp-mates to associate with her. And she responds avidly to each, making him or her think she could be a best friend. She does this genuinely because though she is an extrovert, she is a sensitive and considerate one. She treats everyone equitably. In this way, she spreads herself thinly, but not notice-ably, at least not to the kids. But she exhibits a special regard toward him. If she were older, he would consider her flirtatious, but instead she has a curious ingenuousness, a real desire to share his knowledge. He suspects it is her love of theatre. At the end of the week, when each person in the group "charges" his or her mask, Lizbett is the one who most understands the intimate duality of the mask. It is her grasp of that subtle and com-plex profundity that has so endeared her to him. She becomes her mask brilliantly, impulsively, spontaneously, allowing the mask to take her over. And her mask comes alive. He finds it thrilling just to think about it.

Today the class will be creating life masks: plaster casts made right on their own faces. He will choose Lizbett to be one of the first. It seems appropriate that on such a momentous day, a day of ritual, she will leave her real face behind.

# 2

# THE SAME MONDAY MORNING IN JULY 1986

## *The Warnes*

The first thing she notices is the sky. It is lavishly streaked with crimson, a molten sun in the middle. A pulsating, bleeding sky. It feels violent, ominous, a harbinger of disaster. "Red sky in the morning; sailor take warning ..." Meredith sighs. More storms.

Their house is on a street that climbs one of the steepest hills in the city and from her third-floor bedroom she can see out over the abundant trees (it is a city known for its green), to the office towers of the downtown and beyond that, a sliver of the great lake it sits on. She turns to look at her husband, Thompson, or Sonny, as he is occasionally called, a childhood nickname. He is sitting on the edge of the bed, his head in his hands, yawning. "Still not awake?" she laughs. She goes over and ruffles his fine, dark hair. He is a long, lean man, but soft, untoned with a little bulge above his pantline. Both of them are naked, having just made love.

It was hurried, more sensation than passion. She had, as usual, awakened early. Only this morning, lying there, instead of trying to return to sleep, she had curled herself around Thompson's back and reached over and cupped his soft genitals. He groaned; didn't respond. Mornings were his low point, the first few moments at waking grim.

"What do you think?" she asked. "Up for it?"

"Not sure," he answered, not opening his eyes, not moving.

"Want me to try?"

"If you want. Some people like necrophilia."

She laughed and pulled him over and lowered her head to his groin. This was as much for her as it was for him. She loved doing this, even with his disinterest. She loved his penis, ready or not. She loved the transformation from squishy, helpless thing in its nest of hair to solid, satiny tower. She loved to run her tongue around the precise rim of the glans, immerse the strong shaft into the wet warmth of her mouth. She felt power and pleasure with the possession of him.

His reaction, or *its*, was as she had expected and she reached into the drawer of the bedside table for the tube of K-Y jelly and lubricated them both and then she sat astride him and slid onto him. He still hadn't opened his eyes.

"You know I hate this," he said, with a sleepy grin.

"That's okay," she said, with a laugh. "It's for me. It will soon be over." And it was, she having reached orgasm by touching herself while she was on him, he quickly following her. She always loved sex, even when it was hurried like this. She loved its raw upheaval, the thrill of its temporary exposure. She lay on his lanky body, her own roundness filling his angles while he stroked her back.

"I do love you, you know."

"Terrific," he said, motioning for her to get off. They were both sweaty, more from the humidity than the exertion and she wasn't a lingerer, in any case.

"Okay," she said, sliding off him. "Up and at 'em. Time to get a wiggle on. No dilly-dallying," which is what she says almost every day.

She heads for the bathroom and looks guiltily at the stationary bicycle in the corner. Her nemesis. Her struggle. Her weight. Tomorrow.

Thompson falls back onto the bed and puts the pillow over his head.

In the shower, she lathers her curly, coppery hair and pale freckled body. She is beautiful, but not in the ordinary sense. She is more striking, with round, wide eyes, a small nose with a tilt, and a full mouth. Her face is always animated; her expressions pliant.

She thinks of the reliability of their sex, that it is not so much ardent (not after almost fourteen years of marriage), as loving and easy. Familiar. It isn't boring or perfunctory. She doesn't think that. What she feels is a small gladness for the surety of it; that Thompson would always be available and willing for it to happen.

She wonders if the girls have heard them. Not that they made much noise. She, a little, when she came, maybe, a stifled gasp. Besides they are on the spacious, remade third floor of their Victorian house. It has a large bedroom with a fireplace and bathroom and an office for both of them for their business, Artful Sustenance. He is a photographer, she a food stylist, and they've worked together successfully for six years since Meredith returned to work when Darcy was a year old. Before that, she was in advertising. Thompson has always been a sought-after photographer.

Lizbett, who is eleven, and Darcy, seven, are on the second floor, each in their own bedroom with a shared bath. There are two other bedrooms and another bathroom on the same level for guests.

Still, Meredith is always concerned about having sex when the girls are up. It's better to wait until they are asleep. Thompson prefers that. Inventive, prolonged sex at bedtime. But Meredith is usually tired at night and not up to Thompson's desires. Their best times are afternoons, with a bottle of white wine, when the girls are away or if they can escape somewhere for a weekend or a holiday, but none of these happens as often as they would like. So they compromise, taking turns with each other's preferences and it has worked.

Or at least it is starting to again. Meredith is recovering from a recent six-month affair with a young mystery novelist, a swaggery extrovert who nonplussed her with his overtures and eventually she succumbed. And eventually she was hurt. He was probably a little in love with her, and she more than a little with him, but he wanted marriage and children and even if she were to divorce Thompson, she has had her tubes tied. Besides, she is forty. And she has Lizbett and Darcy, her beloved girls for whom she would do anything, even stay in a marriage that has felt less than full. But she still feels aftershocks from the affair, which was vigorous and inventive.

She had not thought she was unhappy, but she realized after being with Allan, who was a vital, spontaneous man, that Thompson's quiet reticence, his understated responses, if he responded to her at all, have created in her a kind of hunger. Thompson is slow-paced, laconic. Allan was spirited, responsive, both loquacious and an enthusiastic listener. When she talked, he talked back.

Once she said, "I'm not sure why I'm doing this terrible thing."

"Terrible thing?"

"This … being with you. I'm forty years old, married with two children I love … a husband I love."

"Why are you, then?"

"Because you came after me. I was flattered. And intrigued. And it's an added dimension to my life. It's like parentheses filled with ignition and pleasure. Everything in my life has always felt so exposed. It just spills over onto everything. I like the secrecy of this … there's a precariousness that's sustaining … like being abandoned somewhere unknown. I don't know what's going to happen. But that's the thrill. The unexpected. The dangerous."

"Dangerous?"

"Well, in the sense that I am very vulnerable. I rarely feel vulnerable. I mostly feel safe. I organize my life so that it is. No surprises."

"So this is not about me? It's about the risk."

"You're inseparable from it. You invite defiance. You're cocky and assured. You strut."

"Strut! Jesus!"

"Yes. As if you have no match."

"Maybe you're just bad." He'd laughed. She hadn't.

"I hope I don't get punished."

Mostly the affair had puzzled her because she and Thompson had regular sex. Good sex. Sex wasn't the issue. Nor was connectedness. They thought alike. It was really Meredith's need for reaction.

Meredith is an extrovert, a demanding one. Some might call her brash. And her spiritedness needs fuel. When Thompson fell in love with that vivacity, he suspected it might come at a price. She'd offset his emotional timidity with an impetuous, almost ravenous devotion. But when she went after him, though he responded willingly, he did so with deliberate caution, fearing he'd lose something crucial. He lives within himself and does not emerge easily. He is an awkward connector. He doesn't talk because he doesn't like talking, so he rarely does, unless he has something important to say. Meredith was attracted to this quiescence, believing it to be depth, which it was. He was always preoccupied with the contortions and convolutions of existence; how greed and power superseded charity, how influence superseded compassion. He believed humans were primal, that "power over" was the engine of society and that manners and morals, intellectual and philosophical thought, art and music, were attributes of comfort and leisure without which instinct ruled. He was troubled by the fact that connection, the key to life was arduous and tenuous. Life was more about irony and survival than love.

Except where his daughters were concerned. For them he felt a feeling so pure, so clear he could almost see it — as a bright, overwhelming light, all-encompassing, inescapable, which began and stopped with them. They took up all of his deepest vision, the vision that fed his quiddity.

Even though she had always craved, commanded attention, it was a relief for Meredith to be with Thompson. His need for isolation was so embedded that it read like assurance, an independence that was appealing. But lately the restraint she had so admired in him had come to seem like indifference. She adored him, adores him, and she is certain he adores her, but she wishes it were not so complicated, that it did not require such effort to get him to acknowledge her. Sometimes she feels like screaming to get him to interact, to react.

One of the things that redeems Thompson — because almost everyone who tries to talk to him has a difficult time — is his wry sense of humour. He is subtle, quick, and acute. This morning, after they had made love, he had cracked her up when he said, "What took you so long?"

Above all, he loves her for her abundance: abundance of love and generosity, compassion, abundance of spontaneity and spirit, abundance of creative energy. Above all, she loves him for his spareness, his thoughtful withholding. They have had an embedded mutuality. They are like a wooden matchstick. Neither part is useful until the match is struck.

Below, Lizbett has heard her parents' lovemaking. Her bedroom is directly below theirs and their bed has a light squeak. She realizes they are not aware of this or they would do something about it. She is not the least disturbed. She has grown up with an openness toward sex, first, when she was little with *Where Do I Come From?* Now she has thoroughly read

*Our Bodies, Ourselves* and *The Joy of Sex* with her best friends. She has felt that throb between her legs. She has not yet masturbated, but she has had "pretend" sex with her best friend. And she has kissed her best friend's brother, who is fifteen. That was nice, arousing even. She looks forward to knowing what real sex feels like.

She has been awake and up for some time. Ever since she was a baby, she has not been a sleeper. Meredith found her difficult because she was never still; always into everything. Always questioning. She continues to be like that. This morning she has already showered and dressed, tying her still-wet hair, the exact red of her mother's, in a ponytail, putting on her favourite red shorts with a red-striped T-shirt and leather sandals. Before she leaves her yellow-and-white room with the daisy wallpaper, she makes her canopied bed and though she doesn't play with them anymore, rearranges all her dolls in her old bassinette with the eyelet skirt. She loves the dolls. But she will be twelve in a few months and is on an ambitious new track.

For a moment, she sits at the edge of her bed, as if contemplating her next move and idly runs her fingertips across her lips. She feels a tiny bit of ragged nail and bites it, then presses it and bites some more. She does this with all her fingers until one of them is bleeding.

Recently she had the lead in a month-long run of *Annie* at the Nathan S. Hirschenberg Arts Centre and it has given her a kind of celebrity. Not that she didn't earn it. She has been studying voice and ballet at the Conservatory since she was nine and told her parents she wanted to be an actress. Before *Annie* she had already played Gretel in a new musical version of Hansel and Gretel at The Children's Theatre Workshop. She has done two television commercials, one for cookies, the other for cereal. She will go to sleepover drama camp in August, as she had last year. She has been acting, really, from when she could walk and talk and realized her antics got a positive reaction. Anytime she has an opportunity to perform, she does. The part of Annie was hard won. Dozens of other girls auditioned. For Lizbett, the thrill of the exposure has only whetted her appetite for more.

She has no illusions, however. She is astute and practical. She knows life doesn't always go as she'd wish. And she feels divided in courting her parents' pleasure and finding her own way.

Lizbett feels especially attached to her mother. They have a special "oneness"; their ways of being are in tune. Not that Lizbett isn't aware her mother is the adult and she is the child. Her mother can be firm and demanding and she sets boundaries. But she is loose and loud and showy and Lizbett loves how she attracts attention. And Lizbett knows she and her mother think alike, have the same aspirations. She knows her mother is ambitious for her. She is ambitious for herself and she likes having an ally. Ever since she was very little she and her mother have chatted easily and laughed, exchanged feelings and ideas. Lizbett shares all her plans and misgivings with her. They have walked together, shopped together, gone to art galleries and films and the theatre together, cooked together, watched TV together. Before Lizbett was in school all day they even "lunched" together at spiffy restaurants. Though she knows it's maybe inappropriate, she likes to think of her mother as her best friend.

With her father, her relationship is more confined. She does not find him easy to talk to, but he is more affectionate than her mother. He is always available for a tight hug. And until recently, she could climb on his lap and snuggle into him with his arms around her and stay for an indefineable time. He was fun and funny. They used to have a silly game. They'd play it over and over. She never got tired of it.

He would ask, "Lizbett, what's the difference between a duck?"

"Oh, Daddy, that doesn't make sense."

"Then what's the difference between a duck and a train?"

Lizbett would laugh harder. "That's 'dicilous," she'd say.

"Okay, then. What's the difference between a duck and cheesecake?"

As the comparisons got more and more absurd … "What's the difference between a duck and a dinosaur, a sofa, a hamburger with ketchup?" Lizbett would be shrieking and giggling uncontrollably.

She loved their reading and playing the piano together. They just didn't talk much.

In her acting, Lizbett has the ability to enter the character she is playing, slip into her skin and become her. Take on her identity. At the same time as she does this, she also animates the character with her own sensibilities and vitality. The two meld. For this she is praised: for her naturalistic, un-self-conscious portrayals.

Meredith volunteers every second Saturday morning at a settlement house that provides daycare for single mothers. Most of them are teenagers who go off and do teenage things while their small children are looked after. Lizbett sometimes goes and helps out and the thing that most overwhelms her is not how shabby and unclean — even a bit smelly — the children are, but how passive. Their only stimulation has been the television, which they've been plopped in front of from their earliest months. No one has read to them, played hand and face games with them, coloured and drawn with them, performed puppet shows for them. Lizbett does all this with pleasure, but she feels, sadly and with some early cynicism, that it means very little. It bothers her to return to her privileged life when the children have to return to their deprived ones. She doesn't know how to reconcile the imbalance.

Down in the kitchen, she pours herself a glass of milk, then goes into the family room, sits at the piano, and begins to practise. First she does some hand stretches and then she begins the scales, then the arpeggios. She brings out a book of exercises and plays each one, diligently, though not effortlessly. She is a good pianist, but she is a careless one, going through the pieces the same way she goes through life, with enthusiasm and endurance, but not necessarily focus, concentration. Her head is in too many places at once.

She begins a Schubert piece she has been working on for some time.

Upstairs, lying in bed, a Huey Lewis song is running through Thompson's head. "Doin' It All for My Baby." He really doesn't like sex in the morning. He feels groggy, subpar, as if all his neurons aren't firing. He doesn't like the bad taste in his mouth and he doesn't like the smell of Meredith's. He doesn't like that his body feels stale, raunchy. But he is particularly aware right now of Meredith's need for responsiveness and this morning was the best he could do. He knows she has been having an affair or rather he keenly suspects something extraordinary has been going on. Her euphoria, her frequent absences with odd explanations, her heightened attentiveness to family, her increased sex drive, her more than usual garrulousness all suggest this. He was once the object of such excess. Not that Meredith isn't always a bit excessive, but in love she's almost manic.

That's how it seemed when they were in university. She was an exchange student from Australia doing her junior year in Fine Arts as a painting major. He was majoring in photography. They had a seminar together, "Food in the Paintings of the Baroque Era," which they both loved.

He wasn't sure exactly what he had done to attract her. He was handsome in an unassuming, untidy way, but he wouldn't have thought so. He had an ungroomed beard and his dark eyes under heavy eyebrows gave him a gruff look.

He was not used to female attention, having gone to an all-male boarding school from age ten. And he was diffident, a late only child with parents so engrossed in one another that he felt he was a basically a distraction to them. His only contact with his mother — his father only came on weekends — was summers at their island cottage up north. Being alone with her in that isolated setting, in deep silent woods by active, glistening water, Thompson learned something about women ... or his own intimate version. His mother exuded care, but she was removed and he would watch her move about the cottage, on their walks, while they swam, in awe, as if she were something "other," a mystical being. She was elegant and gentle and convivial; she treated him not as a son, but as a companion. She never hugged him, but somehow seemed to embrace him in a respectful, solicitous way. She engaged him, seemed interested in his thoughts. What he felt from her was a kind of power, an intelligent, creative, thoughtful power that reinforced his life, but did not enter it. She was unknowable.

So Meredith's initial undisguised ardor, especially her physical overtures, overwhelmed, but also pleased him. It seemed to require so little effort on his part.

"I'm not used to so much fuss," he said.

"You just don't know how to deal with ..."

"With ...?"

"Love."

"It's not anything I ever imagined having."

She took over his life.

"I'm not sure what you see in me," he said after a session of particularly fervid sex when Meredith was so loud he was afraid the upstairs tenants, a group of earnest student teachers, would hear.

"I'm not sure, either."

"Is it because I'm so eloquent?"

She laughed. "No, you only speak when you have something to say ..."

"Which isn't often," he interjected.

"Which isn't often. Right. My father is a church minister who never stops talking. He preaches and proselytizes and lectures and tells the same stories over and over and we have to listen, my sister, my mother, and I. We weren't allowed a voice. All he had to do to get us to shut up was give us a withering, destructive look.

"He was mean?" Thompson asked.

"Oh, no, never! He was … is a gentle, kind man, but he was a stern lecturer and so boring and repetitive. And from early on, I thought what he said was such bullshit! You have no bullshit in you. I … love how grounded you seem. I always feel as if my feet never hit firm ground … as if I'm … not flying … but moving just above the surface of things, never really in contact. I feel a little as if you pin me down."

"It's nothing I do," he said. "Or mean to do."

"I know. It's me."

"With your father the way he was, I mean, a silencer, how did you get to be such …"

"Such a yakker? From him! Once I was out of the house I couldn't shut up. I think I must be full of bullshit. You haven't noticed?"

"I've noticed!"

"And …?"

"It's okay. It fills spaces I can't or don't want to. And I can tune out."

"I've noticed."

"Sorry," he said.

"I don't mind." she replied. "Because it means the pressure's off me."

"What pressure?"

"The pressure to keep you amused so you'll want to be with me."

"I want to be with you."

"You do?"

"Yes."

"That's the first time you've ever said anything."

"Well, you've never wanted to know."

He senses now that she wants to know. She's gone into retreat mode which is rare for her. Retreat mode for Meredith means she is distracted, distanced. She doesn't talk. She goes to bed. The girls put their mouths to her ear and say, "Earth to Mom!"

He is thinking he should be jealous. That would be the reasonable — or unreasonable and instinctive — way to feel. Perhaps he should be enraged. But he just feels sad: sad at his own passivity, that in some way he has failed her, failed her enough that she has heaped her affection — that's how he sees it — on someone else. Her affection is a loose, lavish, limitless weight. It is not in his nature to ask her what's wrong. If something is wrong, she'll tell him. Or so he believes. Either that or he'll lose her. He feels that actually preventing that is beyond his power. He can only keep loving her as he always has, steadfastly, profoundly, heedfully, and hope it's enough.

Lizbett enters the kitchen where Meredith is studying a shopping list. She and Thompson have a big contract: a five-page Christmas editorial for *RARITY*. She says to Lizbett, "Lovely playing, darling."

"Thanks, Mom. It's Schubert. It's really hard."

"'The Impromptu Number two in A Flat,'" says Thompson. He is making a pile of toast and peanut butter for the table while he puts together the girls' lunches. "It sure was hard."

"Nan-Nan is always telling me how you never practised. How she doesn't want us to end up like you."

"I wish I had now."

"I like your jazzy stuff."

He leaves the lunch-making and goes into the next room with the piano and plays few vibrant riffs from Ray Bryant.

Meredith looks up. "Sonny! C'mon! Has anybody seen Darce? Isn't she up yet? Lizbett, go upstairs, please, and get your sleepyhead sister out of bed."

"Why is she so bad? Do I have to?"

"I already stuck my head in," says Thompson.

"So did I," says Meredith.

Lizbett enters her sister's ocean-blue room with the red plaid curtains and opens them.

"Don't!" yells Darcy. She buries her dark head in the pillow. Dora, Meredith's mother, is descended from the "Black Irish" and Darcy has inherited her colouring. When they are open, her eyes are a deep brown, with black lashes — unlike Lizbett's, whose blond lashes fringe bright green eyes. And Lizbett is pale like her mother. Darcy's skin is olive.

She is like a sprite. Her family likes to say she is "no bigger than a minute."

"C'mon, Darce. Mom said. You'll be late for camp."

Darcy whimpers, "I don't want to," and Lizbett puts her hands under her sister's back and lifts her into a sitting position. She flops back down.

"Please, Darce. C'mon, I'll help you." Reluctantly, Darcy pulls herself out of bed. She is a wistful child. Where Lizbett is impulsive, spontaneous, Darcy is pensive, hesitant, as if she regrets, not her short existence, but any disruption that may occur in the future. This has nothing to do with premonition and everything to do with her view of life, which is essentially sad. She was only three when their beloved Great Dane, Misty, died, but the sorrow that pervaded the house affected her deeply: seeing her mother, father, and sister weep openly. She clearly remembers the dog's enormous bodily absence and the wonder of that. Now she fears separation of any kind, sensing it may be permanent. But she knows her parents, her mother especially, disapprove of any fuss, so she has developed a brave face. Getting up in the morning means she is going to have to put it on.

Lizbett leads her into the bathroom where she fills the sink with hot water, wets a washcloth, and washes Darcy's face. Then she puts toothpaste on her toothbrush, says, "Open," and brushes Darcy's teeth.

Back in the bedroom, she pulls clean clothes out of the drawers, some panties, brown shorts, and a white T-shirt and helps Darcy put them on. By now, Darcy is awake and she bends over and buckles up her sandals.

"Let's make the bed," says Lizbett and together, one on each side of the bed, the sisters pull up the sheet and blue coverlet.

"Careful not to disturb Mr. Mushu and Geoffrey!" Mr. Mushu is their Siamese cat and Geoffrey is a stray tabby who arrived last winter during a snowstorm. The two beloved animals are curled up at the bottom of the bed cleaning each other.

"Darcy, honey, what are we going to do with you?" Meredith says when the girls arrive in the kitchen. "Stephen and his mommy are going to be here soon to pick you up. You barely have time to eat."

"I can take some toast in the car. I'm an owl, like Daddy." It's true the two of them have trouble getting to sleep at night. Thompson reads in bed. Meredith has taken to allowing Darcy to do the same. Better to have her absorbed than tossing and turning. Books are her life, in any case. She often has two on the go. Meredith has tried to help her develop other activities, but Darcy has resisted. Apart from the piano lessons, which she also takes with her grandmother, she is not interested in anything else except the cats. And, unlike Lizbett, who has a group of close friends, Darcy only has Stephen, who has been her friend from nursery school. Meredith thinks this is far too passive a life for a child to lead. Her contribution to family life is being complaisant.

Maybe she is a late developer. She certainly was a late talker. While Lizbett had said words at ten months and full sentences by eighteen months, Darcy spoke few words, even at two years. Meredith keeps watching for an artistic bent to surface. Her artwork from school has shown promise. She is hoping that the art camp she is attending at the City Art Gallery will inspire her.

As Lizbett is leaving to walk to the Courtice Museum for her mask camp, Thompson hands over her lunch. "Thanks, Daddy," she says. "Hope it's good like yesterday."

"Should be. It's the same as yesterday."

Meredith says, "Daddy and I are starting a new shoot, a big Christmas one for an important magazine. We're going to be really, really busy for a while, at least the whole of this week."

"Christmas in the summer?" Darcy asks.

"Crazy, isn't it?" Meredith answers. "Just like Australia. But that's how long it takes a magazine to prepare an article like this. Come straight home from mask camp, Lizbett. Brygida will be here and will get you dinner if we're not home yet."

Brygida Breischke is their Polish housekeeper who has been with them since Meredith went back to work and she is their lifeline. She keeps them corralled the way a border collie herds sheep, with an indomitable, tireless energy. As it is, she is inefficient and hurried, the kind of woman who runs through her work whacking the vacuum against baseboards and furniture and missing dirt and dust everywhere. She breaks a lot of dishes. In a day she can clean the house, do laundry, and iron shirts and pillowcases and still have time to make perogies or a veal-and-pepper stew. When the girls were little, she was doting, but firm, and took them to the park every morning. In the afternoons, they curled up on a sofa with her and watched soap operas. She thought they improved her English.

Her daughter Aniela often came to the Warnes' with her mother during school holidays and Lizbett and Darcy love her. Meredith thinks of Aniela almost as a niece. When Aniela graduated from art school, the Warnes helped her to get a job at a gallery. Both Brygida and Aniela have spent nights at the Warnes' to get away from Tadeusz, the husband and father, when he knocked them around.

Now Brygida only comes in the afternoons and stays to get Lizbett and Darcy's dinner if Thompson and Meredith are late. But they don't like her cooking. They find it greasy and mushy.

"I don't have to eat here tonight," Darcy says. I'm having supper at Stephen's."

"Oh, that's right. I forgot."

"And Mom. I wanted to go to the library to look at mask books. I told you."

"There's going to be a big storm, Lizbett. I think you should come right home."

"Mom! The teacher told us to. I have to. Storms don't matter. I always go to the library by myself."

Lizbett is keen to please her teacher. She has engaged with Mr. Searle ... Melvyn (he has told them they can call him Melvyn) ... with Melvyn in a compelling way. She thinks about him a lot; finds him cute. His suggestions for her work flatter her. He is not like other teachers. He doesn't have that grown-up distance. It's not that he jokes or even fools around. He is simply kid-like, maybe because he is closer to their size, maybe because he has a young face. Maybe because he is right in there with them and seems to like them so much. She even thinks she might be his favourite and she likes that.

Thompson says, "Let her, Mer, if it's so important to her. She's a big girl. And the storm may not happen, anyway."

Meredith acquiesces. The library is three subway stops north from the museum and Lizbett has made the trip many times. Maybe Thompson's right. Maybe the rain will hold off. In any case, she'll be mostly underground.

"All right, lovey, go. Now, off you go, lambies, or you'll be late. Don't dawdle. And Lizbett, take your umbrella."

"I already have it," she says, going out the door where Stephen and his mother are waiting for Darcy.

# 3

# A Monday Afternoon in July 1986

*Thompson and Meredith*

Later, when Meredith thinks about the superficiality of her day — that she was moving pieces of food by centimetres — while her daughter was being violated, she will feel sick with disgust. Her life on her daughter's last day on earth was meaningless.

And after today, July and Christmas will never again be the same for Meredith, but for now she is the only one of the crew on the shoot for *RARITY* who feels Christmasy. It is muggy and dark outside. The air is heavy from the threatening storm. But the heat reminds her of Christmases in Australia when she was growing up. Steamy, debilitating heat. Yuletide heat. On Christmas Eve, her father's parishioners would bring blankets and sit outside in the sultry summer air on the lawn of the church and everyone would light candles and sing traditional carols.

On Christmas morning in the close heat of the white clapboard church, her father, every year, talked of the importance of the birth of hope and grace and how that was what they were celebrating, not the secular festivities. Jesus was our Saviour, he said, because as the Son of God, in giving us his life, he gave us enlightened purpose. His arrival this day was a Supreme gift, the gift of a Saviour.

*Rubbish and bunk*, Meredith thought. The same, year after year. The words fused into a big, boring lecture. They were about duty, not Christian duty, to which she felt petulantly antagonistic, but duty to her father, to appear to listen and understand and believe. When she was young, all she could think of was the presents waiting for her and her older sister Abbey under the Norfolk pine decorated with tinsel and glass balls. As she got older, the words made her recoil because she found them duplicitous. Christian salvation was a misogynist myth and had nothing to do with the actual teachings of Jesus.

What she understood least about her parents was their lack of questioning. How could they trust so implicitly something as tenuous as Divine, immortal goodness when everything about the human condition indicated that it did not exist?

Still, she loved the lush time of year: that it was the end of school and the beginning of summer holidays and she and her sister had free days ahead. Her mother, Dora maintained all the traditions of an old-fashioned English Christmas with Dickens' "A Christmas Carol" and gift exchange, then roast goose and plum pudding after the Christmas-morning service. What was best of all was the afternoon trip to the beach to play in the surf and make sand sculptures. Sometimes, on Boxing Day, if her father could find the time, they'd go off camping.

Meredith is in a reverie, thinking about it. All those joyous Australian Christmases. Now she has to reproduce that spirit in July. She is grateful for the stifling heat.

This is a substantial pictorial Christmas spread. *RARITY* caters to an elite readership accustomed to luxury and excess.

They are unfortunately almost a month late getting started. The long-time lover of Lew Chan, the art director, has died of AIDS and Lew has taken the time to recover. Though Lew had nursed Kirk through obscene suffering for long months before his death, he has been distraught to the point of helplessness.

This is the third friend Meredith and Thompson have lost to AIDS. These days, most social gatherings have the pall of the mysterious new disease. Some people are seeing it as a scourge for a lifestyle. The Warnes see it as something terrifying, ruthless and haphazard.

When Kirk died, Meredith had thought, *What a punishing way to die*, although she did not believe for a moment in the hideous "God's

Punishment" theory of AIDS. But she must have some aggravating, insidious Christian tendrils within her because when she was in the middle of her affair with Allan, she had thought, "Will I ever be punished for this?"

This shoot, which is meant to be about joy and festivity, will be sombre, and Lew, who is persnickety and anxious to begin with, will be feeling pressured because of the delay and the overhang of his grotesque loss. The Warnes are prepared for a rough time.

The menu is one of the most elaborate Meredith has worked on:

Appetizers: mini feuilletés with stilton and pear, smoked salmon cornucopias with lemon cream and capers, buckwheat blinis with crème fraîche and caviar and wild mushroom duxelles in pâte à choux.

Soup: oyster cream soup.

Palate cleanser: champagne sorbet.

Entrée: roast goose with chestnut-and-sage-sausage stuffing, red currant/port reduction, glazed carrots and parsnips, caramelized Brussels sprouts with roasted garlic, butternut squash gratin with pecan dust, mashed potatoes with nutmeg and cream.

Salad: watercress and arugula with lemon shallot dressing.

Dessert: ginger plum pudding, saffron crème brûlée.

It will take at least the week to prepare, style, and shoot the food. Meredith and Thompson will both work closely with Lew and Cindy, the prop stylist who will spend the morning in the studio staging the scene, an elegant dining room in a townhouse.

Mornings for Meredith will mean buying and cooking the food. In the afternoon, for the actual shooting, she will arrange all of it on the designated props and decorate it. Monday, they will do appetizers, which are the most finicky; Tuesday, the soup and sorbet and salad (an easy day); Wednesday, the vegetables and possibly one goose for composite photographs; Thursday, probably another goose and the stuffing for stand-alone shots; Friday, the desserts, although Meredith has already made the plum pudding at home.

The kitchen and studio for Artful Sustenance take up half a floor in a refurbished, four-storey warehouse. It is in a new commercial centre down on the harbour where a number of old factories have been transformed for the business community and Meredith and Thompson get good rent because the complex is out of the downtown area. The kitchen, with vast windows overlooking the lake, has two commercial-size ovens and a large double-doored refrigerator as well as both stainless-steel and butcher-block tables on which to work. It is well-equipped with all the accoutrements of food styling: spices and herbs and vinegars and oils, quality pots and pans, and a set of the best super-sharp German knives. Tweezers are crucial. But so are eyedroppers; spritz bottles; blue sticky tack; straws, X-acto knives; several sizes of scissors; pins; Krazy Glue; cotton swabs; cotton pads; three kinds of tape, Scotch, masking and duct; acrylic glaze; and any other accessories — emergency or otherwise — she imagines might be required. Sometimes the least likely device will save a shot.

Arriving in the kitchen late in the morning, she starts in on the four appetizers. It is intricate work. Because she loves to cook, this is the most creative part for her — beginning from scratch and coming up with beautiful results. It is both sculpture and painting. It is her task to make the food look "good enough to eat," but actually be edible. There is a difference. One is artifice, the other naturalism. The two must form a complement.

She works quickly, instinctively, and deliberately. While she does, she thinks of Lizbett's going to sleepover camp in a couple of weeks and how much she is going to miss her. Without her, the house goes silent and feels empty. Lizbett animates it and the family. She is part clown, part performer, part storyteller. She and Meredith have had a special bond, an unusually intimate companionship since Lizbett could talk. There is a synchronicity.

As for Darcy, sweet, moody, inward, tender-hearted Darcy, she is Meredith's beloved. She makes her heart ache because she always feels as if her daughter harbours sad thoughts and is simply unreachable. Darcy is perpetually curious, but she is also anxious, preoccupied, a little hand-wringer. Her dark eyes are pensive and her brow always knit in a little furrow. And she seems vulnerable. Lizbett is forthright, resilient. She challenges everything that confronts her. Meredith cannot imagine anything untoward ever coming to Lizbett.

It is mid-afternoon and Meredith is behind. She puts all the food on a trolley and wheels it onto the set where the crew is waiting. Lew yells at her to hurry. He is blasting "Synchronicity" by The Police, which she asks him to turn down. Her ears are ringing from the Bruce Springsteen and Phil Collins of the morning.

A dark, highly polished Georgian buffet is decorated with ornate silver candelabra at either end, each surrounded by gilt wreaths. Four strategically placed silver platters rest on the shiny surface in between.

Now comes the part Meredith dislikes: the tedious, meticulous placing of the food, every centimetre of space crucial. Lew hovers relentlessly, tyrannically, wanting this piece closer, this piece overlapping, this piece removed, this piece added, these pieces in a different pattern.

Thompson is pacing. He is irritable and restless, anxious to get going with his camera. Thompson calls Lew the queen of control. "The queen of queens," Lew says.

Working with Lew, orchestrating the food so exhaustingly to get a flawless frame always makes Meredith feel she has sold out; that she should be putting this kind of perfectionist dedication into her own paintings. Once she did that full-time: opulent, intimate, super-realistic still lifes that sold well. When they were first married, she and Thompson were bent on living a true and natural artistic life: he to his photography, she to her painting. And they managed for a time, each of them having a couple of successful exhibitions. But want got the better of ideals. They wanted a house; they wanted to travel; they wanted to be able to give their children a comfortable life, not the edgy, uncertain life of artists.

Meredith heard about an opening in the creative department of a large advertising firm and Thompson began to find successful commercial work and they were off to a measure of affluence they both desired. A year after the birth of Darcy, they took a fairly easy risk — because they were both known — and started their own company.

Six years later, Meredith is still using tweezers to reorganize food on platters. Often, when she is doing this, she thinks of the teenage mothers whose children she minds at the settlement house. They do not have the food or the resources or the wherewithal to think or even care about the aesthetics and ritual of eating. She wonders if she should somehow be cooking for the young girls or at least teaching them how to shop and cook economically. They are hungry for food and direction in their lives. The readers of *RARITY* have surfeits of both.

Finally the crew is ready for Thompson and he whoops with relief and exhilaration. Though he appreciates Meredith's work and knows what he does depends on her artful compositions, he hates the waiting. All he wants is to partner with his camera. He loves his camera, a Swedish 500 ELX Hasselblad. He loves that it is an extension of his creative eye.

Photography is about capturing reality as opposed to reproducing it. He sees every photograph, however inanimate, as a kind of portrait. The food is his focus, as expression is to a face. That the food is arranged on beautiful objects is really only about what face *says*. And what he has to consider is how an initial glance from a viewer will perceive the whole. In this instance, it must be captivating enough to draw that viewer's eye into the detail, to "drool over" the display of food and search out the recipes.

The camera is his voice and it is as eloquent as it is loquacious.

He keeps the mood light in the studio. He doesn't feel his art or his craft are compromised by what he ultimately thinks is mundane work. True, it doesn't have the grit of his previous work, the derelict areas of the waterfront. But he likes what he does enough to keep doing it: the careful, magical transposing of food into print. He loves how the contrast of light and dark makes shapes mysterious, creates depth, and how angles manipulate the eye. He controls all that and it always excites him. Even the simplest, most mundane of dishes.

And he especially likes the lack of financial pressure they feel. But he senses a restless and critical mood in Meredith. He knows she thinks that what they do is superficial and indulgent in the realm of world problems. He disagrees. He feels that life would be bleak without the aesthetics of nourishment and he's glad to be an interpreter of that.

Shortly before 4:00 p.m., Lizbett calls the studio from the payphone at the museum, just to let her mother know she is still going to the library. Meredith tries to talk her out of it.

Sometime after 4:00 p.m. Meredith walks over to the kitchen windows and sees the black, turbulent sky. The lake looks angry. Directly below, torrential rain is flooding the brick walkways. She hears the thunder; starts at the immediate flare of lightning. And her heart sinks. Why did she ever consent to allow Lizbett to go to the library in such weather? Why hadn't she made herself available to pick her up and drive her home?

The shoot finally ends a little after 6:00 p.m. Meredith phones home and Brygida tells her Lizbett hasn't appeared yet, which is odd, since she usually calls if she's going to be delayed or has changed her plans, although allowing for browsing time and travel time, she's not really late.

"She's probably gone to a friend's house or has taken a bit longer at the library," says Meredith. She suggests Brygida look in their address book for the numbers of her best friends — there's a list — and give them a call.

After they have cleaned up, the art director asks, "Who wants to go out for a bite to eat?" Meredith and Thompson both do.

# 4

# A MONDAY AFTERNOON IN JULY 1986

## Lizbett and Melvyn

Lizbett loves the rotunda of the Courtice Museum with its gold-and-turquoise mosaic floor and its soaring dome with the beautiful stained glass. She has been coming to this museum since she was in a stroller pushed by Meredith or Thompson, a Sunday afternoon ritual.

She is just returning from the Chinese garden where she has eaten her lunch with a couple of her campmates. She and her friends had thought they might get rained on, but they were lucky. They have come in early, in any case, to make a quick visit to the mask exhibits, something Lizbett does almost every day. She is in awe of the masks, of their tremendous variety and meaning in every culture. She likes what Melvyn has been telling her about masks: that a mask is something that hides a person, but is also an extension of that person. A mask has one face, but is two people: the one in it and the one it represents.

Lizbett gravitates to the very wild, primitive masks and also the Noh masks of the Japanese theatre. There is a maiden's mask from Mali where the entire face is covered in white cowrie shells and draped over those is a heavy veil of hundreds of thin braids. On top of the head, the hair is formed into a tiara bordered in bright yellow and red beads. And beneath there is a collar of turquoise beads. The Noh mask that most attracts her is also that of a young girl. Playing a young girl was the highest challenge for a Noh actor and the masks only succeeded if the performer's movements were natural and convincing. Lizbett imagines a man making this white doll-like face with the thin red lips and laughing eyes into someone the watchers believe is a happy, innocent girl.

It distresses Lizbett that in almost every culture, only the men wore masks. Even if women took part in a ritual or drama, their faces remained uncovered.

This morning Melvyn had gone over again what mask camp is about. It's not just about making masks, he always says. "What else is it about?"

Lizbett's hand shoots up.

"Lizbett?"

"It's about what masks say. Like they can say who we aren't as much as they can say who we are."

"And how do they say who we aren't?"

Again, Lizbett's hand.

"Jesse?"

"Um," Jesse says, "Sometimes they can be a fantasy of what we want to be, a self in our imagination. Like who we want to be. Like a king mask, or something. Or they can turn us into someone else who is real. Like a mask of someone famous. Or else they can show us to be scary when we're really timid. Or happy when we're really sad."

"Or they can be a spirit or a god or something. Or maybe even an animal," Laurie, in the back, pipes up.

"That's right," says Melvyn. "They can be representations, not of ourselves, but of what we believe. That also is a kind of indication of who we are. We've talked about the two-fold aspect of masks. Masks allow us both to deceive and believe at the same time. The person wearing the mask is the deceiver, but he is getting you to believe what the mask says. Masks can be us, but not us, as creations of our ancestors, our bloodline, or how we imagine them. Masks can be instruments of healing. Warrior masks protect against evil. A mask is a facade that gives us certain powers, the ability to act in ways we couldn't act without it. But do people really believe the one wearing the mask actually becomes the spirit he's portraying? Does that figure then become a way for someone to communicate with the spirit? Next week, our last week, we'll examine spirit masks, masks that are stand-ins, masks that portray something unknown, something we don't really understand. Something spiritual. A god or goddess. Something that might be worshipped or perhaps be a communicator between us and a higher force. And then we'll create our own spirit masks from moulds of what we're going to do today. So far, we've done two kinds of masks. The first week, we carved a mask out of clay to show a self from our imagination. An ideal self, a fantasy self. Last week, we went into our deepest selves to make a mask of an inner feeling, one that we could only express through an art form. We called that an outer creation of an inner core. Many people create invisible masks to hide feelings or their real identity. We created visible ones, ones that actually advertised an emotion."

Lizbett thinks about the masks she has made. She has not found this course easy. She had thought masks were about disguises, like for Hallowe'en. But Melvyn has talked about each mask being a map and that making them is a journey of discovery. The first was a journey outside yourself, so you could see yourself as a fantasy. The second was a journey inside yourself to find a hidden or secret feeling. The first one was the real challenge.

"I really don't know how to make a mask of how I imagine myself," she said to Melvyn. "I sort of imagine myself as how I am."

"Don't you have hopes and dreams?" he asked.

"Well, I'd like to be an actress."

"What kind of actress?"

"A really good one. A famous one."

"And what do we call a famous actress?"

"Oh! A star! I get it. It doesn't have to be realistic. It doesn't have to look like me. It's about a symbol of me as a star. Or a star as me."

After that, Lizbett knew where she was going. She fashioned a plain, smooth face, out of modelling clay, like the Noh masks, because her face had to do or be anything and she wanted her body movements and words to tell the story. After the clay hardened, she painted it white and yellow with a thin gold overlay. And she arranged gold and silver sequins and little yellow jewels in patterns all over that. And then with curlicues of wire, she made a fancy halo, a tall headdress, and wound gold garlands and beads around it, ones she'd found at home in their box of Christmas decorations. And she hung spirals of gold and silver ribbon from the sides. Herself as a star. A star as her.

The second mask was less difficult, although in the meditation session Melvyn always did at the beginning of the class to help them on their journey, she was afraid she might start to cry because she was thinking her deepest feeling was from when their dog, Misty, had to be put to sleep. But that was the mask she wanted to do. A mask of the horrible sadness after something dies.

"Your mask comes from a feeling inspired by death?" Melvyn asked. "That's very serious, Lizbett. A mourning mask. Are you sure?"

"It's my deepest feeling," she replied. "It's a mask of tears."

*Tears are water*, she decided. So she fashioned the saddest face she could imagine, borrowing a little from some carved wooden masks from Switzerland in the exhibit whose furrowed brows and sloping eyebrows and eyes spoke of real sorrow. Using papier mâché, fashioning eyebrows, eyes and mouth in a deep downturn, skin dripping, she painted the mask a pale blue and again used an overlay, but this time in silver. She drizzled clear silicone from the eye sockets. And she found in the trinket box, much to her delight, several little tear-shaped mirrors that she glued down one cheek. And this time she made elaborate, long, drapey hair from strips of blue fabric and silver paper. When she put the finished mask over her face and looked at herself, she actually felt sad. She could feel her whole body droop.

Then Melvyn talked about this week's mask. "We're going to do a special mask that is an exact representation of who we are. Now, how can a mask say who we are, as others actually see us not as we see ourselves? Anyone? Carla?"

"Well, we can make masks of how we think we look to other people."

"Not how we think we look, how we really look. How do we get a mask to be exactly us?"

"Couldn't we get a photograph of ourselves and model a mask of that?" offered Laurie.

Melvyn said, "Wouldn't that still be just an interpretation of what you see? The same goes for modelling a mask of yourself from a mirror. How do you get a mask of how others see you?"

"I know!" volunteered Teddy. "You get someone else to make a mask of you by looking at you."

"But," replied Melvyn, "That would still be his or her interpretation, wouldn't it? We want a mask of the real you, as you really are."

The class was stymied. "Has anyone ever heard of a death mask?" Melvyn asked. No one responded. "Before cameras, people made death masks of their loved ones or someone famous at the exact moment of death by putting plaster over the face and molding it to the person's features. That way they had a perfect representation of the person to remember him or her by. Why would that mean more than a photograph?"

"Because it's the real person," Lizbett said. "Not something fake. And it's you know … full."

"That's right. It's three-dimensional. So is a sculpture, but, as Lizbett says, this is the real thing, not an interpretation. When we put on a mask, we put on another face, a second face. And that mask blocks out the face people know us by and puts in another. But a death mask does not hide, it reveals, it records. So that's our next mask, only it's going to be a life mask. We're going to put wet plaster gauze over our faces. If you've ever had a broken bone, you've seen a doctor mould it on your arm or leg. We're going to mould it to the shapes of our faces, our noses, cheekbones, lips, chin, and so on and let it harden. And very carefully remove it. And there you will have an exact you. It will be more than a likeness of you. It will be you because when you remove the plaster, you remove something of yourself."

"How long will it take?" Teddy asked.

"It takes fifteen or twenty minutes to make the mask, to prepare the face, then wrap the wet plaster gauze all over the face and smooth it into shape. And then it takes about twenty minutes to dry. That's a long time to sit still, I know. If there's anyone who feels uncomfortable about doing it, they can make a self-portrait mask out of clay. Is there anyone who doesn't want to do it? We don't cover the nostrils so you can breathe."

Lizbett said, "Do we have to have our eyes covered? I really don't like my eyes being covered. I hate blindfolds. I've hated them ever since I was little and we played 'Pin the Tail on the Donkey.'"

"Of course, leave the eyes open if you wish. Afterwards, you can fill them in, the way the Egyptians did, and paint them if you choose. Now, let's see, we're how many? Twelve? Pick a partner and decide who gets the mask on first. Then you'll trade."

Lizbett and Carla paired up. And Teddy and Laurie, and Jesse and another boy. The rest found partners except for one girl, Kristin, who didn't want to do it. Melvyn will do the mask on the odd person out as a demonstration.

Lizbett and Carla decided Carla will have the mask put on her that morning and then Carla will do Lizbett in the afternoon.

Coming back from lunch, Lizbett is a little apprehensive about having the plaster covering her whole face. This morning while she was smoothing the plaster gauze onto Carla's face, Melvyn had asked them to think about the geography of the face. "Remember how we said a mask was a map of the face. Well, the face itself is like terrain, with hills and valleys and crevasses and gullies. Feel all that, not only as you apply the plaster, but as you are having it applied. Imagine your face as a landscape and what that landscape reveals."

At lunch, the three who had had the plaster smoothed on them had mixed opinions about how it felt. One said it was warm. Another said it was squishy and weird. The third said it was sort of scary. All agreed it was a long time to stay still and that was boring but then seeing yourself in plaster was so neat!

Lizbett sits in a chair and lays her head back on a small pad on the table. She has tucked her mass of curls into the plastic bag and sealed it with Vaseline. And Carla has also carefully put it on her eyebrows and lips. She will leave the eyes opened, as planned. Melvyn has put on some soothing music … men singing in a low, chanting way. He says they are monks and the music is called Gregorian chants. Lizbett likes it, but her heart is still thudding a bit. How will it feel to have her face all covered for such a long time? Carla covers Lizbett's face with flannel and then begins to apply strips of the wet gauze which warm as they sit on her face. But the gauze falls off and gets tangled.

Melvyn says, "Here, Carla, let me help." Melvyn gently lays the gauze all over Lizbett's face. She can feel Melvyn's careful pressure as he smooths his fingertips across her forehead, over her eyebrows, across her cheeks and down both sides of her nose. With one finger he meticulously follows the contours of her lips and the groove of her chin and then tucks the gauze under it. The sensation is as pleasurable as having her hair washed at the hairdresser, but Lizbett is aware of something unsettling, something more personal. Melvyn is not the hairwasher. He is familiar to her. She realizes she has never been touched with such tender care by a grown-up other than her parents.

"Good girl," says Melvyn. "Great stillness. You're done, Lizbett. Are you comfortable? You have about twenty minutes to wait. You'll feel the plaster begin to harden. Sit up if you want to."

But Lizbett keeps her head back. She has been feeling a bit sleepy with the face massage. Melvyn was very gentle. She thinks again of the fact that all through the history of masks, they were only worn by men. Lizbett read that the Greeks believed that since men's private parts were external, they belonged to the outer world and since women's were internal, they were meant to live inside. And because of childbearing, women were considered closer to nature and needed to be controlled. Men would never allow them to go on display. They themselves played the women. Men wore women's masks to be them, to create them as they wanted them to look and behave. And as women, men could act in ways real women were not allowed. They could break the rules they made for women. Some mask ceremonies were aggressive and violent. Women weren't considered powerful enough to be in them. Men also used masks to make fun of women, to belittle them. All of this makes Lizbett angry and she has discussed it with her mother. Why did men treat women so horribly?

"Some men still do," Meredith said. "They still keep them in a kind of prison. They don't let them have their say. They don't let them do the things they think only men can do. The think women are inferior. They treat them not as people, but as objects, mostly to do with sex. Do you understand what that means?"

"I think it means men think women aren't really people, that they should be sexy, but not smart. Or not the boss, maybe."

"That's sort of it. Some men believe that women are weaker and dumber than they are and they keep them from moving forward. And men still hurt women in terrible ways."

"But why? When it isn't true? Women aren't weaker and dumber. Why do they believe it?"

Meredith said, "I have a theory ... it's not entirely mine, but it comes from what I've read. Thousands and thousands of years ago, when humans were still very primitive, men were in awe of women because they could do two magical, powerful things men couldn't. They could become two people ... when they had babies. And they could bleed for several days ... when they had their periods ... without dying. When men bled for that long from an injury, they died. People had sex, but they didn't know sex made babies or that bleeding had to do with that."

"But then men became farmers, not hunters. And they started to breed animals and gradually they made the connection between sex and reproduction. If I do this to a woman, then she will have another person. So she needs me to do that. And when she has another person, she is weak and not able to get food. So she needs me to protect and provide for her. But how could a man be sure that a woman wasn't doing 'the thing' with another man, as well? And how could he tell if the new person came from him or someone else? A man would want to know the new person came from him so he could give him some of his farm land and share his animals. He wouldn't want to do that with someone else's new person. And he didn't trust that his woman would be faithful to him. Men saw women as temptresses, out to weaken men through their sexiness. So the man said to his woman, 'If you want me to help and protect you, you have to stay inside and only see other women. You may never see another man except a father or a brother.' That's very simple, I know. But it explains to me why men have kept women down and confined. They have had to be sure their son was their son."

"But what about modern times?"

"I think over the centuries it became such a standard for male and female behaviour that even as humans became more sophisticated, they were still wary of women's sexuality, seeing it as something evil and disempowering. And they still believed women were weak and needed protecting and controlling."

As she continues to wait for the plaster to harden, Lizbett imagines a play she is going to write where all the actors are female and all wear masks, male and female. And each character would wear two or three or even four masks, all representing different people ... even though, in the play, they'd actually be just one person playing several different personalities and no one would ever know who anyone really was and one mask-person would know stuff about another mask-person and the person wouldn't be aware of it. It would be a huge mix-up of identities. And people would get all confused and all sorts of things would go wrong. Maybe it could be another world or another species or hundreds of years from now. It would be like a crazy fairy tale, but not for kids, really. She is thinking she will suggest it at drama camp next month.

Melvyn cannot believe that on this day of all days, he has been the one to form Lizbett's life mask, to stroke his fingers over her delicate, lovely face and create the face that would be her, that was her, an essential part of her. The thrill was almost more than he could bear and afterwards he felt unsteady. Her face, the external path to her, had been born in his hands.

He pulls himself out of his reverie and suddenly says, "Okay, Lizbett. Time to look at the real you." Lizbett sits up, excited. And he loosens the edges all around her face and slowly, slowly lifts the mask off. When Lizbett looks at it, she says, "I didn't know I had such a big nose! Or such a pointy chin."

"You don't," Melvyn says, laughing. "It's only that what you're seeing is not what you see in the mirror, which is reversed and then interpreted by you, by how you hold your head, by what light you look at yourself in, by what you want to see. What you're seeing in the mask is exactly how you are."

Melvyn cannot believe how exquisite she is; how serene, how austere, how enigmatic. She is Lizbett, but she is not. What he is regretting is that Lizbett won't be around to charge her mask at the end of the week, make her own "self" live. This has always proven to be a fascinating psychological exercise and most children, wearing their own life mask, lose all shyness and reveal selves that have never been otherwise evident. A lot of anger comes out, in boys especially. But the girls, too, become more verbally aggressive, their body language more forceful. Since Lizbett seems to be so constantly self-revealing, he wonders what inner spirit would have enlivened her mask.

But it is too late for regrets. His plans are set for this afternoon. He is desperate to carry them out.

Near the end of the class he gives Lizbett permission to leave a bit early. She wants to call her mother. But promptly at four, he dismisses the class and goes out to get his car. What luck. Pete is asleep. But as Melvyn clicks the door open, his heart stops. Pete suddenly sits up, his wide eyes seemingly staring at Melvyn. Then, just as suddenly, he falls back with a snort, his head dropping again to his chest. And Melvyn rushes away.

Pete will later swear that the door was never used on his watch.

After talking to her mother, Lizbett comes out of the museum doors at a little after four and stops to chat with several of her classmates at the top of the stairs. Big raindrops are falling. All the kids but Lizbett rush down to waiting cars. At the bottom of the steps, one mother asks Lizbett if she wants a ride. Lizbett indicates her umbrella and says, "No thank you."

The umbrella is green with little frogs at the end of the spines. She puts it up. It's a good thing she brought it because by the time she reaches the corner, there is a great flash of lightning, a violent, prolonged clap of thunder, and the sky opens. The rain that falls is dense and hard. A fierce wind closes everyone and everything in, in silvery, wet sheets. People are scurrying every which way to find shelter. Water flows over the sidewalks and rivers rush along the curbs. Lightning sears the sky again; a crack of thunder immediately follows. Lizbett stands at the corner, hesitating. She can barely see across the road. She wonders if she should simply dash into the hotel that's on the opposite side. While she hesitates, a car pulls up making a huge splash and the passenger door opens. Lizbett hears, "Get in. Hurry!"

Lizbett bends down and sees Melvyn and quickly, gratefully, slides into the car, closing her dripping umbrella after she's in. He pulls away practically as she's doing it. In the confusion and power of the storm, no one has noticed a little girl with a green frog umbrella get into a grey Honda.

"Had to get out of there," Melvyn says. "There was a bus on my tail. Look at you. Lucky I came along."

"Lucky you did. I was getting soaked. I didn't know where to go." The car is cold from the air conditioning and she shivers a little.

"I was just passing when I saw you. How about that? So where to?"

"The library, I guess."

The "I guess" makes Melvyn's heart leap. He sees it as an opening.

"Why don't we drive down to the pier and watch the storm? The waves will be fantastic."

Lizbett doesn't really want to do that, but she doesn't want to hurt his feelings. He is very nice to give her a ride. She says again, "I'm going to the library to get some books on masks."

"I'll drop you there. C'mon," he says. "It will be an adventure."

An adventure. Melvyn is always saying, "Wearing a mask is an adventure. Always keep yourself open to adventure." Her mother says, "Life should be full of adventures." Besides, it's Melvyn. She's seen him all day, every day for two weeks. He works at the museum. She likes him even if it does feel strange to be alone in his car and go to the beach. She says, "Okay."

"This could be a sort of date," Melvyn says and reaches over and pats her shoulder. Lizbett has never been on a date, nor really ever imagined what one would be like, but she doesn't think kids go on dates with their teachers, even ones as nice and friendly as Melvyn. She shrugs.

The pier, a couple of miles southeast of where they are, is in front of an abandoned nineteenth-century knitting mill. The pier extends far out into the lake. Cars can drive out onto it. Since it is so isolated, it is popular with teenagers. Lizbett has been walking there with her parents.

On the way, she chats easily with Melvyn, about making the life mask and how fantastic it was. She also tells him her idea for a mask play. She says how terrible she thinks it is that women weren't allowed to wear masks.

Melvyn says, "Well, women were supposed to be quiet and invisible. Besides, men didn't think women were clever or assertive enough to take on the powers of a mask. Masks were a connection to something beyond women's understanding. Good women didn't know about magic."

"But the men wore masks that were women. Women who got them in touch with spirits or who were spirits. Didn't that show that women were important? That they had powers?"

"The masks showed women as men wanted them to be, not how they were. It was a kind of control. 'We say how you should look and behave. Or we'll make you behave in ways we forbid you to behave.' And you know, they thought women's bodily functions … the way their bodies worked … made them part of nature and nature was something that needed taming or it would take you over."

"It wasn't fair," says Lizbett. "Men had all the fun."

"Masks weren't really about fun. But look in the back," says Melvyn. The two masks he'd chosen that morning were there: masks created from his face, a male and a female. The female was modelled after a Guatemalan maiden's ecstasy mask, meant to represent the wearer's sublime connection to the Divine during mock sacrifices. The male, derived from a Sri Lankan mask, was the lofty lord of the harvest, the supreme overseer, the guarantor of productivity. It was a maniacal face with black-lined eyes, bushy fur eyebrows, and a broad fur mustache that curled at the ends. The mouth was agape in a huge laugh.

"Wow! They're amazing."

"Put one on."

"Really?"

"Sure. Why not? Put on the maiden's mask."

"That's not the one I would have picked," Lizbett says.

She turns around and picks up the mask and ties it to her face. It is quite heavy.

"Look at yourself in the mirror under the visor."

Lizbett pulls it down and stares at the face before her, a beautiful white-faced woman with fur eyelashes and full, bright red lips surrounding a mouth that is open in a poignant cry.

"Make the sound," he says.

Lizbett is startled at the gruff sound in his voice and asks, "What sound?"

"The sound she's making. That's how you'll make the mask come alive; how you'll feel something."

Lizbett is feeling very uncomfortable now and says, "I don't know what sound," and starts to take the mask off.

"Leave it on," Melvyn orders.

"I don't want to."

"Leave it on!" he yells. But she yanks it off.

There are several cars at the pier and Melvyn drives in well behind the mill. Lizbett now realizes something is not right and asks to go home.

"In a minute, sweetie," he says. "We have something to do first." He reaches over into his glove compartment and pulls out latex gloves and puts them on and then gets a roll of duct tape and Lizbett sees all this and reacts instinctively. She opens her mouth and places her teeth on his bare upper arm and bites down as hard as she can, grinding her teeth back and forth.

He tries to pull her off and she clenches harder. He is yelling and knocks her hard on the head with his free hand and she lets go, but she pulls at his hair and starts screaming. In vain. With the wind and the pounding of the waves, no one could possibly hear her. Plus they are all sealed in their own cars.

Melvyn quickly rips off a piece of the duct tape with his teeth and without even thinking he should wipe his blood off her teeth and lips, grabs Lizbett's chin and holds the tape across her mouth. She is flailing and kicking at him, pulling at his face, his lips. He hadn't expected her to be a fighter and he's anxious and angry. This is not his Lizbett, his "Annie," this monster child.

He slaps her across her face. "Stay still or I'll kill you!"

She does. He tears off another piece of tape, slips her little purse over her shoulder and grabs her arms and twists them around her back and tapes her hands. Then he tightly tapes her ankles. Her widened eyes are flitting with terror and filled with tears. He cannot stand that and he suddenly remembers her saying she hated blindfolds and he tears off another piece of tape and puts it across her eyes. Now, there is only whimpering, which he also doesn't like. It reduces her.

He picks up the maiden mask and places it over her face and ties it tightly. Then he puts on the male mask and checks himself in the mirror. He raises his chest, then inhales deeply and exhales making a long, low, forceful roar.

It has stopped raining and he gets out of the car, goes around and opens the door, and picks Lizbett up and carries her with difficulty, as she is thrashing furiously, into one of the side sheds which has a door slightly ajar. He pushes the door and they go in. There is an old mattress at the far end and he goes to it and lays her there. She kicks hard with both feet.

"I'll kill you, I said. Kick me again and you're dead!" he says. He peels off the tape from her ankles. He feels panicky now because of his fear of being discovered. He imagines lots of vagrants come here in the summer. Blood is running down his arm from the wound. A couple of drops fall to the mattress. So he moves quickly. He pulls off her panties and shorts, unzips himself, and shaking, puts on a lubricated condom, leans down, pulls her legs apart and penetrates her vagina, feeling it rupture.

This is right! This is what she is for. He is the supreme lord. He is the mask; the mask is him. His persona is primal, all his power, his inhibitions are released. He is part of a sacrifice of the most beautiful. She is before him: a trade-off, innocence and purity for an expunging of excesses. He wishes he had not taped her eyes so he could see her mask live.

But it's never as he has imagined it. He's imagined her co-operative, ecstatic. Lizbett stiffens suddenly and then goes limp. Good. She's fainted. He puts his hands around her neck and tightens until his hands ache. There'll be no resistance now. He concentrates on the mask, the now beatific mask, whose wail he can hear and pushes into her rectum and finishes. He has kept her from inevitable taint.

Now he has to get out of here. He takes off the condom and sees that it is bloody. He pulls on his pants and finds an old McDonald's bag nearby and he gets it and drops the condom in. Later he will put the gloves in too and deposit the bag in a trash bin downtown. He doesn't want to leave the body in the same place as the act. He looks out and sees the rain is a soft drizzle. He picks Lizbett up and notices a bloodstain where she'd lain. So what? The mattress is covered in stains, some of them probably blood. He picks up her panties and shorts and the McDonald's bag and carries her a short distance away to a sluggish industrial canal, fuller than usual because of the rain. He considers dropping her in the water like the Mayan maidens who were thrown into the cenotes. But he decides not to. He feels a pang of something like sympathy, as if immersing her in a stagnant pool would somehow degrade her. And he decides it would be better, anyway, if her body were discovered soon. So he lays Lizbett face-down on a stray clump of Queen Anne's Lace growing out of a piece of broken concrete. He has to undo the duct tape on her wrists to get off the red striped T-shirt, but he wants it. He takes the mask and hurries back to his car, unobserved, folding her clothing and putting everything on the seat beside him with her purse. Only then does he remove his own mask and before he drives off, he tosses the umbrella in the water.

# Part Two

## FUNERALS

# 5

# WAITING

The rain is still teeming, the walkways flooded as they leave the studio building for the restaurant: Meredith and Thompson, Lew and Cindy, and Thompson's assistant, Polly. They are going to Benvenuto, a pasta restaurant with one of those new, open-concept kitchens where the wine is served in tall balloon glasses.

Thompson is buoyant, and, for him, talkative. The young women are clinging to him and laughing. He even has Lew chuckling. Editorial shoots are a challenge and that loosens him. It is banality that drives him inward. An editorial shoot has a connectedness that a shoot for single or even multiple dishes without a story line does not.

After she orders — grilled quail on a bed of crispy sage noodles — Meredith suddenly feels another pang about Lizbett and goes to the bar phone and calls home. Darcy is back from Stephen's, but Lizbett still has not shown up. It is past 7:30 p.m. Meredith asks Brygida if she has called Lizbett's friends and Brygida says she tried but was unable to get them all. Many people are on vacation. Now Meredith feels a tightening in her gut, a distinct jab of alarm: that thought no parent ever wants to think. *Where could my child be?*

She returns to her table where the banter has elevated. Thompson has finished his glass of white wine and has poured another.

"Do you see that gorgeous woman over there?" Lew asks. "Irme Pormoranska. She's your competition. An up-and-coming stylist. I know her. She's very good."

But Meredith isn't paying attention. "Look, Thompson, Lizbett's not back. I think we should go home."

"You worried she's been kidnapped?" Thompson quips and everyone laughs.

"Come on, Sonny. Let's go."

In the car they are silent. Thompson is peeved at having to leave when he was having a good time. Though she knows she has no right to be, Meredith is piqued with him for his behaviour with the women. She was finding his uncharacteristic gregariousness sexist and affected. All that touching. But she is mostly concerned about Lizbett's whereabouts. This neglectful attitude is so unlike her.

Meredith calculates her possible itinerary. She would have left the museum a little after four, got caught in the downpour, but would have made it to the subway in five minutes or so and been at the library, only two stops away, in fifteen. Then it was another five to ten minutes, depending on her walking speed, which Meredith assumed would be quick, to the library. How long would she have been at the library looking for books on masks? A half hour? An hour?

She could possibly have gotten distracted in another section, fiction, perhaps. She could have lingered there choosing some new novels. Or maybe she went to the children's section to pick out some books for Darcy. She goes through them so quickly. Or she could have met up with someone she knew and they decided to go to the nearby McDonald's so she wouldn't have to eat Brygida's dinner. This was not something Lizbett would normally do, but Meredith is considering all options. Or maybe she and the person decided to look into some of the clothing shops on the bustling street the library's quiet street runs into. One of the stores sells great gear for teenagers. Meredith knows Lizbett likes to go there. That could have taken another hour if they lingered or tried on things. There's also a big drugstore. Perhaps the girls (Meredith is assuming it's a girl), went to the cosmetic counter and put on makeup.

That would make it six-thirty or seven, maybe a bit later. All this time, Meredith imagines that Lizbett is thinking she should call home, but she can't find a payphone or the ones she finds are busy or she doesn't have the right change and decides she'll be home soon enough, so she lets it go. Meredith can get her to seven, seven-thirty if she stretches it, with plausible explanations, but after that she cannot picture where Lizbett might be or what she might be doing. The friend she met up with possibly is new, not on Lizbett's list. Like someone from the mask camp. Yes. That would be it. Lizbett went to the library with someone from the mask camp and they've dawdled. That would explain why Brygida hadn't been able to find her. Maybe her parents are worried, too. Lizbett would be home when they got home, all apologetic or else she would have phoned from the new friend's house.

But Lizbett is not at the house when they get there and there has been no phone call. Brygida is extremely distressed. "I'm just so frantic," she says. "I cannot even think what to do."

Darcy runs to her mother and grabs her. "We can't find Lizbett," she says.

"We will," Meredith replies. She gets out their telephone book and calls all the numbers Brygida already has and adds on a few others. Either no answer or no Lizbett, with those she does talk to expressing grave concern. Now it is eight-thirty. Lizbett should have been in touch by now.

Meredith and Thompson decide to call the police.

Two sergeants arrive in about twenty minutes: young, fresh-faced men in uniform. The Warnes show them Lizbett's head shot from *Annie*.

"How long has your daughter been missing?"

Allowing time for her to get to and from the library plus lingering there, the Warnes say, "Probably about two and a half hours. We expected her at six or six-thirty."

The two cops exchange a dismissive glance. "She ever run away before?" asks one.

Thompson sees red. "What do you mean 'before'? Lizbett has never ever been late. And if she ever had a change of plans, she phoned. She would absolutely never do something like this — go somewhere and not let us know."

Meredith, her anxiety undisguised, adds, "She's a model child, a very obedient child, really very cautious, who simply wouldn't not let us know exactly what she was doing. And she's taken the two 'Street Savvy' courses your police department gives at the schools. She's a very aware young girl."

"She usually travel on her own?" inquires the other.

Thompson and Meredith give each other a quick look. "Like every other kid we know. She's been taking public transport since grade four.

So have all her friends. They're all confident, capable kids. We've encouraged them to be independent and resourceful."

"So she couldn't have gotten lost or anything."

"Not at all," says Meredith. "She takes the subway to the library all the time."

"Could she be at someone's house?"

"Absolutely not. She'd phone. Plus, we've called most of her friends. No one has seen her."

"How are things at home? Any arguments lately? Any ongoing conflict? How's she been behaving?"

Thompson raises his voice. "We told you. This is a great kid, not a perfect kid, but a special kid who always toes the line. She's an actress. She's very keen and responsible. There's no reason to believe she'd do something stupid or defiant."

"An actress?" a cop asks. "Hey. I thought I recognized her," he adds. "I've seen her in that cookie ad. Look, she'll show up. Don't worry. We'll put out a bulletin to be on the lookout for her. That's about all we can do right now."

"You don't understand," says Meredith. "She must be in trouble. We'd have heard from her otherwise."

Meredith calls her sister, Abbey, who is a lawyer in a small matrimonial firm. She comes immediately and rushes in. Tall and angular, she enfolds her much smaller, softer sister in her arms.

Abbey brings Kyle McDonaugh with her, a teacher at Lizbett and Darcy's school and Lizbett's soccer coach. They have been dating, but their relationship is not established. They met last year when Abbey was helping Meredith run a booth at the school's Christmas bazaar. Kyle is one of the many men the police will bring in for questioning regarding Lizbett's disappearance and will actually become a suspect, since he does not have an alibi.

Abbey, who is two years older, is close to her sister. They see each other several times a week. It was she whom Meredith followed when she first left Australia. Though Abbey looks like their mother and Darcy, dark and olive-skinned, she has the formal, solicitous affect of their minister father. She has his beneficent tolerance without the spirituality, which is why she is such a good divorce lawyer. Abbey is as loquacious as Meredith, but she is more thoughtful and contained.

Thompson also calls his mother, Nellie, thinking she can help with Darcy. And they all wait.

At 10:00 p.m., there is still no sign of Lizbett. The police conclude that this is not some resentful, rebellious runaway, not a kid who's miffed at her parents. This is not payback for a family altercation.

This is a kid who would phone. There's not a good reason why she hasn't. They start to put the machinery together to look for a missing child.

Another policeman, a detective from the youth squad, comes to the house and tells the Warnes that the police have contacted the local TV channel. A reporter and cameraman will be there shortly. Could the Warnes give a statement regarding Lizbett's disappearance and appear on the 11:00 p.m. news?

*Disappearance? Vanished. Nowhere but somewhere. Somewhere but where? Where, oh where?*

This is the reality. A roaring overtakes Meredith's head. She sees a black nothingness. She puts her hand on Thompson's arm for support and he pulls her to him. Darcy, who is in a nightie but has refused to go to bed, clings to them. This is a horror of horrors, something too egregious to be believed. Not their eldest daughter. Not Lizbett. *Disappeared.* Meredith only just spoke to her before 4:00 p.m. In six hours she has disappeared? They can't fathom what it means.

"We suspect abduction," the police say.

*Are you worried she's been kidnapped?* Thompson remembers his facetious comment from dinner and feels the horror.

"Omigod. Omigod. Omigod. Omigod." Meredith almost collapses, but then pulls herself together and says abruptly, "Okay. Let's get going. Let's write something."

"Give a full description," says the detective. "And invite the sympathy of the viewers and maybe the abductor. Play on his conscience, his guilt. Be frank, be especially praising of your daughter's accomplishments. We want to make him squirm."

By now, Nellie has arrived and she and Abbey and Kyle take Darcy into the living room. Nellie takes out *The Wind in the Willows* to read to her. Meredith and Thompson go up into their office to prepare a statement. "Make him squirm?" Who is this "him" they are targeting? How can they possibly imagine him? What would he be like ... a vagrant, someone young, a freak, an addict? Someone perverted? Someone insane or cruel?

Some ordinary guy? Someone she knows. Someone *they* know? Why has he picked Lizbett? What can he possibly want with her? They are entirely incapable of thinking about it. They write:

"Our talented, precious daughter Lizbett Warne is missing. She was last seen at the Courtice Museum at 4:00 p.m. today wearing a red-and-white striped T-shirt, red shorts, and red leather sandals. She is five feet tall and weighs about eighty-five pounds. You can't miss her curly red hair, large blue eyes, and bright smile. She is a caring and charming girl who touches everyone who meets her. Perhaps you saw her as Annie at the Nathan S. Hirschenberg Arts Centre. We ask anyone who may have seen her to come forward and if she is with you, we appeal to your compassion and good conscience and pray that you will return her to us safe and unharmed."

Just as they are finishing the composition, the TV crew arrives and they shoot with lights at the front of the house. The rain has let up, but the air is steamy. The reporter goes first. "Eleven-year-old Lizbett Warne, who lives here on this street of elegant, refurbished Victorian houses, disappeared today at 4:00 p.m. from the Courtice Museum where she has been attending day camp. According to her parents, she was heading for the Oakland branch of the public library, several blocks north. It has not been ascertained whether she ever reached there. Police say that the fact that the storm broke shortly after four may make finding witnesses difficult. And since the rain has continued heavily, off and on, that will most certainly hinder search efforts. Lizbett Warne is an aspiring actress who most recently played the lead in the production of *Annie*. Now, here are Lizbett Warne's parents, Meredith and Thompson Warne, to make a statement. For WCHN Channel 11 news, I'm Scott Vivien."

The camera pans to Meredith and Thompson. Meredith reads their statement, the lilt in her Australian accent pronounced, but stony, her body rigid. It is the stance she will adopt as they go through all that they are about to go through.

How will they make it through the night? How can they just sit around and endure the ravages of waiting? Surely there is something they can do.

Meredith thinks of posters. They call a friend who has a printing business and they spend part of the night producing hundreds of posters with Lizbett's vivacious head shot and the statistics helpful to her identification, along with the appropriate police phone number.

And they don't care who they wake up. They phone dozens of friends and acquaintances and convince them to solicit friends and acquaintances. Many have seen the news and have already called to see how they could help.

So a hundred or more volunteers traipse out across the dark city in the unpredictable drizzle and on street after street, neighbourhood after neighbourhood, on telephone poles and trees, on fences and post boxes, they staple or tape up Lizbett's poster. By morning, her mischievous face beams out at everyone who looks, broadcasting her disappearance, inviting them to find her.

And the city rallies. A stolen child speaks to everyone. No one escapes the ominous threat. A stolen child injects terror in all families; explodes the complacency in a sedate city, forces it to think differently about itself. Every child becomes a target. Unanchored men become suspects. This city has always been safe. The Metro police receive hundreds of calls from people offering to help with the search. An officer is appointed to coordinate teams.

The Metro force is fired up. Cops hate predator crimes involving kids. Everything points to Lizbett Warne getting hit by some pedophile. And for all their eagerness to get going, fuelled by the repulsion and hatred they harbour for the perpetrator, they are not hopeful. The victims in such cases are usually killed in the first couple of hours.

She could be anywhere. This is a large city, extensively wooded, with ravines, large parks, a river that runs through it much the way it has done since the city was established. And there is the partially derelict waterfront.

Sprawling suburbs and farmland reach beyond the city and a hilly conservation area just to the north covers hundreds of wild acres. Plenty of places to dispose of a small body.

Plus it has been raining almost the whole time since the disappearance. Any crime scene will be washed clean.

But they begin at the beginning, checking with the library to see if Lizbett ever made it there. None of the staff, most of whom know her, saw her yesterday afternoon. Which simplifies things, but also complicates them because if she never reached the library, at what point did the abductor get her? Right at the museum? Between the museum and the subway? On the subway? Before or after which stop? En route to the library? Hundreds of questions need to be asked of hundreds of people.

As much as the fear for Lizbett has overpowered them, Meredith and Thompson have two inescapable here-and-nows to attend to. The most consequential is Darcy. She is with them, vital and attentive, ardently curious. Suddenly she seems to have become a baby again, though not in how she is behaving. No. She is being steady and brave. But she has become their baby, gone from oh-so-big to tiny, vulnerable, needy, utterly innocent of the immensity of the situation. She has shrunk from precocious to defenseless. If Meredith could attach her to herself in some way, the way she did when she carried Darcy in the baby-pack, she would. She wants to cradle her, coddle her. She feels a fierce desire to protect her, not only from the kind of harm that may have befallen Lizbett, but from the fallout that may result from it.

And what about the shoot? It's crucial to their business, their livelihood. Lew has phoned and said not to worry about coming in. He will find someone to replace them. Of course, he will. What they do is desperately competitive and even though Artful Sustenance is one of the best, there are others waiting in line. Thompson is less concerned about this than Meredith. There will be other jobs. But she is deeply ashamed to admit she is afraid Lew will hire Irme Pormoranska.

"We can't just sit around here all day and wait for news. I'll be hysterical. I'm barely hanging on as it is. Why don't we go in and work? It will distract us. I'll keep Darcy with me," Meredith suggests.

Thompson is reluctant. He doesn't have Meredith's desperate need for activity at the best of times. She zooms every which way. Thompson thinks of her as a blown-up balloon suddenly let go in the air. He can plunk himself in a chair for some time, an hour or two, and just be; mind churning, body static, staring out at their garden. It feels creative to him. He calls himself "a contemplative." Where she is thinking work will be a distraction, he is wondering if he'll be able to concentrate with his daughter's life in his mind.

But he consents, mostly because he wants to keep Meredith as stable as possible and he thinks the demands of styling will do that. Nellie says she'll stay behind at the house and contact them with any news. Darcy is excited to go to the studio, but she is used to going with Lizbett and it will feel funny without her.

When they go out, it has started to rain again. What they hadn't even thought about are reporters. There is a gathering at the foot of their walk.

They have nothing more to say other than what they stated on the television last night. Yes, they are fearful, but they are also hopeful. People are essentially good. This is a good city. They are trusting in someone's humanity. For advances on the search, the reporters should contact the police.

How do you prepare a Christmas feast when your daughter has been kidnapped? Meredith has only her own resources to draw on. She has no God to pray to, no Saviour to implore. She considers trying to pray, but it is anathema to her. "Dear God, if you really are, keep Lizbett from harm and bring her back to us." That is what her father advised her to do when they phoned him in Australia with the news.

"Pray, dear Meredith. You will feel stronger, more able to cope if you do. Pray for the strength to deal, for the understanding of what may be ahead. Prayer gives us hope and courage. Prayer grounds us. I will pray for you. I will have my parish pray for you."

Why would she pray to a God who allows an eleven-year-old girl to be snatched?

She gets to work. Cream of oyster soup. Arugula and watercress salad with lemon shallot dressing. Champagne sorbet. She will make the chestnut stuffing for the goose as well.

Darcy has been set up with a big ball of the leftover pastry dough from yesterday and Meredith has given her raisins and cinnamon and sugar and chocolate chips and cookie cutters and told her to make whatever she wants.

Lew asks, "Music?"

"Something not too loud." He puts on Peter Gabriel's *So*.

When she hears "Red Rain" she almost loses it.

Melt the butter. (Lizbett is tied up and gagged in the trunk of a car.) Add white wine, turn up the heat and reduce. (She is drugged and on a plane being taken far away.) Turn down the heat. (She is imprisoned in a dark closet or a dank basement.) Add the oysters and their liquor to the reduced wine and butter and poach gently. (She is bound and gagged, lying on a filthy mattress in some sleazy motel.) Add whipping cream and ground pepper and turn up the burner slightly just to heat the soup. Do not boil. (She is at the bottom of the lake.)

The morning passes, merges into the afternoon. They shoot the soup in an ornate silver tureen with roaring lions as the handles. Darcy loves it. The salad is in a deep white ironstone bowl. Meredith has decorated the arugula and the cress with mandarin orange sections and toasted, slivered almonds. The greens glisten with the lemony dressing. In fact, they look so good, after they are photographed, they decide to eat them with slices of crispy baguette Meredith bought that morning. It is the first time she has eaten since the sandwiches they ordered in for lunch yesterday. *What a terrible way to lose weight*, she thinks.

This has been an easy day. Tomorrow doing all the vegetable dishes will be more demanding but Lizbett will be back by then, perhaps frightened, but above all safe. She is a strong, purposeful girl. She can survive anything.

# 6

# THE BODY

A little after 7:00 a.m. on Wednesday morning, a homeless teenager, who has spent the night with several buddies in the outbuilding where Melvyn killed Lizbett, goes outside to look for a private place to move his bowels. It isn't easy to find. The area is a sprawl of concrete and asphalt. But he ducks behind a low pile of metal machine parts and while he is squatting, he sees what looks like a head in a bunch of tall weeds over by the edge of the canal. On going to look, he discovers Lizbett's face-down, nude, bound body. He touches it with the edge of his running shoe, lifting it slightly. Then he recoils in horror, shouting and running to get his friends who sleepily stumble over to the body and are immediately repulsed.

Lizbett has been lying in the rain since Monday afternoon and her body is bloated and marbled with veins, splattered with mud. Someone says to turn her over to get a look at her face. They have assumed she is a girl because of the long ponytail with the baubles. Someone else seems to know not to touch anything and they all realize they have to contact the police, which none of them wants to do.

How to do that, anyway? They are a couple of miles from a phone, if they can even find one. The neighbourhood adjacent to this one is down-trodden and will be deserted at this time of the morning. They decide to walk out to the main road, which is actually an underpass and see if they can hail a car. They know that will be difficult because who is going to stop for a filthy, freaky-looking group like them? And it does take a while because there are few cars and even when they try to make a barricade on the road with their bodies, the cars peel past.

Finally an old farmer with a truck stops. It is full of the vegetables he is taking to the market right at the foot of the city. When they tell him they want to go to the police station, he lets them get in the back with the crates of lettuces and green beans and he takes them as far as the market. From there, they walk a few blocks north to where they know there is a precinct and they go in and tell the desk sergeant what they have seen and where. He asks them to wait and gets two uniformed officers who sense from the kids' agitation that they're not fooling around. There are five of them. The boy who first found the body gets in the back of the squad car. The others are ordered to stay.

The boy, whose name is Jackson Lee, has often been in trouble with the police and he is frightened. But he directs the two officers right to Lizbett's body and they call in the find and its location and within minutes several cars and an ambulance are there, carrying members of the team who will begin the forensic machinery that will help solve what appears to be a murder and probably a sexual assault.

Jackson is taken back to the police station and held for questioning with the others, which bums them out as they thought they were doing good. They even hoped they might get a reward. What they don't realize is that people who report homicides are considered suspects. Often they are the perpetrators trying to mislead the police.

The crime scene at first appears to be chaos, a panoply of flashing lights and swarming people. But, in fact, a highly organized system is in place and every individual has a specific role.

Who are these people who have chosen what appears to be a repulsive and gruesome task? They are sharp-eyed observers, relentless searchers with untold patience and perseverance. They are the kind of people who hang obsessively over five-thousand-piece jigsaw puzzles, except a crime scene has infinite pieces and there are inevitably one or two missing.

Pat Toliver and Duff McLeod, the two patrol cops, the first responders, have the responsibility of establishing the boundaries of the crime scene and barricading it. They record everyone's comings and goings and document all activity.

There are three crime-scene investigators, the criminalists: scientists whose duty it is to collect all the evidence that appears relevant and then to analyze it in the lab. They'll take dozens of photographs and make many sketches. They'll hand their findings over to the homicide detectives as armaments in their search to find the killer. Later, they will be used in the prosecutor's efforts to convict him or her.

Crime-scene investigators are the archeologists of pathology. The work is painstaking, tedious, lacklustre, the only excitement coming from a discovery. They have only fingerprints, blood-typing, trace-and-impression evidence to go on. Anything and everything can count, but, as they'll find out, this crime scene doesn't have much. Dave Prentis, thirty-eight, is a former police officer who has degree in microbiology. Sam Jacobson, forty-five, and a bit jaded, was also a cop who went on to get a BSc in chemistry before he joined the forensics division. Both men are meticulous and capable of obsession.

Al Birchler, the forensic investigator and second-in-command to the medical examiner is a fat, funny man who, at forty-eight, has seen his share of violent crimes. He, too, has been a beat cop, but he has half a medical degree. He will examine the body at the scene and even though he's done that dozens of times before, this one will sicken him because he has four daughters, one about Lizbett's age.

Pat and Duff cordon off an extensive area, surmising that the body has been moved. Instinctively, they include the outbuilding where the boys spent the previous night, the place where Lizbett was murdered.

What can Dave and Sam and Al possibly find? The scene has been under siege from rain since Monday afternoon. It is all hard surface, most of it pooled with water. There is no sign of any impression evidence: tire tracks or footprints. The floor inside the small building has been disturbed by the presence of five teenage boys. Who knows what's gone on in there before they arrived? There is a grubby, queen-size mattress and a pile of blankets and strewn garbage, old pizza boxes and fast-food bags and pop cans. Cigarette butts are everywhere, as is broken glass. Dave goes over it all inch by inch.

Outside, Sam establishes a geometric searching pattern, a spiral starting at the body and working his way out.

Al Birchler finds that Lizbett is in flaccid rigor mortis, meaning she's been dead at least forty hours, less possibly since heat speeds up rigor and the temperatures have been in the mid-eighties Fahrenheit. And she is thin. That also makes a difference. There is fixed deep purple lividity on her chest, abdomen and thighs, where her blood has pooled. She was placed face down shortly after she died. She has deep bruises around her neck, round ones in the front, longer ones on the side, indicating she has been manually strangled. Al figures the small bones above her larynx are broken, but the autopsy will confirm that. He removes the duct tape from her eyes and bags and tags it. He notes when he checks her eyes that she also has the burst capillaries that come from a forceful hold on the neck.

Before lifting the duct tape from her eyes and across her mouth, he has dusted the pieces for fingerprints and found none. But miracles happen at the lab. What he does find, which surprises him as there is no apparent injury, is that there are traces of what looks like blood on the inside of the duct tape from her mouth. His TMB test confirms it. There is more blood on her lips, and, when he raises those, on her teeth. It's a brilliant discovery because he can only assume it's from another source, likely the assailant whom she may have bitten in defending herself. He carefully bags and tags all the evidence.

Al does not find any evidence of fluids other than Lizbett's blood in her vagina and rectum, where there have been blowflies because larvae are already present. This would also point to her being dead for some time. Her body temperature is the same as the ambient temperature, which says the same thing.

"What have you got?" asks Irv Mikkelson, one of the detectives who has just arrived. The other is Nick Angstrom. Nick, at thirty-two, is younger than Irv by ten years, but he is the smarter of the two, although Irv is more methodical, less quick to act. Irv and Nick have been together three years and they're a good team because Irv is brusque and Nick is forthcoming.

"I'll tell you what we've got. Goddamn little. The rain's washed away pretty much anything we might have to go on, that's for sure. She was dumped face down, eyes and mouth duct-taped. There's lots of mud and botanical debris on her torso and a whole pile of bugs. We've got it all. COD looks like asphyxia brought on by strangulation. There's extensive damage and bleeding in both the vagina and the rectum, but no evidence of semen. Guy likely wore a condom. We'll look for lubricant at the lab. I can't give you an exact TOD, but I would think sometime between 5:00 or 6:00 p.m. and midnight on Monday. She's been dead thirty-six hours, anyway."

"Any prints on the duct tape?" asks Nick.

"Nothing. Guy must have worn gloves. There is something worthwhile. Under the tape there's blood, not hers, I don't think. And on her teeth and lips. The serologist at the lab will tell us more. She has some abrasions on her buttocks, but not on her back. She must have been wearing a top that he removed later. We're looking for fibres, but so far no luck. I'm certain this is a secondary. It's too exposed for the assault to have taken place here. But the rain's a bugger, as I said. We can't find a thing. Head's soaked. Body's washed clean."

"Anything in that building over there?" Irv asks.

"Dave Prentis is there now. But no, I don't think so. It's a mess."

At the outbuilding, Dave says, "I found some pretty fresh blood near the bottom of the mattress. It's not much to go on but it's something."

"What about the main factory over there?" Irv wonders.

"We've walked all around it. It's all boarded up ... doors and windows," Dave replies. "Sam's working on the outside. I'll do up and down the canal when I'm finished in here."

When they walk back to Al, he is just covering Lizbett's hands and wrapping her body in clean white sheets, which could possibly catch any trace evidence they might have missed. Then two attendants place her in a body bag, zip it up, put her on a stretcher, which they place in the ambulance and they drive off to the morgue.

"I hate these things," Irv comments. "They make my blood fucking boil."

"Yeah," replies Al. "Especially because this guy's a genius."

Ken Kumamoto, the medical examiner, is a soft-spoken, forgiving man, slow to comment and slow to react, which makes him ideal in a crisis. He's well-suited to supervise the crime lab, both in temperament and training. Once he was a surgeon, but he left his practice to do a pathology residency. He's a solitary man who doesn't really like social contact.

He feels very aware of Lizbett's assurance and strength. Her body was healthy and muscular, which shows she was physically active and animated. He recognizes a dancer's, or at least an athlete's, legs. They are well-defined for such a young girl. All her internal organs, including her brain, are in good condition. There was evidence of salami and cheese and chocolate in her stomach contents. The toxicology screen was normal so she wasn't drugged or poisoned.

Her vagina and anus were severely torn, and there was bruising on the perineum and the flesh on the pubis. He confirmed that the perpetrator had used a condom, a lubricated one, as there was no semen, but there were traces of a dilutant in Lizbett's blood, likely a water-based lubricant. He was unsuccessful in finding any pubic hairs or fibres that could have come from the killer.

Since her fingernails are bitten to the quick, he cannot find any defense evidence under them, nothing to indicate she had struggled. There were no bruises or broken bones in her hands. In fact, other than the damage to the lower area and minor scratches on her body, she is free of purposeful injury. There is evidence of an old fracture in her left tibia. Lizbett had tumbled out of a tree when she was eight.

He found bits of dried plaster and Vaseline around her hairline. Ken surmises she was involved in some kind of mask-making.

The cause of death was strangulation, the mechanism cerebral hypoxia. Her face was congested and there were ruptured blood vessels in her eyes. Her neck did have several fractures of the small bones, including the hyoid bone and there was bleeding in the muscles as well as the imprint bruises from the killer's hands.

The face was the surprise. In spite of the distortion and discoloration of death, he saw she was lovely. He saw a visage that he imagined had been lively and curious. But best of all, he saw that Lizbett's mouth, the mouth that had chattered and laughed and sung, was bloody. As Al had already recorded, there was dried blood on the lips and teeth.

Frances Ruffolo is called in. She is the serologist. A former cardiac-surgery nurse, she went on to do forensic training in blood evidence and she is ruthless. Besides fingerprinting, ABO typing is the other key way of identifying perpetrators. She tests Lizbett's blood and finds she has neither A nor B antigens. She is type O and since she has the RH factor, she is O positive. The blood on her mouth is what has everyone excited. It has both A and B antigens. It is AB with a positive Rhesus factor. AB positive. The blood type of only 3 percent of the population. Lizbett had bitten and she had bitten hard a man with the rarest of blood types.

Frances also analyzes the fresh blood found on the bottom of the mattress on the shed and discovers both Lizbett's O positive blood and the AB positive blood of the killer.

Now all they have to do is match it.

# 7

## REALITY

By Tuesday evening, the Warnes still have heard nothing. The rain continues to fall. After the shoot, they arrive home exhausted. Nellie is waiting for them. Darcy had fallen asleep on a couch at the studio, but Meredith and Thompson haven't slept since Sunday night. Still, Meredith does not feel sleep will come to her although her head is throbbing and her body feels leaden. Thompson, who normally doesn't sleep well in any case, thinks he could crash. But they want to hang on for any word. They have talked to the police continually throughout the day, but never with the desired news.

Thompson pours a strong Johnnie Walker Red and adds water and ice. Meredith asks for one neat. Nellie has a glass of white wine. They take their drinks out onto the screened porch facing the garden and settle into the bamboo furniture with the big chintz cushions.

The air is moist and sweet. The trees are dripping, but the rain has stopped. It is very still. Dusk is about to fall and the sky is silver with a horizon of pale orange. There is a cacophony of crickets and birdsong. Nellie makes several beautiful birdcalls in response.

She is a placid, gracious woman whose austere long-necked, long-nosed good looks, accentuated by white hair twisted in a chignon at the nape of her neck, often give the impression that she is imperious. Actually, she is quite shy and soft-voiced, though she has the bearing of the fine concert pianist she was. And she is warm and generous, with an inquiring intelligence and a keen desire to be involved and active. So she gives piano lessons to her granddaughters and plays at the occasional fundraiser.

She was never an available mother to Thompson, mostly because she and his father Theodore did a lot of travelling and Thompson was sent to boarding school when he was very young. Nellie and Theodore were one of those couples whose attachment to each other superseded their child and a regular circle of friends. They preferred each other's company alone and when Thompson did see them, he saw a man and a woman as enamoured and exclusionary as two teenagers.

Not that Nellie did not love her son. But she loved her husband more.

Meredith is imagining, under other circumstances, the four of them walking to Jeremiah's, the ice cream store at the edge of the park. At the store, Meredith would have Jamokka Almond Fudge. Thompson would have Rocky Road. And both the girls would choose Chocolate Smartie Overload. They'd all have sugar cones and walk back, and, because of the heat, the ice cream would drip down their hands if they didn't lick fast enough.

Meredith gets up and lights the candles on the table and the porch closes in.

"So much rain," says Nellie. "I can't ever remember so much rain."

Meredith pictures Lizbett lying out in it.

Thompson decides she isn't. She's inside somewhere. She's not getting wet.

"Where could Lizbett be?" Darcy demands.

The phone keeps ringing. Well-wishers. Inquirers. The curious. Every time it rings, their hearts pound, their breath shortens.

"Hello?" one of them will say, but it never is anything they want to hear.

People dropped by all day, as well, asking how they could help. Nellie says she sent them to the police.

"They brought food. A lot of it. There's a roast chicken and a potato salad. You should eat something."

"We will," they say. But they never do.

Meredith says, "What about a bath, Darce, love? You haven't had one since Sunday night. You should wash your hair."

Darcy says, "It's too hot for a bath."

"C'mon," offers Thompson. "I'll take you. And we'll keep the water cool, cool as you want. You can even have bubbles."

The girls' bathroom has an old-fashioned claw-footed tub, probably original to the house and Thompson fills it and adds foaming green apple bath gel. Darcy undresses, puts her clothes in a hamper, and climbs in. "Br-r-r-r," she says. "Too cold. It feels like the lake!"

Thompson adds some hot, undoes Darcy's braids, and helps her lather her hair, then reaches up for the shower nozzle and brings it down to rinse away the shampoo.

"Ready to wash your body?"

"You can. I feel lazy. But first you have to do conditioner so I won't get tangles."

He laughs. "Okay. I forgot." When he's finished he asks her to stand up. He soaps her all over. "You do your bottom. And be careful. Not too much soap. Little girls with sore bottoms can't get to sleep."

"Mommy says it's special, tender, precious skin."

"Yes, it is."

He thinks of Lizbett. It has been years since he bathed her and sometime since he has seen her unclothed. Soon, he realizes, she will be in the first flush of womanhood and one day, some young man (or men), will be as entranced by her essential core as he is with Meredith's, that very same unique, wondrous place he so delicately and so lovingly wiped and creamed and powdered. And a shattering, searing, ineffable image comes to him: that of Lizbett being violated.

Darcy brings him to. "Daddy! Daddy!"

"Yes, sweetheart."

"You weren't listening to what I was saying. You were in la-la-land."

He laughed. "Yes I was. What were you saying?"

"That you don't have it."

"Don't have what, angel."

"That special, precious skin."

"No, I don't."

"You have a penis and tessicals."

"Testicles."

"Stephen says they're called 'balls.'"

"They can be."

"He says a penis is called a wanker."

"That's not a name I know."

"What ones do you know?"

"Well ... dick."

"Dick! That's a boy's name. A boy with that name probably wouldn't like it."

"No, probably not."

"Daddy?"

"Yes, Darce."

"Could we get a dog? Another dog like Misty?"

"Now would not be a good time."

"When, then?"

"I don't know when. Maybe something will tell us. Now rinse off and out you get."

"Look, I'm a soap-man," she says. "Write my name on my tummy."

"A soap-lady. D-a-r-c-y."

"Now yours and Mommy's"

"M-o-m-m-y. D-a-d-d-y."

"Now Lizbett's."

It's almost more than Thompson can bear, but he writes, "L-i-z-b-e-t-t." Then he says, "C'mon, now. Before you get itchy."

He rinses her off with the shower nozzle and she steps out and he encloses her in a big, fluffy towel, hugging her tightly and he thinks his heart is going to break.

Abbey and Kyle arrive. "I'm so sorry I couldn't get here sooner," she says, embracing everyone, but giving a prolonged, tight hug to Meredith. "I'm in the middle of a horrible divorce and custody case."

Meredith pictures a hostile couple, cruel words flying, some children held emotionally hostage. There's life out there, however sordid. She feels theirs is sordid, too, and cannot fathom how it has all happened. How comfort can so vehemently, so precipitately become dread. She thinks of the randomness of life, how, really, you can count on nothing. What she had thought was happy containment, what she had never doubted would always be, has been shattered and not in the mundane way of a split marriage or even the death of a loved one, but worse, by something atrocious.

That's how she sees Lizbett's disappearance. An atrocity. The word *savage* comes to her and it's like a punch. But that's how — in what has become relentless fear — she sees it. Lizbett okay? Safe and dry somewhere waiting to be found? She wants to think so, but she doesn't.

"Pour a drink," she says to Abbey and Kyle. "Come and sit. It's lovely out here." They do. After a time, Meredith breaks the silence. "I think I should call Dr. Brooks."

"What for?" asks Thompson.

"Valium. I need some Valium. I don't think I can take this."

Thompson has been hoping for, waiting for a ransom call, although nothing has led the police to think this might be a kidnapping for money. For some reason, that would be easier, Thompson feels. Pay us $X$ amount and you get her back. Even though they aren't rich, maybe someone thinks they are. Maybe Lizbett's performing has given her a celebrity that has attracted some low-life to believe there is money to be had in her. That she is worth something. She is, of course, and Thompson believes he would pay anything: mortgage the house, sell stocks, borrow from the bank or Nellie to get her back. So he is more hopeful than Meredith, opting to believe in the dishonesty of humanity rather than the evil.

At midnight, they go to bed with no news. Thompson walked out to the drugstore at the bottom of their street to pick up the Valium Dr. Brooks had phoned in. They both take one and crash. Darcy sleeps between them. Nellie stays in the guest room.

Meredith had forgotten to close the curtains. Thompson awakens while it is still dark and he lies wide-eyed, watching as the light slowly creeps in. He can see a brightly coloured sky with dark striations. He thinks the Valium has not worked; that he was awake most of the night, flopping around to find a position of comfort. Certainly, he has been awake for the past few hours, his body jittery. And rather than feel flat and grim and embedded, the way he usually does when he first opens his eyes, he feels an unease that threatens to unwind him.

How many ways are there to describe panic? Fear? Not enough. How many ways to describe the lurching in his gut, the limpness of his limbs, the thudding of his heart, the tightness in his chest, his inability to take a breath?

He feels as if he is plummeting from the highest point on a roller coaster except this is not sought, this is not a thrill with a finish. A finish that brings euphoric relief. This feeling perseveres, fueled by the ruthlessness of the imagination. It grips like a pit bull. And it's infinite. There's no escape even in sleep because the imagination invades and distorts sleep. He thinks death must be the only way out. But he doesn't want death. He wants his daughter.

He looks over at Meredith and Darcy, both of whom are breathing heavily. He thinks how terrible that the three of them are there. Not that Darcy hasn't come into their bed many times. She's been doing it since she could climb out of her crib. But she hasn't done it for a while and the reason she has done it now is overwhelming. However are they going to guide this fragile, innocent child through whatever is to come? Because even if Lizbett is alive and comes home, she won't be unharmed.

He rolls out of bed so as not to disturb the two of them and pads downstairs to the kitchen. Nellie is there, reading the paper. She has made coffee and cornbread, which smells delicious. Thompson, realizing he is starving, cuts a piece and lathers it with butter.

"It's all here," she says. "Everything they know, which is really nothing. Which is what the police have been telling us. Apparently at the baseball game last night, at the seventh inning stretch, they put up Lizbett's picture on the scoreboard. Thirty-five thousand people saw it. It must have been amazing. Hundreds of searchers have been out in the rain night and day since she disappeared. They've also been trying to find witnesses ... anyone who might have seen her. They basically have no one ... no clues."

Meredith and Darcy sleep past 10:00 a.m. Meredith awakes with a start, feeling groggy and thick-tongued. For a moment the terrible situation evades her, and, glancing at the clock, she wonders why she has slept so late. She feels a sudden concern for the shoot. Then it all comes flooding back and she looks over at Darcy and scoops her up and holds her so tightly that Darcy protests.

"I only just wanted you to know how loved you are."

"As much as Lizbett?"

"Of course, as much as Lizbett!"

"Would you be so scared if I didn't come home?"

"Oh, sweetheart. Don't even think that. But yes, we'd be very, very scared, just as we are with Lizbett."

"Did someone kidnap her?"

"We don't know, angel. We really just don't know anything."

Darcy gets up and goes downstairs, but Meredith lies back down. She cannot move. It's not like a paralysis, the way her legs felt after the epidural for Lizbett's birth. She does have feeling. What she doesn't have is the physical strength to lift herself up from the bed, as if her body has suddenly become like the mattress itself, dense, thickly padded, and weighty. She wants to cry out, "Somebody come and help me," but she can't find her voice. So she just lies there, eyes closed, trying not to think about another day without knowing anything about Lizbett.

Thompson comes in. "You awake?"

"Yes," she says. "I wish I weren't. I'm so exhausted. I might take another Valium."

"Don't."

"Okay. I won't. I'll just lie here in the mire of my suffering."

"We're all doing that, sweetie, in our own way."

"I know," she says. "I'm sorry."

"Can I get you anything?"

"What about the shoot? I can't make it, Sonny. Lew must be going crazy."

"I called him first thing and told him to replace us. We can't do anything else."

"Who will he get this late?"

"I don't know. He didn't say. It's not our problem now."

"Sonny, what will we do?"

"We'll do what we have to. Shall I bring you some coffee?"

Meredith doesn't take another Valium, although she's tempted, but she does stay in bed, drifting in and out of fitful sleep. Mr. Mushu and Geoffrey curl in close to her, purring and prodding. She remembers how Misty used to come up on the bed and if Thompson weren't there, the dog would lie in his place, her huge head on his pillow. She's thinking how it would be to have her there now and how strange it is that it is a dog she is picturing for comfort and relief. But Misty was that kind of dog. Infusive, effusive. She had eyes … the droopy, mournful eyes of the breed … that understood and reciprocated. "You're profoundly loved and protected," they said. The Warnes all used to put their arms around her big body when they needed reassurance.

Thompson has never seen Meredith so incapacitated. Even though she was a mess after Misty died, she was always up and about. Sobbing, but up and about. It's not like her to succumb. He doesn't want to think what it will mean when they have to face the truth.

He goes out to work in their large garden, an elaborate tangle of perennials and annuals, like a wildflower field. Both he and Meredith are committed gardeners, although they often lose plants and don't know why. But they are haphazard. Contrary to the discipline they each show to their respective fields, they go by gut out here. Every spring they go to a nursery and wander up and down the aisles of spectacular plants and say, "Let's take this, and this and this." They don't even think of a garden as a canvas. They simply like an abstract, serendipitous splay of colours and textures. Right now, it all badly needs weeding.

The soil is wet and crumbly and it is easy to pull out the weeds, but Thompson hates them. And he hates the act of weeding: the back-breaking kneeling, the tedium with no reward because the weeds soon come back. They won't use poison because of Mr. Mushu and Geoffrey, who like to hang out in the flowers.

He knows every one of the myriad mass of weeds by name, and, as he pulls them out, he imagines himself as some kind of hero annihilating an invading enemy that threatens to end a culture. This fantasy, along with the monotony of what he's doing — digging and yanking over and over — put him in a kind of trance. The day is close and hot. He feels gritty and itchy and sweaty. His back hurts. A few mosquitoes whine incessantly around him. Probably they should have emptied the bird bath. He wipes his face on his damp T-shirt and looks up.

There are patches of blue. Maybe they'll soon see they sun. Maybe if he perseveres, he can finish the whole garden, though he doubts it. Maybe they can hire a high school kid to come and do it. Maybe Lizbett would come and help.

He can't believe that, for a time, he was so far away from his anxiety that he actually forgot that Lizbett is not with them. He stops and bends forward to the ground in a supplicating position, his muddy gloves cupping his head. And he weeps.

What happens next is a blur. He doesn't know if he went back to work or if he just sat there, kneeling and weeping. He doesn't know how much time has gone by when Nellie comes out into the garden, her face grave. "There are two detectives here."

# 8

# AGONY

Lizbett's body is on a gurney covered in a sheet. It is behind a large window. Meredith and Thompson and Irv Mikkelson are on this side. Ken Kumamoto lifts the sheet. Thompson drops his head. Meredith crumples.

Mikkelson helps her up, supports her, and says, "We're very sorry for your loss," knowing, as he says them, the words are presumptuous, hollow and meaningless. It seems insulting to say them. He loathes saying them. He wishes someone would come up with something else, something more genuine, something with more feeling, but he knows feeling is something he's not meant to have.

He shows the Warnes the way into the big main room. All eyes are on them. There is shock and there is rage and there is sorrow. Not one person feels as if he or she hasn't lost a child. A couple of people approach them and touch them and murmur condolences. Meredith and Thompson are cataleptic.

Mikkelson leads them to a couple of chairs by his desk and asks if he can get them anything.

"A glass of water," says Meredith.

Thompson shakes his head.

Then Mikkelson hands them a plastic bag. "Her effects," he says. Meredith looks in and pulls out Lizbett's green jelly Swatch, her gold bangle from Everard, the red plastic baubles from her ponytail. At the bottom are her red leather sandals.

"There were no earrings?" Meredith asks. "She usually wore little pearl earrings."

"No," answers Mikkelson. "I'm sorry."

"She must've forgotten to put them in. I'll look for them on her dressing table."

"I have a few questions, but I can leave them to another time," Mikkelson says. "I know this must be very difficult for you."

"No," replies Meredith. "Anything that will help."

And the usual questions are asked. When was the last time you saw your daughter? Spoke with her? Did they know if she had any plans after leaving the museum? Was she accustomed to going about on her own? Could she have possibly have changed her plans? Had they seen anyone unlikely near their house? What were they doing at the time of her disappearance? Was there anyone in the realm of their friends and acquaintances, any service people who had been behaving suspiciously?

Thompson comes to. He is aggravated. They have answered all of these questions over and over. What can the police tell them? What have they found?

"We wish we had more," replies Mikkelson. He wonders how much to tell them and thinks not much. They have seen the body. They know where it was found, the manner of death, the probable cause and time. They were told there had been a sexual assault. At this point, the police don't know much more themselves.

Meredith wonders when they can have Lizbett. "Can we go to the place?" she asks.

"I'm afraid not, ma'am. It's a crime scene."

"Not even near it?"

"I wouldn't think so." But Meredith is thinking she will try.

For now, there is nothing they can do but go home. Go home and what? Go home to a house with an unfathomable hole. Go home knowing Lizbett is gone from this earth; that she has been savagely taken from them in a way they could never even have imagined. Go home knowing she's being cut and probed in a morgue, a place that has only ever existed in movies and on TV.

Their Lizbett. Their first-born. Their precious, precious perfect girl. Their star.

Who will hold them up? How can they possibly live?

In the car on the way back, Thompson says, "Whatever are we going to tell Darcy?"

Nellie has called Everard Henley, Meredith's father in Australia. He is the sole caregiver of Dora, Meredith's mother, who has mid-stage Alzheimer's. He will come as soon as he finds someone to take over his church and the care of his wife. Abbey and Kyle are already at the house. Meredith falls into her sister and they both sob.

Nellie has been attending to Darcy, who has been told nothing, although she suspects from the arrival of the two detectives, her parents' immediate departure, the gravity of the atmosphere, that Lizbett is dead. She knows "dead" because of Misty. It feels like that now. And she's even more sure when her parents get home and she sees the slump in her mother's body, in the terrible sadness on her father's face.

"Is Lizbett dead?" she asks.

"Yes, she is, sweetheart," Thompson replies.

"How?"

"A very mean, very, very, very bad person took her."

"Did he hurt her?"

"I'm afraid he did. But she can't feel it now. She's safe now."

"How did he hurt her? Why did he?"

"We don't know why. And we're not sure how he hurt her." Thompson felt instinctively he needed to withhold here.

"But he did it enough for her to be dead."

"Yes."

Darcy bursts into tears. "That is mean. That is very, very, very mean. Now I don't have a sister. I'm all alone."

Thompson bends down and takes her in his arms. "You're not alone, angel-girl, you have me. And you have Mommy. And you have Nan-Nan. And Grandpa Henley is going to come. And Abbey and Kyle."

"And Mr. Mushu and Geoffrey," Darcy says. "And maybe a dog … will that bad guy want to get me?"

"We won't let him," says Thompson. "We absolutely won't let him."

Word gets out. One by one people begin to arrive with food. Soon the dining-room table and the kitchen counters and the refrigerator are laden with donuts and cold-cuts and cheese plates and casseroles and scalloped potatoes and salads. There are pies and cakes, cookies and brownies. Someone brings a whole roast beef tenderloin that they will actually eat.

And flowers. There are so many bouquets, they run out of space to put them. They even have flowers on the bathroom counters.

Brygida comes with her daughter, Aniela, as they had yesterday, to keep order. Brygida is all efficiency, sorrow, and empathy. Aniela has been a wonderful distraction for Darcy. They have visited a couple of pet shops, even though Darcy knows the Warnes disapprove of them, but she got to see puppies and kittens. They have gone to the park and to a coffee house with a Mickey Mouse theme, which Darcy loves.

Brygida had been a hungry and impoverished little girl in Nazi-ravaged Warsaw. Her father, a captured officer from the Polish army, helped build the camps and was killed in Majdanek. Brygida also witnessed, and felt for years, the Russians' brutalization of the Poles. She has an instinct for tragedy and the wherewithal to endure it. She will be Meredith's rock.

Magdalena arrives. She remembers coming here after Misty's death. Then, the household was drenched in tears, a wide-eyed, bewildered Darcy clinging to her mother's knees. The silence in the spaces was stifling. Magdalena sat with the family and no one could speak.

Today the noise is deadening. People are hyper-animated, gesturing excessively. Like too-loud music, the tragedy drowns out words, turns sentences into mouthed gibberish. An unknowing observer might think it was a successful party, the kind where everyone is feeling euphoric, celebratory.

Everyone notices Magdalena's entrance. For one thing, she is taller than almost anyone. She is wearing a long, brilliantly coloured gypsy skirt and an orange T-shirt with a wide belt studded in turquoise at her waist. And she has a gentle, commanding demeanor that brings calm and comfort the way a cool breeze does on an oppressively hot day. Meredith rushes up to her. The larger woman takes the smaller one in her arms. It's as if her uncanny channel with dogs has translated into something humanly therapeutic. Her being offers a momentary easing. Meredith presses into her shoulder, her body shuddering with silent sobs.

Meredith's close friends arrive: Betty Lou, Cynthia, and Diana. They sit by her on the sofa and hold her. The wives of their couple-friends come without their husbands, who are at work. In fact, it is mostly women who come. Neighbours, fellow artists, clients. The mothers of Lizbett's friends all come with their daughters. Daphne, Dominique, Lauren, Jen, and Claire. They are a close-knit group; have been together since kindergarten. Lizbett was their leader.

They are all straightforward girls, assured, certain of their futures. Or at least they were. That has been shattered now. They are all weeping and clutching each other. What have they been told? What can they be thinking? They are all only eleven. Would they even know what sexual assault means? How will it impact on their young lives, being so close to womanhood as they are? Lizbett's little purse with her address book inside disappeared with her. Could the other girls be targets? How can they be kept safe? How can they be kept from being fearful?

Meredith gives each of the girls hugs, says over and over, "Oh, don't cry." She has watched them grow up; feels a special attachment to each of them. They are constantly at the Warnes' house, coming after school to do homework, for meals, for sleepovers, for visits to the cottage. She tells them they are welcome to go up to Lizbett's room, but though they perhaps don't understand the sensation, it feels macabre to them. One or two of them have lost pets or grandparents, but none is yet able to comprehend the immensity of Lizbett's death. There will be grief counsellors at school and Saturday-morning support groups, but it will be years before any one of them can really come to grips with the horror of the event.

For now, they wander around the food table. One chooses a chocolate chip cookie, another a jelly donut and gets icing sugar on her nose. Another asks her mother if she can have a piece of chocolate cake. The mother says, "Really?"

Daphne says, "If I was here all the time, I'd get so fat."

Meredith stares at the girls and recalls seeing them all crushed together one night on a couch watching a movie and being struck by their collective female power, the potential of it. She sensed something crucial and ascendant in their vibrant, intelligent femininity and she was in awe of it.

Precipitately, she feels a surge of bitterness: these girls are alive! These girls will get breasts and their periods and have boyfriends and go to university and have careers and maybe get married and have children. Lizbett no longer exists. She never will exist. Meredith will never see her have any one of these things. She wonders if she can bear to ever see the girls again, as they will be constant reminders of what she has been denied. For a moment, she hates them.

Thompson is in a kind of bewildered, frozen graciousness. Ill at ease at gatherings under normal circumstances, now he must face dozens of people, whose only purpose is to be kind and compassionate, but who seem like alien invaders. All he wants to do is avoid them. What are they doing here? Who are they?

Of course, he knows who they are, or most of them, anyway, but he feels no connection to any of them. Their lips are moving. He hears their words, but he doesn't know what they are. They are muffled, elided. He has no idea how he's responding or if he is at all. His mouth opens, his tongue moves, a sound comes out of his throat, but what it says is beyond him. Does he even feel himself smile? Could he possibly have pulled his lips across his teeth and crinkled his eyes and smiled? What would make him smile?

He is sure, too, that from the sofa across the room, he has heard Meredith laugh. Several times. Heartily. She is sitting with her closest friends and they have been laughing about something. He isn't distressed or shocked by this, merely puzzled. Where does a smile, laughter come from when a person has been tossed into a bottomless pit of horror and sorrow? Can humour actually overpower atrocity? Or does a person's makeup kick in and respond automatically, out of politeness, to protect the teller from the listener's agony? "You must not see that I am about to break. You must not know I am drowning, that my lungs are full of Lizbett's finality and I am gasping, clinging hopelessly to nothing."

He walks from the living room to the kitchen, nodding and murmuring as voices and hands reach out. The kitchen is full of garrulous people, as it always is at their parties because it is big and bright and informal. Were they actually talking about Reagan and Star Wars? A few people hug him. He acknowledges a couple of Lizbett's friends' mothers. One, he thinks, is Lauren's mother and she is sensational. He can't believe the thought came to him.

"Just getting a beer," he says, going to the fridge and taking one out. He sees the fridge is full of beer. Where did it come from? "Please. Help yourselves ... to anything and everything."

At one point he encounters Magdalena.

"Lovely party," he says.

She laughs lightly. "I ... I have no words ..."

"You don't need them. Your being here is enough. I know how much it means to Meredith."

"And you? How are you holding up?"

"Me? I'm not. I've been invaded by some kind of robot who's doing it all for me, all the motions, the talk, the polite connecting. Everything but the feeling."

For a moment they are silent and then in a gesture of ineffable sadness and compassion Magdalena reaches out and pulls the grieving man to her.

Then he paces through the rooms aimlessly until it occurs to him he's looking for something. He goes to the basement door, opens it, and switches on the light. He descends. Why is he going down into the basement? He doesn't know except that he is searching. For what, he doesn't know. For something tangible, something explicable. Some comfort? An answer?

It is chilly and damp and he shivers. Normally he loves the basement. With its high stone walls and thicky planked ceiling, he is reminded of the solidity of their nineteenth-century house, of the care taken to build it. A pungent, acrid odour assaults his nose. The cat litter. He goes over to an alcove and sees a large plastic tub filled with sodden clay and piles of feces. In that instant, he wants to cry. This was Lizbett's responsibility. She was supposed to clean it out every couple of days, but sometimes she forgot. Who knows how many days before her disappearance she had done it? The litter is too solid with urine to scoop so he retrieves a large garbage bag from a shelf and dumps all the foul mud into it. A brown liquid clings to the bottom of the tub. He gags. His eyes are stinging, perhaps from the ammonia, perhaps from the tears he is fighting. He takes the smelly thing over to the laundry basin and runs hot water into it and adds bleach, swooshing it around. He rinses it, wipes it with paper towel, and dumps in a fresh bag of litter and stands for a time debilitated, ashamed, astounded that such a banal, unpleasant task feels so monumental, so influential. There is no more Lizbett. Lizbett will no longer be available to do this. He is fond of the cats, but he does not want to be the one to clean their litter. It is Lizbett's job.

He climbs the stairs back into the kitchen, acknowledges a few more people, and then goes up to the second floor, down the hall to Lizbett's room. She's not there, either. But everything about her is there as if she were just downstairs amusing people at the party: the bright colour is there, the neatness, the sentiment, the smell, her bookshelf, the bassinette lined with dolls, her desk with the Peter Rabbit mug full of pens and pencils. A diary is resting there. Did he know she kept a diary? He doesn't think so. What secrets did she have? He picks it up and turns it over and over as if it were some alien thing. It is pink with daisies and has a lock. He longs to know what's inside. He wants to open it and so he presses the little latch. It clicks. In the deathly silence, he can hear his quickened breathing. He sees that his hands are shaking.

He leafs through, but does he not feel like an interloper. Rather, he is awed. He feels as if he has something mysterious and precious in his hands, an animation of a life, an inner record. But at the same time, he feels no closer to her. There are some longer entries he decides not to read. Mostly there is page after page of "too tired to write." "Too sleepy to write." He smiles wistfully. Lizbett, so responsive, so responsible that even after a long, productive day, even though she was exhausted, would feel compelled to put something down. Not leave an empty page. He closes the little book and lays it down carefully, moving it by fractions of an inch to get it into the same position it had been.

He notices the pearl earrings. He opens her closet and sees her white muslin nightie hanging on the back of the door. He sees skirts and blouses and rarely worn dresses, sneakers and party shoes jumbled on the floor. He pulls out a drawer and there are T-shirts, shorts in another, and jeans in another. He doesn't pull out the top drawer, realizing it would likely be underwear. The room is full of her signs of living, but will never be imbued with her life again. This is what Thompson cannot grasp. This excruciating, indelible fact. Lizbett's life has been lived. It is over. Without his being able to protect her. With a lifetime of things left unsaid and undone. Without ever having said goodbye.

He goes down the hall and hears quiet chatter from Darcy's room and sees her and Stephen seated at a little table, heads together, colouring.

She looks up and sees him and says, "Look, Daddy. Stephen and I are colouring mermaids."

"Those are beautiful, guys. What amazing colours!" Stephen's work is actually a little rough, but Darcy is a perfectionist. "How are you doing, sweetheart? Okay? Anything you want?"

"Fine, Daddy. Could we go to the park? We're getting a bit bored of colouring."

"Oh, I don't think today, sweetie. Mommy and I are busy."

"We could go by ourselves, like we usually do."

"No, Darce. Not today. Why don't you go in the backyard and do something? Could you think of something, maybe?" Thompson is drawing a blank. He cannot think of a thing they could do. Plus, it's steamy hot.

Darcy pouts, makes a face. Thompson says, "No nonsense, Darce."

She sighs. "We should have a dog. I wish we had a dog to play with. Daddy, Stephen says his mother said dead children go into the arms of Jesus. Is that true?"

"I'm not sure, sweetie. I don't know much about Jesus."

"I don't think Lizbett did, either. But it would be good for her to be in someone's arms, wouldn't it? Except, she wouldn't know him very well. He'd be a stranger. She might not like it."

Later, Magdalena wanders out into the garden where she had worked with the Warnes to train Misty. Actually, Magdalena has come with Joan and Hildy. They thought it would be a good test for the dog: the car ride and big-city exposure. They are taking turns connecting with the Warnes and walking the dog along the shady street. Hildy has been calm.

Magdalena sees Darcy and Stephen sitting in the dense shade of the maple tree. She has a flash of something unbearably painful in the otherwise pleasant image of the quiet children, Darcy's dark head against Stephen's fair one, removed from the tragedy and its entourage in their innocence, but, in their vulnerability, an essential part of it. She wonders how they are dealing with such an immense and horrific incident. She has little experience with children; she likes dogs better. Children seem jerky and demanding and unpredictable; they are far more difficult to reassure, to control. In the examining room of her clinic with their pets, the children are disruptive, often frantic that she is hurting the animal. She often has to ask that the child be removed so as not to excite or frighten the dog. She can always read a dog and knows intuitively what to do when a dog mistrusts or is in pain. She would have no idea how to comfort a child, but something about their poignant aloneness, their vulnerability, compels her to approach the two. She remembers vividly the tiny Darcy when she was here training Misty. So wide-eyed and reserved. So intent. What is that little girl thinking now?

"Hello, Darcy. What are you up to?"

"Hi, Maddie. This is Stephen. We're very bored."

"Hello, Stephen. Well, could I sit and chat with you for a bit? I could tell you about all my dogs. I have a new puppy."

"You have a new puppy?"

"Well," Magdalena says, "An almost grown puppy. The people who bought her gave her back because they said she was bad but I think they hurt her and that made her bad."

"Hurt her? How? Why?"

"I wish I knew. I wish she … Hildy … could tell me. Right now, she's very fearful and as a result she sometimes acts really fierce."

"Fierce? How?"

"She growls and snarls and bares her teeth. I have to train her that that is not acceptable behaviour. I have to teach her to trust."

"How would you do that? Will she ever be better?" Darcy asks. "And why would anyone hurt a puppy?"

"Some people believe animals are stupid, lesser beings and they feel smarter and more important if they mistreat them. Maybe someone hurt them and they're taking it out on the dog. I don't really know. But I think Hildy will get better with lots of work. Inside hurt is very hard to heal. I can't see it, but I know it's there. So I have to be very firm with her all the time. She has to learn that being fierce won't make the hurt go away. But I have to love and praise her, too. If she's loved and has rules, she'll be fine. She's a beautiful girl. And very responsive."

"I wish I could see her. I'd like to rescue her."

Magdalena decides to take a chance. She says, "She's outside with Joan. If your parents say it's all right, would you like to see her?"

Of course, Meredith and Thompson want to see her, too. "Can we be rude for just a few moments?" Meredith says to the people who have been talking to her.

When Joan sees the family approach with Magdalena, she high-collars Hildy and commands her to sit.

"Oh, she's so beautiful," says Meredith. "Can we pat her?"

"Reach out your hand palm down under her chin. Let her sniff it. Then scratch her throat."

One by one, Meredith, Thompson, and Darcy take turns introducing themselves to Hildy. Hildy remains passive with only the faintest flicker of her tail.

A day later, when all the visitors have gone, the doorbell rings. Meredith answers it. Melvyn Searle is there with a large bag.

Meredith sees a small, handsome blond man in thick glasses. He half smiles, revealing a dimple.

"Hello, Mrs. Warne. I'm Melvyn Searle. I was Lizbett's mask teacher at the museum. I can't tell you how sorry I am about what has happened."

For some reason Meredith is taken aback. She almost recoils. Perhaps it's because something about him feels out of place. He seems to be just a boy, but he has the confident thrust of a person selling something. She wonders what.

"If only I'd kept her a little longer," he says. "I let her out early to phone you. Or I could have driven her to the library myself. She told me that's where she was going."

"Oh my god," says Meredith. "You were one of the last people to be with her. Lizbett talked so much about you. She loved you!"

Meredith is suddenly overwhelmed with a desire for a familiar connection to this man, this man she on whom she suspected Lizbett had a crush. She wanted to share Lizbett's life with him because he would have stories about her, insights into aspects of her that Lizbett didn't share with her mother. Meredith had seen an expanding self-awareness and attributed it to the mask class. She feels a ravenous, selfish curiosity. What was Lizbett like away from her, especially at the end?

She calls Thompson. "This is Melvyn, Lizbett's mask teacher."

Thompson feels a bit invaded by this stranger. Why hadn't he come earlier, with everyone else?

Melvyn says again, "I am so very sorry. I thought you might want to have these wonderful masks Lizbett made. She was very imaginative. I admired her inquisitive mind."

"Oh, let's see them," Meredith says. "She told us about the star one. I was fascinated. And this one is ... "

"About tears. About her deepest sadness. A visual expression of that."

Thompson examines the mask. "I can't fathom her ever feeling that sad about anything."

"I asked her. She mentioned something about a dog ...?"

Melvyn has taken the time to make his own permanent mould of Lizbett's life mask, so he easily pulls it out of the bag and hands it to Meredith. It is wrapped in white tissue paper, as if in a shroud.

"I hesitated to bring this to you, though you should have it. It may distress you. On that last afternoon, we made what we call life masks. This is Lizbett's face, formed by smoothing plaster gauze over it and letting it harden. It's a three-dimensional portrait, but from reality, not an artist's interpretation."

Meredith looks bewildered and pained. She takes the mask and gingerly unwraps it, holding the face in the palm of her hand as if it were made of eggshell. She examines the flannel interior; touches it tenderly. She feels profoundly the mask's heartbreaking implications; its fragile finality.

"This is Lizbett? On Monday afternoon? This is where her face was?" Then she carefully turns it over and stares. Her eyes are locked to its inert, consequential vitality. "This is her sweet face? This is her dear nose, her lovely high forehead?" She fingers the lips. She wants to put her own lips to them, but instead she puts the mask to her cheek. "This is Lizbett?" she says again. "She's in this? This is her?" Her eyes well. "It's a last record of my beautiful girl."

"It is. We removed it just before she left. It really is her. She was remarkable. So intuitive. So keen."

"Thanks for this," Thompson says. He wants this overbearing, presumptuous man to leave and moves to usher him out of the house.

"I can tell you a bit more about her masks," Melvyn offers. "If you're up to it. It might help. Masks are more complicated than you realize. These are much more than artifacts she's made. She is actually in them. They aren't representations of her, they are her."

Meredith says, "Oh, yes, do, please come in, Mr. ...?"

"Melvyn."

"Melvyn, do come in and tell us about Lizbett."

As he enters the living room from the front hallway, Darcy comes down the stairs and he stops. He sees a wide-eyed, wistful, exquisite little girl. And he says hello.

On Sunday, Thompson and Darcy fetch Everard at the airport. He is a wiry, erect man with a handsome, crinkly, open face, a face that invites confiding. His hair is redder than Meredith's. He is a tennis player and his skin is ruddy-bronze in the way redheads tan. When he comes through the door, Meredith, who has been holding things together in a distracted sort of way, bursts into tears. Everard takes her in his arms. "Oh, my poor pet. Oh, my poor, poor pet." He releases her when Abbey comes forward, weeping as well, and he embraces his elder daughter.

"Hello, Nellie," he says, seeing her.

The Warnes have requested no visitors, so the house is quiet today. Thompson makes Bloody Marys and they take them out on the porch.

"Lovely garden, kids," says Everard.

"A little weedy," replies Thompson looking at the pile of weeds he was building when the detectives arrived. When was that?

"Yes, well, one of a gardener's trials. You should spray," Everard says.

"Oh, god, no," Meredith exclaims. "We have two cats."

"Then get the cats to weed," Everard says.

The conversation stalls. No one knows what to say or rather there is nothing to say that hasn't already been said. They do not see Everard often, every two years or so, less now since Dora has been ill. And Abbey and Meredith are not close to their father, in any case. Both rejected his life, the life they had grown up with, long ago. He knows this and is always careful not to impose, though it disappoints him to have two daughters who have left the church. He is a steadfast minister, although some of his liberal thoughts distress his congregants. He does not take the Bible as gospel, for example, but simply as an occasional, appropriate guide. He more views it as fine spiritual literature, Judeo-Christian history.

But he has a keen sensibility, having dealt with death dozens of times over the years, though never as close and horrific as this. And he knows certain things must be talked about.

"So what are your plans?" he asks.

"Plans?" Thompson wonders. "What plans? To survive. To make it to the next hour."

Meredith gets up. "Should we eat lunch first? There's so much food." Nellie finds a Salad Niçoise and some cold asparagus. Thompson finds some white wine in the fridge. It is lovely and dry and cold.

As they are eating, Meredith says, "Daddy, we don't want a service."

Everard contemplates this. "I see. And what do you propose to do, then?"

"We thought of a private farewell at the funeral home, maybe with a couple of poems. Then we'd like to go straight to the cemetery. Just family."

"You're in accord, Thompson?"

Thompson nods.

"Hmmm," says Everard. "Is that the wisest, most considerate thing to do? You're sure, are you? You'll be denying an awful lot of people the chance to say their own farewell. You're ignoring Lizbett's legacy, her connection not only to friends, but to the many, many people she touched.

To the community. You're ignoring people's love for her and their love for you. They will be searching for some kind of simultaneous comfort, some kind of sorting out of their questions and their grief."

"They can do that on their own," says Meredith.

"There is enormous power, enormous healing in the collective, Meredith. Not everyone feels as removed as you do from the goodness of the church."

Meredith rolls her eyes.

"This is no time for faces, my dear! Don't you think you have an obligation to share with others Lizbett's wonderful life and to offer the chance to acknowledge the tragedy of her death? Many, many people are mourning. I believe a whole city must be mourning."

"Why should I care about them?" Meredith asks.

"Don't you think Lizbett is owed some reverence, some tribute? Why not set aside your irreverence, your personal scorn for the sake of your dead daughter and all those who loved her and want to see some valued, time-honoured ritual in her dying, some celebration of her life."

Meredith now feels too disabled to respond. "Sonny?"

Thompson, as well, is feeling too defeated to object. "Ev may be right, Mer. Maybe we can't think only of ourselves. Lizbett touched many people. I can see how her death might be … might just stay a horrible headline if we don't take the time to talk about her life."

"What do you suggest, Daddy?" Meredith asks.

"I have a colleague here. I know him from ecumenical conferences. His name is David Burkleigh. Perhaps you know his church. St. James the Apostle. I believe it's quite large."

"I do know it," Meredith replies. "Sonny, it's that big stone one with all the gardens downtown. It is beautiful."

"It's the society church," says Thompson.

"Does that matter?" Everard asks.

"Not really. Except we'd never go there."

"You don't go anywhere," says Everard. "This is for Lizbett."

"But we have gone there," says Meredith. "That time we went to the Mozart Requiem. Remember? There's a magnificent pipe organ." She is silent for a moment. And then she acquiesces. "All right, Daddy. We'll have two then. One just for us. And one for everbody else. It's all a kind of theatre, anyway. Lizbett would like that."

The following Friday, at 11:00 a.m., eleven days after Lizbett's death, nine days after her body was discovered, the family gather in the non-denominational chapel of the Woodward Funeral Home. It is an austere room with a lot of pale wood and crystal chandeliers, although today there are many candles. There are tall, abstract, stained-glass windows, lit from behind, along the side. At the front, there are two massive floral arrangements on pedestals at either end of the white coffin. It is closed. The Warnes, with Darcy, have spent the previous couple of hours with it open, but they want it shut for the little ceremony.

Nellie is playing the piano. She has chosen the adagios from three Mozart piano sonatas. Along with the Warnes and Everard, there is Ruth Warne Sanderson, Thompson's father's sister; her husband, Todd; their four sons and their wives; and a number of children ranging from an infant to several teenagers. And Abbey and Kyle.

When Nellie finishes, Everard gets up and turns on a tape machine and plays "Turn. Turn. Turn," which borrows its lyrics from Ecclesiastes 3:1: "To everything there is a season and a time to every purpose under heaven/A time to be born, a time to die, a time to plant and a time to pluck up that which is planted/A time to weep and a time to laugh/A time to mourn and a time to dance/A time to cast away stones forever ..."

Then Everard speaks: "Dear family of our beloved Elizabeth Louise Ellen. Thompson and Meredith have asked me to say a few words to you in a farewell to their precious daughter, but also in acknowledgement of her fineness, her accomplishments, her concern for others, her joyous embrace of life."

Though she has tried to contain them, Meredith's sobs are audible. Everard moves to comfort her, but Thompson surrounds her shaking body in his arms.

Everard continues, "Shakespeare wrote, 'Praising what is lost/makes the remembrance dear.' That's what I want to do today. Make our remembrance dear. Wordsworth also wrote, 'There is a comfort in the strength of love/'Twill make a thing endurable, which else/Would overset the brain, or break the heart.' Our brains have been overset. Our hearts broken. We are enduring the unendurable. 'No worst there is none,/Pitched past pitch of grief,/More pangs will, schooled at forepangs, wilder wring,' wrote the poet

G.M. Hopkins. 'Pitched past pitch of grief.' That's us, isn't it? We're mired in grief. How do we go on?

The thought strikes everyone in the small gathering. How will the Warnes go on?"

"We go on 'in the strength of love'; the strength of our love for Lizbett, but more important, in the strength of her love, not only for all of us, but for all she believed in, all she endeavoured to achieve. She is no more, but she remains a beaming example of the fact that love has no capacity, no borders, no restrictions, no rules. She loved genuinely, with a spirit of adventure and a sense of responsibility. She put back enthusiastically and conscientiously all she was given. And then some. And that's what we must do to heal our hearts, to restore our trust, to begin to endure again: we must love capaciously, unconditionally, responsibly. With beloved Lizbett as our example, with the memory of her vivid in our hearts, we must live each day riding, soaring on the strength of love. Let us bow our heads:

"O Dear Life, that art in me/precious be thy presence. Thy inspiration come/thy gifts be done on earth,/ as it is forever./Help me this day find bread, strength, wisdom, comfort, calm./Forgive me my frailties as I forgive others theirs/Strengthen me against temptation/Help me fight evil/For Thine is the universe, the power and the self/Forever and ever. Ah-me. Ah-you. Ah-us. Ah-them."

Everard looks to Meredith. She looks up at him and smiles.

"I believe Darcy has a few things to say," he states.

Darcy is clear-eyed, her voice strong. She reads from a piece of lined paper: "Hello. My name is Darcy Alison Emma Warne. I am seven years old. Once I had a big sister called Lizbett. She was eleven years old and she was a star. But she died. A bad person killed her. Killed is when someone hurts you and makes you die. You don't die because you were sick or old. He was very mean. Now I don't have a big sister. I am very, very sad. She looked after me. I miss Lizbett a lot. My Mommy and Daddy are very sad. They are crying. They miss Lizbett. I could be the big sister now, but I don't have a little sister. But I will be a big girl. I will be good. I will help them not be sad. Goodbye Lizbett. I love you, wherever you are."

Meredith and Thompson rush up to her and gather her in their arms. "We love you, Darcy," they say. "You don't have to be a big girl for us. Be who you want to be."

Everard gets up for the last time and turns on a recording of Lizbett playing the piano at her last recital: the mournful adagio cantabile from Beethoven's *Pathétique* sonata.

At one time in the nineteenth century, the cemetery was a two-hundred-acre farm on the outskirts of the city. Now it is a vast groomed park in its middle, with myriad statuary and elaborate crypts and twelve miles of winding roads. Great hardwoods loom over the well-tended graves. There are little streams with waterfalls and bridges and a large pond with graceful weeping willows and several pairs of swans. It is a beautiful place to be dead.

The sun glares mercilessly on the day of Lizbett's burial. The humidity is suffocating. It is actually visible in a hovering haze. Were it not for the protection from the cavernous oaks and a slight breeze because of the height of land, the gathering of her little family would be suffering as much physically as they are emotionally. As it is, faces streaming with tears are also wet from perspiration. Clothing clings.

Everyone circles around the coffin resting above the opening of the grave. As the coffin is lowered, each in turn picks up a handful of dirt and tosses it on the top. In the stillness, the sound of pebbles on the wood is jarring. Some also throw in a flower. Some people say a few words: "Goodbye, Lizbett."

"I love you, Lizbett."

"We'll miss you, Lizbett."

"You were special, Lizbett."

"Go with God, Lizbett."

Thompson is holding Meredith up. Darcy sobs. No one, no one feels capable of what they are doing: watching the coffin containing a young girl, their Lizbett, mutilated and slain, go deep into the earth.

# 9

## MELVYN: AFTER LIZBETT

**M**elvyn gets back to museum a little after 5:30 p.m. in an agitated state. He hadn't counted on rush hour to hinder his getaway and he hit it full on: a line of cars inching all the way into the city. He struggled to contain his aggression. All he wanted to do was ram the guy ahead. But an incident would prove he'd been away from the museum. His nerves were screaming with frustration and fear — fear that he wouldn't make it back to the museum in time to connect with someone on the staff who would confirm his alibi that he had been in his studio all afternoon. And his arm was throbbing. The wound was bleeding. The napkin he had been using to staunch the blood was soaked.

No one sees him come in from the parking lot and let himself in the service door to the basement. He is certain of that. Fortuitously, Pete had left. And the general alarm wouldn't be turned on until 6:00 pm.

The rain had subsided to a drizzle and he is a little wet, though not noticeably. And he must quickly attend to his injury. Fortunately, he has an extensive first-aid cupboard. Kids were always gouging themselves.

He turns on the tap and runs warm water liberally over the bite, watching the blood swirl around the drain. He winces, sees an essence of himself disappear. He recalls his shock and disillusionment with Lizbett's attack. He had not anticipated it. He would not have thought she had it in her. The other one hadn't. But she'd been younger.

The flesh is deeply punctured, ragged and ugly. He pulls it apart and exposes the raw, crimson tissue. He is concerned because he knows how prone human bites are to sepsis. He wonders if he needs a couple of stitches. But he can't take the chance of going to emergency. So he pours on antiseptic, grimacing. When it looks as if the bleeding has stopped, he considers using several butterfly bandages to close it, but it occurs to him it's probably better to keep it open so he squeezes on an antibacterial ointment, covers it with a gauze pad and wraps gauze around his arm. Then he puts on a lab coat in case anyone wanders into the studio and wonders what happened.

He is lucky he is so isolated down here. It is off-limits to museum-goers and rarely does any member of the museum staff come down. His colleagues seem to know he likes to be solitary. Except for weekly department meetings, he has little to do with them and though they welcomed the idea when he came up with it, they are not connected to his mask workshops, which are essentially part of the children's division.

After he gathers up the bloody gauze, which he puts in a plastic bag in his satchel, he goes up to the rotunda and chats with the front security guard and the woman on the admissions desk who is just closing up.

"Hey, Melvyn," says the guard. "That was some storm."

"I barely saw it," says Melvyn. "The studio windows are so high up. But the thunder was loud enough."

"Wasn't it? It shook me a bit. And there were killer winds," says the guard. "Apparently there are big tree branches down all over the city."

"I guess we were lucky to be inside," Melvyn says.

Saying good night, he exits the museum from the front door, as is his usual habit. It doesn't occur to them to wonder why he is wearing a lab coat. He is a weird guy. When they are questioned, they will attest that Melvyn had been there all afternoon as he always was because they have no reason to think otherwise.

On the way home, he regains the well-being he felt with Lizbett. Apart from the pleasure he gets in planning his exploits, their success elates him more. He feels like a conqueror.

He pulls up to a random city garbage bin outside a McDonald's and deposits the bag from the crime scene and the plastic bag, making sure they are well buried in the other rubbish.

His accomplishment, which is how he looks at it, feels easy now, and leads him to imagine himself a mastermind of crime … not that he thinks what he did was criminal. To him, it was a sacrifice, sending a beautiful child to something higher. He has spared her the iniquity of womanhood. And he has preserved her for himself. He was her last witness, her last connection. He! Melvyn Searle. The man who has given Lizbett Warne eternal childhood has given himself indelible memories.

But he has more to do. He is convinced he will be questioned soon, as he is among the last people to see Lizbett. His place must be clean of any traces of her or his other girl. He takes the photos from the refrigerator; he takes Lizbett's clothing and her purse along with the other little girl's articles he has stashed and puts them in his wooden souvenir trunk. It's hidden away in the crowded storage locker in the filthy basement of the house.

Then he dusts everything with Pledge and vacuums his flat thoroughly and cleans his bathroom with bleach and Ajax. He washes the kitchen floor with Pine Sol. He spreads Mop & Glo on his floors.

He wonders if he should eat something. He has a pizza in the freezer. Or he could make Kraft Dinner and add some tuna fish. He only had an apple and some yogourt at lunch as he was keyed up with his mission. How perfect was it that he got to make her life mask, or death mask, as it turned out to be? He couldn't have planned it better if he had tried.

But that is where he excels, he decides, as he pours himself a glass of red wine. He spreads part of a tin of sliced mushrooms and several slabs of cheese on the frozen pizza and puts it in the oven and turns it on. His plans. Like the last one in the other city where he lived before he moved here two years ago.

He had had a relationship with little Audrey Tovarek, as well, but not with the same intellectuality and creativity as he did with Lizbett. He's not sure why he was attracted to her at that particular time in his life. He'd had longings, urges, but he had never before been compelled to act on them as he was with Audrey. And Lizbett. It occurs to him he is only attracted to exceptional girls, girls who exude love.

Nine-year-old Audrey had only just moved with her mother Mariska to an apartment building a couple of streets over when he encountered her in a park he used to frequent. The park was nearby. Audrey came there most days after school and on weekends. Melvyn often saw her. He was teaching cultural anthropology at a university and had flexible hours.

From the beginning, Melvyn saw Audrey was a shiner. She was petite, agile, and effervescent, with short blond hair held to one side by a barrette. She had penetrating brown eyes and a winsome smile. Melvyn kept his eye on her from spring to mid-summer. In the park he would sit on a bench and though he rarely talked to anyone except to say hello, people accepted him as a regular fixture — the boyish guy with the thick glasses and a book. Sometimes he would watch a baby in a stroller while a mom went to push another child on the swings.

Audrey's mother was not always with her. She was single and worked as a salesperson at a large department store. Audrey went to a babysitter in her apartment building, but if the weather was fine, the babysitter let her come to the park.

Early one Saturday morning, near the beginning of August, Melvyn saw Audrey approaching the park. He had been out walking. He went up to her and said, "Shall I walk with you?" Audrey had had little conversations with Melvyn before. Once Melvyn brought her a barrette with sparkling rhinestones, which he said he'd found.

"I just live over there," he said. "I'm going shopping. I forgot my wallet. Want to come by and wait for me while I get it?"

Audrey hesitated.

"It's okay," he said. "I won't be a minute. And I can bring us down a Popsicle. I have some in my freezer. Or you can come up with me and get it."

Audrey saw that his house had a garden with pretty flowers and little elves and mushrooms.

"Don't you like that?" Melvyn asked. "I think it's real cute. My landlord puts them there. He has a cat named Pookie. Maybe if you come in, you can see him in the hallway."

Audrey did think the ornaments were cute and she liked cats. She wanted one. She wanted to see this one so she walked up the stairs onto the porch of Melvyn's house and followed him through the front door and down the hall to his doorway. They didn't see the cat.

"Come on in." And she entered into his world, three small rooms, a kitchen, a living room, and a bedroom looking out onto the alley. "Have a look around," he said. "I have some neat masks in my living room. You can try one on if you want." Audrey wandered confidently into the living room and took a glittery Brazilian half-mask with long feathers off the wall and put it over her face.

He said, "Wow! You're fantastic. There's a long mirror in the bedroom where you can look at yourself. Here, let me tie it on."

While she was in the bedroom, he went into a drawer in the kitchen and took out a roll of duct tape and some scissors and pair of kitchen gloves, which he put on. He cut off a piece of tape and went into the bedroom and before Audrey could realize what was happening he placed his hand over her mouth and slapped on the tape. She stood there in the mask, immobilized by shock. He quickly cut another piece of tape and pulled her arms around her back and wrapped her wrists. She was whimpering. Through the mask, he could see terror in her eyes and tears running down her cheeks from under it, but she wasn't trying to get away. He took her by the shoulders and pushed her onto the bed.

He had a mask on his dresser, a Mexican carnival mask, a glossy, handsome male face with heavy eyebrows, a wide, leering red mouth and mass of black hair — horsehair, probably. He put it on and looked at himself in the mirror and laughed. Then he pulled off Audrey's panties (she was wearing a pink sundress with a sequined cat on the bodice and the words "pretty kitty") and unzipped his fly and yanked down his chinos, and, reaching for a condom, ripped open the package and put it on. Like the one he used with Lizbett, this was lubricated. And like his invasion of Lizbett, he followed the same pattern. He brutally penetrated an opening not much bigger than a thimble. Her vagina tore in two places. This sensation empowered him as did the fact she was bleeding. He was as rough with her rectum. Audrey threw her head back and tried to scream. Her eyes rolled upwards and he wondered if she was unconscious. All the better if she was. He put his hands around her neck and squeezed, pressing with his thumbs onto the carotid arteries on either side of her larynx. When she was no longer breathing, he released his hands and then took his time finishing.

Melvyn did not feel pleasure. He felt dominance, an ascendancy unleashed, but he was, of course, not himself, but a celebrant taking part in a religious festival. The mask was him, he was the mask.

The easy part now over, he began to think about how he could get away with this. He believed no one had seen him with Audrey. The park was heavily treed along the edges of the street and there weren't many people there anyway. His landlord was at work. The condom, duct tape, and gloves he removed and placed in a grocery store plastic bag that he would dump near the store when he went shopping. He took off Audrey's dress and stuffed it, for the time being, with her panties in a drawer. From the kitchen he brought a large, heavy-duty plastic bag, the kind used by contractors. He curled up Audrey's body, stuffed it in the bag, and tied it closed. He carried the bag out the back way to the alley where his grey Honda stayed and he dumped it in the back seat. That night he would drive around the city or the outskirts looking for an unlikely place to leave a dead little girl.

He was questioned, but never held. No one doubted this reticent, ingenuous man. To his knowledge, they have never found the body, which he tossed under a bridge on a remote rural road about forty miles outside of town.

*Ping! Ping! Ping!* The timer goes off on his pizza. He pours more wine. He is now feeling inordinately removed, calm, like a depleted star athlete who has expended himself past his limits and won by seconds. His body and mind have moved into a resting mode, a retreat, really, from the pure, sublime exertion of earlier. It is as if he is in a state of suspended animation — alive and thinking, but inert, unresponsive. The event is history, can never be repeated. When he thinks of the stilled body lying face down by the Queen Anne's Lace, being cleansed by the rain, he sees an artifact, the precious detritus of an architectural site, another time, an object full of experience, of tales, now powerless to express them except in its delineated perfection. He notices Lizbett's life mask on a table. He goes over to it and looks at it with a sense of wistful elation. He still possesses her. He gently places the mask over his face and walks to the mirror and sees that he is Lizbett. While her face is on his, she overtakes him and lives.

He returns to his pizza. He is hungry, he realizes. He needs sustenance, so he cuts a limp piece, takes a bite and chews it with deliberation and distaste. He peruses the newspaper, thinking he might go to the late showing of a film. His neighbourhood theatre is small and plays second runs and art house movies. He can choose among *Hannah and Her Sisters*, *Platoon*, or *Labyrinth*, a Jim Henson film with David Bowie. He has already seen it four times, but the movie always overwhelms him. It will be a perfect way to lose himself after the pressures of the day. He is not feeling stressed, but still, an escape like *Labyrinth* would be regenerative. The theatre has an espresso bar.

He looks forward to getting one and an iced brownie. The ones they have there are so moist.

From the opening credits with the overlay of flying white and gold owls, he is mesmerized. He will drift in and out of his reality and the movie's all night. Jim Henson is a genius. The phantasmagoria of characters thrill him because they exist. They are not animated. They are three-dimensional, real. True, as puppets, their existence is enlivened by humans, the way masks are. But it's that vitality, that palpability that makes them so believable. They truly are alive. The watchers believe they are alive. The watchers believe *in* them. Melvyn does, implicitly. The creative interdependence excites him. Like it did with Lizbett. Without the mask it would have been an assault.

In the film, there is a seduction scene between Sarah, the young heroine and the king of the goblins, played by a fantastic David Bowie. Melvyn becomes the king. Sarah has eaten the "peach of forgetfulness" and is in a trance. He wills the act to happen; the goblin king and the maiden. A magical man and a girl-child. Merged. David Bowie is mersmerizing with his mane of platinum spiked hair and his cocky stride. Melvyn imagines himself as compelling. He believes he is. Didn't both Audrey and Lizbett come to him willingly? He didn't have to cast a spell. He is a superior being with ultimate control.

"I have been generous," says the Goblin King. "But I can be cruel." And then the Faustian temptation, "I'm offering you your dreams. Just fear me, love me, do as I say. I'll be your slave ..."

"You have no power over me," says Sarah.

But Melvyn has shown he does. The excitement of the day and the inspiration of the movie have made him feel he will again.

## 10

## ST. JAMES THE APOSTLE

The soaring stone church is packed. Flowers spill from silver urns, the fragrance of the Oriental lilies pungent. There are wreaths of miniature white roses on the ends of the forward pews. Dust motes dance in beams of sunlight from the rose window over the altar. A blow-up of Lizbett's head shot stares out from an easel where the coffin would have been. It is the same picture that still remains on a lot of telephone poles across the city. The organ is playing Ravel's "Pavanne for a Dead Princess" as the mourners file into the long nave, both sides of the transept and the upper galleries. A crowd has gathered on the steps outside.

Lizbett's friends and their families have come. All of Meredith's and Thompson's friends are there. Some have brought older children. Brygida, Tadeusz, and Aniela have come. The cast and crew of both *Annie* and *Hansel and Gretel* are there and the television people who worked with Lizbett. There are the Warnes' work associates and many clients. Magdalena has come with Joan. Allan, her former lover is there. And Irme Pormoranska. Meredith is momentarily shocked. And most of the Metro police department, who are looking for anyone suspicious. Whoever that could be.

Melvyn Searle is there. And why wouldn't he be, the cops think? He was Lizbett's teacher. He liked her. The police have interviewed Melvyn at length three times: once at the museum, once at the station, and once at his flat, where they had a close look around. He could be a suspect, but he is not. He will never be a suspect. There is not the probable cause necessary to investigate him. He was in his studio at the Courtice Museum at the time of Lizbett's death. Two witnesses have corroborated that.

Mostly the church is filled with strangers, strangers with daughters and granddaughters and nieces and sisters, strangers who have lost children, strangers whose once taken-for-granted security is now overturned, strangers with public profiles, everyday strangers whose hearts have been torn by Lizbett's shocking story. When they enter from the vestry, the Warnes are overwhelmed by the mass of faces and momentarily, their composure, which they have been carefully guarding, wavers. But they regain it and sit in stiff silence in the front pew, gripping each other's hands. Once Darcy pulls her mother's head to her mouth and whispers something and Meredith clutches her head and kisses her face.

Though the church is awash with black, Meredith has chosen to wear a simple yellow silk dress with black flowers. Darcy picked a smocked dress that had been Lizbett's, pale blue with sprays of white daisies. All three Warnes are in sandals.

Then the Reverend David Burkleigh enters, followed by Everard Henley in church raiment. Meredith was disarmed when she first met Burkleigh. She didn't know what she was expecting ... a squat, bald man with puffy face, bulging eyes, a bulbous nose, full lips, and a pompous, posturing manner or a skinny, pinched-looking man, mincing and sanctimonious with close-together eyes, a long nose, thin lips. But not what she saw ... handsome! Very handsome! A silver-haired man: tall, tan, well-built with a fan of beguiling lines around his dark, penetrating eyes that never left her gaze. He had pock-marked skin, lending him an appealing, resilient vulnerability, and a square jaw and chin with a cleft. His perpetual smile accentuated his sensuous mouth and big white teeth. He was demonstrative, almost flirtatious, a man who used a gentle touch to advantage, and she liked him, in spite of herself.

Reverend Burkleigh speaks. He is magnetic. His voice is a buttery baritone. "The Lord be with you."

The mourners say, "And with thy spirit."

The Reverend says, "Let us pray."

*I can't*, thinks Meredith.

"O God, whose beloved Son did take little children into his arms and bless them: Give us grace, we beseech thee, to entrust this child Elizabeth Louise Ellen to thy never-failing care and love ... out of the dark have I called unto thee, O Lord/Lord hear my voice ..."

Meredith hears an inexplicable clamorous roaring. It infiltrates and resounds in her whole being. Is it the protest of her own sensibilities or simply the pulsing of her blood? Why has she consented to this sham, this violation of her essential self? Where is the comfort? Where are the peace and acceptance? She hears a barrage of meaninglessness. She hears emptiness, pretense, platitudes, posturing. Make-believe. *I'm not capable of this*, she thinks. She tries to close herself off.

A soprano sings: "The Lord is my Shepherd, I'll not want/He maketh me down to lie/Beside the still waters ... " The music and the girl's sweet voice enter Meredith's body and she feels some redemption.

And then she is suddenly overcome with a shattering fear: what if Lizbett's death is a punishment from God for her adultery? Or her blatant disbelief? What if God is scourging her, showing His power over her scathing attitude, her cynicism? What if she believed? What if she'd gone to church week after week, year after year, as in her childhood? What if she'd taken the girls to Sunday school? What if she prayed? Would Lizbett still be here? What if she said now, with every honourable intention she could muster, "Dear, dear God. I am so very sorry. Please forgive my years of scorn. Please forgive my inability to see you, to believe in you. If you are there, Dear God, show me some sign. Give me some answers."

The congregation is asked to stand and sing hymn number six hundred in *The Book of Praise*:

"Lead, kindly Light, amid the encircling gloom/Lead Thou me on/ The night is dark and I am far from home ..."

She cannot sing. She cannot sing for tears and a dam in her throat. Nothing comes. *Comes*. She has a bizarre thought. Appallingly inappropriate, but vivid. Her trying to believe is like during sex, being so aroused and desperately wanting an orgasm, desperately trying and trying, frustrating yourself and your partner, feeling on the brink, but never the welcome, euphoric explosion. Why won't God enter her if he exists?

The Reverend Burkleigh continues. "Be seated. It is with the gravest sorrow that I welcome you, dear friends, to this sacred house to mourn the tragic and egregious loss of a precious and innocent child, Elizabeth

Louise Ellen Warne. We are here to commemorate her dear life; to offer our love and support to her fine family, and to find some comfort for their and our suffering.

"But we do not want to be here, do we? Do we?

"'O, my God, my God, why has thou forsaken me … and the words of my roaring?' Did Christ not call out those excruciating words? '… the words of my roaring …'? We are all roaring are we not? Did God not hear the roars of that wonderful child? Where is God in all of this?

"The answer is He is here, with each one of us. But He is here, too, for the sinner who has taken Lizbett from us in such a violent way. We are all God's children.

"But we are not His puppets. God has given us choice. The choice is ours, dear friends, whether or not to follow Jesus's teachings and be saved. We have the choice whether to sin or not. We are all part of the ageless sins of mankind. They began with the most original of sins and they are perpetuated, over and over, through the ages. Unspeakable evil is perpetuated over and over. Why? Because we do not follow His way. We do not CHOOSE to think and live through the life of Jesus, who DIED, dear friends, yes, was tortured and murdered, dear friends, so that we might make the right choice. The generational sins of mankind can end with each and every one of us, right here, right now, as we remember the life of Lizbett.

"Sin is not a single act. Yes, we have a primary sinner, but the secondary sinners are myriad. We even may be among them as people who do not choose God's love; who do not choose to reach out and offer help and spiritual sustenance to the misguided, the poor and damaged, the wrongdoers.

"We are all feeling a paralyzing grief and fear. These are God's incentives. If we let God remove our feelings of terror, abhorrence, of contempt, of revenge and we become freed, yes freed into love and tolerance. And through God's guidance, the sinner who has so brutally taken our sweet Lizbett will be apprehended and treated according to the ways God has so ordained in our fair and democratic society.

"Let us remember today, a beautiful, loving child, a child who lit up everyone she touched, who is now in a state of supreme grace and love, at the hand of our dear Lord. Do not perpetuate generational sinning, but stop it, stop it every minute of every day by believing in Him. Let Elizabeth

Louise Ellen Warne's short, charmed, and charming life be your inspiration. Remain innocent of sin, trust in God and His son, Our Lord Jesus Christ, and love wisely and well, not just God and his beloved son, but yourself, your family and friends, and those who sin or have sinned against you.

"Go gently and thoughtfully today, dear friends, with your hearts full of the memory of Elizabeth Louise Ellen, but fuller still in the knowledge that as she was loved by God, so are you. And that He is with you. May His way be yours forever more, in the name of the Father, the Son, and the Holy Spirit. Amen."

Meredith is suffocating. Her chest feels bound. Her heart is racing. She tries to find her breath, but it is not there. Arrogance, presumption, delusion, and lies have invaded her being. How could an intelligent person believe such despicable things? Generational sin? We are collectively responsible for Lizbett's being slain by some monster because we have not followed God's path? Every word was an assault to her and Thompson's way of being. She glanced over at him several times during the sermon, but he chose not look at her; merely squeezed her hand. Was he not as enraged as she? She wants to leap up and scream; throw her head back and let out a long raucous call of protest from her deepest recesses. She wants to pommel the Very Reverend David Burkleigh; beat his chest over and over for spouting his invidious, manipulative, ingeniously calm tirade. She looks at the end of the pew and plans to flee; to escape what she feels is a mire of righteousness. She feels enmeshed. But Darcy's head slides toward her shoulder. It was bowed the whole time. Meredith realizes she must be very sleepy. Meredith strokes her hair and Darcy looks up and gives her a wan, compliant smile. Meredith cannot imagine how all of this is affecting her. She hopes most of it has gone over her head. Meredith wishes it could be that way for her. How could she have thought she had it in her to be a believer when she inherently is not? It's not that she chooses not to believe. It is that she is incapable. Nor, after that sermon, does she want to be.

The soprano sings "Ave Maria."

Meredith submerges herself into the music. It makes her think of Christmas, the only time, really, that she plays religious music. Then a wave of pain rushes over her again. Christmas. No Lizbett. Christmas. No Lizbett. Christmas. No Lizbett.

Another song. The mourners rise.

*Oh good*, Meredith thinks, *Cat Stevens.* "*Morning has broken ...*"

Now Reverend Burkleigh pours forth more words she chooses not to hear, in the way she responded to her father's sermons when she was young. She shuts down. If she could put her hands over her ears, the way children do and say, "La, la, la, la," she would.

She is trembling and it occurs to her suddenly that her anger has overridden her sorrow during the whole service. In this important commemoration for Lizbett, the one for all to share, Meredith has lost sight of her. She has been so self-preoccupied! Whatever she may believe, as her father had urged her, the day is for Lizbett, and for others, to receive comfort for their pain. Who is she to stand in judgment of those who are finding solace in the words today and who are here out of love for a wounded child? Would that she could be one of them.

*Forgive me*, she thinks.

Meredith has an epiphany. Lizbett's presence in the church, her palpable vitality, evident in the concern of every one of the people who have come to say their own form of goodbye, is what she should have been concentrating on all along. Today is not so much about the fact she has gone, but about the glorious fact that she was.

Throughout the ceremony, Melvyn has felt supreme elation. It is actually he who is being lauded. This day is a celebration of his handiwork: his cleverness, his finesse, his creativity. He is the true believer, the one who understands the crucial trade-off of power and submission. But for him, this elaborate, ancient ritual would not be taking place. He made the sacrifice. He released Lizbett's life force to a higher purpose. He gave her the gift of ascendency, transporting her to the beyond with his mastery, a mastery he deftly took from the mask. He was the mask; the mask was him: a being, a lord who manipulated life and embedded it forever in the present.

Irv Mikkelson had been on duty at the church, scanning the mourners for anyone suspicious. The grandness of the holy dwelling, the magnificent stained-glass windows evaded him. The powerful words that had everyone weeping floated past his ears. The music, the emotive notes that swelled in the great space was mere noise, not even a distraction. He had one purpose. To scrutinize every individual in the crowd for strange, revelational behaviour. Was he looking for someone jittery and anxious, someone aggressive, someone unduly gregarious and cheery, someone sobbing excessively? Was he looking for an unkempt derelict? Though he knew he could be looking for someone who didn't belong, he felt innately that it was someone who did belong, someone who blended in. But who? If only he knew.

Now he is sitting at the bar in a big, fancy old hotel near the church. An older woman in an evening gown is playing show tunes on the grand piano in the lobby. Irv is a big man, and though very tall, he appears hunched, contained, and cautious within himself. But he is soft and appealingly personable. Women find him sexy. Maybe it's because he sometimes appears wounded and secretive. He has greying hair with an unruly lock covering his forehead and a grooved, pliant face, the skin shiny, almost rubbery. His nose is sizeable, with broad nostrils. Only his thick moustache, darker than his hair, gives him any age. He has heavy brows and deep-set, pillowy brown eyes that don't crinkle when he laughs, as if they're on a different nerve centre. But he does laugh, not so much a jokester himself, but as someone who enthusiastically appreciates others' humour, as if not to laugh would hurt their feelings.

After two rye and ginger ales, the emotion he didn't feel, couldn't feel, during the service now overtakes him. He is as close to tears as he has ever been. He tilts his head back so as to prevent any that might escape from rolling down his cheeks. He swallows and clears his throat over and over to avoid them. He is not allowed to feel. He does not permit himself the burden of emotions. He sees shocking, savage murders, murders beyond believing, and consoles distraught relations constantly, and yet he remains visibly removed, devoid of the pain he has witnessed, absent from the repulsion most would experience.

But with Lizbett Warne, he has felt it all. He is unaccustomed to the vice clamped on his chest, the stinging in his eyes, the dead weight of his being. He has never before felt disconsolate, unutterably devastated, and overwhelmed with helpless horror. He has never before been felled by the command of a tragedy. But now he feels as if an evil has been unleashed. It pours into him. And with it has come a rage so violent it thrashes his senses about like a kind of storm, a hurricane with fierce winds that snap trees and lift roofs from housetops.

How could he find this monster? How could he recognize him? Where is he right now? Is he tall, short, stout, thin, fair, dark, old, young, handsome, hideous? Black, white, Asian, Native? Is he her doctor, dentist, agent, teacher, friend's father, uncle?

Even though Mikkelson knows the majority of pedophiles have themselves been violated, he feels no tolerance or understanding. He cannot see the bewildered, wounded child. A sexual predator is a degenerate low-life, iniquitous, barely human, and not worth saving. An act of pedophilia is a choice, not the act of a damaged soul behaving from experience.

How many interviews would it take until he recognized him? What did he have to go on? A rare blood type. An instinct that Lizbett knew the man. But what man convinces an intelligent, aware young girl to go to that desolate place? Why would she go? Did he kill her immediately? Why did no one see anything? How did he get her from the museum, from the subway, from the library to the deserted factory? How could someone commit such a sick, violent act and not show symptoms of weirdness, of perversion, to someone? How could someone with such a hideous psychopathology live a normal life?

Because likely this asshole was. Living a normal life. Smiling happily. Celebrating. As Mikkelson orders his third rye and ginger, he pledges with a passion that is alien to him to get the son of a bitch, but at the same time he feels his gut plummeting. He has fuck all.

# 11

## AFTERMATH

They have gone to an island north of the city, a half hour from shore. The Warnes and Everard, along with with Abbey and Kyle. Nellie is already there. The island is in a sparkling bay of islands, many still wild. There is some boat traffic, so they are not isolated, but they are alone.

The cottage is old, used by the Warne family since the 1920s, when it was bought by Thompson's grandfather with money from his successful construction business. Thompson came to the cottage as a boy, as did his father and his father's sister, Ruth, who built another spacious dwelling at the opposite end of the island for her large family. Thompson is an only child so the first building does not have to be shared with siblings, although Nellie normally spends the summer there with her two Labrador retrievers, Havoc and Rowdy. Theodore has been dead for five years.

The place is a rambling, dim Arts and Crafts house covered in weathered shingles. A broad, screened verandah runs around three sides. The many bedrooms with their large sash windows are tucked under steep gables.

Downstairs there is a spacious sitting area with overstuffed, faded chintz furniture dating from Thompson's boyhood. A large stone fireplace with tall, full bookshelves on either side occupies one wall. Nellie's old baby grand piano sits near the windows facing the lake.

In the dining room opposite stands a long walnut table with several leaves and at least a dozen Windsor chairs around it. Beyond is a big kitchen with a wide enamel sink, wooden countertops and exposed shelves, a wood-fired range, and an old stove and fridge about to die. No one has ever considered upgrading anything. The shabbiness is a record of years of summers. The wicker that fills the porch is original.

The Warnes have capsized and are deluged with pain. Perhaps the rituals of cottage life will offer them a lifeline. At least it will remove them from the immediacy of Lizbett's death, let them breathe in the wild space. There are early-morning and late-night skinny dips, meals on the stone terrace under the pines and poplars, fishing for bass in Thompson's secret spots, reading in the hammock or on the verandah. Meredith and Thompson go for short paddles in the early evening when the water is like glass, just before cocktails, as his parents used to do. Meals are simple: grilled meat and the succulent seasonal corn and field tomatoes. Sometimes they cut up the tomatoes with chunks of Brie and have it on warm pasta. Or they will just make a big potato salad with ham and hard-boiled eggs. It seems Nellie is always baking bread.

And after dinner, they all play games of bridge and euchre and gin rummy, and, with Darcy, hearts. Or Trivial Pursuit. Then, it's early to bed to listen to the frogs and the wail of the loons.

Most days everyone stretches out on towels on the flat rocks or on the dock. Thompson swims and swims, out deep, back and forth, his stroke smooth and mechanical. Closer in, Meredith and Darcy and Abbey try to do water ballet. Kyle will sometimes take out the Sailfish, though there hasn't been much wind.

But now, in this particular time, this unforgettable summer, every once-upon-a-time pleasure, every chore, thought, and motion, however routine, is overtaken by the image of Lizbett. It's as if what has made them all vital: their cells, their nerves, the pulsing of their blood, their breathing, their organs: the brain and the heart above all, their every extremity have been constrained by the horror of her death and by the inability to imagine it. By the ability to imagine it. A wire, wound tightly around and around them, is cutting deeply into their flesh, their very essences. But there is no bleeding. And there is no escape. Nowhere. Not in any way.

And each is a prisoner of his or her own isolation, as well, unable to reach out or share feelings. Even as they go about the brilliant days, with the gleam of the bay and the incessant slap of the waves along the shore reinforcing the privacy and privilege of where they are, even as the soft pine-needle paths under their bare feet and the cedar smell of the cottage walls and the dozens of photographs on them remind them of all their joyous times there, they are continuously tortured.

None of them can remember this kind of heat on the bay, and the cottage, even with all the open windows and screen doors, feels stuffy. The days have been still. A relentless, almost brutal sun heats the flat rocks so that they can almost hear their feet sizzle as they race into the water.

The heat has a clarity that hard-edges the grey rocks and ridges, the dark, crooked trees and the tangled, unwelcoming shorelines. And it is quiet. The water, though sparkling, looks solid. It doesn't have the aquamarine translucence of the sea. Meredith misses the sand and salt and tides of her childhood. She would like to see a school of porpoises leap by.

Thompson loves the raggedness of everything here. He loves that the water is deep and dark, like obsidian, that the woods are overgrown, almost impassable except through the paths they've made. He is the one in the hammock staring into the wilderness.

He is thinking that he does not want to think. Swaying gently, he tries to empty his mind, to concentrate on the feeling of being in the cooler woods where the sunlight barely makes it through the huge pines. His gaze follows them up to the sky and he marvels at the flicker of rays breaking through the dense needles. Then he is thinking about evil — what evil is. He realizes he has never thought about evil before. Or witnessed it.

Evil is what is in the newspaper or on TV. He thinks of his — before now, unfathomed — concepts of evil: unfettered power and greed, corporate transgressions, war, violent crime, fundamentalism, anything that impinges upon or destroys equality, privacy, rights, and freedoms, anything that imposes upon others a belief system that denies individual thought or action.

But he has never before thought of evil in the personal sense, that physical or mortal harm would be done to him or someone he loved. That there would be someone out there with the desire and the capacity to destroy his world. He has led a sequestered life, he realizes, a life of ideals, creativity, connectedness. Cruelty, despair, rapacity, perversity, and psychopathology were not in his realm of comprehension.

Lately, he has been questioning his own goodness. A gun has been invading his thoughts. He doesn't know anything about guns except maybe the toy six-shooters with which he used to play cowboys and Indians when he was a boy. Or the guns he's read about in detective novels: a Luger, a 38-calibre, an Uzi. Now he conjures something substantial, a large, square handgun that would feel weighty, lethal, in his hand. He'd like the resources to be able to find his daughter's killer and put bullets into him, purpose-fully, one at a time. His brain. His heart. Then he'd blow away his groin. Though he is a passive, conscientious, compassionate man, these thoughts, which in another time he'd find heinous, do not disturb him. They comfort him. They make him feel less useless.

He hadn't known what to expect from fatherhood. He had no siblings; little experience with younger cousins. He saw Lizbett from the moment of her "crowning," the appearance of the impossibly tiny round head. And the quicksilver emergence of the body: his utter surprise that it was a girl. It astounded him that he found the infant instantly, avidly engaging. He remembers changing her diaper for the first time and being in utter awe at her perfect intricacy — what would one day be her full pleasuring womanhood.

He was only too eager to do the middle-of-the-night feeding when Meredith pumped her breasts so he could give Lizbett a bottle. That was as close as he could imagine to the sublime privilege of maternity.

Lizbett cried incessantly for three months. Meredith sometimes lost it. But he never did. He paced with the baby in his arms, rocked her, even took her out in the car. And then, at three months, she miraculously stopped crying and became the achiever she was, sitting up, talking and walking early, amusing them with elaborate gobbledygook that soon became little stories. Whatever she did enthralled him; caused him to reach deep within himself for a reasonable understanding of human behaviour. Who was this complex creature, this random product of him-self and Meredith? How could he even begin to fathom her purpose, her separate place in the world? Because she forged her way with decisiveness and ingenuity, as if in her developing mind there was already a fixed, unerring path.

Was she ever naughty? She was headstrong, independent. He had several times whacked her behind (cringing at the thought), but he can't recall why. Once, when she was about Darcy's age, she had chalked "fuck" on the sidewalk up and down their street. That had required a lot of scrubbing and apologizing to the neighbours.

Only last year, she and a friend had been caught shoplifting a couple of chocolate bars from a pharmacy. The confrontation with the police, the threat of a criminal record, had unravelled her.

And now, not only did it all feel like a blip on a radar screen, it felt like it was in vain. For what had he committed an essential part of himself, if the object of that desire to nurture and protect had been obliterated? It left him bewildered, bitter, totally devoid of any sense of life's purpose.

But there is Darcy. Normally pensive, ultra-sensitive Darcy with her little "Darcy-scowl." Darcy had been a placid baby, such a late talker that they had wondered if there was a problem. In a sense, she had been a background baby, one whose needs were easily met, who responded to being amused not with glee, but with curious reticence. She seemed to have a childlike stoicism that protected her from hurt, from being overshadowed by an effervescent, ambitious sister. Darcy didn't plod. She was an achiever, too. But she did everything without ceremony, as if the simple act of doing was reward in itself.

Thompson wonders what's going on in her head. Instead of seeing brooding sadness, teariness, which he would fully expect, he has seen her become more outgoing, projecting herself on everyone not with her usual endearing, solemn sensibility, but with an uncharacteristic cheeriness. It's as if she's attempting to override the pall of despair by being spirited and effusive, seemingly taking it upon herself to banish all the bad and replacing it with her own version of how Lizbett always seemed to invite only enthusiasm. Lizbett had been the gregarious daughter. She was the one who kept everyone entertained with her bright ways and clever antics. She lived life in overstatement. Darcy is modest. She usually retreats into a quiet politeness, speaking only when spoken to and not saying much when she does talk. Now she is talking, telling amusing little stories, being silly. She is responding to conversations. Instead of having her nose in a book, she is out and about, playing with her cousins, the way Lizbett used to.

Just before they left, she had put on Lizbett's star mask and her too-large dress from *Annie* and demanded that everyone watch her sing "Tomorrow." It was poignant in its absurdity.

And only yesterday, she had gone into her Nan-Nan's dress-up trunk and found a black silk dress with jet beading, a black, feathered hat with a pink velvet rose and a rubber Hallowe'en witch's mask. She had wandered about the cottage, cackling to herself and rubbing her hands together. Then she had approached everyone with a basket of peaches, saying in a gruff, raspy voice, "Try one of my magic peaches. If you eat one you live forever and ever. But take care! One of them is poisonous and if you eat it you die!"

Where has this come from? Where has it been?

Thompson doesn't know how children mourn, what is normal behaviour. When their dog had to be put down, the girls were inconsolable. Even at three, Darcy seemed to understand loss. But now he can't tell if Darcy is filled with sorrow or even if she's terrified deep down. So far, she has shown a remarkable resilience, as if she has distanced herself from the shocking events. He wonders if she's feeling anything. He thinks he should really ask her because he's worried she's not okay.

He knows how Meredith is feeling. She is utterly destroyed. She says she cannot get Lizbett's final moments out of her head. The thought of the horror she must have endured undoes Meredith. She weeps without restraint. She is also overcome with guilt for allowing Lizbett to go to the library after mask camp, instead of going straight home. "I never wanted her to go," she says. "I knew there was going to be a bad thunderstorm. I should have said go another day. And while she was being mutilated by that monster, I was pushing around bits of caviar and smoked salmon. I feel so useless. All I've ever done feels useless. I don't know how to get rid of my vicious thoughts. I don't know how to move forward."

And he says, "Go on for Darcy."

Thompson knows well enough how to go on. Dailiness. Just keep doing what you have to do and the days will go by. He has wood to split and stack, boards to replace on the wooden walkways, windows he could wash, screens Mr. Mushu has torn to repair, paths to clear. What he doesn't know specifically is what to feel and this surprises him. Grief. That's obvious. This he feels with a weight in his chest so leaden, he cannot inhale. But should he cry? He feels as if he should, but he can't. Even at the funeral, seeing the white coffin leave the funeral home, though he wanted to sob, to collapse and curl up into himself and heave out tears, he could not. He could only stand ramrod straight and watch, jaw clenched, face expressionless, one arm around Meredith, the other around Darcy. He wonders if there is something wrong with him.

And what about his rage? He feels as if an explosive has entered his being and gone off, but not has not killed him. He is paralyzed. He is paralyzed to adequately support Meredith, to understand Darcy. He is paralyzed to do anything but lie in this hammock and try not to think of his daughter who was ripped from his life.

Darcy lies in the hush of dawn in her white iron-framed bed. The light is dim. The trees are silhouettes. And she can't, as yet, hear any of the birds she has been listening for, the ones whose calls Nan-Nan has been teaching her. Especially the one they call the "Boogie woogie woogie" bird, whose real name they don't know. She has been trying to ignore the mosquitoes that come in Mr. Mushu's holes in the screen.

She has been thinking about the hummingbird from the day before. She was watering her grandmother's geranium-filled urns on the terrace and suddenly a hummingbird flew into the spray from the hose, and hovered there, its whir of wings making a fine splash in the sunlight. So close to her! She was mesmerized by its luminescence, its tininess. The bird lingered in the water for what seemed to Darcy the longest time and then it flew away. She heard the buzz of its wings. She had seen the hummingbirds come to the feeder filled with sugar-water outside the kitchen window. But she knew this was special. She loved telling the story to everyone, loved their pleasure at hearing it. If Lizbett were here, she'd be jealous.

She is confused about her sister's death. She knows she was murdered. She knows what murdered means. She knows that the police do not know who the person is who did it. What if he murdered her, too? She also realizes she will never ever see Lizbett again. This should make her very, very sad and it does. But not all the time. What she doesn't know is if she should think about Lizbett all, all of the time. Sometimes she forgets about Lizbett and thinks about something else: trying to see the fish with her mask, getting her hands all floury when she kneads the bread with Nan-Nan, teaching her to sing "Karma Chameleon." She forgets when she reads *James and the Giant Peach* or when she plays long games of Monopoly with her cousins. Would Lizbett mind if she knew Darcy sometimes had fun? Would Lizbett think that meant Darcy didn't love her enough? Darcy has never really thought about loving Lizbett. She knows she must because Lizbett was her sister. But it doesn't feel like loving Mommy and Daddy. That is a huge love because of how they love you and hug you. But a sister? Sisters sometimes can be mean. And if she doesn't feel sad, is she bad?

She thinks if she shows too much sadness, it will upset people. Already everyone is very sad. And Meredith has never liked "long faces." She has often said to Darcy, "Try to keep a smile on your face, darling." So that's what Darcy will do. She'll be cheery and tell stories just like Lizbett used to do and try to make people laugh even though she doesn't really know how.

Her father peeks his head in the door and says, "Ready, sweetie?" Darcy leaps out of bed and puts on shorts and a T-shirt and her running shoes. She and Thompson are going fishing in the canoe. The fish haven't been biting because it has been so hot, and her father thinks that very early in the morning would be a good time to catch some. Everyone has missed the floured fillets of bass fried in butter they often have for breakfast.

They anchor the canoe in a narrow, vacant bay and cast. Behind them the forest looks impenetrable. Their lines whiz and the lures pierce the glassy water sending out a pronounced splash and gentle circles around it. Then they wait. Darcy knows it isn't a good thing to talk so as not to scare the fish but she needs to. She hasn't been able to speak to her mother. Her mother seems too spacey.

"Daddy, is Lizbett in heaven?"

"If you think she is, Darce."

"No, really. Mommy says there's no such thing as heaven."

"Heaven is there for anyone who wants to believe in it," Thompson says.

"But what is it?"

"Well, it's a place you go ... where some people think you go after you die."

"But is it a world? Or a country? Or a city? Or what? And where would it be? If it were up in the sky, wouldn't we be able to see it, like Mars or a star? Or is it far, far away where it can't be seen, in another universe like *Star Wars*? And how would a dead person get there?"

"I don't think the people who believe in it really know any of that. They can only use their imaginations. Or what they call their faith. Like there are gates made of pearl."

"Well, who would go there?"

"Well, supposedly people who are good."

"Who decides? And how do they know who's been good? And how long have people been going there? Has heaven always been there? Who made it? Did a good caveman go to heaven? I learned in school that was thousands and thousands of years ago. Heaven must have to be really huge to fit in the gazillions of people there. And do people know each other? If Lizbett were in heaven, would she meet someone from the olden days? Like Christopher Columbus? Is everybody just wandering around or do they do stuff? And do kids grow up there or do they always stay kids? Is there more than one heaven?"

"Oh, sweetie. So many questions! And I don't know the answer to any of them. I'm so sorry. I can only say I'm not sure I believe in heaven, myself."

"But where else could she be?" Thompson doesn't reply. He has never heard such a barrage of words from Darcy and he feels a heart-twisting helplessness. He feels sick that he is failing her at a time when she seems desperate for support, that he cannot give her answers that might comfort her, but he cannot. Even with his own crippling grief unassuaged, he cannot simply say, "She is somewhere safe and beautiful."

"Daddy ... Daddy ... I said where else could she be?"

"I don't know, precious. I simply don't know."

"I hate her staying in the ground. Is it true worms will eat her body?"

Thompson can't bear this. He hasn't known from the beginning how much truth to give Darcy when the truth is impossible enough for them to face. He wonders if they are paying for their beliefs, or their lack of them, and if they have made a grave mistake in not giving their girls some spiritual instruction. But Meredith was adamant and years of daily chapel at boarding school helped him agree. "The coffin is very thick," he said. "And sealed really tight."

"Why didn't we have her burned up ... cre ... cre ..."

"... mated. Cremated."

"Why didn't we have her cremated like Misty? And we could have had her ashes in vase, like Misty."

"Would you have wanted that?"

Darcy thinks of the floor of the fireplace, of a vase holding her burned-up sister, all ashes, like the logs. She wonders how a burned-up body can go to heaven. "No. I don't think so."

Thompson says, "Darce, you should talk to Granddad about these things. It's what he does. He might have better answers than I."

"Daddy, would Lizbett mind us fishing? Would she mind us … you know, having fun, instead of feeling sad?"

"She would want us to do things as we always have."

"Even if she weren't there?"

"Even if she weren't there."

"Sometimes I think I'm not feeling sad enough. Sometimes I forget to think about the horrible thing that happened to her. Or sometimes I don't want to think about it, so I make myself not to. Is that bad?"

"No, sweetheart. Everybody's sadness is different. I know you feel really, really sad when you need to. When you don't, that means you're moving on with your life. That's what we all need to do."

"Mommy's feeling the saddest, isn't she?"

"I think Mommy shows her sadness the most. I feel very, very sad, too. But it's not as easy for me to say so."

"Is that because you're a boy?"

"Why do you say that?"

"When we were all crying so much after Misty died, you only cried a little bit. And Mommy said boys were taught that crying is bad."

"It isn't, Darce."

"What does 'axess your grief' mean?"

"Why?"

"After Misty died, that's what Mommy said you didn't know how to do."

Frank Sinatra is singing in the kitchen, "You make me feel so young …" Rowdy and Havoc are lying on the rug in the doorway.

"Oh, dogs," says Nellie. "Why are you always in the way? And you're so stinky."

Darcy and Nellie are making chutney and jam. Peaches are in season. They slice them on their cereal or have them with sugar and cream. There are pies and crisps that Nellie and Darcy make. And now the canning.

Peaches simmer on the stove. The rising steam is redolent with their sweetness and with the cinnamon and ginger and cloves that make them chutney. More peaches bob in a huge bowl of boiling water, getting blanched for peeling. Nellie and Darcy find the ritual of removing the slithery skins from the warm peaches satisfying.

"Nan-Nan, what about Queen?"

"Queen?"

"Freddie Mercury."

"I don't know it. But we could try it," says Nellie.

Darcy goes into the sitting room and finds the new *A Kind of Magic* cassette and takes off Frank Sinatra and puts on Queen. She starts to dance and sing the words to the title track into her fist, as if she were holding a microphone.

When she's finished Nellie applauds and says, "Wow!"

Darcy tucks in her head and smiles shyly. "It's Mommy and Daddy's favourite. It was better with Lizbett. She practised. She was a better singer than me."

"Than *I*," Nellie says.

*It's true*, Nellie thinks, that Darcy is not a natural singer, as Thompson is not. She remembers, in this same kitchen, trying to sing songs with him and Ruth, Thompson always a tone off. Lizbett was a clear, bold soprano with nearly perfect pitch. She was an agile dancer. She had a gift.

But she did not have Darcy's gift of abundant warmth, her capacity to love. Lizbett was a natural performer with an innate sense of her audience, but it came from a need for reaction. Darcy has no self-concern. Though reticent in a group, she is entirely spontaneous one on one. From the moment she began to understand human connection, she has reached out and offered something, something effusive and reassuring, expecting nothing in return. Darcy wraps her arms about your waist, rests her head against your torso, leans into you and squeezes. She is a connector. This is the essence of her. This and her extraordinary ability to read other people's feelings and respond appropriately. When Nellie's brother Lucas, to whom she was very close, died the previous year, Darcy said to her grandmother, "I can't make you feel better, Nan-Nan, but I can stay with you and give you lots of love."

"Nan-Nan, what will Mommy and Daddy do?"

"What do you mean?"

"They won't have anybody who can do all the things Lizbett could. They won't have anybody to show off."

Nellie fights tears. "They will show you off, angel, because that's what you are. You will be their angel who helps them with their grief."

"Well, they should get me a dog."

That afternoon it is too hot to be in the sun so everyone is on the screened verandah through which there is a faint breeze. The big pines enclose it and it is always cooler. Actually, Darcy and Nellie are inside, sitting at the piano. Darcy is learning a Chopin étude Nellie has adapted for her.

Meredith and Abbey are doing a jigsaw puzzle of a Jackson Pollock painting and are finding it slow going. Everard is asleep in the big rocking chair, his head thrust back, mouth open. Every so often he chokes and snorts. Thompson is stretched out on a settee, reading.

The quiet is shattered when Kyle comes in, booming, "Hey! Who wants to come to the marina with me to get some more bait?"

"Not me," say Meredith and Abbey, in unison without looking up.

Kyle leans back against the wall and asks, "Anyone? Darcy?"

"I'll come," she says and slides off the piano bench. Then she hesitates. "Is that okay, Nan-Nan?"

"Sure. You go. You did very well today."

Darcy rushes up to Kyle and he puts his hands on her shoulders. "That's great, Darcy-cat. Thanks for the company." And before anyone realizes, they are out the door and down the path to the dock.

Meredith leaps up. Precipitately, from a deep-down, fearful, untrusting place, she thinks the unthinkable. She doesn't want Darcy to be alone with Kyle. "No! Wait!" she shouts after them.

"No Darcy! Stop!" Thinking she now wants to come, Darcy and Kyle stop and turn, wide grins on their faces. "Hurry, Mommy," says Darcy. And Meredith is instantly appalled at her suspicions and ashamed. Is every male now a predator?

"Darcy, don't forget your lifejacket. And put on your sun hat," she calls out, still uncertain, but feeling as if she must be realistic and see such fears as absurd. She cannot keep Darcy from life.

When she returns to the table where Abbey is waiting, she buries her face in her hands and sobs. "Oh, Abbey. I'm sorry. I'm so, so sorry."

Abbey embraces her, crying, too. "It's okay," she says. "I was thinking the same thing."

Everard is on the verandah sitting on the swinging couch when Darcy gets back from the marina and she sees him and goes up.

"Granddad?"

"Yes, precious."

"I have some questions Daddy said you could answer."

"Well, I'll do my best, but I'm not an expert on anything."

"Not on God? Mommy once said you thought you were."

Everard laughs. "Your mother and I don't agree on God, but she's mistaken about me."

"I want to know about heaven. What is it? Where is it?"

"That's a very deep and difficult question. Come up here and swing with me and I'll see if I can answer it … heaven isn't an actual place. It is all, all the energy of dead people's good spirits … since the beginning of humans … come together all around us. It is a palpable — something you can feel — vitality that simply exists … has always existed. It's what we call collective goodness, the goodness of the ages concentrated into a universal concept. That's pretty tough, huh? Very big words."

Darcy nods, looking confused.

"Let me see if I can put it another way. When a good person dies, like Lizbett, her wonderful spirit lives in a kind of bank of goodness, of peace, of grace, that gets recognized forever. It's something most of us would like to have and I believe after death, our spirits do … they go into a bank."

"So it's not a place where people wear clothes."

"Not exactly, no."

"That's good. Because I was wondering where they'd buy them and who would wash them."

Meredith and her father are reclined on chaise longues on the long dock. The raft beyond is a bobbing black oblong.

The air is calm and Meredith can hear the soft clutter of voices carried over the water from other cottages, other islands. On this limpid night, the islands rise from the water like dark, jagged monoliths. Recognizing those tops is the way to find your way in a boat at night. There is no moon, but the stars are so congested, so defined in the black sky, that to Meredith, they seem like minute, glittery orbs she could reach up and clasp. That they are light years away and actually flaming suns seems unfathomable. A star falls above her, leaving a shimmery, ephemeral trail. She wonders if it is a sign. She has been looking for them incessantly. She wonders if, in some abstract or surreal way, it could possibly be Lizbett.

"Where has she gone?" The question obsesses Meredith. Harasses her. It seems like a living entity. She wants an answer. She longs for — is desperate for — an answer.

Energy cannot be destroyed. Isn't that true? Is she a mass of energy floating around in the air, the universe?

The simple truth and the one easiest to face — because of its finality — is that Lizbett is in a white coffin deep in the ground of the cemetery with the towering, protective oaks. She will one day be the earth itself.

The most painful truth is that Meredith does not know, cannot know, where Lizbett is, if she is anywhere beyond the ground. But what she deeply desires is that Lizbett be somewhere; that she find comfort in that.

A fish jumps just beyond the dock, its splash like the pluck of a violin string, a pleasant reminder that the lake has life. Staring into the solar system, her father quiet beside her, Meredith imagines that Lizbett is with them, beside them, not in spirit, but physically, in an unseen body, trying to transmit to them a measure of comfort. But Lizbett would not want to be where she is; she'd be fighting to get back into life. "Let me out!" she'd yell. At least, that's the disturbing thinking Meredith comes to. That Lizbett is not where she wants to be.

Is she way, way up there, then, in some sort of celestial landscape, still whole, still vital? Would she sleep, eat, have friends? What would it look like? Meredith thinks of all the artistic representations of heaven: infinite green pastures and vibrant gardens, gauzy clouds with people in ethereal robes walking on them, vast white tropical beaches on the edge of luxuriant jungles, lions and tigers placid and friendly, the turquoise sea filled with gregarious dolphins ... the latter being Lizbett's idea of heaven. Once, in Florida, they'd visited a place where you could swim with them. She hugged and stroked the rubbery, curious, squealing creatures when they approached her, unapprehensive, believing that being with them was a privilege. "I hope I get to do this all the time when I die," she said.

But Meredith cannot go there. She is too rooted in her life, in the way she lives in the world, the way she knows the world ... and science ... to believe in heaven as a physical place.

So there is no heaven for Lizbett and no consolation for Meredith to know she is there. What Meredith most wants to believe is that Lizbett has been born again, that her energy will go into another life. Some newborn baby, somewhere, will have inherited Lizbett's spirit and will contribute to the world the things she did, will have Lizbett's accomplishments, her goals. Not that the person will *be* Lizbett. She will be her own self. But she will have Lizbett's essence, Lizbett's light within her.

But what if Lizbett could transcend death, be with them, near them? And visible. A ghost. Occasionally, she has looked up from doing something and thought she's seen a bit of Lizbett whipping by to somewhere, as she always was. But she has always put it down to a play of light. Would Meredith want to see a vision of her murdered daughter? Would Lizbett be as she had died, nude, bloodied, mutilated? Or would there be some sort of spiritual clean-up?

Of course, there will be no ghost of Lizbett. But the vision of her brutalized daughter stays and Meredith is beset once more by thoughts of her daughter's fear and suffering. These images Meredith cannot banish. As much as she wonders where her daughter is, she more often conjures her ordeal, the explicit ineffable horror of it. Softly, embarrassed, she begins to weep.

Her father reaches out his hand and lays it on her shoulder.

"Oh, Daddy. Where is there comfort? If God is a comforter, where is He? And how could that God allow such an atrocity? It's a cliché, I know. But how can you believe in Him?"

"Because it has nothing to do with God, Meredith, dear, and everything to do with life, with one of life's abominable assaults over which we have no control. An assault based mainly on a perverted, likely damaged, angry individual and his unfortunate life and those in his life. Why Lizbett? I don't have an answer for that. Time, place, circumstance. The unknowable. But God? Not the God of my understanding."

"And He would be …?"

"You know, Merry, neither a He nor a She."

Meredith and her father never discuss God. Growing up with his sermons, she eventually considered them blather. She doesn't know when that happened, when she began to find them hollow, dogmatic (though her father is more liberal than most), but she turned her back on the church when she left Australia. She has no concept of God. She dislikes collective righteousness. She has no need for it and is scornful of those who do. She and Thompson married in a civil ceremony. Lizbett and Darcy were not baptized and did not go to Sunday school.

Her father went on. "A supreme, removed force more powerful, more infinite, more influential than humans can perceive. It's a force beyond us, an inexplicable force that can never be completely understood, but it's also something within each of us, the potential for goodness, for compassion, for creativity. St. Paul said, 'Faith is the substance of things hoped for, evidence of things not seen.' Perhaps that is what God is: hope and wonder. But an overseeing God attached to each and every individual, a caregiving God who has the ability to cause or not cause things to happen? A judgmental God who grants and who punishes? No, I don't believe in that. You know I don't and I never asked you to."

"What about prayer? You've prayed your whole life and asked others to pray with you."

"Prayer is about self-motivation. It is an invocation, to our best selves, through the power of the universe, for the strength, the insight, the wisdom, the comfort to survive something or do something. I don't believe there is a God who does *for* us. We have to find things for ourselves by believing in and doing good things. By self-reliance and reaching out to help others."

"I was so angry at the memorial service. I was so angry at you! I couldn't pray. I couldn't sing. All I felt was rage. Rage and a savage pain."

"Could you pray with me now?"

"I don't think it would do any good. What would I pray for, anyway? Finding the guy and killing him, watching him be killed, maybe. I imagine torturing him, doing the worst things to him."

"Then pray for understanding and the ability to forgive him."

"Forgive? How can you even suggest 'forgive'? Forgiveness is too easy. Too good for him."

"You think forgiveness is easy?" Everard asks. "Forgiveness is one of the most difficult acts in life. It requires extreme effort and thought. It requires your acceptance that the man who perpetrated Lizbett's heinous death is a suffering, severely ill human being. Forgiveness is not condoning, forgiveness is freeing yourself from the entrapment of pain and rage. If you concentrate on allowing yourself to forgive, give yourself the gift of forgiveness, you will eventually alleviate the pain."

"I can only see her suffering."

"That will disable you. Replace that with the knowledge she has been released from the suffering."

"I could never concentrate hard enough to forgive such evil."

"Such evil doesn't simply exist. He wasn't born evil. Perhaps he was predisposed because of some genetic mental disorder, but the evil was imposed by others. Who can imagine what was done to him? Punishing him and torturing him won't bring Lizbett back."

"How can you not believe in evil?"

"I believe in evil acts, not evil people. Evil is human, earthly. And I believe human behaviour is made."

"So people aren't born evil."

"Evil comes from circumstances. Poverty, deprivation. Or, as I said, a person may be born with a mental deficit that in other circumstances would be treatable, but sometimes it simply gets exacerbated by events in a person's life so that his or her capacity to cope with reality, with justice, with goodness, with what is right gets all skewed. I'm not a psychiatrist, Meredith. I've only studied a little psychology. But what I have done tells me humans go off track for a reason."

"You think this monster should be helped?"

"I believe he is suffering. I'm not sure he can be helped. The recidivism rate for pedophiles is high. But he should be incarcerated, yes, so he doesn't hurt others. But don't perpetuate his act, Meredith. Only goodness must come from this tragedy. Not more violence. Vengeful thoughts destroy Lizbett's life as we knew it. They submerge her goodness. Take the goodness, the light, from Lizbett … and pass it on. Pass it on, Merry. That's how you'll heal. Pray for the goodness in you, the goodness that's possible in life and let Lizbett's life be about that and not about what was done to her."

"What if I can't?"

"You have to, Meredith. You must. Because you have Darcy. Darcy is the one who will be most hurt if you stay mired in revulsion and vengeance. Matthew said, 'If therefore the light that is in thee be darkness, how great is that darkness.' He also said, 'Keep thy heart with all diligence for out of it are the issues of life.' Keep your heart, Meredith. Think of Jesus. Think of his unendurable suffering. Yet he has endured. And that suffering is our path to redemption. To forgiving and being forgiven. He is our Saviour."

"Not mine. I want to watch the bastard die," Meredith says, in a snarl from deep in her chest.

Then the night becomes ugly and oppressive, the darkness a pall that can't be lifted. The water, though lapping gently beneath the dock, looks oily and menacing. The stars, which offered something, if not positive before, then something magnificent, have simply become vacant, unreachable, and meaningless. The loons' cry becomes a keening, aural trajectory of her mood. She wants to leave this place, to go into the brightly lit cottage up the stone steps. She has suddenly become terrified of what the night contains: not danger, but dangerous thoughts. She hates them. Her brain has been gored by them. She can feel them. They are like skewers, twisted in and pulled out. But they are her thoughts. The iniquitous loss of Lizbett has planted them there and she must live with them. She decides she will, for now, think about the monster-man and what he did to her daughter, what Meredith would like to do to him. She will think the worst; she will torture herself with brutal, repulsive, disgusting, damaging images. She will make herself sick. She will want to die, too. She will let herself picture it all, over and over again. And then maybe it will go away.

# Part Three

## BRUNHILDE

# *Interlude*

## HILDY AND MAGDALENA

Magdalena and Joan's farmhouse is filled with the roar of electric fans in all the rooms. Sticky coils covered in dead and buzzing flies sway from the kitchen ceiling. When the women go outside, the wet heat overcomes them: it feels solid, entrapping, like one of those vast nets fishermen toss out over the sea. The incessant wails of cicadas and tree frogs fill the air. The dogs are immobilized in the deep holes they've dug in the shade.

Magdalena has been working with Hildy daily, tirelessly, since she retrieved her in the spring. She is resilient and determined, spraying herself liberally with repellant against the swarming mosquitoes. The dog continuously pants, her tongue lolling out the side of her mouth. Magdalena is drenched.

Each morning they go out to a mowed field away from the house. The dog is off leash, staying close to Magdalena's knees.

"Heel," "sit," "stay," "come," "down" ... these are commands that Hildy now obeys with a graceful, easy precision. Magdalena's voice is low, quiet, firm. The dog hears reassurance. Magdalena believes if a dog hears a high, whiny voice he/she hears anxiety and submissiveness.

The two repeat the exercises together over and over in the shade of a sprawling maple. Hildy feels Magdalena's strokes on her ears and muzzle, she sees intensity and sternness in the trainer's eyes and she responds, not out of fear, but out of the desire to please. The dog seems — not to understand her trainer — but to read her, to trust her, and feel in sync with her. Hildy can reason. She understands cause and effect. She sees that when Magdalena smiles, which is frequently, her face spills over with affection and encouragement. To Magdalena, the dog smiles back, her expression gleeful, her body language eager, her tail whipping back and forth.

Magdalena does what she is doing out of love and ambition, but also out of a sense of redemption because she believes implicitly that the dog has a right to a good and normal life, which she hopes she can offer, or rather, to which she can condition her. Otherwise, the prognosis is not good. As an untrustworthy, unpredictable dog, one who may attack not only people, but other dogs, Hildy can only expect a life of confinement. Or perhaps the ultimate safety of being euthanized. Magdalena has had to euthanize irredeemable dogs.

Her attitude toward dogs is practical, her ability to comprehend them, uncanny. She does not romanticize or anthropomorphize them. An abused dog is not an abused child. Unconditional love is no tool. Dogs are unique companions, but they are animals with ancient, embedded instincts. They are not family members, as Joan would have them. Joan is a mollycoddler, a cooer. She lies on the floor with the dogs, spoons with them on the bed. Magdalena's affections, though deep, are reserved. Her dogs are her life — of it, but apart from it. She loves dogs as she loves people: sparely, discriminately.

She does however, sometimes indulgently bend down and put her face close to Brunhilde's muzzle, and, after asking, allow the dog to kiss her. Or she will embrace her enthusiastically, her arms circling the great chest, her lips on the dog's head.

And she clearly adores the breed. Their nobility, their curious, loving, docile personalities infuse her days with challenge and an overwhelming sense of communion. She knows that they are intelligent, but not brilliant, that their loyalty, calm affection, and confidence are a reflection of their own sense of their stature. She manages them with her inflexible strictness because they are headstrong and powerful. She has seen a bolting Great Dane on a lead pull a large man to his stomach.

But with Hildy, will her hard work be successful? What if she fails? What if Hildy were to attack someone? The element of unpredictability will always be there.

Magdalena has started to take the dog walking up and down in the main street of their small town. People are always attracted to Great Danes and Magdalena, with her own height and grace, is a vision with the dog. Hildy is beautiful and still puppyish, with gangly legs and oversize paws. So when someone stops and wants to pat her, Magdalena encourages them, making sure she has the dog under control. Over the past couple of weeks, Magdalena has seen Hildy's tail *thwap*, the most positive sign that the dog has recovery in her. She has seen the dog lean fully into an admirer, a habit of Great Danes. The same thing is happening in the schoolyard. Since school began, Hildy has been going with Magdalena to visit the children. Holding the dog on a tight rein, Magdalena watches as they swarm eagerly, little arms reaching out every which way. It is Hildy's biggest test and so far she has passed.

# *12*

## SEPTEMBER

What can Melvyn Searle, murderer of two little girls, have been thinking and doing?

After the mask camp, he takes a two-week vacation, renting a small cabin at a family resort. In his affable way, he manages to make some connections by telling people his wife and small daughter had to go to England at the last minute to tend his wife's ailing parents and that he hadn't wanted to waste the rental. Yes, he minds being alone. Though people do not feel comfortable with him (there is something awkwardly insinuating about him), he is so good with their children that they often invite him to dinner. They think his job is interesting. Once or twice in the evenings, the parents ask Melvyn to sit with their kids while they go dancing in the bar.

Melvyn likes the resort. There is lots of opportunity to watch little girls run around in their bathing suits. He'd like to touch them, hold them on his lap. He stays close to them on the sand where he shows them how to sculpt different faces instead of sand castles.

Mostly, he has been thinking about sweet little Darcy. When he first encountered her at the Warnes' home, he was instantly overwhelmed. Since then his image of her has been incessant. The attraction is pure narcissism.

In his imagination, she reminds him of himself as a child. She is shy and intense, bookish and solitary with a keen intelligence, and, beneath her wistfulness, he thinks he sees an assertiveness that would surface if she were challenged. This appeals to him most of all. Darcy has hidden moxie.

That hidden moxie was something he didn't have. He was always very thin and small for his age and his thick glasses made him look odd. Kids made fun of him, calling him "frog-eyed-squirt" and "bug-eyed pipsqueak." He felt a sickening rage when they did this, the way he felt with his father and Stacey and this was heightened by his helplessness to do or say anything. All he wanted was the power to alter who he was, the ability to overpower his offenders, to obliterate them.

In high school he pretty much got lost among all the other weirdos, but by then his bitterness had been fertilized and had grown into a vengeance he was desperate to assuage. But in his fantasies he didn't strike out at those more powerful. No, he annihilated the defiant weak.

He has been trying to figure out how to connect with Darcy. He has thought the Warnes might have him over after that first time, but that hasn't happened. Perhaps he didn't make enough of an impression on them, even though he stressed his unique relationship with Lizbett. What he wants now is to be a part of Darcy's life, or more precisely, to make her a part of his.

At the beginning of September, he telephones the Warnes. Meredith answers.

"This is Melvyn Searle," the voice on the other end of the line says. "I was Lizbett's mask teacher at the museum." For a moment, Melvyn's high voice makes Meredith think it is of one of Lizbett's friends. "How are you?" Melvyn asks. "I hope things aren't too rough."

"Thanks for asking," says Meredith.

"I wondered … I was wondering if Lizbett's sister … Darcy, is it … I wondered if Darcy might like to attend my Saturday morning mask class? She seemed quite interested that time I brought you Lizbett's masks. I thought she was very bright."

"I saw the brochure from the museum," Meredith says. "But isn't she too young? The age limit suggested was ten to twelve. Darcy's only seven. She won't be eight until the end of the month."

"Wow. She seems very mature."

"She seems to have become so."

"I think she'd love the mask class."

"Lizbett did. She went on and on about it. And she really liked you. What will you be doing this time?"

"Well, for one, we're going to do an animal mask."

"Darcy loves animals."

"I'm sure I could make an exception for her. She seems very intuitive and responsive."

Meredith doesn't know whether to be pleased or not. Her main preoccupation is keeping Darcy busy, so busy she won't be able to think about the loss of Lizbett. She has her enrolled in kung fu, a beginner book club at the library, piano twice a week with Nellie, and a pottery class given by an artist who lives down the street. Something on Saturday mornings would complete the week. Meredith is sure Darcy will think the mask class would be fun. She is always trying on the ones Lizbett made, especially the life mask, and looking at herself in the mirror.

Darcy is trying to be Lizbett. She thinks that if she puts on the life mask, the one that is Lizbett, that came right from her face — the one made just before she died — and if she wishes hard enough that maybe the mask will have the power to turn her into Lizbett. With it on, she imagines being Lizbett, imagines what it is like to think her thoughts, live her life. She tries acting like her. But one thing troubles her. If she becomes Lizbett, what will happen to Darcy?

Meredith has an unsettled feeling about the mask class. Is it jinxed? It's ridiculous, she knows, but since it represented Lizbett's final burst of creativity, she wonders if it somehow doesn't have an aura of doom. As if it were somehow responsible for what happened to her. She realizes that's not possible, but is it normal and healthy to send a daughter into the same activity another daughter was doing just before she was slain? Is it foolish or is simply like climbing back up on the horse? And is she being paranoid?

Actually, Meredith no longer has any idea what is healthy or normal. She feels as if she is living in the midst of madness. She has not returned to work with Thompson. He is grateful for the diversion of the job, but worries about Meredith not working. He's using Irme Pormoranska, who is gorgeous and whom he likes. And she is good, but she is boring. He and Meredith are a seamless team. "Artful Sustenance." It's what they're all about. The aesthetics of nourishment. It's how they connect: tone, texture, light, colour, balance, proportion. They know how to make roast beef and potatoes and gravy look

like a Fantin-Latour. He understands her creativity; she appreciates his tech-
nique. And he misses her cocky banter, the way she infuses a shoot with
ribaldry. Especially when so many art directors are tyrants.

He realizes he is now dealing with an absent wife. As if dealing with
Lizbett's absence isn't painful enough. Meredith is just gone. She's gone in
her head. She's gone in her body. He can see her, but he can't hear her
because she doesn't speak. And he can't touch her because she's always out
of reach. It's almost as if she's an apparition, which is ironic because if he
were to see a ghost, he'd imagine it would be Lizbett. With much despair,
he has accepted the finality of the loss of Lizbett. What is harder to accept,
what is exacerbating his agony, is the loss of Meredith.

She's fixed in a routine and that is all she can manage. She gets up,
dresses, comes downstairs, and makes breakfast for Thompson and Darcy.
Or rather, puts out juice and milk and the cereal boxes. Meredith only
drinks coffee while she makes a little lunch for Darcy.

There has never been such silence in the house. For a while, Meredith
tries turning on the radio, but it is too jarring. So they sit quietly, chewing. Darcy sometimes hums. She would like to read a book, but she is not
allowed to read at the table, even though Thompson reads the newspaper.
That is something grown-ups do, Darcy is told. So Thompson hands her
the comics.

But no one shares any thoughts or asks any questions. No one tells
any stories. Each is full of his or her own unique, indefinable pain and
each is wondering how to avoid it. Each is self-absorbed, or rather, Lizbett-
absorbed, trying not to think about the empty place, the bleak disruption
of what was once a lively time, usually because Lizbett and Meredith were
going on about something. Often, Lizbett, having already eaten, would be
practising the piano.

Darcy occasionally has tried to open up. "Hi, guys," she'll say cheer-
fully. "How was your sleep?" Sometimes she'll tell them about a dream.
"Is it okay to dream about Lizbett?" she asks. "Because she's always in my
dreams. We're usually running somewhere or else we're with animals.
Once she was on the ceiling. Another time, I dreamt we were in a roomful
of tigers and they were all friendly and they purred and let us pat them.
Once she came and took Mr. Mushu and I was so mad. And she saved me
from a bad person. She hid me in a big box. When I got out, she was gone,
but I was safe. I cried in that dream."

And in fact, Lizbett's place at the table is not empty, not at breakfast or dinner. Darcy has insisted on setting it for every meal. Sometimes she draws a picture or puts a little token there.

Last year, Darcy was bused to school. Now that she's in grade three, she's obliged to get there herself. Were Lizbett here, they'd go together on the city bus, the one Lizbett had been taking on her own since grade four. Lizbett and Darcy's school, a private school for girls, is not in the neighbourhood. Many of the parents drive their daughters, but Meredith and Thompson believe in independent and resourceful children. Their daughters have been given many talks about being streetwise and the school is always offering programs. Lizbett had taken several. And so public transportation was fine for her.

But it's not fine for any little girl after this summer.

"Will I ever be able to take the bus by myself?" she asks.

Meredith and Thompson can't imagine when.

Meredith has cut her hair very short. She has lost ten pounds. She's who she was before her babies. She looks like a boy. And now she has the incentive to use her stationary bicycle. After she returns from taking Darcy to school, or after Darcy leaves with Thompson, she goes upstairs and for an hour blasts exercise tapes and pedals and pumps until she is gasping, dripping with sweat. She would like it if her mind went numb or at least into a kind of neutral when she's on the machine, but it doesn't. Thoughts of Lizbett get tangled up in the lyrics of the songs: Bruce Springsteen, Creedence Clearwater Revival, The Who, Phil Collins, Robert Palmer, Huey Lewis. If it's thudding and fast, it works to use up her body but not her mind. She hears "Lizbett, Lizbett, Lizbett, Lizbett," to the heavy beat of the songs. She doesn't know how to use up her mind.

After she showers and gets dressed again, she goes into Lizbett's room and lies down on the bed and stays there until it's time to leave to pick up Darcy. The room is unchanged. Nothing has been touched. The hamper is still full of dirty clothes. Brygida still comes a couple of times a week to clean and Meredith has instructed her not to alter a thing.

To Meredith the room feels as empty, as echoey as a tomb. The brightness is the washed-out brightness of winter. Harsh and bleak. In fact, she always feels cold there. And everything feels flat, delineated. She feels flat and delineated, as if she were in a photograph. But still, she spends all her time there not because she's trying to be with Lizbett in some way, not because she's trying to call her up or because it gives comfort, but because all the other rooms remind her that there is life beyond Lizbett. They scream at her to get on with her life. At least, in Lizbett's room, time stands still.

She has a big bottle of Valium, only one or two of which she's taken and she carries it around with her. When she's lying in Lizbett's room she clutches it in her hand and stares at it and imagines emptying the whole thing into her mouth. Several times she's had the pills in her hand, counting them, wondering if there were enough.

Sometimes she cries and wonders why her body can still produce tears. Sometimes she sleeps. Sometimes she has dreams so real she thinks she may actually be awake and that they are hallucinations. Her sorrow has gone wild.

*She is encapsulated in a vast, empty, icy storage locker. There is a frozen blinding white glare and she is filled with dread. She feels raw, as if her inner core is exposed. She is a carcass of bright red meat on a stone slab, ready to be butchered. Then she is butchered, but it is bloodless and she is racing around trying to find the frozen pieces of herself to put herself back together again.*

*Lizbett is a beautiful grinning baby. They are going somewhere and she is wearing a sweet white knit dress embroidered with silk rosebuds with delicate green leaves. But she has soiled her diaper and a yellow stain has oozed out into the white tights with the little ruffles. When Meredith goes to change her, Lizbett has shrunk to the size of Meredith's thumb and Meredith is weeping with frustration as she tries to change the minute diaper on the perfect, tiny Lizbett.*

*Darcy has disappeared. Meredith searches for her in the oddest places: the top shelves and the back of deep, dark closets, in a non-existent attic filled with antique trunks and boxes and racks of vintage clothing, under the stored*

*jumble of furniture in their damp basement, in the garage inside the tool counter. Finally she finds her. She is with Lizbett in the garden shed behind all the urns. The sisters are saucer-eyed and terrorized and they say, "Go away! We aren't safe with you. You can't protect us."*

Sometimes Meredith lies in a willed, masochistic paralysis of re-imagining the crime, going over Lizbett's entire day to the final gruesome moments. Sometimes she thinks about what it would be like if Lizbett were still here, what her future would look like. Occasionally she thinks about her and Thompson. They don't talk. Well, they never did, but they had their work as communication. They shared an artistic vision. She knows he must be suffering too. But he doesn't show it. He's the same Thompson he always was. Tender in his glances, resolute in his quiet.

But something about him angers her. She wonders if it's because he's male and all males repulse her right now. All she can see is swollen, menacing penises, the damage penises can do. She wonders how he now views his own maleness, the maleness of others. Does he see potential threat, as she does? Does he in any way blame himself, his sex? She also resents the fact that he talked her out of not letting Lizbett go to the library after mask class. If he'd supported her, their daughter would still be here.

She does appreciate, though, that he is hyper-attentive with Darcy. He has always engaged with the girls in a more physical way, hugging them, holding them on his lap, dancing with them. Meredith is verbally affectionate and generous of her time and creativity, but Thompson envelops.

Since Meredith no longer sleeps with Thompson; since she sleeps in this same bed where she spends her day, she doesn't even know if he sleeps. Or if he dreams. And he would never say.

She is held hostage by the duality of without and with: without Lizbett's easy acuity, her inchoate, earnest wisdom; without her questioning conversations of her world. Without purpose. Without joy. Without the physicality of Lizbett: the tight hugs, being touched by her essence, without her palpable, creative energy, without all the years to come when she had so often envisioned for her daughter a lifetime filled with accomplishment and goodness. She lives without the hope that she will one day heal, that days will become fluid again.

And there is life with: with the insistent, torturing image of Lizbett's last moments, with the knowledge the killer may be laughing, with a destitute spirit, a hollow heart, with torpor, an overpowering sense of guilt and uselessness, with an irrational, irrepressible belief that what happened did not happen, that Lizbett still thrives and will walk in the door any minute. With a solitary, sombre Darcy. It shocks Meredith that she is now the mother of an only child. "I have a daughter," she hears herself saying. Does she then add, "I did have two, but the eldest was raped and strangled"? Darcy's oneness makes them both more vulnerable, and her baby more precious. Like having a single kidney. If it goes, you die.

Meredith feels utterly inadequate to protect her little Darcy, her silent, unreadable baby. Her attempts at gregariousness touch Meredith deeply because it seems such an effort for her.

Sometimes when Meredith picks Darcy up at school, she comes charging out and practically leaps into her arms. Other times, she is removed and formal. "Hi, Mom," she'll say, and continue walking.

"How was your day?" Meredith always asks.

"Fine." "Good." "Okay." "Not bad."

"Anything interesting happen?"

"No. Not really."

"Not really?"

"No," replies Darcy.

Sometimes she volunteers information about the grief support group the school is offering. "They always ask us how we're feeling. If we have any problems," she says.

"Do you?"

"Only that I want to talk about Lizbett; tell stuff about her. So today we did a remembrance list and everyone could tell anything they wanted about what they remember about Lizbett. It was neat. I said she was famous and everybody always wants to be her friend. I said how sometimes I felt as if she bossed me, but that I liked it that she looked after me. Claire said she and Lizbett's friends are sort of breaking up because everyone being together without Lizbett makes them feel too sad, as if there's an empty space. She said they're afraid to do normal girl things because it looks as if they don't care. One girl, I didn't know her name, said she and her friends used to be jealous of Lizbett and her friends because they were stuck-up and now she was feeling bad. The leader said it was good to talk about it.

Daphne told about a time they all tried to smoke! Lizbett tried smoking, Mom. And Lauren said Lizbett had a boyfriend. Tommy, her brother. Did you know that?"

"About Lauren's brother? I knew Lizbett liked him."

"He liked her. Lauren said they kissed!"

"Did they!" exclaims Meredith.

"Are you mad I told you this?"

"Of course not, lovey. Lizbett was her own person. We're all remembering her in our own way. I'm glad her friends and you are able to share stories."

Once home, Darcy practises the piano before going off to whatever activity is set for that day.

At night, in bed, after Thompson reads to her (they are reading *Heidi*), Darcy's little head whirls with her day. She is very, very tired, but not sleepy. If she can get him to stay, Mr. Mushu curls up in the crook of her body. Most nights he's there. Sometimes, so is Geoffrey. As much as a seven-almost-eight-year-old can, she is feeling as if she has too much to do. She has a project on India for geography. She likes kung fu and pottery and mask class and piano with Nan-Nan. She doesn't mind practising because she wants to get good. But she really just wants to sit and rest. She has often heard her mother say, "I'm so busy I don't have time to think." That's how she feels. That she "doesn't have time to think." She doesn't actually know what she wants to think about. About animals, maybe. About how much she wants a dog. She would like time to imagine that: having a big dog like Misty to walk and to hug and to play with. But she wants to maybe do nothing. She just wants to lie on her bed with a book and read the way she used to, not have all these things to go to. She wishes Lizbett were around to make her parents happy again, to take their attention from her. She wants to make them happy, but she doesn't know how. She can't think of things to say. All she feels is that there's a big black space where Lizbett used to be and no one can fill it.

In grief therapy they talk about the things it's okay to be feeling. Like it's okay to be mad at Lizbett for not being here. Sometimes Darcy wishes she weren't here, either. Sometimes she wishes she were invisible or that she could just vanish to some secret place and be alone. It's okay to think that, they said, as long as she tells someone about it. It's okay to not cry. Darcy feels she hasn't cried as much as she should have. It's okay to want some of

Lizbett's things, like her radio/tape player and her green jelly Swatch and her gold bangle. It's okay to want to wear some of her clothes, even though they're too big. And it's okay to be afraid of the man who killed Lizbett, but not to go overboard and never go out and do things. And to always go somewhere with a friend or grown-up. It's okay to feel certain she'd be happier if they got another dog like Misty.

On Saturday nights they eat dinner in the dining room. It is the one thing Meredith can rally to do. On this night, mid-month, she has made spaghetti carbonara and a spinach salad with toasted almonds and grilled pear. For dessert, she has concocted her own version of spumoni in their ice-cream machine, with candied orange and lemon peel and ginger and hazelnuts. It was one of Lizbett's favourites.

It is a lovely warm night and they are eating on the screened porch with the oil lamps lit. Thompson asks Darcy about mask class.

"Lizbett already told you everything."

"Yes, she told us a lot. But could you try to tell us your version?"

"Melvyn ... he said we could call him that ... he said he likes the kids he teaches to not think of him as a grown-up, but to think of him as another kid. That way, we won't be afraid to express our ideas. Melvyn told us about animals and their spirits ... the thing that makes them what they are. He said lots of people worship animals and think they have powers and can speak and talk. Some animals bring good luck. And some animals can heal sick people. When they put on an animal mask, the person becomes the animal and takes on his ... his cha ... chara ..."

"Characteristics," says Thompson.

"Yes," replies Darcy. "Those. Like in Africa, they have lion masks. And leopard masks. There are even elephant masks with real tusks. And Indians make wolf and eagle masks. They're always animals who are fierce and strong so the people turn fierce and strong."

Meredith asks, "What animal did you pick?"

"Oh, I'm making a mask of Misty."

"Of Misty!" Thompson exclaims.

"Yes. So I can bring her back. Or at least pretend there's a dog like her in the house. It'll be a magic mask."

Meredith and Thompson are a bit taken aback and Darcy jumps in. "Couldn't we get a real dog? Couldn't we, please? For my birthday. We should get another dog just like Misty."

Thompson says, "Another dog wouldn't be 'just like' Misty, sweetie. Another dog would be who he or she is. Probably quite different."

"You mean like 'replacing' Misty. We talked about that in grief group. About trying to replace a dead person. And we learned that you can't. That everyone is irr … irr …"

"Irreplaceable," says Meredith.

"Ir-placeable. But," says Darcy, "another person can add on to the memories of the dead person, make them better."

"You maybe mean 'enhance,'" Thompson offers.

"Yes, 'enhance.' Just like a baby sister would enhance how much we loved Lizbett."

"Oh, Darcy, sweetest girl. There'll never be a baby sister. Daddy and I —"

"Well, how about a dog, then?"

After Darcy falls asleep, Thompson comes into the den where Meredith is watching TV. She does this night after night until she falls asleep. She watches cop shows, mostly. *Cagney and Lacey. Hill Street Blues. Miami Vice. Magnum P.I.* She also likes *Moonlighting* and *Remington Steele.* It distresses him to see her so absorbed in stuff that would, at one time, have bored her. It pains him to see her so deadened. She used to read novels: new ones, the best ones.

"Could we talk about tonight?" he asks.

"We could."

"Could you sit up and turn that off?"

"I could." But she doesn't move.

"Mer …"

"I'll turn it down," she says.

He comes and sits beside her on the couch. She moves away. "What would you think about getting a dog?"

"I wouldn't."

"Just like that?"

"Oh, Sonny, please. I'm in no shape to give out the love and time and attention a dog needs. I'm barely hanging in, as it is. A dog needs so much. And besides, what if … what if it got sick and died, like Misty? I couldn't go through that again, especially not after Lizbett."

"That's no reason not to get a dog: because it might die. I think it would be so good for Darcy, Mer. She talks about it every chance she gets. I think it might be good for all of us. To get us out of ourselves."

"I just don't think I have the wherewithal … the emotional or physical stamina. My brain is pudding. My body is filled with glass shards and hurts all over. I have a continuous banging headache. I have vertigo when I stand up. I feel as if I'm hemorrhaging my life blood."

"I know."

"I'm grieving, Sonny. I'm grieving my guts out."

"So am I, Mer. For god's sake. I can barely make it out of bed in the morning."

"You never could."

"This is not the same. This is like I'm dead. Or in a coma."

"Bringing a dog into such an emotional mess isn't a good idea."

"I think it is. I'm going to call Magdalena."

Meredith had not grown up with dogs the way Thompson had, but she had loved Misty in a way she would not have believed possible. Besides Thompson and the girls, Misty had been her life. All their lives. But Meredith knew what kind of energy and commitment that required. Three daily walks, obedience training, and, if they got a puppy, all the trials of puppyhood: the pools of pee, little turds in corners, the chewing, the rambunctious mischief where nothing was safe, not toilet paper rolls, cushions, shoes, wicker baskets, rugs, furniture legs. Puppies took over. How could she care for an animal when she could barely take care of herself? And it would be her, during the day, at least. She remembers that from Misty.

# 13

## OCTOBER

J ust driving up the lane of Celestial Kennels lifts the Warnes' spirits. Not that Darcy's aren't already flying, in any case.

The sky is unbroken azure. The sunshine is giving the day brilliance and warmth and the maples are in full garish colour: bloody crimson, orange, and yellow festooning the way.

When they reach the farmhouse, the barking is deafening: five Great Danes. Magdalena and Joan come out with Hildy on a leash.

"Oh, there she is! There she is!" exclaims Darcy. "She's so sweet!"

Magdalena has warned them to exit the car cautiously and approach the dog slowly. She has told Hildy to sit. "All right," Magdalena says. "Come up to her one at a time. Put out the palm of your hand for her to sniff. And you can offer her a treat. Praise her in a low, calm voice, 'Good girl, Hildy. Good girl.'"

Meredith goes first and Hildy stands and tries to back off. Magdalena corrects her and she sits again. She accepts Meredith's treats. With Thompson, she stands and attempts to get behind Magdalena, who issues another correction. The dog sits again and takes Thompson's treats. Darcy is very excited and has trouble containing herself. She wants to throw her arms around Hildy's neck, but she practically tiptoes up to her and offers her treats and the dog is more than happy to receive them.

"That's great," says Magdalena. "Now we can all say hello!"

Meredith embraces her. "Oh, Maddie. It's so good to see you."

Magdalena says, "Why don't we go for a walk up to the top of the hill with Hildy on the leash? And if she does okay, I'll let her off."

When they all reach the top of the hill, Darcy leaps on a swing hanging under a cavernous maple and asks Thompson to push her.

"That's the same swing I had when I was a little girl," says Magdalena. "My father used to push me."

"I can't believe how beautiful it is," Meredith says. "You could live up here!"

She has an overwhelming and comforting sense of the assured continuity and mystery of countless decades of life. Lustrous cornfields and golden swathes of wheat stretch for miles. Hardwood stands blaze between them. Sheep and cattle punctuate rolling pastures. Interrupting the bucolic panorama, stolid farmhouses and their shimmering silos rest where they've been for decades. Families: so many personalities have come and gone, fought and loved, lived and died. Meredith envisions women harvesting laden gardens, canning and baking in hot kitchens and labourers out beyond, sweating for the land. Occasionally a steeple rises and she can picture the dark graveyards filled with toppling, mossy stones and she momentarily thinks of all the dead children, of the frequency, the commonality of that. In the distance, she can just see the Victorian rooftops of the little town and the lake, so blue and gleaming, it almost disappears into the sky.

There is a prolonged, painful silence. Joan, accustomed to such moments, asks Meredith, "How are you coping?"

"I feel unstable. I'm not doing anything worthwhile. The days are pretty long."

"Give yourself some time."

"Let's let Hildy off," suggests Magdalena. She unfastens the dog's leash and Brunhilde leaps up into the air and tears around the top of the hill as if she'd been imprisoned for weeks. Then she comes bounding toward the three women.

"Just wait," says Magdalena. "Let's see what she does." The dog stands there in a crouch position, eyeing them and Magdalena tells Meredith to call her and then give her a treat.

"Come, Hildy. Come, girl. Come." Hildy hesitates and then comes up to Meredith. Meredith gives her a treat and the dog wags her tail, nuzzling for another.

Magdalena shouts to Thompson and Darcy to call the dog. When they do, Brunhilde runs to them.

Magdalena says, "I think she may be okay."

On the way down, Hildy races around them and Magdalena talks about the responsibility of accepting an abused dog. "You'll always have to be vigilant and strict. And consistent. Training an abused dog isn't about being flexible. No spoiling. She must never think she's in control. Work with her on obedience every day. Take her to a class or even a couple of them, if you can. Expose her to other dogs … good dogs, of course. Dogs you know are socialized. Especially let her meet as many people as possible, always making sure you have her in a high collar at first, just to see how she reacts."

"Can't we just give her lots and lots of love?" asks Darcy, who has reached out a couple of times when Hildy came by, which the dog accepted.

"Lots and lots of love is fine as long as she knows it's love that does not allow any wrong behaviour. If she misbehaves, say in a strong voice, "'No!' Or 'Wrong!' If she persists, you can take her muzzle in your hand and apply pressure and say the words again. She must be perfectly trained, partly because she's going to be big, but partly because of her background. There may be an unpredictability there we have to watch for."

"She wouldn't be dangerous?" asks Meredith.

"Not now. She's come a long way."

"I mean, she won't ever bite us."

"Not you. No. Not if you establish leadership from the beginning. I've worked and worked with her every day and she's been socializing with all the other dogs. She was … could have been a dog like Misty. That nature is still in her. It just needs to be constantly reinforced. I've got so that I can take a bone out of her mouth. You should be able to do that. Why don't we go and visit with the other dogs and watch them all interact? And then come into the house for tea and we'll see how you all do inside."

"Be careful," Magdalena says as she opens the gate to let the other Danes out. "There are several hundred pounds of exuberance here!"

The huge dogs bound out and then stop short upon seeing the Warnes. They give a few deep barks and then come wiggling up to the three of them, five tails whipping against their legs.

"Ouch!" says Darcy. "Their tails hurt!"

The Danes are lovers and leaners and they all vie for everyone's affection. Zeus is as tall as Darcy and he gives her face a few slurps and soon

Artemis has joined in. And Hildy, well accustomed to them all, dances eagerly around them. Soon she has joined the pack, demanding attention. It's as if their acceptance of the strangers has added to her confidence to be with them.

Inside the house, she is even more relaxed. She wanders from person to person sniffing, leaning in to be stroked. Darcy scratches her ears and wants to give her some cake.

"It's very bad for her," Joan says. "You don't want her to get fat. That's very bad for a dog's hips, especially a big dog."

Although they already knew, Magdalena tells them again about "bloat" and the twisting of the stomach.

"We don't know what causes it or why Great Danes are prone to it ... maybe their huge chests ... but it's often fatal," says Joan. "Fast eating, exercising too soon after eating, free access to water. Nothing's been proven. Get her an emergency fast if it happens. My dog, Daphne, died of it."

"They're such risky dogs, aren't they?" Meredith says. "That really worries me. And they live such a short time."

"My last male, Apollo, was eleven," Magdalena offers. "But he was an exception. You can expect seven or eight years. Do you want to walk to the end of the lane and back with Hildy before you decide?"

"I've already decided," says Darcy.

In the back of the Warnes' station wagon, into which she jumped willingly, Hildy doesn't settle and whines continuously during the first portion of the drive home. Then, partway through, she climbs over the back seat to sit beside Darcy, who puts her arm around the dog.

Thompson looks back. "How's she doing?"

Meredith says, "Do you think that's okay, sweetie? Isn't that spoiling her?"

"Just 'til she gets used to me," say Darcy. "I think she's very happy now. Wouldn't this be so perfect if Lizbett were here?"

If Meredith and Thompson are despondent and anxious over the police's inability to find Lizbett's killer, add rage and frustration to the investigators' state of mind. They have talked to dozens and dozens of people. Known sexual predators, for example. They were even certain they had caught the guy, a man sentenced to fourteen years for the violent rapes of two teenage girls who was out on parole. He had no alibi. But they subpoenaed a blood test and the type didn't match. They have interviewed as many men as they could who were associated with Lizbett in any way: fathers of friends, husbands of friends, relatives, the crew and cast of the two plays she'd been in, the TV techies, teachers, her dentist, her doctor, the head librarian at the children's library, even their Chinese dry-cleaner, who always gave Lizbett candy. They questioned Tadeusz, Brygida's husband. Kyle, Abbey's boyfriend, was a prime suspect. He was well acquainted with Lizbett and had had no alibi, but he willingly volunteered a blood test and he was O positive. Melvyn has not volunteered for a blood test and is not required to. Since he has a twice-verified alibi, the police have no reason push it, nothing to justify disbelief or suspicion. But he has stated that his blood type is O positive as well. Melvyn seems a rational, conscientious man, obviously distressed by realizing he had been one of the last to see her alive.

It would be so simple if they were able to test the blood of every person they talked to. But they need a warrant and for a warrant they need probable cause, potential proof. They certainly do not have that with Melvyn Searle.

They are convinced Lizbett knew the killer. They thought this even before they brought in the FBI profiler who asserted the same thing. Criminal profiling is new in 1986 and considered uncertain, hocus-pocus, but the police are stuck and need all the help they can find. The FBI expert, Frank Milner, is known to city homicide. He had done work with them two years before: in the case of a serial rapist who was attacking women in one of the northern suburbs. The man was never caught.

In Lizbett's case, Milner suggests this was a carefully executed crime, indicated by the killer's precautionary use of gloves and a condom. He probably kept a kind of "kit," which included the duct tape, in his car. He is likely a man of above-average intelligence, a personable man, a trustworthy man, whose car Lizbett would have had no trouble getting into. He could be someone used to working with children, someone who knows how to attract them. Above all, he is someone who knew Lizbett's daily patterns. Milner believes it is not a coincidence that the perpetrator happened to apprehend her after her mask class.

And, given the secluded location of the crime scene, he is a man who knew the city and planned to use the spot he did.

Milner also asserts that heinous as this crime is, the killer is "conservative." There was no kink. The body was intact. There was no purposeful mutilation, no evidence of torture. He does not think there was rage or vengeance attached to the act. He also believes that the perpetrator may be a man of some conscience, maybe feeling some guilt about what he did. Rather than dumping the body at a faraway, isolated site; rather than burying it; rather than throwing it into the canal, he has left it in plain view, as if he wanted it to be found. That, says Milner, indicates conscience. Milner feels too, that because of these things, the man is likely not a serial killer. He probably has not killed before, says Milner, but with the success of Lizbett, he may be feeling encouraged to do so again.

Mikkelson scoffs. He had thought of all this before, many times. This profile applies to most of the men in Lizbett's life.

Meredith and Thompson talk to the police as often as they can. Meredith thinks they're slacking.

"Why would they, Mer?" says Thompson. "I don't think so. They need to find this guy. They have over a hundred people on the job. They talk to people every day. They go over and over what little evidence there is. They've offered a $50,000 reward. They want the guy as desperately as we do."

But detectives Irv Mikkelson and Nick Angstrom are facing a brutal truth. Unless an informant comes forward, the odds are slim they'll find Lizbett's killer. The case is almost cold.

The Warnes have two enormous crates for Hildy, one in their bedroom and one in the kitchen. Darcy wanted one of them in her room, but Thompson and Meredith feel that, for now, they should be the ones in control. The first night she's home, Thompson is awakened by the dog's screams. She has been gnawing at the wire on the door of her cage and her upper and lower canine teeth have gotten hooked. Her jaws are locked in open position. Thompson leaps out of bed. Meredith and Darcy come racing. They can't pull the door open because Hildy is stuck there. They reach through the narrow openings in the wire and try to pry her jaws off but they won't budge. The dog is frantic.

"Where are some goddamn pliers?" Thompson shouts.

Meredith has no idea where pliers might be. In the garage? In the basement? In some junk drawer in the kitchen? She and Darcy are trying to soothe Hildy, who is terrified. Thompson frantically searches for pliers and finally finds some in the kitchen. He bends the wire away from the teeth so that they can lift them away. They let Hildy out and she wiggles and wags and kisses their faces. Not once in their attempts to free her has she growled or protested.

That night she sleeps on the bed with Thompson.

Meredith can no longer spend long days in Lizbett's room. Unless she leaves Hildy in her crate, which she doesn't want to do, the dog has to be watched every second. She trots about the house looking for mischief and, if no one is watching, finds it. She can unmake a bed and rip open a pillow in seconds. She likes wicker hampers. She pushes open the top with her nose and strews the dirty clothes everywhere, proudly bringing Meredith one of her bras or a pair of underpants, which she often eats. Chair legs attract her teeth. So do shoes someone has forgotten to put away. They call her "the Shredder" because that's what she does to all loose newspapers and magazines.

One morning, Meredith lets her out in the backyard and discovers Hildy has dug up the dozens of parrot tulip bulbs she and Thompson planted in September. The day before she had ripped apart Darcy's bed, chewing through to the mattress. Meredith phones him at the studio in tears.

"We cannot keep this dog."

Still, after her workout, she walks her all over the city, sometimes for two or three hours. October is a beautiful month. The skies are clear; the air has only a promise of the cold to come. Chestnuts crash to the sidewalks. The fallen leaves crackle under their feet. They walk throughout the university campus, with all its evocative Gothic stone, around the massive Victorian government complex, through Chinatown, Greektown, the Italian neighbourhoods, the old Jewish market. She finds pockets of the city she didn't know existed and beautiful parks everywhere. People stop to ask questions about the dog, to pat her. Hildy sits and endures. She's never friendly, but she never growls.

Lizbett is in Meredith's head the whole time. She feels weighted, solemn, without joy.

In the afternoons, after getting Darcy to her activity, she takes Hildy to a dog park a couple of blocks away from their house. It is actually a huge grass bowl, surrounded on three sides by ravine and fenced on the fourth. Meredith and the dog descend steep steps to reach it. At first she keeps

Hildy on a leash when they're inside, carefully watching her reaction to the other dogs who all come up to greet her. Her tail goes in between her legs; she tries to wedge into Meredith's legs. Meredith commands her to sit until all the dogs have sniffed her and trotted off. Then Meredith walks up and down, across and around the perimeter of the park, over and over until she senses Hildy is beginning to relax. After about a week and a half, Hildy seems comfortable there and Meredith sets her free.

As she did on top of the hill at Magdalena's, Hildy breaks into a full tear and streaks every which way with a number of dogs in pursuit, which she seems to like. Even at eight months, Meredith can see the beauty of her stride. Her musculature is silvery and sinewy.

Hildy makes some friends. A shepherd/collie mix, a Staffordshire terrier and a yellow lab are all up to her boisterous level of play.

She gets attacked by a fierce white husky, but she falls into submissive position and the husky backs off.

When Magdalena sees this, she says, "That's great." She is staying with the Warnes for a week to see how the training is going.

"My father believed in the spirituality of animals," says Magdalena. "He was a dour, quite crotchety man, but with animals he seemed to light up ... actually be enlightened. He loved that dogs are deeply linked to the primal, yet perfectly adapted. He thought dogs, particularly ... but cats, too ... enhance ... enlarge ... our spirits because they connect us to something beyond ourselves. They're complicated and mysterious. We can't know what's going on in their heads and yet they seem to know what's going on in ours. How can they be so instinctive, yet so equally responsive? How can they detect our moods, read our expressions so astutely? They live by their need to survive yet their capacity to give is infinite. How do they know what they know, understand what they do, when they can't speak? Why is it not uncommon for a pet to die soon after an owner dies?"

Meredith says, "Lately I've been thinking so much about Misty and remembering my grief when she was put down. I've told you, for days I lay curled in fetal position on all her sleeping places. It was just before Christmas when she died and the tree took up one of those spaces. When the season was over, I took off the decorations, but left the tree until spring, as a kind of, I don't know, memorial. That was such agony, the loss of that dog. Even now, with the savage hole left behind by Lizbett, the memory stabs. How can there be two such unrelated, raw grievings?"

"I don't know," replies Magdalena. "I don't have children, but it seems to me that love for a child is instinctive and urgent, fused by flesh and blood. Ironically, the second a child is born, they begin a journey to independence. A parent's job is to love and encourage that separateness, in fact, sometimes enforce it, to make themselves dispensable. Love for a child is embedded, I think, but it is also external and as infinite as the universe. Love for a dog is internal and confined. A dog co-opts ... invades your way of being. It's dependent and unconditionally adoring. A dog only wants a life with you and mourns in separation. A child is of you ... an extension of you, but eventually grows from you. A dog becomes you ... like an infiltrator. Dogs don't leave, emotionally or physically."

"Except when they die," Meredith retorts.

"That's simply unexpected loss. A dog stays. My father thought a person was made better by that bond. From it, from the animal, you find compassion and tolerance and patience. A sense of humour, even. You can't be self-preoccupied with a dog, for example. It needs you and being needed feeds well-being ... self-worth. Being responsible for an animal takes you out of yourself and into its life. It's a kind of embracing ... an enlarging trade-off. My father loved it, even with the cattle and sheep he raised to sell for meat. He felt great gratitude for their 'sacrifice.' That's what he called it. More than anything he recognized and valued the interdependence of people and animals, whether for food or emotions."

Meredith says, "It's a bit scary because I feel so vulnerable. Some sort of transformation has taken place here. Our feelings for Hildy have gone beyond mere attachment to something ... something more profound. It's hard to express. She's beneficent and omniscient, really, the way she oversees our moods, our gestures, our voices, our needs. She just seems to 'get' them. Her solidity has filled us ... to overflowing, it sometimes feels like. She is just so wonderfully 'there.' Thompson said the other day, 'I don't think I could possibly love her more.' It's not that she's relieved our pain so much as she has been sharing it, in a kind of understanding way. Her devotion has been sustaining us."

After Magdalena leaves, Darcy says, "It's not fair, Mommy. You get Hildy all day and I have to go to more school after school. I want to come to the dog park with you." So Darcy gives up kung fu and book club and pottery, but keeps piano lessons with Nellie so she can go to the dog park.

They go every weekday. The three of them develop a kind of communion, Darcy holding on to the leash and Meredith's hand, Hildy sniffing her way along. It is companionable and telepathic in its contentment. Hildy is loved. Darcy is joyous. Meredith is released.

They all watch for squirrels.

"Be prepared, lovey. She'll bolt."

Once Hildy does see a big black one, but Darcy has seen it, too, and quickly high-collars the dog, who lurches and stops. "Leave it!" she commands.

The dog park becomes a fascinating new world for them. It is an odd assortment of canine lovers and dozens of breeds and mutts with a great range of behaviours. Like loquacious MaryBeth with her two giant schnauzers. And Colin, with his ball-obsessed Britanny spaniel. And Thelma, who is as enormous as her Great Pyrenees. There is Evelyn with her two nasty toy poodles. Sometimes the place is a sea of yellow: labs and golden retrievers. And there are too many fat black labs to count. Hildy loves Romeo and Juliet, two huge Harlequin Great Danes. Neither Meredith nor Darcy like anything that resembles a terrier. Jack Russells, those feisty, hyperactive runts, are the worst.

Both of them are agreed. Many of the dogs are obnoxious. They charge into people and jump up (sometimes knocking them over), they never ever come when they're called, they steal other dog's toys and tennis balls, and they dig huge holes for people to trip in.

An unneutered Doberman called Cyril always snarls and lunges at Hildy. She is terrified of him.

"You should control your dog," Meredith tells the owner. "He's vicious."

"Not really."

"What do you call what he does to my dog?"

"You should have seen him a year ago," says the man. "I couldn't even bring him here. He was abused. I work with him every day."

"Well, so was ours. And she doesn't attack."

"Well, just keep your dog away from mine."

It's a place a bit like the old West. There are no rules and no one to enforce them if there were. The only enforcement comes from vigilantes, responsible owners who object to a dog's bad behaviour, which usually sets up an altercation. Dog owners are hostile to having their dogs criticized. Since it is a "dog park" where anything and everything is allowed, the onus is on the offended person to accept an assault. "What do you expect?" the nasty dog's owner says. "It's a dog park!"

While they watch Hildy play, Darcy and Meredith are drawn into all the preoccupations of the owners: the consistency of dogs' stools (the most popular — diarrhea is always the worst concern), dog obesity (the biggest problem), dog diets, dog antics, dog neuroses, dog epilepsy and diabetes, dog breast and bone cancer. They learn of all the dog deaths that have occurred, the most recent a West Highland terrier with a brain tumour. There was a memorial service. They hear any number of stories about dog delinquency: the Airedale who ate a whole leather belt and had to have surgery; the Jack Russell who has eaten through the wall from the laundry room to the kitchen, the springer spaniel who demolished a down comforter; the border collie who put the car in gear and it ran down the driveway.

Occasionally, there's a new puppy and all the dogs and owners rush in to greet the newcomer. Orbison is the newest, another rambunctious yellow lab.

The common connector is love. There is not a person at the park who would not die for his/her dog and who would not feel like doing so should anything happen to the beloved pet.

"It's *Days of Our Lives* for dogs," Meredith says.

One time, Joy, the owner of three yappy Pekinese, came up to Meredith and said, "You're that woman, aren't you? The one whose daughter was murdered last summer? I remember. I saw you on TV. We felt so bad for you. It was a terrible thing."

"Yes," said Meredith. "Thanks for your concern."

"I don't know how you stood it all those days she was missing before they found her. I would have gone crazy."

It happens: the unwelcome celebrity. At the grocery store. At Micky's Chikin 'n' Ribs. At the pharmacy. Even at the dog park.

But in fact, on the surface, the Warnes look like a happy, loving family with a magnificent, obedient, gentle dog. No one would ever know.

The profiler was right about the killer being high on his success and wanting to experience it again. Melvyn's urges feel explosive. He loiters at the park in front of his house. He visits schoolyards. Above all, he continues to fixate on Darcy at the Saturday class. He has taken pictures of the kids attending and put Darcy's on his fridge. He hovers around her all morning until she begins to wonder. She says to Thompson when he picks her up, "I think Melvyn is worried about me. He always stays way too close to me."

Melvyn can't believe how precious he finds Darcy. She is so unlike Audrey and Lizbett. Rather than being shining and extroverted, she is velvety and inward, mysterious even for an eight-year-old.

Melvyn wants the little girl close. He pictures bathing her. He likes the natural smell of her hair. He imagines having her on his knee, hugging her. He can see them listening to his children's records in his living room. He wants her desperately, but he has no idea how to get to her.

Late one morning, he leaves his office and drives to a park where he knows the girls from Darcy's school go running at that hour. It is a wooded park, thick with undergrowth and a narrow, winding trail. He is all in black and he puts on a Darth Vader mask, hiding behind some bushes. He hears the girls' chatter, the thudding of their sneakers on the dirt, but he waits. A line of girls passes by. Then there's a short break and another group passes. He still hasn't seen Darcy, but soon two stragglers appear, well behind the others ... just what he was waiting for. He comes out of the bushes with his erect penis exposed and begins to masturbate.

"What is he doing?" says one little girl and she stops. The other runs on. Melvyn grabs the little girl and claps a hand over her mouth and drags her into the bushes. He jams his other hand down her running shorts and penetrates her as deeply as he can with his fingers. She urinates on his hand. This shocks and repulses him and he throws her down and runs off into the woods, pulling off the mask and backtracking until he gets to his car.

He has failed! He is disgusted with himself. He compromised his standards. This was not how he usually performs his rituals. He doesn't do "snatches." He has an amiable — dare he think it? — affectionate relationship with his girls. They willingly go with him. He will continue to work on Darcy.

The school calls the police. They search the area for clues and find nothing. Neither little girl can make an identification because of the mask. A Darth Vader mask. Ubiquitous. Commercial. Worn by countless kids on Hallowe'en. Not an artifact. The police put the attack down to just another perverted jerk-off fucking up a little girl's psyche.

# 14

## NOVEMBER

Darcy announces she wants out of the mask class on Saturdays. She wants to be at home with Thompson and Meredith, having fun with Hildy. And she thinks Melvyn is creepy.

"I'm so sorry, Melvyn," Meredith says when she telephones. "Darcy is mad for this dog and we think it's good she's showing such spirit."

"I'm disappointed. I really like her. She's a wonderful, intriguing kid. She'll be missed." Melvyn hopes he has hidden his distress. He feels unfairly rejected and panicky.

In fact, Darcy's opting out of the class is very convenient for the Warnes. They've been offered a ski cabin northwest of the city in the snow belt, by friends who are going away on sabbatical. They plan to use it on the weekends. The deal is they have to cut trails.

If it's possible for someone who has just lost a daughter in a vicious way to feel ecstatic, Thompson does. He sees their getting away into neutral space as a way out from the oppressive mood in their house. He hopes it will be a sort of rehabilitation. In spite of Hildy's takeover, there is no escape from the overhang of Lizbett's death. Or not so much her death, per se, as the absence of her life in every room, in every situation. It is as if the absence itself is alive and clinging and won't let go.

Meredith is trying to look forward to the cabin, but she is disturbed about going. She is actually afraid to leave their house, leave Lizbett's things, for long, as though she may return and not find her family there. Meredith sees a weekend away as an abandonment not only of her daughter, but of her grieving for her.

But she likes the cabin. They have stayed there before. It is a big log structure with an open main floor. A huge antler chandelier hangs from the middle of the cathedral ceiling. Three bedrooms are attached to the living space, and, above, there is spacious loft with three sets of bunk beds and floor space for air mattresses and sleeping bags.

Being active in the wilderness, in the creeping cold, will be restorative. There's just that ruthless pang: no Lizbett to share it.

Arriving Friday night in the piercing air, the sky almost solid with stars, the Warnes enter a world removed. The cabin is on a hundred acres, deep in a forest. The trees rise in a melded mass, their branches splayed against the lighted sky. There is nothing else around. The black, sonorous silence swallows them completely. They break through it, invade it with the *crunch-crunch* of their boots in the light virgin snow, the heaving of their frosty breath as they unload the car. Hildy doesn't quite know what to do in such a wild space.

Indoors, they start a fire in the stone fireplace and warm the place up. Thompson makes a martini, Meredith pours wine, Darcy huddles down into one of the overstuffed canvas sofas with a plaid woollen blanket, Hildy as much on her lap as she can be. They eat a late dinner by the fire, takeout from a French restaurant in their neighbourhood at home. If Darcy falls asleep, Meredith and Thompson will have a brandy. They sleep in the same bed with a chasm between them, or rather with Hildy, snoring and stretched out there, jerking them roughly with her legs when she dreams.

In the daylight, the forest seems bleak and monochrome. Black trunks rise straight from a dead floor into a metallic sky. The air is sombre and harsh. The terrain is challenging, with steep slopes to manoeuvre. Jagged granite boulders loom and here and there, in the north shadows, snow has drifted in elaborate sculptures. Thompson's chainsaw whines; Meredith hauls away the severed pieces, and Darcy clears the branches. Sawdust blows everywhere in the brisk wind. Hildy does not take off. She actually helps by picking up big sticks and carrying them off. This is where they

will cross-country ski when the snow is deep enough. The family is lay-
ered in winter gear, some of which they've removed from their efforts.
Their cheeks are bright red and their spirits even.

One evening, in the city, Meredith invites Lizbett's closest friends over
with their mothers. They have sweetly and casually been dropping by since
Lizbett's death, singly or in pairs, talking about school, mostly, how their
French teacher, Monsieur Bluteau, is being really strict and mean or about
whether Dionne Warwick singing "That's What Friends Are For" is as good
as Whitney Houston singing "Greatest Love of All." They mention how
hard grammar is in grade six. And that none of them is as good at math as
Lizbett was. Sometimes they'll go up into Lizbett's room and Meredith will
hear hushed words.

In fact, the girls love Meredith. She is high-spirited and playful and
always engages them in lively talks. They've always loved the Warnes'
house, too, because of its embracing warmth. Anything goes. They would
come more often and they'd come all together just to hang out, but they are
worried about disturbing Meredith.

When the girls arrive, Hildy greets them cautiously. She actually wags
her tail. But when she sees Lauren, much taller than the others with glasses
and blond, short hair, she growls and backs off.

"Wrong!" Meredith says in a low voice and clasps Hildy's muzzle.
Hildy whines and sits. "Here, Lauren," says Meredith, handing her a treat.
"Give her this." But Hildy growls again and refuses to take it.

"Wrong!" Meredith says again, and, to the gathering adds, "I'm so
sorry. She's been abused. We're just training her. I'll put her in her crate."

All together like this, in this seemingly purposeful gathering, without Lizbett, the girls are shy. It's difficult to remember that they used to
run around the place as if it were their own. The mothers, most of whom
Meredith only knows from the occasional phone call, seem standoffish.
They're wondering why Meredith has invited them.

Meredith isn't really sure, either, except that she wants to see the interac-
tion of Lizbett's friends with their mothers, to get a picture of how it would
be for her if Lizbett were still here. Lizbett would have been twelve at the end
of August. Would she have changed as much as these girls seem to have?

They are taller, more contained. Their faces seem serene, less childlike. All have dressed for the occasion and are wearing skirts and blouses or sweaters instead of jeans. Are those little buds she sees on Jen's chest? Breasts? Already? Would Lizbett's have begun? She cannot remember any signs.

She offers the mothers white wine, which they all accept. There is juice for the girls and the dining-room table is covered with thawed goodies left over from the funeral.

"Tell me, tell me, how you are all doing?" What is she expecting? That they are a mess? That they can barely function without Lizbett? Is that what she wants to hear? Some reassurance that she's not alone? Or are they more resilient, more detached than she and are leading back-to-normal lives? Do children have a natural armour or are they less vulnerable because they are less emotionally developed?

Would that distress her, to know they're not suffering?

She has no idea what they've been told or even if they've all been told the same thing. Have some parents been more protective? Do the girls compare what they know? With their just-burgeoning sexuality, what do they think? How is a young girl — who is just beginning to have an awareness of her body — affected when a close friend has been violated? Is she terrified? These are the questions Meredith wants to ask. She wonders what she would have told Lizbett had some other girl been killed. She is appalled, but she wants to pry.

If she did, the girls would tell her they've been told Lizbett was raped and strangled, and yes, they know what rape is. Mostly they think about it as something violent, something really painful. They don't think about or discuss the details. They've heard rumours: that Lizbett was chloroformed, that she was actually dead. Once somebody said the guy used a big stick. One girl would tell Meredith that she has a terrible recurring nightmare that she is being raped, always by a different man: her father, her uncle, her teacher. Another dreams she's being smothered by someone she knows, but she can never really see the face. Since they know it is likely that Lizbett knew her killer, they can't help but view all males suspiciously and will for a long time.

Dominique is the first to speak. She is chubby, with a blond bob. "I don't ever feel happy anymore. Nothing is very much fun."

"I feel happy sometimes," offers Lauren. "When I don't let myself think about it. When I do, I get sad all over again. I'm tired of being sad. I'm tired of crying. I didn't know my head could hold so many tears."

"So am I," says Jen. And Claire concurs. They are both dark, with pony-tails held by baubles. "We do all of the same things as we did, but we get into fights. We sort of fight about who was her very best friend."

"That's because if you're a close friend you get to have private time with the grief counsellor. If you're not, you have to go with the group," Claire says.

"That's no big deal," says Daphne. She has brown curls and a quiet voice.

"It isn't. But some people make it out to be," says Lauren. "Anyway, we used to get into other fights, but Lizbett made us make up. No one does that anymore."

A mother, Monica, says, "I think the girls have lost their footing a bit. It has been enormous to deal with and no one actually knows how to. I'm very concerned about the girls' safety as well as their emotional health."

"In grief group they tell us to talk about Lizbett and what happened. But it feels like we have. Over and over. And sometimes it just feels like gossiping," says Dominique. "And I don't know much more to say."

Lauren says, "I don't like those girls who try to be our friends just because we knew Lizbett. It's like we're special or something. Just because she was my close friend doesn't mean I want attention."

Daphne adds, "I don't like feeling like I stand out. Those girls think we want attention. They think we think we're sort of famous because of how good friends we were. But we're the same as we always were."

"Yeah. We're just normal girls who had something horrible happen to them," says Claire.

Another mother offers, "I think Monica's right. The big issue is safety. Lizbett's purse with her address book was never found, was it? I think about that every day. Our girls used to be able to go everywhere and anywhere on their own. Now they have to be guarded all the time."

"Mom!" says Dominique. "We do not! The school says we're fine if we're with a partner or a couple of other kids. I don't think we should feel like we're in prison."

"I don't want to feel like I'm in prison, but I'm scared," says Lauren. "That guy is out there. Maybe he's after one of us. How do we know? There are a couple of police cars at the school every day. That freaks me out. You know what else is sort of freaky? Like, how we sort of try to be like Lizbett. We kind of, you know, say things she used to say and act like her."

"No, we don't," says Dominique.

Claire says, "Well, maybe not actually be like her, you know, on purpose, but sometimes when I say something, I realize, 'Wow. That sounded just like Lizbett.' It just doesn't feel right without her."

"I thought you were saying we were trying to bring her back or something," Dominique says to Lauren.

"That's not what I meant," she replies. "It's just … it's just that we were so close to her, some of her rubbed off on us and now she's not here."

"I really, really miss her," says Daphne. "It's hard to have fun without her because it makes me feel bad that she's not with us."

Meredith turns to Lauren and asks, "Wasn't your brother Lizbett's boyfriend?" There is dead silence. Right away, she realizes she has made a mistake. "Oh, I'm sorry," she says. "I only wondered. I know Lizbett liked him."

"They weren't like, you know, real boyfriend and girlfriend."

"I'm sure," says Meredith. "But soon you'll all be thinking about boys."

"We already do," says Dominique. The girls all laugh. "Sometimes it's all we talk about … who likes who … who is going with who … who has broken up … "

Meredith says, "I'm glad what happened to Lizbett hasn't kept you from normal things." Again, there's silence. "You know, one of the reasons I invited you all here was to ask you if there is anything of Lizbett's you'd like. Please feel free to go up into her bedroom and look around and take anything you want. Really. Anything. It would make me feel so good to know some of her things were still being used."

The mothers all watch the girls leave and one offers, "Children grieve differently. In spurts, almost. When my first husband died, Jen was only six. She was all over the map with her feelings. Sometimes I thought she didn't have any. It's normal. There are lots and lots of setbacks for a while. And sometimes you have to realize you can't always fix it. It's theirs to fix. My experience is that they do fix it eventually."

Upstairs they hear the girls chattering and giggling. Meredith thinks it sounds like music.

The girls pull open drawers and rifle through the closet. They pick up the dolls and stuffed animals from the bassinette. They find her jewellery box and carefully choose things: earrings, a thin strand of pearls, gimp bracelets. They try on shoes and sweaters and jeans, but not skirts or dresses. They check themselves out in the dressing table mirror. They say things like, "Remember this?" Or, "this is what she wore to your birthday, Claire." Or, "I was always so jealous of this." Finally they come downstairs. Jen is wearing Lizbett's favourite blue cardigan. Dominique shows her mother a pair of earrings, little silver cats. Lauren has chosen a stuffed golden retriever puppy. "I hope this is okay," she says to Meredith. "Lizbett always used to let me sleep with it." Daphne and Claire, closer to Lizbett's size, have each chosen similar jeans, one dark blue, one light.

"Oh my goodness, loveys, is that all?" Meredith asks.

"Really. It is. Her things really just belonged to her," says Dominique.

"It was sort of funny. It almost felt as if she were there … that maybe she'd just gone to the bathroom or something and that we were all there trading like we usually did," adds Lauren.

A few nights later, Meredith comes from the den into the living room where Thompson is trying to read.

"Darcy and Lizbett's school phoned me today. One of the booths from the Christmas fair just cancelled. It's really short notice. Two weeks, but they wondered if I'd like to do the booth I did last year."

"Remind me again what you did."

"I did a bake table with Abbey. But I've been thinking. I've been thinking about that mask teacher …"

"That weird guy?"

"Yes, he was weird, but also intriguing in an eccentric sort of way. I can't seem to get him out of my head. Maybe because of his final connection to Lizbett and the fact that he seemed to find her so appealing. Maybe it's a way of holding on to her, through someone else. But I'd like to see him again. And I've been thinking about masks … how fascinating they are and how humans are so drawn to them, so inspired by them. And I thought, why not do a mask table? You know, offer to do those fabulous life masks for people. Those plaster ones. We couldn't do too many, so we'd charge a lot. Maybe twenty-five dollars per mask. Melvyn Searle could direct. And maybe Abbey could help again. And you. And Aniela, Brygida's daughter. She's such a good artist. Don't you think people would really be keen to see their own faces reproduced? And how hard can it be to smear plaster bandages on somebody's face?"

"I don't know, Mer. Isn't it kind of spooky?"

Melvyn can hardly believe what he is hearing when Meredith telephones. The words blur.

"Christmas bazaar … mask booth … do life masks … would you be interested in helping?"

"We'd have to get going on the planning right away. Could you come over this evening?"

As soon as he enters the house, Hildy goes berserk. She lunges and snarls and snaps at him. Meredith can barely restrain her and yells to Thompson to help. He and Darcy come running. They try to get Hildy to sit, but she is in a frenzy of barking and growling, pulling hard at her collar. She is very strong and determined to get at Melvyn. Thompson grabs her muzzle and squeezes. "Wrong, Hildy! Wrong! Enough!" Hildy tries to extricate herself. Meredith runs to get her leash and Thompson high-collars her and pulls her away out of the room. Meredith and Melvyn and Darcy can hear her deep, angry bark even with the door to the den closed.

"That was too scary," Darcy says. "I thought she was really going to bite you."

Melvyn is shaking. He does not like dogs. "I thought she was, too. She's pretty vicious."

"Oh, Melvyn. Are you all right?" Meredith asks. "I am so, so sorry. We're so sorry. She's really a lovely dog. She's been abused. We've been working extremely hard with her. She's been so good. This is a real setback. You must remind her of someone."

"Maybe the guy who was mean to her," says Darcy and goes into the den with her father and the dog.

# 15

## DECEMBER

**M**elvyn constantly relives that terrible night at the Warnes' house. Not only was he almost attacked by a savage dog, he did not ever get to be with Darcy. She was the reason he was so keen to go over to the Warnes' home to help Meredith plan the mask booth. He imagined Darcy would be around and that he'd get to be playful with her. But she stayed with her father the whole evening and then went upstairs to bed. She did come into the dining room where he and Meredith were working to say good night.

She kissed and hugged her mother, who said, "I'll be up in a minute."

Melvyn had never experienced such longing. He could feel her arms about his neck, her breath against his face, her sweet lips on his cheek. He thought she might come over to him and he could at least put his hand on her arm, but she merely turned to him as she left the room and said good night, without even saying his name.

He is beside himself with frustration and desire. He does not recall feeling this way after Audrey. No little girl had caught his eye. He lived his life. Until Lizbett. His experience with her has aroused urges in him that he feels he cannot suppress. Perhaps it was seeing the mesmerizing Darcy so soon after. Perhaps because it is the same family. There is a sibling magnetism he can't get out of his head. And with her docile, dark radiance, Darcy has become the more appealing.

But he's being blocked at every possible opening. First, the withdrawal from the mask class and now what appears to have been a kind of dismissal at Darcy's house. He can't figure out what's gone wrong.

Usually when he selects a target, everything falls into place.

Even the possibilities for connection with another girl are limited now. Winter is closing in. The parks are empty. His mask class is finished for the term.

He has taken to hanging out in shopping malls, which are crowded with parents and their children because of Christmas. They are gaudy, gilded places, noisy with Christmas music. The lines for Santa are long; the waiting children restless and recalcitrant. And they are little and only interested in giving their gift orders for Christmas morning. He looks for young girls and occasionally will see an appealing group hanging around one of the jewellery kiosks or the racks of clothes displayed outside the stores. But he never sees a girl alone; never has the opportunity to start a conversation with one. Not that that would be possible, in any case, without arousing suspicion. That is something he doesn't do. Arouse suspicion. He must always be beyond suspicion. So he just wanders around, lingers where he sees potential connections. And feels more and more thwarted.

At home, he has magazines, lots of them, with graphic pictures of girl children involved in some kind of sexual act. These only increase his urges and make him jealous. That should be him! He buys little girls' dresses and imagines Darcy happily putting them on for him.

His cravings are so powerful that he is considering a girlfriend. He has only ever had one girlfriend. She was a classmate in university. He had not felt any need to be with the young women in his classes. He was living at home and often went into his stepsister, Alice's, bedroom, as he had been doing for years. But one girl, Marta, he thinks her name was, was nice to him and since she was petite with a soft, babyish voice, he went along with her as best he could. He wasn't a good conversationalist. Talking to adults stopped up his throat. He could talk to children easily because they were so expectant and uncritical. But adults judged his responses, which he thought were never articulate or thoughtful enough. He could always hear his father's scathing comments.

But Marta seemed shy, too, and he discovered if he talked to her the way he'd talk to a child, simply and animatedly, she responded. They had their anthropology class in common and he loved what he was studying.

They went to a couple of movies and drank a lot of coffee in the student cafeteria, but when she invited him up to her room in the dorm, he panicked. She wasn't the little girl he fantasized her as being. She was an adult with an adult female body and strong female responses. He couldn't handle her deep breathing, her sighs, the undulating of her hips. He stopped seeing her.

But he is older now. More assured, he thinks.

When he shows up at the school to help Meredith set up the mask booth, he is feeling full of himself. Not only will he be applying plaster bandages to the faces of a number of girls, he is going to be seeing Darcy.

There are a couple of dozen booths in the school gym, all hung with white lights intertwined with pine garlands. The enticing scent of cinnamon and cloves from the hot spiced cider fills the room. Each booth offers a way to spend money: jams, jellies and relishes, brownies and cakes and pies and chocolate chip cookies, silk floral arrangements, candles, perfumed bath products, several displays of jewellery, some in sterling silver and semi-precious stones that are quite expensive. Large cedar wreaths with big red satin bows are available. People line up for the carnival games and the chili and beer booth. In the centre of the room stands a tall, twinkling tree covered with decorations made by the students, all of which are for sale. The choir sings carols on the stage, and then the gymnastics team gives demonstrations.

Besides the flea market, the life-mask booth is the most popular at the bazaar. Meredith is thrilled that she had the idea. Melvyn is thrilled that the booth is near the stage where he can watch the young gymnasts perform. And he gets to meet Aniela. With her art-school expertise, Meredith has asked her to help with the masks. Aniela is a pretty slip of a thing, barely five feet and skinny with long, brown hair that gathers in becoming wisps around her wan, freckled face. Her eyes are light and seem haunted. Her mouth has distinct curves, but is thin and often pursed, giving her an air of concern. She could be the suffering maiden in a pre-Raphaelite painting.

She has almost no breasts to speak of, which Melvyn notices first thing. Breasts and pubic hair are repugnant to him. Aniela has a shy confidence: she opens up superficially, but guards what's within. She is not a little girl, but she looks like one and she's much younger than Melvyn, maybe ten years or more. (In fact it is eight.) He has the idea it would be easy to pretend with her.

Even with Aniela, Meredith, Melvyn, Abbey, Kyle, and Thompson applying the plaster, they still cannot accommodate the number of requests. It takes a while to prepare each person: cover the hair, smear on the Vaseline and place the pieces of flannel before actually smoothing on the bandages. And there is the hardening time, at least twenty minutes before the mask can be removed. But then, there it is. A beautiful, smooth white visage, not a representation, but the face itself. Many, many faces have been given eternal preservation. People think they will make a great Christmas presents.

Melvyn does a number of girls. They are squirmy and giggly, self-conscious at having their face repeatedly stroked by a strange man as his fingers delicately find the contours of their faces. Having the lips traced makes them feel the most awkward. But since Melvyn is so encouraging and talks to them just as a friend would, they relax.

"You're doing just great. No laughing, now. C'mon. Just be cool and relax. Wow. You're such a good girl," he says.

Later, Melvyn says to Meredith, "I was hoping to do Darcy for you."

"Oh, thanks," she replies. "I offered it to her, but she said she didn't want it. Meredith didn't add that he gave Darcy "the creeps."

Melvyn invites Aniela to visit the mask exhibits and she gives him a tour of the art gallery where she works, which is in the same district as the museum. They go for walks nearby on a street of elegant shops and look in all the extravagant Christmas windows. They eat lunch in the museum cafeteria. He takes her to see *Labyrinth*, which she loves. They go to a performance of *The Messiah* with original instruments at the Church of the Redeemer. Finally he gets up the courage to invite her to his flat to see his mask collection. He pours them wine and they sit in his living room and talk more about masks, his masks.

He asks her if she'd like him to do her life mask. She does not like the idea of being confined in this intimate space with plaster on her face.

"Oh, I don't know," she says.

"Why?"

"Maybe … maybe … I'm claustrophobic. I might feel trapped. I'm not sure."

"Don't you trust me?" Melvyn asks. "It's not painful."

"Oh, no. No. It's not that. I just don't know about lying still for twenty or so minutes being unable to see."

"Why don't we leave the eyes open, then? You'll actually like it. It's very soothing. I'll put on some nice music. And you can always take it off at any time, if you feel uncomfortable."

She consents, still somewhat reluctant. He leads her into the kitchen where she sits with her head back on a pillow on the table. First, she tucks her hair into a plastic bag and smears Vaseline on her face, and Melvyn goes back into the living room and puts on a tape of the same Gregorian chants he had played for Lizbett.

"Here," he says, pouring her some more wine. "Drink this while you can."

A few quick gulps loosen her.

Then she reclines her head and he delicately applies the pieces of flannel over her face. She closes her eyes feeling uncomfortable staring into his eyes and at his face, which is set in concentration. The plaster bandages warm as he smoothes them over the planes of her face. Would she have ever thought there were so many nerve endings there? With each careful, tender, implicit stroke of his fingers, she feels heat, not only on her face, but in her whole body. Her face, all its dimensions, the rise of her cheeks, the sweep of her forehead, the curve of her chin, the impressionability of her lips, have all merged into an organ of arousal. She opens her eyes and sees in his a heightened look of intent, which unsettles her, but his words are soothing. He almost coos. "You're doing so well. Just lie still. You're such a good, sweet girl … a good sweet girl."

She has never heard these words from a man before, said with such soft urgency. She feels trust and relaxes.

Next they go to a performance of *The Nutcracker* and she invites him to the Christmas party at the gallery, and he takes her to the museum's party. Back at his flat once again, they drink wine and he takes the maiden Noh mask from the wall and puts it on her. He then puts on his lord of the harvest mask and slowly begins to undress her, looking purposefully into her eyes from behind his mask, into hers behind her mask. He feels both masks charge. His look, or rather the look from the mask, disturbs her.

She feels she is with a leering stranger. She starts to pull of the mask and he says gruffly, "Leave it on!" which startles her. She is actually timid with men, always uncomfortable with them. Her father, Tadeusz a poet, is a tormented, fractured man, and his creativity often turns surly and destructive. At five, he and his family of six were interned in Auschwitz. Only Tadeusz survived. Thus, he can flail in unpredictable rage and strike out. Aniela and her mother both have had the contusions to show for it, the sorry, wary sense of self.

Aniela likes Melvyn because he seems so gentle and solicitous, so predictable, treating her almost the way you'd treat a child. This allows her to behave in a girlish, receptive way, something she's never had the freedom to do and not feel threatened. So she's not quite sure how to react when she hears the harsh voice. What kicks in is fear, obedience, and she whimpers, "Please don't hurt me." This excites him and what follows is a brutal sex act she had not anticipated.

But she remains drawn to him, compliant, compelled to do what he asks. He is what she knows, after all. And when it is over, when they are out of the bedroom, he is engaging and attentive, quite fun, really, and very affectionate, and she is lonely. He continues to call her "his sweet little girl." This alone, is seductive.

They continue to do social things, the theatre, concerts, but his sexual demands escalate. Even though he says he loves her, he is extremely rough. He attaches her to his bedposts with duct tape. He inserts foreign objects into her vagina. A carved piece of wooden dowel. Once he forced a glass pestle into her. She often bleeds. He insists on anal intercourse, which offends her. He tells her what a good, good girl, what a sweet girl she is. And she submits. They always wear masks.

Melvyn is not thrilled with Aniela, but he is pleased with her availability. And she gives his life a degree of normalcy, which he likes. Like the way he and Stacey used to take little Alice for walks. They spend most weekends together and he expects to have sex frequently. What amazes him is she is so yielding. He asks her to protest, to beg him not to hurt her. And she does. And then he does.

Even Darcy is not looking forward to Christmas. She feels instinctively that what is usually a joyous and extravagant time will be solemn and austere without Lizbett. How can she feel excited about presents and her stocking and singing and celebrating with a dead sister? She always takes over everything.

Meredith is particularly dreading it because it is an insidious reminder of what she was doing when Lizbett died. Christmas now means Lizbett's death to her. Nothing more. The garish signs of the season all around her are an affront, the ubiquitous music an assault. She remembers vividly the steamy July day, her Australian Christmas reminiscence that had so put her in the mood. She remembers the Christmas set, the lavish decorations, the elegant serving pieces. She remembers the black clouds, the teeming rain, and worrying that Lizbett was out in it. She remembers that last phone call.

She is walking to the dog park with Hildy and Darcy. The wind is harsh. Only Hildy loves the new snow. She tunnels her nose into it; rolls in it, snorting like a horse.

Darcy says, "I guess we won't have Christmas this year."

Hildy is pulling at the leash, barreling into the banks of snow along the sidewalk. "Don't let her pull, sweetie. Hold her back. Make her heel."

"You didn't answer. I said, 'I guess we won't have Christmas this year.'"

"I was thinking, I'm sorry. I don't know what we'll do, lovey. It's going to be a very difficult time for all of us."

"Why don't we go someplace she never was so we don't have to think of her there. We could go to the ski cabin. She was never ever there, was she?"

"No, I don't think so."

"So, it's just our place. Our place with Hildy."

They invite Abbey and Kyle and Nellie to come along. And Lew Chan and his new partner, a florist called Selby Ransome.

From the moment they arrive, they feel freed. The landscape is cushioned in deep snow. There are massive drifts, whose edges look sculpted in the sunlight. In the woods, the rises are defined by the soft purple shadows of the trees. The whiteness is infinite, its icy starkness a welcome contrast to all the showy artifice they left behind.

Selby is accompanied by his two six-month-old bull terriers, Vita and Vanessa. Hildy is besotted. The dogs spend most of their time tumbling out the door into the snow and back in again, over and over.

There are no Christmas decorations. Selby has brought leftover flowers from his shop: long-stemmed crimson and creamy roses, and he makes a bursting arrangement with pine boughs. Darcy pushes for a tree. So they cut a small one in the bush, stick it in a bucket of potting soil, and decorate it with strings of popcorn and cranberries. Darcy makes a star out of cardboard and tinfoil. There are few presents this year and when they put them under the tree the dogs keeps getting into them and shredding the paper. They have to be put on the mantel. Not only that, the dogs like the popcorn, but spit out the cranberries.

The cabin has a small electric keyboard so Nellie can play carols and after Christmas Eve dinner, with a fire blazing, they sip egg nog and brandy and they sing and sing.

Darcy opens her standard Christmas Eve gift, a new nightie, and though she protests, they send her off to bed. Hildy goes with her. Abbey suggests charades and they play until after midnight, rowdy from all the alcohol. Selby stumps his team with, "Now is the winter of our discontent made glorious summer by this sun of York ..."

Meredith hangs Darcy's hand-knitted stocking on the mantel. Undone by the abject aloneness of the festive object where normally she would have placed two, she caves.

Christmas morning brings streaming sunshine. The glittering snow is broken by Hildy's great leaps when Thompson lets her out first thing.

Darcy gets up and goes out for her stocking. The room feels very, very quiet and empty. She sits on a sofa with Hildy beside her, sucking on a candy cane while she begins to pull out the goodies. She gives the dog a gumdrop, which gets stuck in her teeth.

Memories of this stocking ritual every year with Lizbett overwhelm her. Of taking out the little treasures at the top and then of finding in the toe an Asian pear, a huge navel orange, and chocolate bonbons. This is the first time since Lizbett's death that she has felt impossibly alone. An only child. A child with no sisters or brothers. She sees herself suddenly in that big space, which could be life, really, all by herself. Before, she has thought about Lizbett's being gone, but not about her own loneliness. She was used to being by herself with her parents, when Lizbett was at lessons or rehearsals or performances. Whatever. Lizbett was coming. Lizbett would be home. On this Christmas morning without her sister, Darcy is aware of how profoundly this aloneness is going to affect her life. She has lost someone to share things with, to compare notes with, to tell secrets to, to hear secrets from. From now on, for festivities she shared with Lizbett, like opening her stocking, like looking for eggs at Easter, there will be only her.

After Thompson pours Bloody Marys for everyone except Nellie and Meredith, who have champagne and orange juice, they all sit down to unwrap. Thompson gives Meredith a Chinese ivory fan with a jade inlay. She gives him a yellow cashmere V-neck sweater to add to the drawerful he already owns and a book about Georgia O'Keeffe and Alfred Stieglitz. Selby and Lew give each other leather handbags. Nellie gets flowered gardening gloves and a coffee-table book with Audubon birds. And Kyle gives Abbey a ring, a sparkly oval citrine with diamonds. She doesn't know what hand to put it on and he slides it on her left and says, "Marry me," and everyone cheers. Meredith leaps up and hugs her and Abbey apologizes. "Oh, Mer, I hope it's all right."

"Losing Lizbett doesn't mean we should stop living," Meredith replies.

Darcy gets books, books, and more books, and a little stereo for her room.

But Hildy. Hildy gets dog chocolates, a leather collar studded with crystals, a sheepskin cover for her bed, several new squeaky toys, a massive rubber bone, a big stuffed elephant, and a bag full of rawhide candy canes. And Lew gives her a sterling-silver dog tag in the shape of a fire hydrant.

Vanessa and Vita get sheepskin coats.

Hildy sits snuggled on the sofa between Thompson and Darcy, her eyes seeming to reflect her pleasure at being given so much love and attention. It's hard to imagine her ever having had cigarettes stubbed out on her flesh. In this lively, loving gathering, it's hard to imagine anyone is missing a murdered girl.

After a brunch, they take off skiing. Thompson, at the head with Hildy, has to break trail. The snow is deep, dry, and powdery. The wind lifts it in glistening gusts all around them. The dogs dart and dodge in and out between the skiers, ruining their tracks, and they shout, "Get out of the way!" The short-legged terriers have trouble keeping up. Once Hildy stopped mid-trail to do a poop and Selby skied right into her and tumbled. Darcy does very well. Their school has taken them cross-country skiing at a conservation area so she knows how to handle her skis.

Thompson finds a comfortable, rhythmic glide. *Swish-swish. Swish-swish*, poles squeaking as they dig. He hears a waltz in his head. Above the black mesh of barren branches, the sky is an unsparing blue. Embedded in it, the sun glares. It skitters playfully in and out of the trees, as if it is chasing them. But the golden brilliance is deceiving. Even as it glazes the snow, it withholds any warmth. Thompson is perspiring, but his breath is frosting his scarf and eyelashes and his fingers are tingling.

He can hear the harmonic rasp of the others' skis behind him. Ahead, he sees their magnificent dog making great, graceful leaps and he feels a rush of gladness to see her there. He is thinking how lucky they are to have her. In fact, he is thinking about luck. Is it something you inherit, something you find, or something that finds you? Does it have to do with choice? Has he made lucky choices or have these circumstances just fallen upon him, beneficently, willy-nilly? He wonders if it is about being blessed or is that purely spiritual? Or is luck something more crass, more earthly, more defineable? If so, how would he define it? The possession of good health, good things, being attendant to good events? He is thinking how lucky they are to have the secluded, shimmering beauty of these woods; how lucky to know people with a big ski cabin they can share. The aesthetics and plenty of their Christmas feel lucky. So does having as companionable a friend as Lew Chan and as charming and devoted a mother as Nellie. He feels lucky to have a job he loves, that pays so well. And though she is distant and sorrowful, he feels lucky to have Meredith because he loves her deeply. And he feels luckiest of all for his darling Darcy, whose bravery and curiosity have sustained him.

He is not going to think how unlucky they are.

# 16

## JANUARY AND FEBRUARY

Melvyn Searle is making new masks. He is bored with the ones he has been using. For himself, he is making a wolf mask using pieces of unplucked beaver. For Aniela, he is making a fairy-tale mask … a creamy-skinned, innocent princess with puckered ruby lips, cherry cheeks, and thick black lashes. He has used a form from his mould of Lizbett's face.

The wolf mask gives him a feral confidence. He likes the sense that he is not human; that he is pure instinct, with no thought or emotion interfering with his takeover of the delicate princess. He becomes all flesh, all muscle, subduing, penetrating, devouring. He could rip her open. He could consume her. Instead, he grips her throat with savage force until she passes out.

"Thanks for this, Thompson," Irme says to him. They are having lunch at a little pasta restaurant near the studio, the one he and Meredith always went to.

"Well, I just wanted to say thanks to you. You've really been good to work with. I appreciate it."

"But not as good as … Meredith. You surely miss her." There is a lilt to her words, a subtle, appealing little accent. And she is extremely beautiful: full-figured with luminous, pale skin, dark, deep-set eyes, one slightly wandering, and masses of chestnut hair that she wears loose across her shoulders. Her teeth aren't perfect, but her plump lips are. Thompson now feels comfortable with her, though not particularly stimulated. She is an unanimated woman, slow and terse in her responses, lackadaisical, almost. He knows she's not disinterested. In fact, her keenness is something he is aware of.

"We were a great team," says Thompson, surprising himself with the past tense. "We've worked together for a number of years and know instinctively each other's techniques and flaws. I admire her work … I admire her very much. Meredith is one of the best, for sure."

"I'm working on getting there, myself," Irme says.

"Can I give you a tip?"

"Sure."

"Try to put some more zing in what you do. Reach a bit. Study the old masters. That's what Meredith did. She actually used to paint exquisitely detailed still lifes of food."

"I've heard she was very good. I'll try her focus. I majored in graphics. I'm more about line. Do you think she'll come back?"

"Think more about balance and also contrasts of shape and of tone and texture," Thompson suggests. "And proportion. And harmony. And drama. In the end, it's all fine art … Will she come back? I hope so. But I don't know. I'm not sure. We don't talk about it."

"She maybe has to find her own way."

"I'm sure that's what she's trying to do. She was such an affectionate screwball. I mean, she's still amazing, really, when you think about it. She volunteers every Saturday at Settlement House. And she's always doing stuff at Darcy's school: field trips and fund-raising. Right now she's painting sets for the school play. And we go away on the weekends. Plus we have this dog who takes up most of her time."

"You have a dog?"

"She's a Great Dane … just a year. Brunhilde … Hildy."

"Oh, great name. The warrior princess. I love Great Danes," says Irme. "We had them when I was growing up in Poland. The tan ones. They have wonderful personalities."

"This one's called blue. It's actually a steely grey. But she was abused. She has a tendency to be aggressive … especially with teenage boys or anyone who resembles them. Don't get me wrong. She's wonderful. I don't know how we could have got this far without her. Especially Darcy. The dog is kind of like an absorbent. All our anguish … the misconnection … the misunderstandings and unsaid words go into her. And she takes them and gives us back what we need most. Not love exactly. That's a given. But solidity … stability … security, maybe. And, well, big slurps."

He felt he has never talked so much in his life. Irme has broken a dam.

Irme laughs at the slurps comment. "Don't forget the drool."

"Yes, when she shakes her head, it splatters on the walls."

"But dogs are such healers, you know? Aren't they?" she continues. "That sounds kind of, well, crazy, but they have a sort of power to understand and give comfort … to actually … what is the word … salve … pain. I hope that doesn't seem like hocus-pocus or something."

"No, it seems like exactly what's happening at our house."

Irme reaches out and places a hand over Thompson's. "You know," she says. "I am a very good listener. I will be very happy to hear about what you are going through … what you've been through. Everybody needs to talk about what's going on inside them; to connect on a certain internal level, I mean. If Meredith isn't able to give you that, I … well, I'm already a sort of substitute for her … I will love to be your friend."

Allan phones and asks Meredith to lunch.

"What for?" she asks.

He laughs. "No reason."

She feels an inexplicable rash pull and says "Sure."

They meet on a dreary, drizzly January day at a sushi restaurant they used to frequent. The street corners are blocked with piles of filthy slush. Jumping over them lands Meredith in a puddle. She feels a little rush when she sees him. She knows instantly why she gave in. He is effusive, magnetic. He is a little shorter than she, and sturdy. His hairline is receding, but the rest of his dark hair is pulled back in a ponytail. He is wearing a buttery tan leather jacket and brown cords. His eyes flash with his big smile.

"Mrs. Warne," Allan says after giving her a hug. "You look absolutely fabulous."

Her heart is racing and she hates it. "You're not supposed to say that to women who have lost weight. It encourages eating disorders."

"Well, you looked good before, too."

They sit down at the sushi bar and order a warm sake. "I think about you a lot," he says, taking her hands in his.

She pulls them away. "I have other things to think about."

"Sorry."

"No. I am," she replies. "I thought a lot about you, before … too. I mean, right after. In fact, I was determined to win you back. I started looking for apartments."

"You could never have left Thompson or your girls."

"The girls would have come with me."

"That was never us," he offers. "We were never about permanence. We were about sensation."

"It was sensational, wasn't it?" He gives her a wry smile, a wicked seductive smile. "What …?" she asks.

"I'm thinking about you naked," Allan says.

She is instantly, brutally grounded. "Don't," she says harshly. "I don't do naked."

"You have sex with your clothes on or you don't have sex?"

"I don't have sex," Meredith says.

"Ever?"

"Ever."

"Since when?" he asks.

"Since the day my eleven-year-old daughter was raped and sodomized and strangled."

"Oh, god, Meredith. Oh god. I am so sorry. I am so very, very sorry."

"I can only see a penis as a cruel weapon."

"And Thompson is …?"

"I don't know. We don't talk. I sleep in Lizbett's room."

"That doesn't sound … healthy … you haven't considered counselling?"

"I don't want to have to go and talk about my thoughts after already thinking about them all day long. It seems like twice-over misery. Besides, I have faith it's all going to wear off, you know? Once, when I was a kid doing calligraphy with a straight pen at the kitchen table, I knocked over the India ink and it spilled all over my fingers. It wouldn't wash off and my mother said, 'It will have to wear off.' And it did. Gradually, it was gone. It just got sloughed off. That's how it will be with Lizbett. The memory will be there, but the pain will … wear off. And we have this dog. She really helps."

He had to laugh. "Your dog is a therapist? I don't get it."

"Have you ever had a dog?"

"No."

"Then you wouldn't get it. And I couldn't explain it."

"Try me," he says.

"Well, she … her name is Brunhilde … Hildy … is a Great Dane, so her presence is already huge. She's really demanding, but she's also very giving."

"What can a dog give but shit and shedding and a nose in your crotch?"

"Massive, massive love, patience, humour, empathy, a listening ear."

"C'mon, Meredith. Empathy? A listening ear? You're joking."

"No really. It's just that she's so receptive and seems to understand everything. You have to see her face, the way her eyes wink and her eyebrows twitch. And those droopy, penetrating eyes. She has a huge number of expressions. I see the empathy in her face, poignancy, concern. She gets really upset when I cry."

"I'm glad for you, Meredith."

The Warnes have invited Lizbett's five friends to the ski cabin for Lizbett's birthday. They had to rent a van to fit everyone and their equipment in. But they arrive and unload and immediately the place changes from a serene retreat to a girls' camp with whoops and shrieks and everyone talking over everyone else. There are elevated discussions over who gets what bed in the loft. In the end it is decided that the oldest girls get the top bunks. Darcy wants to sleep up there with them, but Meredith feels that would inhibit the girls so she says no. Darcy has a tantrum and the girls say it's all right, really. She can sleep with them. So Darcy does.

Hildy accepts all the girls, but Lauren, of whom she is still wary, but at least she doesn't growl.

For dinner they make pizza. Meredith has brought all the usual ingredients, plus things like grilled artichokes, pineapple, and gorgonzola cheese. They make four different pizzas, each thick with a spontaneous pile of toppings. And then they say, "Let's make one for Lizbett! Let's make her favourite."

They put together a fifth pizza with bacon, onions, spinach, and extra mozzarella.

Everything tastes delicious at the cabin.

The girls have as much fun making ice cream sundaes for dessert, swirling spoonfuls of hot fudge on the ice cream and taking turns squirting the whipped cream into each other's mouths.

Thompson suggests they walk to the end of the lane and back, and, swathed in all the requisite gear, they exit the bright warmth of the cabin for the frigid blackness of the wilderness. There is no moon and no stars. The January thaw is over, the way is icy. Their footing is precarious on the hard surface, but it is exhilarating to be out in the inky, biting air. Unless they walk backwards and look at the comforting lights of the cabin, they can barely see the person in front of them. "I can't see a thing. Help! Hold on to me! This is so scary!" They move forward slowly, placing each foot carefully, holding hands until they make it to the end of the lane, and, turning around, they see a spectacular display of the Northern Lights: great, luminous, voluminous undulations of colour. They whip extravagantly across the dark sky, trailing streamers of green and white and rose.

The girls erupt. "Omigod. That is so amazing. I can't believe it. I've never seen anything like this. It's magical. It's like fireworks!"

That night in bed, listening to the restrained hysterics of five sleepless preadolescent girls, Meredith thinks what a pleasure it is to have elated, innocent female sounds above her. Lizbett would have been twelve. Lizbett, twelve! The last year of her girlhood. Next year she would have been a teenager with all its attendant hurdles and pitfalls.

Lizbett had been so self-assured, so guaranteed of her future. Guaranteed by whom? By what? By her looks, her charm, her brains, her ambition, her talent? By her fortunate birth with loving, successful parents? The older sister of one of Meredith's friends was in rehab for drug abuse. She'd been an A student, a champion gymnast. Lauren's parents were as ordinary, as privileged as the Warnes. What were guarantees? They didn't exist. Life was about never knowing, regardless of seeming certainties, about never knowing what was ahead or above or around the corner. All one had were the successes, failures, pleasure, and pain of what lay behind and the here and now. This second. This minute. That was all. One could trust nothing. Because in a nanosecond, life could turn unbearably, shockingly cruel.

Meredith was fearful. Every day she was fearful. She had never felt this way before. She'd been blithe, sanguine, overreaching. Ignorant. Now she was fully, mercilessly knowledgeable that there was absolutely no knowing. Most of all, she wanted the past obliterated so she didn't ever have to look behind to their loss and feel the agony.

She brings herself back to the girls, the hullabaloo above. How different would it be if Lizbett were up there? Would her spirited voice carry over the others? Would Meredith fall into a restless sleep, knowing the girls would talk all night? Would they keep her awake and annoy her? Would she and Thompson talk about the evening, the unexpected beauty of the Northern Lights? Would they make quiet love? Would Lizbett have allowed Darcy up with them?

She is overcome with an uncharacteristic, unsparing bitterness, not against the girls whose presence she finds so elevating, but against life itself, for hurling her into this tarry abyss. She cannot move for the black, engulfing matter. How can she possibly extricate herself? Will she ever?

Thompson is not thinking about the giddy girls. He is not thinking about the sensational Aurora Borealis. He is wondering, as he has so many times before, where Meredith has gone. Because she has … gone. Disappeared. He feels he has lost her, not that he ever "had" her in the possession sense, but in the sense of communion. They had a perfectly tuned connection. Like good improv. They anticipated one another's thoughts and actions and were usually synchronous. Now, where once there had been a vibrant, overt, forthright being, there is a tuned-out, mute automaton. What has happened to her boisterous voice, the clever ripostes, the obstreperous laugh, the one that made everyone turn their heads?

He sees her interact with Darcy, but she simply doesn't "click in" with him. She negates him. She communicates to him through Darcy. "Tell Daddy to do …." "Remind Daddy he needs to …." "Ask Daddy if …." He has tried to interest her when they are alone, which isn't often. "Mer," he says, "let's …." And she always too automatically responds, "I'm busy. I'm tired. I'm on my way out. I've got a load of laundry in. I have to get some dog food; we're almost out. I'm engrossed in this book, this program. I'm just going to bed …." And so on.

He can't figure out why, given their former closeness, their keen ability to read each other's needs (they were like mutual seismographs), she won't let him comfort her, why she won't comfort him. It's as if she does not believe he is grieving. It's as if she's been reborn into an insentient being; someone he can't fathom. Can one alter one's own persona, instigate a sea change, or is such a phenomenon spontaneous? How can a being be so completely transformed into an entirely different one and still inhabit the same body?

That body. He is thinking about how much he misses the contact of her once-receptive body, not only for affirming hugs and light, casual kisses, but lingering ones. For sex. He has been thinking a lot about sex, how desperately he wants to have it. It has been six months since he and Meredith last made love and even then it wasn't great. It was a perfunctory morning quickie. He wonders if there's something inadequate about his character that he wants sex so badly when he had a daughter killed for sex. He wonders if he's evil. He wonders if his grief is flawed or shallow. Or is he simply wrong? But he doesn't think so. He could not possibly feel more sorrow, more despair, more agony ... there aren't enough nouns to describe how he feels about Lizbett's death. But he sees his preoccupation with sex as an appetite, like eating, something separate from suffering, something necessary, and, yes, pleasurable, even in the midst of dire pain. Does a grilled filet mignon oozing red juices and drizzled in Béarnaise taste any less fine if one is mourning? Granted, appetite recedes in the beginning when the shock flattens everything. He can remember feeling anaesthetized. All his senses were dead. Light was grey. Sound was muffled. Food was tasteless and odourless. All surfaces were without definition. But after a while he needed light. He craved music. He was hungry for the flavours and scents of eating. A simmering lamb stew. An apple pie. Bacon and eggs. Did that mean he missed Lizbett less? He couldn't miss Lizbett more. He aches for her. But he is really horny. At home he would masturbate. He has done so frequently. Even here, he might think of reaching over to Meredith and trying to initiate something, but what does he do about the 130-pound beast breathing heavily between them?

He starts to think about great sex: not kinky sex. Not acrobatic sex. Just plain old great everyday sex. The lights are low. No, maybe it's a hot, sunny afternoon, the bed an expanse of cool white. There's an icy bottle of Sauvignon Blanc, some kind of quiet, easy piano jazz ... Don Shirley. Start with just drinking and looking and slow touching, a bit of teasing. Lots of tender lingering. Move to soft kisses, then hard, long, deep ones, as deep as possible, endless kisses. Time with the breasts, the lovely breasts with the taut nipples. Cup. Stroke. Nuzzle. Suck. Pinch the nipples, rub them between his fingertips and hear her moan. Then down, down, lips on her smooth stomach, face in her already damp pubic hair, then gently part her, now mouth and tongue inside, delicious firm knob, not knowing if it's her moisture or his saliva making the wondrous slither. Then she pulls him up and kisses her taste from him and goes down on him, prodding his balls, nibbling the rim of his cock, then taking all of it down her throat and back up, mouth tight on him, pulling up hard over and over. She starts to slide up to him but changes her mind and goes back down and gives him more and more.

"Too delicious," she says.

He warns her he's about to come and she leaves him and lies on her back and opens her legs wide, wide and says touch me, make me come. And he puts his fingers deep in her heat and then finds her clitoris and she says oh, yes, like that, and he strokes and strokes and slips his fingers in and around and feels the silken, swollen flesh and her hips thrash and she throws her head back in a roar. More, more, she says and he keeps going and she roars again and then she climbs astride him and rides him hard, breasts swaying and then she says omigod three times and he rolls her on her back and enters her and she holds her legs high and he pounds and he pounds and he pounds until he roars.

The girls were up most of the night, finally falling asleep in the early morning. Meredith left them until after 11:00 a.m. They all descended in their nighties, yawning and starving and Meredith says, "Why don't you make pancakes? There are blueberries in the fridge." And the kitchen becomes a frenzy of six girls, six incessant voices, twelve hands sifting flour, breaking eggs, pouring milk, and beating the batter. The counter is a mess. Then the griddle sizzles and smokes and again and again, someone drops a spoonful of batter onto the browning butter, enough times to make two or three or four each. They eat in shifts, as the pancakes are done, lathering them with butter and maple syrup and when they are finished everything is sticky and greasy and Thompson says, "Now, I'll help you clean up."

They go out skiing in the afternoon, but rather than do the up-and-down trails in the woods, Thompson takes them out across several fields. There is a crust on the surface of the snow that gleams like glass. At the end of the third field, there is a relatively steep hill and they take off their skis and climb it and snowplow down. The snow is fast and the girls are full of daring. On the way back, by the frozen pond, they light a bonfire in the pit.

Meredith pours everyone steaming cocoa from a Thermos, and when she returns from finding sticks to roast the marshmallows, she hears Lauren say, "I'm having so much fun that I've barely thought of Lizbett."

"Neither have I," says Dominique. "I feel terrible."

So does Meredith.

The girls have been asked to come prepared to perform, and, after dinner that night, all five of them do a lip synch of Cyndi Lauper's "True Colours." Thompson plays a ragtime piece on the keyboard and Darcy dances. Meredith reads a passage from *Little Women*, which she'd seen on a bookshelf. All of the girls are curious to know what happens. Claire says, "I wonder what Lizbett would have done?"

"She wouldn't have lip synched," replies Daphne.

That night the girls do not talk for long.

The next morning there is a haze of flurries, which, by the end of bacon and eggs and clean-up, have become large flakes. A strong wind hurls them into a whirling, opaque screen. They obscure the row of maple trees on the far hill.

"It's a whiteout," says Thompson. "Best not to leave."

The snow falls heavily all day. The windows seem covered in gauze. A big drift piles against the door and they have to shovel it away to let Hildy outside. As they sit down to a dinner of chicken noodle soup and hot dogs, the power goes out.

The girls cry out. "Yikes! This is so spooky."

Fortunately, the table already has some lit candles and Meredith scrounges and finds more. As well, there are several oil lamps and when those are going, the place glows with coziness. Thompson builds up the fire and it blazes and crackles, giving even more light. The only thing to worry about is the electric heat.

After dinner it is noticeably cooler and they all curl up with blankets before the fire.

Then Meredith says, "I have a great idea! Why don't we get out the Ouija board? I saw one in the games closet. Who has ever done a Ouija board?"

No one had.

"Well, it's a sort of magic board that talks. It's really fun."

"I don't know, Mer," Thompson says. "Do you really think it's such a good idea?"

"Oh, Sonny. It's just a game. It might not even work."

They set up the board on the floor in front of the fire. Each of the five girls places an index finger on the wand. Meredith and Thompson and Darcy watch.

"What do we do?" asks Lauren.

"Ask it a question," Meredith replies.

"Like what?"

"Well, ask, 'where are we?'"

"Okay," says Daphne. "Where are we?"

The wand doesn't move. Meredith says, "Ask it again."

"Where are we?"

Slowly the wand begins to move, randomly at first, and then it goes quickly to the letters *f-o-r-e-s-t*.

"Whoa! That was really amazing! How did it know that?"

"Ask 'who is here?'" Meredith suggests.

Lauren asks and nothing happens. "Ask again," Meredith says.

"Who is here?"

Suddenly the wand moves again and the girls scream.

"Keep your fingers on!" Meredith says. "Lightly."

The wand moves rapidly now to the number 5 and the letters *g-r-l-s*.

"Five girls!"

"Ask who they are."

The wand spells out, *D-o-m-L-a-u-D-a-p-C-l-a-i-r-J-e-n*.

"I wasn't moving it, I swear," Claire says.

"I sure wasn't."

"It wasn't me."

"I wasn't doing it."

"I know I wasn't," they all insist.

"Ask who else is here."

The wand points to *S-o-n-D-a-r-c-y-M-e-r*.

"How is it doing that?" Dominique asks.

"Isn't it amazing?" Meredith says. "It's a magic force."

Thompson says, "It's the force of one of the group. Everyone else follows."

"Well, it's not me!" the girls all say again.

"Ask if there's anyone else here."

"Like who?" Jen asks.

"Just ask," says Meredith.

"Okay. Is there anyone else here?"

The wand goes to *I-m-h-e-r-e*.

They're right into it now. "Who's I-m?"

*L-i-z-b-e-t-t*.

The girls scream again. "No way! That's scary! That's impossible!"

"Mommy. Mommy. What did it say?" Darcy asks.

"Girls," Thompson says, "I don't think —"

"Sh-sh-sh, Sonny. Let them. It said 'Lizbett,' lovey."

"I don't get it. Who spelled it?"

"It's pretend, sweetheart. Just pretend," Thompson says.

"Are you really Lizbett?" Jen asks the board.

*Y-e-s*.

"Where are you, exactly?" Dominique asks.

*N-e-a-r-y-o-u*.

"What are you doing here?"

*W-i-t-h-y-o-u*.

"Are you always with us?"

The wand doesn't move.

"Ask if she's happy," Meredith says.

"Lizbett, are you happy?"

Nothing from the wand.

"Lizbett, are you happy?"

*N-y-e*. And the wand stops. They repeat the question and nothing happens.

"Lizbett! Lizbett! Do you miss us?" Nothing.

"Lizbett! Are you still with us?"

The wand remains still.

# *17*

# MARCH

Meredith and Abbey are on the plane to Australia. Their mother, Dora, has died of a stroke. She was only sixty-six. It was a sad adjunct to her escalating Alzheimer's.

More than ever, Meredith has been trying to stay collected. Lizbett's death was a searing premature rupture that catapulted her into unfathomable helplessness and despair. Her mother's was anticipated, and, to a certain extent a blessing, though undoubtedly a great loss. Meredith's mother was beloved to her, but she had had a life with her, until the crest of adulthood and had accumulated treasured memories. And they had been apart for a while.

She and Lizbett had been denied that privilege of time.

"I've been thinking, Abbey, about the different kinds of death and one's feelings toward them. Death isn't just death. Each death has its own characteristics; its own identity. And that's what influences your response. I've come to realize that sadness is commensurate with the loss; it isn't absolute. I was feeling horribly guilty that my feelings over losing Mummy don't come close to what I've been through with Lizbett. And this is going to sound terrible, but even with Misty. It's strange, isn't it, but to a certain extent, it's the life — not the death — that defines the mourning. Or maybe, how much life was invested in the death. No, that's not it. It has to do with how the death took the life. Or maybe it's both."

"Mummy was very ill with a really nasty disease," Abbey replied. "And she did suffer. But imagine how you would have felt if she had died when you were a child. I think it's more how much you, yourself, have invested in the one who dies. The closer they are to you, the greater the sorrow. We've been removed, really, for many years from our mother."

Meredith says, "But death is really an assault, isn't it? It ravages you, leaves you in painful, helpless bewilderment. Lizbett's death was vicious. But so was Mummy's. Her Alzheimer's kidnapped her, held her hostage, tortured her. Especially when she was lucid and knew what was happening. And what about Kirk, Lew's lover? His AIDS death was horrific. So prolonged. And he was such a lovely man. Really undeserving of such an end. And there's Eunice Hirsch, that wonderful food writer. You know. We did the photos for her last cookbook. She was killed at a crosswalk. She had two young children."

"Not all death is an assault. Grandma's wasn't."

"But she was old. And lucky … just to go in her sleep. And do you know what else? I've been feeling lots of self-pity for violently losing a daughter and a mother within months of each other. But then I think of Brygida and Tadeusz, whose whole family was killed in a concentration camp. And there are so many survivors like them who saw horrors we can't even imagine. What right do I have to feel such despair when others have suffered much more? Ours is just one small family tragedy."

Abbey says, "Tragedy isn't a contest, Mer. You're allowed your grief. You've been through something unspeakable. No one would expect you not to be a mess. I've been amazed at how well you seem to be doing."

"Not really. And do you know what else I obsess about? HIS death, how much I want it. I want to see him suffer. I want to watch him be afraid to die and then watch him die. But even his death must surely make someone feel sad."

"Your feelings make me sad," Abbey responds.

"I know," Meredith says. "They're not admirable feelings. They're not how we were raised. But they're very real. The other thing I feel, besides revenge, is indulgence. That I'm not getting it together fast enough. My coping is all surface. I'm constantly struggling. Most days feel unbearable. What keeps human beings going, anyway, when they've experienced something devastating? When everything they knew and every assumption they've ever made is destroyed? Surely it isn't just the simple will to live? Since Lizbett I haven't had that will. I'd just as soon give up. I really would."

"Why haven't you, then?"

"I'm a coward. Giving up requires more than intent. It involves doing. Then the *how* gets in the way. But it can simply be trying to be dead, I suppose, lying as lifeless as you can make yourself all day long, blanking out all your thoughts. I did that for a while. Tried to be dead. Tried to disappear into some unfeeling, uninvolved state. A deliberate coma."

"What brought you back to life?"

"Hildy. I didn't want her to poop all over the house."

"Plus there was Darcy," Abbey says.

"You know, what I most regret is that Mum didn't ever have the chance to love her granddaughters the way she did us. And at the time of Lizbett's death, she was not really aware enough to mourn it. Thinking of our childhoods, thinking of life now without her, I'm so much more conscious of being a mother ... of the influence I have with Darcy ... had with Lizbett. What can I do for her? Lizbett was so good, so intuitive, she almost raised herself. I'm not sure how I influenced her except to love her deeply and encourage her in all her endeavours."

"And be ambitious for her," Abbey says.

"Was I? Oh, was I really? I'm aware I wanted the most for her, but ambitious? Maybe I'm ambitious for Darcy, too. Ambitious that she be spared any long-term harm from Lizbett's death, ambitious that she be content, useful to herself and others, the way Mummy was ... and also Lizbett."

"Darcy isn't Lizbett, Meredith. Darcy is a subtle giver. Some of her contentment comes from her special ability to connect, I think. She has a forceful sensibility. She's a Bodhisattva."

"A Bodi ... what?"

"A kind of living Buddhist saint."

While Meredith is away, Hildy is injured at the dog park. A new dog has arrived, an "intact" Rottweiler/bull mastiff cross named Attila. He is a bruiser of a dog, tan with a black scrunched-up face and cropped ears and tail. He is almost as tall as Hildy, but outweighs her. He has a massive chest and shoulders and sturdy legs. His head is like an anvil. Hildy, though strong, is lean with racehorse legs.

Attila's owner seems to have him in control and if Attila gets snarly with another dog, which he seems to do quite often, his owner commands, "Leave it!" And Attila backs off. With some dogs he is friendly and plays well. They wrestle and race after each other and there are no altercations.

Hildy plays with these dogs, too, and one Saturday afternoon, when she is tussling with a golden retriever, Attila bounds up and either tries to join in or to intervene. No one is quite certain what happens next: who escalates what. But there is a dog fight, a ruthless, snarling, snapping, leaping, and lunging battle. They are brutal, primal things, dog confrontations, with the animals fighting for their lives. The golden backs off and runs to her owner, cowering. But Hildy and Attila go at each other, the sounds vicious and chilling. Attila's owner is yelling, "Attila, leave it! Leave it! Enough! Attila, come!" But Attila is intent on damage and is deaf to the commands. Hildy is instinctively, fiercely defensive. Their bodies are a tumult of ruthless canine survival.

Thompson, who has been depositing a doggy bag in the trash can across the way, hears Darcy's screams first and then people shouting and the terrifying noise of the dogs. He runs over, adrenaline pumping.

"Somone get that big dog off! He started it!" a man yells. Thompson isn't sure to which dog the man is referring.

"Daddy! Daddy! He's going to kill her!" yells Darcy and it appears that Attila has overpowered Hildy because she is down on her back yelping wildly and the hulking male is at her throat. His owner grabs his collar and tries to pull him off, but the dog has Hildy's flesh in his jaws. "Release!" he commands the dog.

"Release!" Miraculously, Attila does, but not before leaving a gaping U-shaped tear on Hildy's throat, which is spurting blood. She doesn't attempt to get up.

"She okay?" Attila's owner asks. "Sorry about that. Bit of competition over the gold one."

"I don't think so," replies Thompson. Someone removes a scarf and ties it twice around Hildy's neck, but the blood seeps through. "Wait here!" Thompson orders Darcy. "I'm going to get the car." He drives it as close to the play area as he can.

Hildy is unsteady on her feet and several people have to lift her in, but never once does she protest. The scarf is now soaked with blood.

"She's lost some blood and she's very bruised," the vet says, "But I think she's going to be okay. She'll be pretty weak for a while. It took sixteen stitches to repair the hole. It went right into the muscle. And there were a couple of other gashes I stapled, as well. We'll keep her here overnight. She'll need to be on these antibiotics for ten days. That must have been some fight."

"It was really scary and awful," says Darcy. "This huge, fierce dog just attacked Hildy and another dog."

"Is that what happened? Really, Darce?" Thompson asks. To the vet he says, "Unfortunately I didn't see it begin."

"Yes! Yes! Hildy was just playing with Sadie and that other dog came and interfered. Sadie got away, but Hildy couldn't. That other dog was just too mean and strong."

"He is a scrapper, that big dog," says Thompson.

"Oh, Daddy. What if Hildy had died? What if she had? What if she just bled and bled and died. I would have wanted to die, too."

As soon as all the snow has melted and the sidewalks are dry, it begins to snow again. Melvyn looks out his front window into the Friday evening gloom and sees glaucous fans of flakes under the streetlights. Already the grass in the park below is solid white. The forecast says it's supposed to snow all night. Melvyn is feeling restless. The bare streets had brought with them the promise of the park's being full and active again and his excitement rose when he thought of the possibilities for connection. Maybe there would be new girls. He would start walking to and from work again and pass by Darcy's house. It's not too much out of his way. Perhaps he might get a glimpse of her; get a chance to walk and talk with her.

But now, another snowstorm. Tonight it irritates him and makes him feel confined. He's feeling edgy and trapped anyway because of Aniela. She is practically living with him and he's grown tired of her and wants her out. He's suggested as much to her and she clutched him and cried and begged him to let her stay. She says she loves him, but he doesn't believe her. How can she possibly love him when he almost kills her every time they have sex? He has even taken to making small cuts with a razor on her breasts and inner thighs. Seeing Aniela's flesh ooze the bright red drops infuses him with a sense of real connection to her body, as if releasing some of its fluids brings her closer. *There is power in blood*, he thinks, and seeing it gives him an intimate link to its source, her heart. Not that he associates that with love, but rather with something more sublime, being part of her life force.

He has been reading about the Mayans in preparation for an upcoming mask exhibition. The Mayans had a large pantheon of gods to whom they felt intimately connected. The gods required blood in return for their bounty. Blood was a means of making contact. The Mayans provided it by self-mutilating: piercing parts of the body with the spears from sting rays and shards of pottery, twine with thorns. They cut the ear-lobes, the penis, drew rough rope through holes in the tongue. The opening up of the flesh allowed them to receive revelations, beneficence. It was an honour to offer one's blood. For kings, it solidified their link to the Divine. It sustained the universe. The blood was collected on bark cloth and in ritual vessels and placed on an altar. This blood for that rainfall. That blood for this crop. Aniela's blood for his potency.

And the victims the Mayans sacrificed on top of their pyramids were symbols of the god for whom they were to die. They took on the god's qualities. Neither had life without the other. So the beating heart was extracted from the victim by the priest and his blood and flesh tasted. Then the body was rolled down the steps and the priest would skin it and dress himself in it for the powers it relayed.

Melvyn thinks about sacrifice, about how it is fair trade, showing gratitude and devotion to the provider for his gifts. He thinks about the young girls thrown into the cenotes, of their flailing bodies in the deep green water. They were part of a continuum. They gave sustenance to the gods, who in turn gave sustenance to the people. A sacrificial maiden was a nurturer, an assurer of a way of life. Much of the Mayans' strength and fortune came from those who died.

He and Aniela will wear Mayan harvest masks tonight.

Aniela is taped to the bedposts and under her mask he has put more duct tape across her mouth. Usually he doesn't bother, but tonight, well, you never know. He has a kitchen knife. He longs to cut well into her. He can only imagine reaching her beating heart. But he is thinking of the blood. It would be more than he could handle. Wearing gloves, he makes small incisions, a little deeper than he has done previously. The tape muffles her screams. He does all this while he is inside her. He thinks it is quite possible that he loves her or that for now, anyway, she is important to him. He needs her to do what he must do. He is both the sacrificer and the receiver of the sacrifice. For him, neither can exist without the other. His supremacy depends on Aniela and only he can deliver her.

Aniela dies the same way Audrey and Lizbett did. Her neck is not even much larger.

Afterwards, he feels a strange mixture of euphoria and melancholy. He realizes he will miss her, but he is thrilled with the ritual and the fact he has felt so profoundly connected to her. She has fed him and he is grateful.

He is also grateful for the storm. It has closed everything in and kept everyone confined. He goes out his back door and shovels off the stoop and the stairs leading to his car. Aniela is wrapped in an old quilt and she is heavier than he expected. It is a struggle carrying her down. Basically, he drags her. Even cleared of snow, the steps are slippery. But he gets her in the back seat.

In his flat, he washes the kitchen knife and puts it back. He gathers the duct tape and Aniela's clothes and puts them in a plastic bag, puts on a coat and leather gloves, and goes down. The snow has covered the car and has to be brushed off. While he's doing this, his landlady sticks her head out her door and says, "Not going out in this, are you?"

He jumps when she speaks, momentarily losing his composure, but then replies, "Have to. I've got an important appointment."

"Can't let the girlfriend down, eh? You're a good man. Be careful out there."

Shaking, Melvyn gets into the car. His wheels spin as he tries to back up, but he goes back and forth a few times and finally is out the driveway. The roads are treacherous. The snowplows haven't been by and the few cars out are crawling, their tires crunching on the accumulated snow. Melvyn feels frightened. His landlady has caught him off guard and he hasn't planned where to take Aniela. The storm is howling around him. He doesn't want to go far. He can barely see the road. Then he thinks of a waterfront park in the west part of the city. He'll aim for that. There's a break-water and if he can manage to get Aniela out to it, he can dump her into the lake.

The park is lit, though deserted as he has imagined it would be, and driving into the deepening snow, his car fishtails several times. He's terrified he's going to get stuck. Better to stop where he is, he thinks, and carry her the rest of the way. Well, haul her is what he does through the drifts in the grove of trees across to the wall rising from the thrashing waves. Huge ice floes crash against the cement. He tosses the body into an open patch of oily water, sees a chunk of ice crash over it. Aniela won't be discovered until the ice is completely gone more than a month later.

Melvyn returns to his car and almost doesn't make it out of the park. His heart thuds as fast as his wheels scream and spin in the snow. By morning, all his tracks will have disappeared. Closer to the city, he dumps the garbage bag with Aniela's things and the remnants of the ritual into a trash can.

Back in his flat after a harrowing drive, he pours a glass of wine to regain his equilibrium, to try and process what has happened. Aniela is gone. He will miss her childlike malleability, her eagerness to please. Her immediacy. Sometimes she even had a touch of gaiety. But the sacrifice was worth it. Now he can move on.

He is acutely aware he will be a suspect in Aniela's disappearance and he must clean his apartment once again of anything that could be remotely construed as a connection. Mostly, he has to get rid of his "little girl things" and his magazines. These he collects and puts in the trunk in the storage room in the basement, but realizes if he is ever searched, this would be a logical place. So he puts the trunk in the car. He will rent a public storage space in the morning. Aniela's remaining things, of which there are few, he leaves. After all, she was his girlfriend. At 11:00 p.m. he phones Aniela's home, where she lives with her parents, and asks to speak to her.

"I thought she was with you," says Brygida.

Melvyn has never met Brygida Breischke, but he knows she and Aniela are close.

"She should be. She was supposed to come over after her classes, but she hasn't shown up. We had a bit of a tiff. I was thinking she'd gone home to you."

"A tiff?" Aniela has spoken to her mother of Melvyn as a nice person.

"Nothing serious. Just about what we were going to do tonight. She wanted to go to the movies. I wanted to stay in because of the weather. It's fierce out there."

"Maybe she went to the movies in any case."

"She probably did," Melvyn says. "Let me know if she comes home."

Brygida calls at 10:00 a.m. the next morning, just after Melvyn has returned from renting a storage locker. "Is she there?" she asks.

"No, she's not," says Melvyn. "She's not. She didn't show up?"

"I went to bed after I talked to you. I simply assumed I hadn't heard her come in. Just now I went to check on her and I saw she wasn't there. Now I'm worried."

"I am too," says Melvyn. "I think you should call the police."

"I expected her around 5:00 p.m., after her classes," Melvyn tells the two cops who come to his door. "As I said to her mother, we'd argued, and when she didn't arrive, I thought she'd probably gone home. I called about 11:00 p.m. to talk to her ... to, you know, apologize, and Mrs. Breischke said she wasn't there. We both thought maybe she'd gone to a film by herself or with some friends. That's what we'd disagreed about. She wanted to go and I didn't."

"Is that usual behaviour for her?"

"Not really. We pretty much agree most of the time. We've only been going out since December."

"How much time does she spend here?"

"The occasional weeknight. Weekends, mostly. Look around if you like. You'll see she keeps a few things here."

The police wander around, in and out of the rooms. "Nice masks."

"Thanks. I collect some and make some. I'm in the education department at the Courtice Museum. I teach a mask workshop."

"That's where that little girl disappeared from last summer, isn't it? The one who was murdered?"

"Yes. She was at my camp."

The police do come back with a search warrant and go into his closets and all his drawers. They take apart the basement room. Melvyn is livid when they don't put anything back.

A cop says, "Your landlady says she talked to you as you were going out the night of the storm. She said you said you had an important appointment. What time was that?"

What time was it? Melvyn hadn't really kept track. He quickly recalculates the evening and figures it was 8:30 or 9:00 p.m. He lowers his head and says so. "I'm embarrassed. I was going to the liquor store to get some wine. I wanted some for ... you know ... later. I didn't want to look desperate to my landlady."

"The weather didn't stop you?"

"It should have. I was foolish to go. It was hairy."

"Did you get your wine?"

"Yes. A couple of bottles of Chardonnay."

"Was it worth it?"

"Well, I had a glass later."

There's nothing. Nothing obvious, nothing tangible, nothing concrete for the police to go on. Not a thing: no body, no blood, no weapon, no signs of violence, no apparent motive, no indication from witnesses that it was a conflicted relationship. No indication from anyone that Melvyn Searle was not a nice guy.

But it all seems too clean and that frustrates the police. And there is the connection with last summer's murder. This Searle is supremely confident, not the least bit anxious about his girlfriend's disappearance. Instinctively they feel he is manipulating them.

Later Mikkelson says, "I have to say I'm liking the mask guy for this. He's too smooth. Gotta gut feeling. He gives me the creeps."

Angstrom responds, "But whadda we got? Zero. He's clean. Squeaky clean. There's nuthin' to pin on him. Same for that little actress last summer. Nuthin'. Lot of coincidence here. Lotta connection. A whole lot. It's staring us in the face, goddammit."

"But no evidence. Nothing to go on. Lookit. No blood, no body, no witnesses, no motive. Fuck all. Nada. Zip. Zilch. We got nowhere to go."

"He's got a solid alibi for the girl. Two reliable witnesses."

"Too bad we can't find some way to prick his finger."

"Yeah. Too damn bad."

Mikkelson feels an enraged surge of frustration. He has felt it before, when an investigation has been stalled because of legal constraints. But he knows only too well, if he somehow "accidentally" acquired some incriminating evidence … he can't conceive of what … like maybe he'd instigate some kind of fight with Searle and knock him in the nose and make it bleed and then test the blood on his knuckles … it would never hold up in court.

The same snowstorm that covered Melvyn's dumping of Aniela's body sees the Warnes creeping east along a dark highway with lanes obliterated by sweeping drifts. Thompson hugs the barely visible tail lights of what looks like a Volkswagen in front of him. It is the only way he can move forward. Meredith is full of fear and tries not to let it show.

It is March Break. They are on their way to drop Darcy and Hildy at Celestial Kennels and then he and Meredith are going to Ste. Agatha's, an inn in the northeastern hills. Hildy has recovered from the dog fight with scars and some regression in her behaviour. She cowers at the dog park, and, a couple of weeks ago, when two personable Seventh Day Adventist missionaries came to the door, she was vicious, terrifying the young men and Meredith.

Magdalena has suggested immersion training and since Zeus and Minerva's "P" litter is now eight weeks old, she has invited Darcy to stay, as well. The four male and six female puppies need lots of socializing and Darcy can play with them all day long.

A neighbouring farmer has ploughed Magdalena's lane earlier and Thompson has little difficulty staying on track. Their station wagon has front wheel drive. Magdalena and Joan rush out. "Oh, we were so worried."

Hildy leaps about in the snow, joyous to be in a familiar place. Magdalena tries to convince Thompson and Meredith to stay, but Thompson is determined to make it to the inn, which is only about three-quarters of an hour further.

The highway this far east is deserted. Quite often they see the whirling lights of a tow truck and a car or several in the ditch. Meredith wants to go back to the kennel.

"We're more than halfway there," says Thompson. "That would be dumb."

She hates him. She looks over at him hunched over the wheel and feels pure rage at his stubborn recklessness. He is endangering them. She could pummel him and feel pleasure. She closes her eyes and says, "Please don't let me die on this highway."

*Or get stranded on this winding back country road that has not been cleared.*

Snow flails from every direction out of the darkness onto the windshield, obscuring his vision like a curtain in the wind. The headlights barely illuminate a roadway blanketed with snow. Thompson grits his teeth and grips the wheel and keeps going at a pace fast enough so that he doesn't get stuck, but slow enough that he doesn't spin out. Meredith's hands hurt from squeezing them together.

Finally they come to the gauzy lights at the stone gates of the inn. It has a long, uphill lane but it has been ploughed. They just keep going and hope.

The stone inn is large and plain, a former convent/girls' school that was bought by a wealthy industrialist after the nuns left in the early sixties. It has only been an inn for ten years.

Meredith feels giddy with safety and, in fact, dizzy, when they arrive in their room. All those hours of staring into spinning snowflakes, trying to see the road.

There is a crackling fire in the fireplace and a champagne bucket full of ice, which Thompson had pre-arranged. A four-poster king-sized bed is piled high with down cushions and a thick paisley duvet. There is a plush Oriental carpet. On either side of the mantel are shelves filled with books and, in front, two wing chairs. Meredith pulls open the heavy chintz curtains to reveal broad French doors that go out onto a walled patio.

"Oh, Thompson," she says. "This would be so perfect if I didn't feel I was about to vomit."

"What? Are you okay?"

"I just have a bit of vertigo from the drive."

"But we made it. We're here now. Let me pour you a glass of champagne."

"And I think I'll take a Dramamine for this nausea."

The champagne with the pill gives her a buzz and she feels a newborn carelessness at this escape.

That night, for the only time they are there, they eat dinner in the dining room. They are almost the only diners in the great hall with its ornate wooden arches and panelled walls. Meredith can picture long tables with nuns and girls in prim uniforms. There is an immense stone fireplace that rises to the ceiling, blazing with logs the size of small trees and they ask to be seated near it. They have changed out of their jeans for dinner.

Thompson is wearing a tweed jacket and he has put on one of Meredith's favourite silk ties. This one is from a Picasso sketch. She has chosen a long black silk skirt and lace T-shirt. Dangling from her ears is a pair of antique ruby and pearl earrings Thompson had given her that she hasn't worn for years.

"You look so beautiful," he says.

"So do you."

It is as if they are on a first date — no — a blind date where each has been prepped, but neither can find the footing, the opening to connect. They are uneasy with each other, but they are not strangers. They don't really feel like strangers. Everything about this, being away from the girls …

from Darcy ... the luxurious ambience, both of them dressed up, radiating an attractive confidence, is a familiar scene.

It's as if they're in a play they've rehearsed over and over, but now it's opening night and they've forgotten their lines. And there is no prompter behind the curtain. They have to strain to find from that vital but unused portion of their brains the words they haven't said, that may not even be there.

They order a bottle of Chablis and the waiter brings them a silver wine cooler. They start with oysters on the half shell and Dover sole with beurre blanc for their main course and they linger, saying nothing, but thinking frantically, with a tinge of fear, trying to enjoy the good food and the grand room. For dessert they share a poached, caramelized pear with a dense chocolate sauce.

Afterwards, they retreat to two leather club chairs near the fire and nibble on candied walnuts while they sip a ruby port.

"I wonder what happened to all the nuns?" Meredith says. "Did they die off? Why ever become a nun?"

"For the same reason as someone becomes a priest."

"Which is ...?"

"Someone who loves God enough to give up earthly delights to serve him, I guess, although I've never really understood the celibacy thing. Jesus never asked anyone to be celibate, I don't think. Did he? It's pretty unnatural and unreasonable to deny a life force like sexuality, and for what? How does denial of something so human make you holy? And anyway, most of the time no one paid attention, especially the male clergy. Who'd ever want to give up sex, for god's sake?"

"Maybe someone who finds sex repugnant," Meredith says.

"Well, who'd ever find sex repugnant?"

"Some ... people. Someone who has been violated or knows someone who has been violated."

At once a look of pained, sad awareness comes over his face. He hesitates. "Do you?"

"What?"

"Find ... find sex repugnant?"

"Now I do."

"Wow, Mer. I had no idea. I just thought you were grieving. Do you find ... do you find me repugnant?"

She looks away.

"Look at me."

She tries, but she cannot. With her head lowered and in a voice so pained, so subdued and reticent he can barely hear, she says, "No ... not you ... your penis, maybe. It seems ugly and harmful. And destructive. A weapon. I can't help associating all penises with his and what he did with it to Lizbett. I can't get out of my head how much she must have suffered."

"Oh Mer, I don't have any idea where to go with this. I don't know how to help you."

She shakes her head. "You can't ... but, well, you don't want sex, do you?"

"Yes, I want sex!" he answers.

"Why? I don't understand. Don't you get that terrible picture when you think of doing it?"

"No. I think of you. How much I love and want you. My desire didn't die with Lizbett or with what happened to her. It waned, but it came back. I feel about the way Lizbett died the same way I'd feel if she were run over by a drunk driver or reckless teenager. Enraged. But it wouldn't mean I would avoid driving or even booze, for that matter. Lizbett died in a sex death, but I focus on the death, the brutality of a sick, sick man, not on the sex. I like sex."

"But the one is fed by the other," Meredith says. "You can't separate them."

"I can. I do, Mer. I have to. I want to live a normal life and have good, normal sex. Preferably with you."

"Preferably?"

"With you," he says.

She fights tears and buries her face in her hands. "I don't know if I can do it, Sonny. I really don't."

Later, when she climbs in under the crisp cotton sheets and heavy feather duvet, Meredith says, "Ooh, I don't believe it. The bed is spinning. Why did I have that port?"

In the morning, breakfast comes to their room: bowls of strawberries, raspberries, fresh pineapple, kiwi, and orange sections. There is thick yogourt, the kind where the liquid has been strained. And warm pastries, pain au chocolat, and almond croissants. Thompson pours coffee from a silver carafe and adds steaming milk from a pitcher. Meredith, in a white robe, sits cross-legged on the bed and keeps saying, "Mmm. This is heaven. It was such a good idea to come here."

"You're okay, then."

"As okay as can be expected. No. A little better than that. I think it's really good to do things that have no relation to Lizbett. I feel less guilty about feeling pleasure and missing her because she wouldn't be here anyway. She'd be at Magdalena's with Darcy."

"Or else we'd be on a beach in Florida."

Thompson comes and gently pulls Meredith, dripping wet, from the shower. She resists, afraid of him, afraid to trust him. Afraid to feel undeserved pleasure. She sees his erect penis and recoils.

"Sonny, I can't. I can't. I just can't."

He feels confident that he can reclaim her here. Now. "C'mere, Mer. It's all right. It's all right. Just let me hold you. That's it. I'll just hold you." She moves into him and he wraps his arms as tightly as he can around her body, his face in her wet hair. She is rigid. "Oh, Meredith, my sweetest girl," he says. She buries her face in his chest and relaxes a little into the familiar flesh, something she has not allowed herself with the constancy of the brutal, obscene images that have skewered her to blame and pain. She feels his hardness against her belly and something in her stirs. But then the grisly image intrudes.

How to allow herself the ecstacy of an act that destroyed her daughter?

How to welcome maleness into the place that had born that daughter, the place that maleness had destroyed in her daughter?

Thompson leads her to the bed. She lies there frozen in his arms and then says, "Come into me." He wonders if she is ready but she says, "Sonny, please."

He is more than ready and does not last long and when he rolls off her he says, "Sorry."

She is only thinking, *I survived.*

A while later he is awakened by her kisses on his face. He clasps her cheeks and brings her mouth to his and kisses her the way he has been imagining all these months, journeying deep into her with his tongue. He has forgotten how good she tastes and he keeps tasting until she pulls away, gasping. Now it's her turn to find him again. She follows his whole body with her nose and lips, nestling into his smooth hollows, the hairy parts with their separate smells. She has forgotten the distinct geography of him, his curves and dips. In a surreal way, she shrinks into her own fingertips, into the thin tissue of her lips. She becomes electric, the nerve endings themselves. She finds his cock and kisses it, holds it tenderly to her cheek, remembering how much she does love it. She cups her breasts around it. "So exquisite," she says. But she does not take it in her mouth. She comes back up and kisses him some more and then she says, "Fuck me." And he does, slowly, slowly at first, waiting to feel her excitement mount.

"Wait for me," she says and he begins to glide more purposefully. She says, "Sonny, oh Sonny, so wonderful. So wonderful." Then her motions change. She becomes more vigorous, more demanding, pulling at him and she says, "Hard, hard now!" He thrusts with a force he had almost forgotten, as if he could crush her. She reaches out to him finally in a release that rips through her body.

Afterwards, she lies tightly pressed into him, her head nestled cozily against his shoulder and once again feels the voluptuous tenderness that always follows lovemaking. She had forgotten the "oneness" of it ... how for a few moments she feels infinitely inseparable, like conjoined twins. She is surprised to realize he has lost weight. He doesn't feel thinner as much as harder. His soft edges have become angles. He, too, has found eating a burden. Why hadn't she noticed? There are little spaces between them now.

"Should we talk?" Thompson asks.

"About what?"

"About Lizbett ... about anything."

"We never have," she says.

"Maybe we should," he replies.

"What would you say?"

"Probably what you would say."

"Which would be ..."

"That I've felt crudely and cruelly dislodged. That I'm at a total loss as to how to move forward."

Meredith says, "That the hole Lizbett left is unfillable."

"We shouldn't even try, I don't think."

"I'm deep in it," she says.

"Climb out."

"I can't. I've tried. I was the mother."

Thompson flares. "You think maternity gives you a monopoly on grief? Jesus! I was the father!"

She is struck by the real anguish in his face, his dear, mellow, normally passive face, the face that had been above her, below her, right beside her, across from her, in her, a face she has seen at breakfast, lunch, and dinner for years, a face she has worked with, a face she thought she was as familiar with as her own. And yet, here is a face of twisted, excruciating pain she doesn't recognize. He's hidden it well. And she is upended. *How presumptuous*, she thinks. How ignoble, how ignorant that she should believe, because of his sex, that his suffering would be less than hers, that hers was paramount. Her self-absorption appalls her.

She suddenly sees him in a different light, not as a man, but as a vulnerable, doting paternal being, one half Lizbett's creator. Lizbett was "of Thompson" as much as much as she was "of Meredith." So imprisoned by her own suffering, Meredith has negated his "fatherness," the physical connection he had to Lizbett and how that fostered his unbreakable attachment. Lizbett was not born of his body, but he had born her, the joy and weight of her life, with as much adoration and responsibility as Meredith had. She feels ashamed.

"Let me help you," he says.

"You can't."

"I can throw you a rope."

"Even if I could manage to climb up, then what? Then I'm up. We can't simply live with a big gaping hole. What do we do? Walk around it? Try not to look down it? Try not to trip and fall? Try not to plunge?"

"Couldn't we cover it over?" he asks.

"With what?"

"With our lives. With love, Mer. With love. For each other. For Darcy. For Hildy. For all we have. For a future for all of us … one where we can feel safe and comfortable walking over the hole."

"Isn't that a negation?"

"The hole isn't Lizbett! It's her terrible absence. To cover it over would be an affirmation of our ability to build over something achingly deep. If we try hard enough, what we build will support us … all of us, even if sometimes it feels shaky. I can't go on and not rebuild. I can't. I can't go on skirting the hole, its danger and destruction, the terrible lethal pull of it. Because it is lethal. It will kill us. I've been down there. I know. We need to cover it over as best we can and salvage what's left around it."

"You've been down there?"

"Many times. You're surprised?"

"You always seem so composed."

"Seem is the operative word."

"I've been very, very selfish, haven't I," she says.

"Yes."

"I'm so, so sorry. I can hardly explain it. I've been beside myself."

"I know."

"No," she responds. "I mean literally beside myself. One of me is outside the other, looking in. One feels. The other does what needs to be done. Neither is very reachable."

"And where are you now?"

"Here, with you."

Thompson's eyes well, but he smiles.

Another time, after making love again, Meredith says, "I had an affair."

"So did I."

"Sonny! You didn't!"

"Okay, I didn't."

"Did you?"

"No."

"Why did you say you did?"

"Because you did." Thompson says.

"But I did," replies Meredith.

"I know."

"How?"

"Mer, give me some credit for something."

She looks away. "It's long over. It was over before Lizbett."

"Why did you do it?"

"I ... I don't know. I wanted ... some reaction."

"Did you get it?"

"Yes," she replies. "Are you angry?"

"I was. But I figured there wasn't anything I could do. That it would run its course."

"It did," she says.

"I'm glad."

"So you're not mad now."

"If it's over, it's over. It was a lifetime ago. There are too many other important things to think about."

"Don't you want to know who it was?"

"I couldn't care less."

"So you forgive me?"

"Mer, the important thing is not that I forgive you, but do you forgive yourself?"

For four days they do not leave their bedroom except to go to the indoor swimming pool, once used by the girls, then refurbished by the industrialist to look like an Algerian bath. It is a vast, steamy room with a long turquoise pool decorated with intricate blue and green and gold mosaics and surrounded by a mini tropical forest. Brilliant coloured parrots screech from large, ornate cages. Wooden chaise longues with white canvas cushions are everywhere.

Meredith and Thompson swim leisurely lengths in the pool, lie dozing or reading on a chaise until a touch or a glance makes their cores pulse. They embrace in the warm water or Meredith runs a bare foot up Thompson's thigh and into his bathing suit and touches his genitals with her toes. And then they go back to the room and make love again. They eat all their meals in front of the fire in their room, usually in their plush robes, which are never on for very long.

Meredith has a sense of salvaging something fierce and needy as if Lizbett's death, the nature of her death, had cruelly imprisoned it and now she is split open, her insatiable desire exposed.

Thompson is just glad to get laid.

On their last morning, he reaches over in the bed and finds her spot empty. Meredith is in a bathrobe, her knees up in one of the wing chairs with a cup of coffee from the carafe in the room.

"I've had an idea," she says.

"I didn't think there was much more we could try."

"Don't be so sure," she replies. But then says, "No, I was thinking about moving forward. How to do that." Her voice quavers. "I thought I might turn Lizbett's room into a studio."

"Oh, Mer. That's huge. Are you sure you're ready?"

"No," she says, bottom lip quivering. "But I want to start painting again and it's the most logical room."

"Come down to the studio."

"I couldn't leave Hildy. I need to walk her, take her to the park."

"Bring her."

"She's not good enough with strangers ... all those people coming and going would make her anxious. Anyway, I want to be home."

"What sort of painting are you thinking of doing?"

"Portraits," Meredith says. "Large, detailed ones. Blow-ups. Five feet by six feet. I'll start with Lizbett."

"Sounds good."

"I think I can do it ... and taking over Lizbett's room ... well, it's a kind of regeneration. Right now, its emptiness is simply a cruel reminder. That's where I feel the loss most, when I look into that pretty, pretty room and she's not there and all her things just sit there in a kind of horrific mockery."

"What will you do with everything?"

"Give the furniture to a women's shelter. Most of the clothes can go to Goodwill. I'll keep some things. And the animals and books, well, I thought ... I thought ... I've been thinking ..." she hesitates. "Oh, Sonny, why don't we adopt? I've been thinking of adopting."

"Mer ... Mer ... sweetheart ... I couldn't even begin to ..."

"Not right away. Just think about it. Would you? I was thinking of a little Chinese girl ... maybe a baby. The orphanages in China are full of unwanted girls. Abandoned ones. The Watsons down the street just came home with one ... the sweetest one-year-old. They said it was devastating, how many there were. Think how happy it would make Darcy to have a little sister."

"I'm not sure I'm capable of adopting," says Thompson.

"It would take time. A year, maybe more. Maybe by then you'd be ready."

"I'm just not sure, sweetheart. It just feels ... it just feels ..."

"Like what?"

"Well, are you trying to replace Lizbett?"

"No. No! I was thinking it was like honouring her ... to bring a little abandoned orphan girl into our comfortable, loving space. I think Lizbett would be thrilled. I know Darcy would."

On the way home, they stop off to pick up Darcy and Hildy and spend a night at Celestial Kennels. Hildy has responded anew to Magdalena's discipline.

Magdalena says, "She's a wonderful dog. Her initial good and trusting nature have taken over, but she'll never be a normal dog. You have to remember that and always be hyper-vigilant. Watch for signs of fear, aggression ... ears back, lowered stance."

Darcy can't wait to show Meredith and Thompson the puppies, who are ready to go to their new owners. A tumbling, silvery wave of ten baby Great Danes, each weighing about eleven pounds, comes to greet them as they enter the puppy "nursery." They have floppy, velvety ears, gangly legs, and outsize paws. Some are solid blue, others have white stars on their chests or white markings on their toes. Darcy knows all their names: Penelope, Pearl, Peony, Persia, Persephone, and Paulina are the females; Perseus, Priam, Petrarch, and Prospero are the males. The puppies are gregarious and rowdy, but already have been discouraged from biting, growling, and jumping up. "It's never too early for them to learn good habits," says Magdalena and she gives a sharp "Off!" to Perseus, who has his two front paws on her knees. "Four on the floor, always."

Darcy gets down on the floor with them and they climb on her and lick her face and sit on her knees. She plays "tug" and throws rubber toys, which they all chase as a wobbly pack. Paulina, much smaller and more reticent than the rest, is the runt and she stays quietly back in a corner, although she wags her tail eagerly when Meredith approaches her.

"She's the only one we haven't sold," says Joan.

"Oh, Mommy. Couldn't we have her? Please, please couldn't we have her? I love her so much."

Meredith says, "I don't know, lovey, if we're ready to take on a little puppy. They're a lot of work and we already have our hands full with Hildy. She needs all our attention."

"Oh please, please, Mummy. Please think about it. Couldn't you just think about it, please?"

They are shaken when Brygida tells them about Aniela's disappearance. The police have already put up posters in areas Aniela was known to frequent. They have questioned anyone connected to her and include the Warnes now that they are back in the city. Since they have no body, there is very little to go on. Meredith and Thompson offer Brygida and Tadeusz anything that will help. Meredith tells Brygida not to worry about coming to work, but Brygida wants to keep busy. And there is support in being with Meredith, who has experienced the same thing. Meredith doesn't really know how to comfort Brygida when she is still barely a comfort to herself.

# 18

## APRIL

*Melvyn and Hildy*

The daffodils are proclaiming the warmer weather in the Warnes' garden. Fountains of yellow forsythia echo their brilliance. Blue Scilla carpets the lawn. Soon the dozens of tulips will trumpet their colours: the blacks, the bright pinks, the whites. The plump buds on the magnolia have unfurled into creamy flowers. The other trees are lacy with buds.

It is such a pleasure for Meredith not to have to pile on layers of heavy outerwear or bend over to pull on boots before walking with Darcy to the bus stop to go with her to school. Meredith and Darcy sometimes skip on the sidewalk, feeling light and freed.

On one of those occasions they hear a funny male voice. "That looks like fun." And they turn around to see Melvyn Searle a few steps behind them.

"Hello," says Meredith uneasily. She knows he was dating Aniela at the time of her disappearance. Instinctively she says, "Oh, Melvyn. It's terrible about Aniela. You must feel frantic."

"Thank you," he responds .Then he says, "I often see you. I walk by here on my way to the museum."

"Really? I didn't know you lived near here."

"Oh, I live farther west and a bit north of here. This is a bit out of my way, but it's such a lovely route by the ravine. It's so gorgeous this time of year, don't you think? And hi to you, Darcy. How are you? Did you have a nice holiday?"

"Yes, thank you," says Darcy.

*Is this effusive man a man whose girlfriend has just disappeared?* Meredith wonders. She feels offended. "Please excuse us. We're just on our way to the bus stop so we shouldn't dawdle."

"Where is it?" Melvyn asks.

"Just down there … down the street a bit."

"Well, I'm going in that direction," Melvyn says. "Why don't I just walk with you there? I'm sure all this business with Aniela must be stirring up some horrible feelings."

He shows up several mornings a week, completely ruining Meredith and Darcy's time together. Not that he is rude or overbearing. In fact, just the opposite. There is something insinuating and insidious about his friendliness. It feels inappropriate and unseemly. Meredith doesn't really know how to talk to him. For all his openness, he seems forced, insincere. She actually — and this is rare for her — loathes him.

"I was extremely fond of Aniela, you know," he says. "I was thinking of marrying her. She was so sweet and girlish, which appeals to me, but she had an underlying creative intelligence that I admired. Her name means *angel* in Polish. Did you know that? I felt she could keep up with me. We had a lot in common. I miss her terribly."

"I'm sure you do," Meredith says, willing him to go away.

"And how sad is it that Lizbett and Aniela were connected? They were close, I believe. Aniela mentioned the girls often. Is it more than a coincidence, do you think, this terrible similarity?"

He talks incessantly about masks, about the Mayan exhibit coming up. A lot of the time he chatters amiably and fluidly to Darcy, who is not the least responsive, walking along holding her mother's hand, giving one-word answers. And yet he doesn't seem to get it and persists in keeping them company. Meredith would like to ask him not to, but can't seem to find a reason and she doesn't want to be rude. She does feel a little sorry for him. She realizes he must be hurting and likely is lonely.

But she and Darcy now watch for him out the window, hoping he'll pass by, but they never seem to catch him and he always comes up behind them, almost as if he's been lying in wait.

He's taken to giving Darcy little gifts. A bag of jelly Teddys. A tiny book called *Noble Dogs*. A pair of shiny barrettes with owls on them.

And so on the days he shows up, usually three, sometimes four, they endure him. It's only a short distance to the bus stop, after all. Still. "I hate him," says Darcy.

Meredith confides how she is feeling about Melvyn to Brygida, which is a mistake. Brygida is defensive. Though she had never met Melvyn before her daughter's disappearance, he has been considerate — solicitous, really — phoning her frequently to see how she is.

"Aniela used to say how nice and kind he was to her, that he treated her like a little girl. She liked that. She needed that with a father like Tadeusz," says Brygida.

For his part, Melvyn believes he's making inroads. Darcy certainly isn't the shiner Lizbett was. She's more subtle, inward, dark. But that's her appeal and his challenge. Winning her over. He's sure he will. He always has.

Mid-month he telephones and tells Meredith, in a shaky voice, that Aniela's body had been found washed up on an isolated part of the beach at Waverley Park. The police won't say any more. Meredith's first thought is for Brygida and she resents hearing the shocking news from Melvyn.

"Just like Lizbett," he says. "I'm completely devastated. I didn't know who to turn to. I have no family. I thought you might be ..."

"Oh, Melvyn. My god. How terrible for you. Of course, you're devastated. But Brygida ..."

"Yes, yes. Mrs. Breischke. She's upset, of course. Her friends are all around her. She has a sister coming. But I'm not really family and I have no one. You've been through this. I thought talking to you might help. I hope it's not an imposition. Presumptuous, you know? As if you haven't been through enough. But you were close to Aniela. I thought you'd understand what I'm going through."

Meredith is livid. How dare he? She hardly knows him well enough to share his grief, but then she remembers all the strangers who helped them during the ordeal with Lizbett. The least she can do is be empathetic. "Well, I really don't know what to say except I do understand. It is a debilitating, shocking kind of loss. And the recovery isn't easy or quick."

Then he brashly says, "Have the police anything further on your daughter's murder?"

Meredith wants to hang up. This feels like some kind of weird obscene phone call.

"It's quite astounding, isn't it? That someone she knew, that you probably know … who committed a grievous crime … is walking around leading a routine life. Does it make you angry?"

This invidious familiarity upends her. "Melvyn, I'm extremely sorry you've lost your girlfriend … you've lost Aniela. We have, too. I have to attend to her mother."

"I was wondering if you attend a grief support group that might give me some comfort."

"No, we don't," replies Meredith and hangs up.

She is shaking with repulsion. She can't figure out how Melvyn has become such an intrusion in their lives. She wants to be rid of him and doesn't know how.

Meredith has been dismantling Lizbett's room. Or at least making an effort to. And after Melvyn's phone call and Aniela's death, it feels more torturous than it has been. What was beginning to be calm has been churned up again. And Melvyn is making it more raw. But why? Why is he invasive? Surely, as a person who has experienced the recent violent death of a loved one, she is a legitimate resource for comfort. She should feel an outpouring of empathy, the way she does for Brygida, whose heart is as shattered as hers. But she does not. And Brygida, whom she should be comforting, is unreachable. Even the loud and looming Tadeusz has been reduced.

Melvyn may have been kind to Aniela, as Brygida has said, but to Meredith he feels like an interloper with an agenda.

With difficulty, she goes back to Lizbett's room. Hildy is lying stretched fully out on Lizbett's bed. She follows Meredith around all day long. Even into the bathroom. Meredith lies on the bed beside her.

*This is the room Lizbett came home to at three days old,* Meredith thinks. It was a real nursery then, smelling of baby powder, with a changing table and a mobile of china alligators, a padded rocking chair, and a large hooked rug with daisies and white ducks. She remembers placing her new bundle in the bassinette with the eyelet skirt, where all the dolls and stuffed animals sit now, and having the sudden realization that every first-time mother has: there was now a separate life in this room, of her but no longer in her, already beginning her own journey towards selfhood. She felt the full weight of knowing everything she did from then on would affect that life.

She pondered baby Elizabeth Louise Ellen and tried to picture who she would be, what role Meredith would play. What kind of mother was she capable of being to this innocent, receptive, responsive wee female? How would she help her? How would she fail her? What strengths could she impart? What frailties could she avoid? She hoped she would become a resourceful, independent, caring woman. One thing Meredith knew for sure: that she would try to offer her new daughter the fullest, most challenging, most loving life she could and she would teach her that with her gifts (because Meredith was sure she would have many), she must give back in some way.

In this same room, Lizbett vomited into a bedside bowl from the stomach flu. It is where she scratched her chicken pox scabs and got blood on the sheets. It is where she had mumps and lay in bed several times with hacking bronchitis, the walls wet from a vaporizer. The pediatrician said it was exacerbated by the cats, but Lizbett screamed at any mention of getting rid of them. On this bed where she lies with Hildy, Thompson and Meredith read to Lizbett books of nursery rhymes, fairy tales, animal and adventure stories. On this bed Meredith lay with Lizbett when she couldn't get to sleep and stroked her back and sang to her.

This is the room where Lizbett will not become a teenager, not squeeze pimples, not put on deodorant, not wake up with bloody sheets from her period. She will not dream about boys, nor experience sexual longing, nor try touching herself. Here she will never slam the door in a rage over a curfew, in tears over a heartbreak, in disappointment over a lost role. Here she will never gather with her friends and gossip and giggle and wonder about sex. Here she will never be.

Meredith has been taking every single item out of the drawers, stroking it fondly, holding it in front of her, smelling it, trying to picture when it was last worn. She makes little piles on the bed of sweaters, T-shirts, blouses, shorts, jeans, socks, underwear. The white cotton panties with the rosebuds and the lace trim are particularly poignant to her. Was Lizbett that small? She stares and stares at everything, with eyes brimming, heart torn.

Getting rid of them feels as if she is getting rid of Lizbett. It feels like an obliteration. And yet to cling to them, to hoard them, feels like mawkish materialism. A vain attempt at earthly preservation. Lizbett is not going to live on in a pair of denim shorts, a pink gingham blouse, some lacy underpants.

Meredith wonders how long she could, how long she would continue to come in this room and open these drawers and see the clothes exactly as they were when Lizbett died. Months? Years? She thinks of the rarely opened trunk of baby clothes in the basement, likely a bit mildewed.

Maybe she should pack all these things from Lizbett's last summer in a special trunk that she could occasionally go into for remembrance. Maybe just knowing everything was still in her possession would be comfort enough. She decides to keep one or two things like the dresses from *Annie*, the Black Watch pleated kilt and yellow angora sweater (these were Lizbett's favourites), and pack up the rest in cardboard boxes and deliver them to Goodwill.

Meredith will keep the pictures and books and the bassinette full of dolls and stuffed animals just in case. She has already called a mover to take the furniture to a women's shelter.

She sees Lizbett's diary. Meredith has looked at it time and time again, desperately wanting to open it, not to read it, but just to see Lizbett's hand, the neat, round delineation of her dreams, her fears. Did she have fears? Meredith does not know. She talked about her dreams but never about what distressed her. She cannot imagine Lizbett ever being fearful. She is struck by the irony of this.

But Meredith will not permit herself to open the diary, seeing it as a violation and she wonders if she ever will.

By the weekend, the room is empty. Meredith and Thompson and Darcy sit on the hardwood floor in the middle of a surreal space that reverberates with a reality beyond their experience — something implausible. They feel as if the plug has been pulled from their life force, depleting it completely. The emptiness feels bizarre, like a place they've never been before. But not as if in a dream. It's tangible. They are ineffably there, the walls and windows and mouldings are there. They've been there many, many times before and always felt happy. But nothing remains of Lizbett now. Not even memories. It is too bleak for that. They try to picture the room as it was, cluttered and bright and cheery, but it's a vision that has vanished forever. Meredith and Thompson paint the pale yellow walls a stark white and staple heavy canvas drop clothes along the baseboards to cover the floor. Meredith finds her easel in the basement and brings it up along with an old round paint-spattered table to hold her paints and brushes and a stool. She buys a big, round bed for Hildy.

Hildy. Better, but still not great with strangers. One day Meredith is kneeling in the front garden with the dog lying near her, tied to a stake. An elderly jogger runs by and Hildy leaps up and charges, barking fiercely. The jogger is so startled to have a 140-pound animal lunge at him that he steps backwards, loses his balance on the edge of the curb, and falls. Meredith races over and sees he is grimacing in pain. He says he can't get up because he has hurt his elbow. Neither he nor his wife (from down the street), will let Meredith accompany them to emergency. Even though she has apologized profusely over and over for Hildy, who in fact was never even close to the man, they reject her offer of help and seem terribly embarrassed to have caused all this fuss.

The fuss ends up being a broken elbow that requires surgery and a pin and four or five weeks in a cast and weeks of physio after that. A regrettable, albeit temporary, sentence for a vigorous man in his eighties. Meredith and Thompson are filled with anxiety. Not only do they feel guilty about Hildy, they are terrified about a lawsuit, which in fact, never comes.

Their insurance settles the business very quietly but the Warnes feel they've had a close call. What if the rope had broken? What if the stake had pulled out? Would Hildy have actually attacked or would she have just stood her guard and barked? Should they muzzle her? It's a dicey situation because though Magdalena has cautioned them to be vigilant, she has also said that the more exposure Hildy gets to people (in a controlled situation), the more her trust will increase. Since the incident in March with Attila, Hildy has been fine at the dog park, friendly both with the other dogs and their owners. But then, the park isn't her territory and obviously, when the jogger ran by, she thought the front garden was.

Meredith has a loving dependence on Hildy and cannot imagine having to give her up. Alone with her in the house during the day, Meredith finds in Hildy a friend, some solace. She talks to the dog constantly. Her physical presence is large; her emotional presence larger. Hildy listens and leans, cuddles and seems to care. In her intelligent gaze, her wrinkled, twitching brow, Meredith thinks she sees the dog responding to her moods. She is very concerned when Meredith cries, burying her muzzle under her arm and wagging her tail frantically. If Meredith screams out in anger, the dog seems to try to calm her.

On long walks, she is congenial company and a connector. Meredith has met many interesting people because they are attracted to Hildy.

But Darcy is the one who is most besotted with Hildy. And Hildy with her. Maybe it's because they are the same height, their eyes at the same level. If Darcy is home, Hildy abandons Meredith and stays by Darcy's side. Darcy romps with her out in the back garden; she brushes her and snuggles with her when she's reading. Hildy walks with Darcy when they go to the park (with Meredith or Thompson along). Darcy throws the Kong for her there. Hildy has actually become an extension of the little girl, drawing her out of herself and giving her strength and a certain stature. Darcy desperately wants Hildy to sleep with her at night, but Meredith and Thompson say "not yet."

The love affair that has them all astounded is the one between Mr. Mushu and Hildy. Hildy could crunch the Siamese in one bite. In fact there's no reason they can understand why Hildy doesn't just take the cat in her jaws and shake her, the way she does her stuffed elephant. But Mr. Mushu rubs his body in and out of Hildy's legs and butts Hildy's face and when she's lying down, cleans her, and then curls up with her, purring like a turbine. Hildy, in return, takes Mr. Mushu's fur between her front teeth and nibbles up and down and all over him, the cat prodding deliriously away. Geoffrey, on the other hand, runs when he sees Hildy, so Hildy always gives chase. But Geoffrey will come into a room if Hildy is asleep and touch noses with her. They think it won't be long before the cat loses his fear.

They question whether or not to take Darcy to Aniela's funeral, but she pleads and Meredith and Thompson decide the finality of the ritual will help her to accept the frightening death of another beloved person. In fact, Meredith and Thompson are resistant to going themselves, fearful that the wound they have been so painstakingly tending will split open again and their suffering will spill everywhere. They're not sure they are collected enough yet to gather it back in.

The service is at St. Irene's, in Polish. Tadeusz and Brygida are part of a large Polish community and have received unending support for the loss of their only child. The Warnes feel like outsiders.

On the opposite side, a few pews ahead of the Warnes, sits Melvyn Searle. At one point, he turns around and sees them and gives them a small nod. Meredith feels an antipathy that disquiets her. Thompson and Darcy ignore him.

She listens to the priest drone on in the strange language, presuming he is saying the same kinds of things as the minister said at Lizbett's service. She is glad she can't understand. What's important today is not to question, but to be here for Brygida, who is sitting at the front of the little church with Tadeusz.

She wonders if the Breischkes are devout. She and Brygida have never spoken about religion, but Meredith recalls how unsupportive and accusatory the priest was to Brygida when she went to him for refuge from Tadeusz's violence. The priest reminded her marriage was a state overseen by God and her duty was at the side of her husband. He cautioned her not to make her husband so angry.

Aniela was twenty-four. Lizbett was eleven. Meredith asks herself whether Brygida's grief is thirteen years more keen for all that extra time she had with her daughter. She saw Aniela grow into a lovely, thriving young woman, something Meredith would never have with Lizbett. She doesn't know which is worse: to lose a young child and never see the years of growth or to lose an older child after having shared those years.

Darcy has been sitting on Thompson's knee during the service, attentive and still. He is overwhelmed with the desire to cry. He was fond of Aniela and this thing they are sitting through today is too close to Lizbett's funeral. He knew if they came, feelings he thought he had subdued would rise up.

He is convinced now that in the first weeks of the ordeal with Lizbett's death, his body had produced some kind of anesthetic that numbed his emotions enough to allow him to get through all those ... all those ... the word "festivities" comes to mind. Sometimes it felt like that: all the people, all the heightened chatter, the booze, and food. Even the ceremony in the big church had an air of theatre. Today that anesthetic isn't protecting him and it is taking all his will not to lose it.

He thinks about Aniela's disappearance and murder; how similar it feels to Lizbett's though he has not read the forensics, only the newspaper and it is probably not similar at all. But the fact there are no leads in either case and that weather played a large part in the destruction of evidence seems eerie. Lizbett's body was in the rain for three days; Aniela's in icy water for how long? Both vanished in a storm, a storm that seems to have given the murderer cover.

Thompson wishes he had access to police files. He feels he could make more progress than they have, which is ridiculous, he realizes. And arrogant of him to think so. But he can't help sensing they must be missing something obvious that is preventing them from moving forward. Or maybe, instead, they are hanging around going, "Ha-ha-ha, the killer is long gone and will never be found and is committing more atrocities somewhere else. It's out of our hands."

Thompson wonders if he cares; if he'd feel less grief or even more, or a morbid satisfaction in seeing the man who violated and killed his daughter brought to justice. The need for vengeance he'd felt last summer has dissipated. Yes, if he's caught, he'd like to see the man suffer, but no longer at his own hands. He can't imagine he ever thought that way.

Thompson watches as the attendees line up at the front for communion and wonders if the idea that they are eating the flesh and drinking the blood of Christ is giving them comfort. He hopes it is, for their sakes, because it is a primal, absurd concept to him. He wishes he could find comfort that easily. Is that how it works? If you believe, if you have faith, your pain will be lifted? Do they really believe God or Jesus actually can do that or does the believing act as a placebo? Whatever. He wishes he could access it and envies those who can.

Will Brygida be able to cope better with Aniela's death than they have been with Lizbett's because she accepts the dogma — if she does? *If so, how do I get some of that*, he thinks, *because it's surely better than what we've faced.*

How unlikely, how grim, it is that he is sitting here in this church at the funeral of another lost girl — a girl they knew well, not some name in a newspaper — when just nine months ago they were doing the same thing for their very own daughter. How unutterably grotesque if they were connected.

He looks over at Meredith and sees she is fighting tears and he lets his own run down his cheeks. He takes her hand and Darcy looks up at him with a look of utter concern and he feels comfort. *This is what I believe in*, he thinks. *I believe in the here and now.*

On a bright Saturday, late in the month, Darcy and Thompson and Hildy go on a long city walk. They stroll on the main avenue where all the glitzy stores are. The warmth has brought out the shoppers. It is just past Easter and the windows are filled with flowers and mannequins in pale clothing. One display has a small corral with live rabbits.

They stop at their favourite bakery in the market and buy cheese pastries, and, for Thompson, a latte. They sit in the sunshine for a bit, accepting the overtures passersby make to Hildy. "Is she friendly?" they ask. "Can I pet her? She's so beautiful." Hildy is always reserved, but her ears are forward and she placidly accepts strokes on the head. She is quite pleased to be offered a treat. With other dogs she is more outgoing and curious, wagging her tail when she sniffs them.

They walk past the stalls of daffodils, tulips, and pussy willows. They peer in the butchers' windows at the great hanging carcasses. Darcy always wants to see the pigs' heads with the eyeballs still in. They pick up some runny Brie and some ash-covered chevre at a cheese stall. The windows of the seafood stores are stocked with every kind of fish, including huge whole salmon, swordfish steaks the size of a platter, and thick, purple-fleshed tuna.

They walk quickly through the textiles and leathers and clothing and housewares. Hildy is getting restless from the dawdling and they decide to take a brisk detour up through the university to the dog park.

When they get there, they are panting and Hildy is pulling to get inside the gate. She has seen a Rhodesian Ridgeback who is one of her friends. When they release her, she runs over to him and immediately the two go on a tear from one end of the park to the other. Thompson sees some people he usually hangs out with just down from the entrance and goes to join them.

Darcy spies a new puppy by one of the picnic tables and rushes over. She is a twelve-week-old Irish Setter/Newfoundland cross, hefty and furry and black with tan markings on her face and paws. Shy from all the attention, she is hiding behind her owner's legs, a tall, obese man with long grey hair and a beard.

Darcy kneels down and speaks in a soft voice to the puppy. "Hello, sweet girl. Hello, baby girl." She puts out her palm and scratches the puppy's ears. The puppy is all wiggles. Darcy is about to get up when she feels a presence hover over her, almost bumping into him when she does. She hears a familiar voice.

"Well, isn't that precious?"

Melvyn is right there. Where did he come from? He wasn't here minutes ago.

"Darcy," he says. "How great to see you. I was hoping I would. I'm thinking of getting a dog and I thought I'd come and do some observing. I bet you could give me lots of advice."

"Hi, Mr. Searle," she replies. She doesn't know what to do. She wants to walk away, to walk away quickly and go over to her father. Melvyn is standing very close to her, almost barricading her.

Melvyn says, "I guess you come here a lot with your big dog. Where is she?"

Darcy points to the other end of the playing field where Hildy and the Ridgeback are running toward them. At a closer range, Hildy begins to pull away and edge her way over to where Darcy and Melvyn are standing. She is full out and looks as if she'll ram into them, but she stops short and immediately starts to growl at Melvyn. Darcy is frightened. She shouts for her father and clutches Hildy's collar.

"No, Hildy! No! Hildy, leave it! Leave it!" she commands.

Hildy's growl escalates to snarling and Melvyn says, "It's okay, girl. I'm your friend. Don't worry. It's okay."

Thompson has heard Darcy's cry and comes running just as Melvyn puts out his hand to placate Hildy.

She lunges away from Darcy and grabs it, pulling on his arm. He yells.

Thompson grabs Hildy's choke collar and tries to pull her off, continuing to command, "Leave it, Hildy!"

But Hildy's jaws are locked into Melvyn's flesh and by now he is screaming, trying to extricate his hand. Thompson puts his hands on Hildy's muzzle, pressing her jowls hard into her teeth, trying to pry her mouth open. But she resists.

A crowd has gathered and finally someone dumps a bottle of water on Hildy's head. She is momentarily shocked and loosens her grip and Thompson immediately puts Hildy's collar high behind her ears, hauling her away. She is snarling viciously, but Thompson has her under control and commands her to lie down and stay.

Melvyn collapses to the ground, writhing in pain. His hand is mangled and spurting blood. A woman with a stroller reaches into a pouch behind it and pulls out a diaper and hands it to Melvyn, but he is too shaken to apply it and someone bends down and does it for him. Someone has raced up the ravine stairs to a nearby house and called the police and an ambulance. There are sirens in the distance.

Suddenly Melvyn stands up, shakily but with determination and pronounces himself to be fine. He insists on leaving, saying he'd rather take care of himself.

"Please leave me alone," he says. "This isn't a police matter and I don't need an ambulance. I know this dog. I likely provoked her. Please. I'm fine." But his knees buckle. Another man rushes in to support him and leads him over to a bench and tells him to put his head between his legs. The man, who says he is a doctor, has a look at the hand and says, "That looks bad. You're losing blood."

Thompson and Darcy have been standing by helplessly, holding Hildy, who is still growling. They have been surrounded by people, as if they might try to get away when all they want to do is help Melvyn.

There is no access to the dog park by car and the paramedics bring a stretcher from way over at the car lot. They strap Melvyn onto the stretcher and immediately insert an IV in his arm and wheel him, with difficulty on the uneven ground, to the waiting ambulance.

Thompson shouts, "What hospital?"

"Templemount."

Two police sergeants want to know what happened and everyone has an answer. In fact, only the puppy's owner and Darcy have seen what really took place. Darcy tries to talk through heaving sobs.

"My dog ... she was abused ... we've been training her ... she doesn't like people who remind her of ... she attacked Mr. Searle when he reached out to pat her ... she tried to warn him not to."

"Is this true?" One of the sergeants asks the big man.

"Well, I don't know about the abused part, but the dog did attack when the guy put his hand out. She just grabbed it and wouldn't let go. Pretty damn vicious, I'd say."

One of the cops looks at Hildy who is now lying calmly and asks Thompson if she's dangerous.

"Not at all," Thompson says. "It's true she was abused, but she's been rigidly trained. We're extremely careful with her. She's never done anything like this before."

"Never attacked anyone?"

"Never. She's only fourteen months … still a puppy, really."

"A giant one with big teeth," says the other cop.

Someone says, "The guy said he knew the dog."

"Melvyn is … is a friend. Once when he came to our house, Hildy … the dog was very distressed by him and we put her in her crate. We think Melvyn reminds her of the person who abused her. She has scars all over her body."

"What would happen if I tried to pat her?" a cop asks.

"Just make sure to put out your hand palm up, under her chin. She'll be fine."

The man puts out his hand as Thompson suggested and Hildy sniffs it and wags her tail.

"Good girl," he says. "Here's what's gonna happen. She's gonna have to be quarantined … you know, confined for a time … a month probably, maybe six weeks … to make sure she's not dangerous. There'll be charges. She up to date on all her shots?"

"Absolutely," Thompson replies.

"Good. Now, you take her home and someone'll come to get her. We'll call you." He writes the necessary information in a notebook.

The lingering crowd is both sympathetic and hostile. Those who know Hildy are distressed because she has seemed like a gentle, disciplined dog. "Never seemed like the kind that would bite," they say.

Others mutter about "untrained, ferocious dogs who shouldn't be let out" and they yell at the three of them as they exit the park.

At home, utterly distraught at Hildy's unacceptable, frightening behaviour and all its implications and sick with worry about Melvyn's condition, they wait for the police to come and get their beloved dog. Hildy looks back over her shoulder in great distress as they lead her to the van.

That evening, they want Darcy to go to Abbey and Kyle's while they go to Templemount Hospital to find out about Melvyn, but she has a screaming tantrum and they feel they have no choice but to take her.

But it doesn't matter, in any case. They are not related and not permitted to have any information. When they explain the circumstances, it doesn't make any difference. The sergeants from the afternoon are there and they sympathize, but say there is nothing they can do. Meredith and Thompson notice several other policemen and wonder what else is going on.

Magdalena is completely shaken when they call her.

"Oh, Thompson," she says. "In all my years of breeding Great Danes, I've never had this happen. It's my fault. She was a generous, effusive, trusting puppy. She should probably have always stayed with me. I simply can't imagine what was done to her or what was going on in her head. Please let me know as soon as you can what will happen to her. I'll take her back, of course. I am so, so sorry. As if you need this."

Darcy asks to sleep with them that night, though none of them sleeps. Each lies silently wondering how they got to this terrible place. They feel entirely to blame.

Meredith says, "Oh, Sonny, I don't think I can stand this."

"Me, either. Me, either."

"Will they have to put Hildy to sleep, Daddy?" Darcy asks.

"I sure hope not, sweetie. But we won't know for at least a month. Maybe she'll be the best girl ever in the police kennel and win everyone over."

"Do you think she meant it ... to hurt him, I mean?"

"I'm afraid so, sweetie. I think she meant to hurt him badly."

"Then even if she could say sorry, it wouldn't be true."

Meredith gets up and goes downstairs and looks at the clutter of Hildy's things everywhere: rubber chew toys, squeaky toys and balls of all shapes and sizes, pieces of rawhide, stuffed animals, some with the stuffing pulled out, lengths of rope, marrow bones, even a crushed plastic milk jug, one of her favourite toys. Meredith bends down and picks each one up and puts it in the toy bin, made of wood because Hildy had gnawed through several wicker baskets. The tidiness afterwards makes her think of life before the dog, how much calmer, neater, and cleaner it was. Their white canvas furniture is covered in drool and dark hairs. A couple of chair legs have deep tooth marks and the corners of some cushions are torn. The garden has big holes.

And yet where would they be without her, without her big, comforting body, her endearing antics, her tremendous capacity to give love? She has brought them out of themselves, their crushing grief, their sorrowful, debilitating indolence. If she has not yet brought them full happiness, simply because they are not ready for it, she brings a reassuring, dominating presence and occasional joyous moments. What will happen to them without her?

At breakfast the next morning, the doorbell rings. It is early: eight o'clock. Darcy is not yet up and Thompson is barely awake. Meredith goes to the door in a daze and a dressing gown and sees Irv Mikkelson and Nick Angstrom. She stands staring at them for a minute.

Can they be smiling?

They both speak at once. "We've got him!"

Meredith calls Thompson.

"You better sit down," Irv says.

"Actually, your dog got him. The guy she attacked in the park. Searle. Melvyn Searle. He's our killer."

Meredith's breath leaves her body. Thompson feels like he has a pile-driver in his chest.

"It was his blood. His blood type," Mikkelson says. "About the only thing we had to go on. We knew the killer had a rare blood type ... AB positive ... from the traces of his blood on your daughter's mouth from when she'd bitten him. We just didn't know how to find him without getting a warrant and testing everyone, which we couldn't do."

Angstrom adds, "He even has a dark bite-scar on his right arm. But the hand is severely lacerated. Your dog's teeth almost went right through and cut deeply into muscle, almost severing a couple of extensor and flexor tendons and actually clipping some nerves. Some small bones are crushed. She's got some strong jaws, that dog. She really meant business. Anyway, the injury required surgery ... a couple, probably, and some skin grafting ... he may not regain full use of the hand. He lost some blood and in the routine blood test to prep him before going into the operating room they discovered Searle was AB positive. All the hospitals had been alerted to watch for it. They called us right away."

A tsunami of feelings overcomes the Warnes. So much to take in! So much involved! Hildy! Melvyn! Meredith remembers the dog's reaction to him when he came last December. Why is she not surprised? She had come to loathe the man, to find him repulsive. What to think now that he has been accused of committing those unspeakable acts on Lizbett? Righteous pleasure? Rage? Vengeance? Relief? What she feels is numb.

"You okay, Mrs. Warne? Mr. Warne? This is the best possible news," Angstrom says.

"What happens now?" Thompson asks.

"He'll be in hospital for a while. Like I said, he needs a couple of surgeries. When he's recovered enough he'll go to the prison hospital. He'll likely be arraigned right away where he is, by special arrangement. We want to keep him confined. There'll be no bail, I wouldn't think. The evidence is pretty conclusive."

"I'm not sure there'd be anyone to pay it," Meredith says. "He has no family."

"You know that?"

"Only because he told me. You know, he was dating my housekeeper's daughter ... the one whose body was found on the beach at Waverley Park. He used to phone me after ... after Aniela died. I was never sure why. Now it seems as if he was taunting me. But I sort of thought he was grieving and wanted sympathy. I had a hard time giving it to him. Actually, I think he's been stalking my other daughter and me."

"You should have called us."

"I couldn't be certain. I thought I was being paranoid. I can't believe it. We've been waiting and waiting for this and it feels so ... so right."

"That's what us cops go on. Gut feelings. But this guy was a sick, slick one. There was absolutely nothing to tie him to it," says Mikkelson. "His alibi was solid."

"What are the chances the blood isn't his? Thompson asks.

"Three percent, like I said. Don't forget, we got the bite mark."

No one has noticed Darcy standing by, still in her nightie. How long has she been there?

"What will happen to our dog ... what is going to happen to Hildy?" she asks.

"That's the tough one," Mikkelson answers. "What she did ... attacking and gravely injuring ... likely crippling a human ... is criminal. We'd love to assume she knew Searle was the killer, or at least that he was making an effort to get at Darcy, but how can we know? Hell, she probably did. Dogs are brilliant. They detect natural disasters, cancer, and seizures in people. We use them to solve real complex crimes. They get stuff we don't, by what? Smell, body language, a person's inward behaviour, like nervousness, potential aggression, fear. Yours reacted to an evil man in an instinctive way. Did she sense something? You say you even did. Anyhow, given the law, I don't know if they'll make exceptions here. That's up to the Crown Attorney. Until we know anything, the dog'll have to stay with us."

"She's in jail?" Darcy asks.

"No, honey, she's at camp."

The officers of the K-9 training division of the Metro police think of Hildy as a great and magnificent hero. She is treated with respect and careful affection. She is one of many dogs at the kennel, most of them German shepherds but there are a few beagles and a couple of golden retrievers. All of them are being schooled for specific duties: tracking, corpse searches, crowd control, drug and contraband detection, guarding. A couple of the dogs Hildy is with were used to help find Lizbett. Except for the training, Hildy is treated like one of these special dogs: she is fed, walked, and given play time in the field with a couple of rookie German shepherds about her age. Every day she is taken out and tested for behavioural problems. Except for being slow to pick up tricks — the trainers have been trying to teach her "high five" — she is responsive to all commands. She is not gregarious, but as she learns to trust the trainers, she begins to exhibit the affectionate, playful nature the Warnes so love. Never once has she shown herself to be vicious or unpredictable. All the officers think she is a good dog.

A couple of prosecutors hash it out. The fact that Hildy attacked a murderer doesn't affect the fact that the damage has crippled a man's hand. But the dog has done them a huge favour. Could she possibly have known Searle was a dangerous man? They would love to think so, but it's hardly provable. No, the dog couldn't have known. And you can't have huge dogs biting guys' hands off. Nor can you have owners who are aware they might.

Thompson is charged with criminal negligence causing bodily harm.

Many people testify on his and Hildy's behalf: the officers of the K-9 team, Thompson's cronies at the dog park who have known Hildy and seen her play with their dogs, neighbours, the veterinarian who sutured Hildy after she was attacked by Atilla. Even her previous owner, the Laverne boy, when called, confesses to her mistreatment and the fighting he subjected her to.

Magdalena documents the history of the Great Dane, that it originally was used to hunt wild boar, that it has been a "war dog," but most recently, it has been bred as a companion animal known for its placid and gentle disposition. She says in her six years of breeding and training Danes, she has never had one attack. The prosecutor asks if she is aware that Great Danes were eighth on the list of the ten most dangerous dogs, a list compiled by the National Association of Veterinarians and the National Humane Society. Magdalena doesn't know about the list.

Meredith explains the circumstances that made her believe she was being stalked by Melvyn Searle.

Darcy relates how Melvyn, from out of nowhere, was standing right over her at the dog park, how he had made her uncomfortable as her mask teacher.

His charge of first-degree murder is brought to bear.

A canine behaviourist, a Dr. Morton Jamieson, testifies. "A dog's perception of people … of individuals in particular … and their surroundings differs vastly from a human's. For one thing, their sense of smell is highly developed. A dog has many thousand more sensory receptors in its nose and it can detect the faintest of scents, even through supposedly impermeable barriers like glass and metal. Does the human body exude an odour to match an emotion, one that humans can't detect, but a dog can? Can a dog smell fear, aggression, harmful intent? I would venture to say a dog can, that a dog can sense danger in unlikely circumstances. And then, of course, there is a dog's perception of human emotions: its ability to read feelings and body language and respond accordingly. There is real evidence a dog does so brilliantly. Can I attest without a doubt that this particular dog … that Hildy … knew Mr. Searle intended to harm the young girl? No. Not in so many words. But I can attest to the fact that there is scientific proof a dog is capable of detecting threat where a human might not."

Over the strenuous protestations of the defense who states prior "similar acts" are inadmissible, the judge makes an exception in this case because the accused is, in effect, an animal. The prosecution calls the elderly jogger who states Hildy snarled and lunged at him as he passed by her property and was injured as a result.

The judge states the circumstances of the attack on Melvyn Searle: it was unprovoked and caused severe bodily harm. Thompson knew Hildy had previously exhibited the potential to bite. The judge finds him guilty. There is an uproar in the court.

She says, "This is a grave offense. This was a grievous injury. A man who uses his hands to make a living has lost partial use of his right hand, his dominant hand. The fact that this man is currently being held without bail for the heinous murder of a young girl has no relevance here. But taking into account all the evidence: the fact that the dog has been abused, the fact that this is its first offense, the fact that experts have indicated a second offense is unlikely, the fact that it is suspicious that a man who has no dog, a man who purportedly has been stalking the little girl in the family, the sister of the aforementioned murder victim, just happened to be in the dog park hovering over the little girl leads me to believe there are mitigating circumstances here. Normally I would recommend the dog be confined to a yard and never exposed to strangers or else that it wear a muzzle. But taking into consideration the time and dedication the family puts into the dog and the importance of the dog to the family's well-being, I am going to allow the dog to return to the family with the caveat that should there be any incident whatsoever involving the dog and aggression, that the dog be destroyed. This is an enormous responsibility, but I believe the family has exhibited their vigilance where the dog's behaviour is concerned."

"As for the charge of criminal negligence causing bodily harm, the maximum penalty for this offense is ten years, but taking into account that the accused has shown deep remorse and demonstrated he is a responsible dog owner, I sentence Thompson Warne to three months in prison and fine him the sum of $5,000. Which sentence I herewith suspend."

# 19

## July

The city is lush and sodden. The heat that clung the previous summer has been replaced by a persistent coolness. The sun, if it arrives at all, does so first thing Monday morning or mid-week, and gets covered again by low clouds on the weekend. Lawns are thick; gardens vibrant; vacations ruined. People are grumbling: as if the winter weren't bad enough with all the snow and bad storms. Now this.

What has changed about the Warnes over the course of a year, through three deaths, all of them rupturing? For one thing, the exuberant love that once made Magdalena so envious has been tamped. Once a bubbling-over pot of affection, it now only simmers, although the contents are more concentrated.

Above all they are like a body missing a limb. Every moment of every day they realize that limb is not available to them and they must adjust their behaviour and feelings in order to function without it. Because there is no prosthesis for this limb. There is the chronic pain, usually dull, but throbbing nonetheless. There is the mourning for the absence of something loved and needed. Something crucial. There is the doing of things they were accustomed to doing with the limb that they now must figure out how to do without. Like walking with crutches with no hands free if it's the leg that's lost. Or trying to do things one-handed if an arm is missing. Something as easy as opening a window is a problem. It's that way with simple everyday connecting. They feel handicapped a lot of the time and frustrated and angry because of it. They want to lash out and often they do. Mostly they just look at the body of their family with its missing vital part and feel helpless, knowing it will never be the same again.

Darcy has taken over some of Lizbett's qualities. She is now effusive, with some of Everard's insistence and a lot of Thompson's wit. She proclaims, exclaims, praises, and disdains. Her stories have no endings. They call her "the stand-up." Though she says Stephen will always be her best friend and that she will likely marry him, he is a "boy," a word she utters with some distaste. She has found a girl friend, Roberta Collingwood, called "Bobbie," who also loves to read and draw and paint. Their giggles run down the Warnes staircase in a stream. Roberta's family are churchgoers and Darcy has asked to attend Sunday school. Though Meredith and Thompson are chagrined, they recognize it is essential to give her the choice. She thinks she might like to be a minister like Everard when she grows up. She is only trying to convert them a little.

Darcy also wanted her room changed. The walls are now white. On one hangs an early still life of Meredith's with roses in a glass vase. On the bed is a white lace bedskirt and a white duvet covered not only in rosebuds, but Hildy's and Mr. Mushu's and Geoffrey's hairs.

She gets up on her own and can make it through her morning ablutions. She wears a lot of Lizbett's clothes. She is still pretty much incommunicative at breakfast. "Give the girl a cup of coffee," Thompson says. She now reads Ann Landers as well as the comics.

There is no indication that she has been traumatized by either Lizbett's or Aniela's deaths. Accepting? Not really. She talks about them constantly, especially Lizbett, and is always trying to find an answer to what makes someone like Melvyn a killer.

"What makes a person who was once a little baby go bad?" she keeps asking. "How does the badness get into them? God doesn't make someone bad. Can someone else make a person bad? And why would they do that?"

"Perhaps *bad* isn't the right word," says Thompson. "Maybe he was born with something wrong with his brain, like an engine in a car with faulty spark plugs. Or maybe his brain is missing the part that decides what is good. Remember that baby bird we found with only one wing?"

"But can he be fixed?"

"That I don't know," Thompson says. "But I doubt it. Can you put a wing on a bird?"

Meredith and Thompson have traded traits. She is now the withdrawn one, living in silent self-retreat as Thompson has always done. Her energy is still always fired up and she spreads herself too thinly, but she does it with an inward reserve. A lot of the time she seems to be in a bit of a daze. Neither Darcy nor Thompson knows what she is thinking and have to prod her to "come to." She has almost finished her portrait of Lizbett, a five-foot-by-six-foot meticulous reproduction of Lizbett's head shot from *Annie*, which she has worked on night and day.

It is spectacular. Already she has two commissions.

She has also put together a proposal and is looking for funding for a Child Care/Home Care program for the teenage mothers at the settlement house. She has realized, looking after their children every Saturday, how much they could benefit from learning about how to use their welfare checks to efficiently buy nutritious food, how to cook it, how to keep a house, how to provide not only a healthy and disciplined lifestyle for their children, but how to stimulate their learning and their play. She would like to teach the cooking/food management part. She has talked to some of the mothers about this and they seemed keen to learn.

For the most part, Artful Sustenance is thriving. Thompson has taken on Irme Pormoranska as a permanent employee. He has also been asked to do the photographs for a book on fences by Edward Bloom, a novelist who is enchanted with the concept of beautiful barriers. Do they keep things out or keep them in? It will require quite a bit of travelling, but Meredith and Darcy could come along for some of it. Meredith is thrilled that Thompson has a chance to use his creativity on something other than food.

He doesn't know how he could love her more. She is as inspiring as she always was and if the mania — which he misses — has gone, it has been replaced by a measured enthusiasm to which he can still attach himself. But he realizes he was dependent on living her emotional life, that he let his stifled affect be stirred up by her instead of trying to stir himself. At least he thinks it was stifled. He wonders if his childhood was akin to yelling in the desert. Now he has never felt more embraced. But he still hates sex in the morning.

Tadeusz Breischke has a debilitating breakdown. He is hospitalized at Elmhurst Lodge for eight weeks and improves. He continues counselling with Brygida. She seems braver and more resilient than Meredith remembers herself being. Brygida admits her attachment to her faith has saved her. She does believe Aniela is in a better place, as she believes God will forgive Melvyn Searle.

Meredith has not forgiven him. She knows it is corrupt, but she has thought and thought about it and she can't help herself. She thinks he should pay for Lizbett's life with his own. This is one of the few things she and Thompson and Everard argue about.

But for all that, she respects Thompson's compassion, his innate belief in the sanctity of life. She, too, has a deepened love for her husband. Whereas she always used to see him as an anchor to her flightiness, she now feels she is intimately and purposefully connected to him on the ground. She sees them each as embedded posts, side by side, joined by an immeasurable sadness, but also by a cautious gladness and an indelible, fierce love for Darcy. And the bond of their precious Hildy.

They have gone to the cottage for the month of July. Abbey and Kyle come on weekends. At forty-three, she has just found out she is pregnant and she and Kyle are shocked, and, they think, delighted. Everard is with them. He has found a young minister to take over his parish for a month. He and Nellie seem to have a rapport. She doesn't like his ramblings and says so, but she admires his wisdom. He is enthralled with her piano-playing she performs almost every evening. They have discovered they both like birds and Nellie has taken Everard trekking and canoeing to see them. He has become quite competent at bird calls.

Abbey sits endlessly working on the Jackson Pollock jigsaw puzzle. She has stopped smoking because of the baby and is cranky. Darcy is hardly ever there. There is no baking bread or canning peaches with her Nan-Nan this year. She is over at the other end with her cousins. Her friend Roberta came up for a week and the two of them would talk late into the night, until Thompson had to come in and threaten to separate them if they did not go to sleep.

Swimming is an ordeal, the water so cold it steals the breath, but they have established the rule that everyone has to have at least one swim a day.

It is hardest for Everard, who is used to the tropical sea. Meredith is a bit of a beluga in that once she's in she stays in and does her water ballet. Darcy now manages a slightly crooked backward "dolphin," which is a rite of passage for the island. Abbey has defied the rule and has yet to go in. She says the shock of the cold water might harm the baby.

On the anniversary of Lizbett's death, the sky breaks and the sun pours out. The day heats up and they all go for a picnic to Elias Island because there is a secluded bay there with a sand beach and spectacularly clear water. They make a huge number of sandwiches: egg salad, tuna, roast beef and horseradish, cucumber and mayonnaise, peanut butter and Nellie's strawberry jam. They take icy cava to drink and lemonade for Darcy. There is a boxful of Nellie's chocolate chip cookies and a basket of strawberries.

The warm sun penetrates their bodies, which have felt constantly chilled for days. The lake is dazzling, crystalline. The light feels blinding after so many grey days. It is calm in the shallow bay and the water is warmer. Sweaty from the sun, they all wade in, plunging when it finally becomes deep enough. Meredith feels febrile in the cold water, almost delirious, infused with a kind of ecstatic torment. This a day of pain-sodden memories she can't escape and yet its clarity, the sudden piercing heat, have invited a happiness that feels new. She swims out deep, and, over and over, curves herself into the sparkling waves. They are almost bath-tub-clear and beneath her, the sun's myriad reflections dance as if alive. A cloud's path across the generous orb replays its journey far below. Some big fish stirs up billows of sand. Even so deep, they catch the light and glitter. She lies on her back, arms stretched above her head, and stares at the turquoise heavens. After a while, she begins to feel she is the water itself: fluid, engulfing, easily-entered. She loses the morbid, corroded boundaries of her being. She begins to understand how life transforms itself, how a thing that was once solid, becomes liquid, becomes air. Becomes nurturing spirit. She feels the lake and the sky come and lift something from her even as she offers it to them.

Shivering, hands and feet all wrinkly, she emerges, placing each foot carefully in the hot sand and feels for the first time in a long while that the earth is there for her.

That night there is a full moon, incandescent, with a luminous white halo surrounding it. All its orifices are delineated. It leaves sharp shadows on land and a bright path on the lake. It upstages the stars. It is shining in on Nellie and Everard playing gin on the porch. It is shining on Abbey and Kyle, who have gone out in the canoe. Thompson and Meredith are sitting with Darcy and Hildy on the still-warm dock, their feet dangling in the water. Hildy is sitting with her head resting on Darcy's shoulder.

"The man in the moon is laughing," she says.

"He always does," says Thompson. "Have you ever seen a sad moon?"

Meredith thinks about the moon, how it really has no character on its own, yet with the gift of the sun's glare, it becomes magical, mythical. Nothing in the universe stands alone. As on earth, interdependency affords definition. She imagines all the places on the planet where the moon is shining. She pictures it shining on Lizbett's grave under the oaks, near the stream on the former farm.

Twelve moons like this one have passed since her terrible death, twelve glowing, magnanimous moons, shut out by clouds, perhaps, but free of the earth's shadow, nonetheless. When she looks at it this way, she sees the passage of time as something emancipated and purposeful, not as something that steals hours, days, months, but something that offers them. That's what this moon is assuring her now: "I will be back."

She can trust this, at least. There will be a full moon regardless of events on earth, regardless of celebrations or tragedies, life or death, savagery or benevolence. Twelve moons ago she was mired in suffering and could not begin to contemplate seeing another. Under the moon before that — if she was staring at it — she could not have imagined Lizbett's life would be destroyed and through that, their own. And yet, here is that moon again, reliable, magnificent, detached, serene. She knows now how precarious, how precious existence is. Who can know if she will ever see another full moon? What she can know is that the moon will always be there, creating an infinite, undisturbed continuum of the ages. It's not that the moon recognizes existence, but that existence itself lives on in the continuum. This moon has seen the beginning and end of all that has ever lived, will continue to see the beginning and end of all that will ever live. The same moon under which a dinosaur stood, the same moon under which Cleopatra mourned the loss of Antony is the same moon she looked at with her mother as a child in Australia and sang: "I see the moon/the moon sees me/high up above in the old oak tree/please Mr. Moon shine up above/shine on the one I love ..." She and Darcy and Lizbett have sung that song under that same moon: this moon. It is shining on the ones she loves now. This moon, which is so mesmerizing her, is being looked at by some other mother — a Masai mother, a French mother, a Chinese mother with her child — somewhere on earth. It may be that Darcy will look at this moon with her children. This moon will always link people to what was, what is, and what will be. She thinks of Lizbett in this context, that in twelve moons she has faded and will continue to fade, but as surely as there will be twelve moons more and twelve moons after that, the 132 moons that blessed her have also preserved her.

Darcy whisper-shouts, "Oh, look, a shooting star!"

"Oh, good," says Meredith. "That means we can kiss. Shooting stars mean kisses." And each takes turns making little smacks on cheeks. Meredith and Thompson's kiss is on the lips and Darcy says, "Ooh, mushy." Even Hildy offers a few slurps.

Up at the cottage, they hear a screen door slam and the padding of footsteps down the path, and then the *click-click-click* of paws along the dock.

"Lina! Paulina!" Darcy says. "Come here, girl. Come here." The puppy prances up, crazy with excitement. She had been sound asleep in a chair when they came down.

She squeezes her way in between Darcy and Thompson and lies half and half on them.

"Help," says Thompson. "I'm going to get pushed off."

"Let's go for a skinny dip!" Meredith says. "C'mon, let's show Daddy how girls do it!" They take off their clothes and pile them on the dock and jump in. The splash reverberates; seems phosphorescent in the moonlight. Meredith and Darcy gasp with the shock of the icy water.

Thompson rushes up to the cottage to get towels and returns undressed with one around his middle. He whips it off and dives in, whooping and yelping when he comes up.

They get used to it, and, awed and wordless in the astounding light, they breaststroke round and round in a circle, gently breaking the surface of the water in little glistening waves. The silence amplifies their tiny splash. The water is like cool silk against their bareness, almost sweet on their lips. Each is feeling a joyous unleashing, but at the same time an intense and marvelous intimacy they will never experience again. They are at one with the water in this great lake and at one with each other.

The moon beams down on a perfect, perfectly happy family. Except.

# Epilogue

Finding twelve impartial jurors and three alternates for Melvyn Searle's November trial takes two weeks. The trial itself takes only a few more.

He pleads not guilty by reason of temporary insanity, stating that in putting on the mask to show Lizbett (to which he has confessed), he was transformed by the mask's inherent powers, from the person he was into the person the mask represented: the "lord of the harvest" of a culture that sacrificed maidens to their god of crops to ensure a bountiful season. He swears he has no recollection of the act itself and that it was fear — after he had removed the mask — that made him dispose of the body as he did.

Expert witnesses, psychiatrists, and anthropologists testify that indeed, a mask can alter a wearer's personality; that is the purpose of the mask. To allow the wearer to become someone else. To the extent that the wearer would lose awareness of his innate self? Possibly, they say. The Mayans believed that the priests wearing deity masks took on the characteristics and the powers of the deity. In effect, they became the deity and, hence, acquired his rights. There are specific masks that induce a trance, transporting the wearer into the mask itself and affecting his behaviour accordingly. For all intents and purposes, then, it is the mask that performs.

Melvyn confronts the courtroom, boldly making contact with his magnified eyes. His face is expressionless, almost as if he were wearing a mask of neutrality, except to use the eyes to pierce and defy.

The jury finds Melvyn's plea preposterous and in just two days comes up with a verdict of guilty. Initially there were two holdouts: a book editor and a violinist. They believed there was reasonable doubt, but were finally overturned by the others.

Melvyn Searle, murderous pedophile, once a tow-headed, timid boy, a curious and creative boy who loved books, receives a life sentence.

Thompson comes to find forgiveness, but Meredith does not ever. They both do, however, find distance.

# Acknowledgements

All writing is solitary, but no novelist creates a work alone. A number of books armed me with the resources to make No Worst, There Is None credible, especially Doug Clark's thorough and affecting account of the Alison Parrott investigation in Dark Paths, Cold Trails. Journey Into Darkness by John Douglas was also helpful. So was The Unknown Darkness: Profiling the Predators Among Us by Gregg O. McCrary and Katherine Ramsland. You Shall Be Holy by Tony Philpot and Grace All Around Us by Stephen Paul Bouman both enlarged my understanding of aspects of Christianity. For forensic information, I read The FBI Handbook of Crime Scene Forensics and The Crime Scene by W. Mark Dale and Wendy S. Becker. Masks of the World by Douglas Condon-Martin and Jim Pieper and Masks by John W. Nunley and Cara McCarty were spectacular. The inspiring Faces of Your Soul by Elise Dirlam Ching and Kales Ching gave me the idea for the "life mask." And for trying to fathom grief, I relied on The Worst Loss by Barbara T. Rosof and Beyond Tears, a collaboration of bereaved mothers as told to Ellen Mitchell.

Without the extraordinary talents of my third daughter Clara, theatre artist, mask-maker. and mask teacher at RADA in London, U.K., I would never have understood the nature and scope of masks.

And her generous sharing of the pain sustained as a result of the murder of her good friend Alison Parrott was invaluable. The astute editorial advice of my second daughter, Celia, theatre artist and playwright, gave me important insights for rewrites. The enthusiasm and direction that came from my friends Michael Harris Bond, professor of cultural psychology in Hong Kong and Deb Klein, law teacher, former prosecutor, and character *extraordinaire* helped stave off the desire to give up. Ian Montagnes and Elizabeth Wilson lent expert surveillance, correcting a crucial flaw. The inestimable emotional support given me by psychiatrist of nine years, Dr. Emily Forcade of Chicago consistently affirmed my creativity and my purpose. Julie Aldis, former food stylist, provided me with detailed descriptions of that exacting job. Any mistakes are mine.

And I am devotedly and infinitely grateful to my wonderful husband Terry for "letting me be me." His generous patronage and ongoing encouragement and avid support of my work have seen me through periods of doubt and discouragement.

*More Great Fiction from Dundurn*

## Surface Rights

### Melissa Hardy

Middle-aged Verna Macoun Woodcock returns to the family cottage for the first time in thirty-eight years to scatter the ashes of her husband, father, and twin sister. At first she is alone except for her dad's dog, the lake, bitter memories, and a barely hidden drinking problem. But soon Verna is forced to open up her tightly shut world to others: strong-willed handy-woman Winonah; the neglected children of her sister, each lost and broken in their own way; even the ghost of Winonah's dead brother, Lionel, who can't seem to make it to the Sky World. Just as Verna is starting to accept this newfound family, she discovers a menacing prospector who posts a notice on the cottage door, stating his intention to dig for ore. As it turns out, the Macouns hold the surface rights for the land, but not the mineral rights. For the first time in her life, Verna has something to fight for and family at stake.

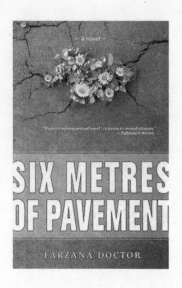

# Six Metres of Pavement

### Farzana Doctor

*Winner of the 2012 LAMBDA Literary Award for Best Lesbian Fiction and of the 2011 Rainbow Awards*

Ismail Boxwala made the worst mistake of his life one summer morning twenty years ago: he forgot his baby daughter in the back seat of his car. After his daughter's tragic death, he struggles to continue living. A divorce, years of heavy drinking, and sex with strangers only leave him more alone and isolated. But Ismail's story begins to change after he reluctantly befriends two women: Fatima, a young queer activist kicked out of her parents' home; and Celia, his grieving Portuguese-Canadian neighbour who lives just six metres away. A slow-simmering romance develops between Ismail and Celia. Meanwhile, dangers lead Fatima to his doorstep. Each makes complicated demands of him, ones he is uncertain he can meet.